An Air That Kills

A catalogue record of this book is available from the British Library

First Edition: December 2004

ISBN: 1-84375-125-9

Also by Craig Brown

Monaco Grand Prix - Portrait of a Pageant (non-fiction: 1989)

Available in Hardback ISBN 0-947981-30- 6 (MRP Ltd)

To order additional copies of this book please visit:
http://www.upso.co.uk/craigbrown

Published by: UPSO Ltd
5 Stirling Road, Castleham Business Park,
St Leonards-on-Sea, East Sussex TN38 9NW United Kingdom
Tel: 01424 853349 Fax: 0870 191 3991
Email: info@upso.co.uk Web: http://www.upso.co.uk

With love to Eugenie, who encouraged me all the way, and to Pete, Tom, Jan and Amy

I hope you enjoy this book

Craig
x

An Air That Kills

by

Craig Brown

UPSO

For Valerie

With eternal love

Acknowledgments

I would like to thank my wife Valerie for her sympathetic and constructive help in checking the manuscript of this book, for occasionally pointing out errors of fact - and for her unstinting support throughout.

Thanks also (and apologies) to Dr Jim Pritchard of the Gustav Mahler Society of the United Kingdom for waiting so patiently for work from me, delayed by my preoccupation with this task.

The title of this book is taken from the first line of a wistfully evocative poem by A E Housman. I have chosen not to reproduce the poem, but I am nonetheless grateful in this connection to Lisa Dowdeswell of The Society of Authors for her helpful advice.

Finally, but importantly, I thank my friend Teresa for her enthusiastic encouragement after reading the opening chapters.

If there are others I really should have mentioned, I can only hope they will understand, and think no less of me.

CB

Chapter I

1960

Meeting Archie

I would always remember it as the big brown house. I realise now, with the benefit of maturity's perspective, that it could not have been very big, and I am almost certain that the paintwork outside was green. But inside the impression was of gloomy hallways, and doors and walls and rails painted brown and the unwelcoming chill of redundant rooms into which I would peep round the door and hardly dare to enter. There was much heavy oak or mahogany furniture, a dark, winding staircase, a long, cool pantry and the frightening black hole of the cupboard under the stairs. The house smelled of mothballs and damp and old newspapers. The name-plate over the front door said *Arcadia.*

I am trying to remember. I think it was about a month after my grandfather died in the cottage hospital that my grandmother, perhaps fearful of being alone at night and presumably in need of money, first introduced me to her lodger.

"This is Mr Archibald McLeish, Neil. He's come to stay for a while – just for lodgings."

The sunlight streaming through the window of the small room where my grandfather had slept seemed to dance and sparkle in Archibald McLeish's auburn hair. I put out my hand in greeting, but Mr McLeish ignored it and, instead, placed a thick, heavy hand on the top of my head.

"Very pleased to meet you, lad," he told me, in a gruff Scots burr. "I'm sure we'll get along just fine."

Since I habitually spent only a few hours a week at Gran's, I found this assurance somewhat disconcerting. What commitment did Mr McLeish expect of me? Little did I know then, of course, how pivotal a figure he was to become in my burgeoning adolescence.

"My grandson visits me every Saturday," Gran explained. "He's a good boy."

"I've no doubt," said Mr McLeish.

"Will you be eating with us this evening?" my grandmother asked him.

"I think not," Mr McLeish replied, still with his hand on my head. "I have a prior engagement."

With that, Gran nodded and left me alone with the lodger. He smiled, showing yellowish teeth, and tousled my hair with his strong fingers. "Sit down, lad," he bade me, indicating the edge of the bed. "I'm sorry I've no chair in here. I have requested a chair, but so far..." and he spread out his hands towards me.

So there, in a shaft of summer sunshine, I perched on the side of Mr McLeish's bed, the day's warmth and my nervousness together painting a thin lacquer of perspiration on my forehead. I wetted my lips, and felt a cold bead of sweat trickle down my back, a sudden, darting tickle, light as a spider.

"The sun in your eyes, lad?"

I shook my head, staring at the carpet. "No, I'm all right."

"You'll be missing your grandpa. I hear he was a fine man, a gentleman."

"Yes, sir."

A sudden snort of convulsive laughter made the bed shake. Mr McLeish slapped my knee playfully with the flat of his hand. "Lord! You don't have to call me *sir!* You're Neil and I'm Archie. Come on now!"

"Yes – Archie. Are you from Scotland?"

And the lodger turned to face me with a broad grin that highlighted the pale furrows in his cheeks. "Aye, laddie, I am. From the most beautiful country in the world."

"My dad's a Scot," I told him, proudly. "He's from Aberfeldy."

Mr McLeish nodded. "I know, Neil. Your gran said. I'm thinking it's a small world."

I stared at him. "How do you mean?"

"Because I was raised in Kinlochrannoch, just along the road a piece." He reached out and squeezed my hand. "Perhaps you know it?"

"I don't think so," I replied. "But I've been to Pitlochry and Moulin. And to Killiecrankie."

He nodded thoughtfully. "Glorious places, Neil." Then he clapped his hands together. "Tell you what. One day I'll take you to Kinlochrannoch. We'll go fishing on the loch. D'you like fishing, Neil?" He didn't wait for an answer. "We'll go walking out on the moor – magnificent desolation."

"Is there a monster in the loch?" I asked, hopefully.

"In Rannoch? Not to my knowledge – but you never can tell, in all that dark water. We'll go at night, when the fireflies are like comets – or perhaps in the evening, with the light going down and the water misty as velvet. You'll love it, Neil. It's a grand experience."

I felt I could grow to like Archie McLeish. Maybe we could even become friends. As for going fishing with him in Scotland, I could not imagine my parents allowing anything of the kind; but his good-natured offer, and the dreamscape pictures it painted in my imagination, would sustain me for weeks to come.

I found Gran in the kitchen, ladling sheets and pillowcases into the bubbling copper with a pair of wooden tongs. "Gran," I asked her, "how long will Archie be staying?"

Gran pulled a face, a kind of knowledgeable smirk. "As long as he pays his rent," she replied, ever the pragmatist.

At six o'clock my father came to fetch me home in our battleship grey Hillman Husky. The car, I remember, was very like my father; it was square, practical, unimaginative and uncompromising. Often we travelled home in awkward silence, but today I was able to tell Dad about Archie McLeish.

"A lodger, you say?"

"That's right."

"What's he like?"

"He was really nice to me. He said he would – " I checked myself.

"Said he would what?" Dad turned his face from the road to glance at me. "He didn't touch you, did he, this McLeith fellow?"

"McLeish. I don't know what you mean."

"I don't trust these lodgers," my father said. "They can be peculiar."

Upon what prior experience of lodgers he based this assertion, I could not imagine. I refrained from comment, whilst suspecting that my father had never met a known lodger in his life.

"I asked you a question," he persisted, with slow, laborious intonation.

"You mean – "

"I mean, did this fellow, whatever he calls himself, did he attempt to touch or rub you – in any way whatsoever?"

I swallowed hard, momentarily speechless from embarrassment and indignation. The car suddenly swerved to avoid a gaggle of teenaged cyclists, who rang their bells defiantly. Dad cursed them under his breath. "Wee basstarrds!"

I felt myself shrinking down in my seat. "He only patted me," I said, my voice trembling slightly.

"Patted you? Hmmh. His hands – were they very small?"

"What?"

"Did he have small hands? Did he wear after-shave?"

"I don't know. I think his hands were quite big."

"Was he perfumed?"

I heard my voice rising as my distress increased. "I don't know. I don't know these things. Why are you asking me, Dad?"

Dad sniffed noisily, jutting his jaw, something he often did before making a declaration. "Because I am your father," he said. "I have a responsibility to protect you. Your mother would expect no less of me."

"But I don't need protecting," I insisted; but my voice came out as a reedy whine, which merely made me sound feeble.

"I will be the judge of that, Neil."

Over the hump of a railway bridge, we travelled so fast, I was jolted almost to the roof.

"Got to get you home," Dad muttered. He darted me a quick glance. "Are you all right?"

I nodded but said nothing.

"Tell me now...all this *patting* that went on..."

I ground my teeth together in miserable frustration.

"Where exactly did he pat you, this McLeith fellow?"

"We were on his bed," I said, and immediately bit my tongue, at once realising that, of course, his question was intended to establish not a location, but a part of the body. Now, thanks to my foolishness, the damage was done.

A deep intake of breath sounded above the drone of the engine. "What on earth...?"

"No, we were just sitting there. He hasn't got a chair," I added, lamely.

"You try to tell me you don't need protecting, then in the next breath you say this chap pulled you on to his bed. You must – "

"I didn't say that, Dad. It wasn't like that."

"I think I get the picture, Neil. Remember, it's you who needs protecting, not him."

"Your picture's all wrong," I said, sulkily. "He's just a lodger."

"Aye, and not for much longer, if I have my way. Do you want to stop for anything?"

"What? No."

The faded muslin light of a summer's evening draped itself over the window as we turned for home. My eyes, as I peered out, were fogged with tears. The day's pleasures were tainted and defiled; I just wanted to forget them. I did not want to talk to my father any more.

Another sniff, and a sharp intake of breath. "I'm afraid we may have to review these Saturdays in the light of what's happened."

"But nothing's happened," I whimpered. "Please, Dad. I like going there. I love my gran."

"Huh. If only it were that simple," he said, with a snort of derisive laughter. "Frankly, I'm surprised at your gran for allowing such goings-on in her house."

"But Da-"

"I've not finished. You'll have to watch this answering back, Neil."

I hung my head and fiddled with my fingernails. The car jerked forward as Dad accelerated into our road.

"I shall consult with your mother regarding future visits to your gran's house," came the stentorian declaration.

I groaned inwardly, for I could see where this exchange was leading us. As in a kind of punitive relay, the baton of parental disapproval would now be passed from my father to my mother, who would wield the same stick against me all over again.

We lurched into the driveway, and Dad switched off the engine. I reached for the door-handle, but he put out a hand to stop me. "Next Saturday," he said, staring ahead through the windscreen, "you will remain at home. After that, we will decide."

For a moment I sat in silence. A light flicked on in the front room, and I saw my mother's face tilt towards us at the window, querulous, like a small bird. It was suddenly very quiet in the car. I could hear my father breathing, and the slow, uneven ticking of the engine as it cooled.

"Gran'll miss me," I said, trying to prevent my voice from cracking.

"That's as may be. She should have thought of that."

"How d'you mean? It's not her fault."

"Oh? And whose fault is it, eh? Tell me that." Dad's voice was rising to a screech. "Is it your fault? Are you to blame?"

"No!"

"Did you encourage this Mc-whatever his name is?"

"What d'you mean, encourage him?" I asked, knowing perfectly well what he meant. Now I could taste the tears in my mouth, the salt-and-metal bile of my despair. I felt angry at my helplessness, and helpless because my anger was impotent. I stared grimly at my father's face in the gathering gloom and tried not to hate him, or to feel a sullen contempt for his mindless intolerance, his insensitivity – and for his stubborn belief that people he disliked could somehow be atomised or dismantled by the childish device of pretending to forget their names.

A tap at the window drew my attention. My mother was standing there. "Aren't you coming in?" she asked, smiling.

Dad waved at her dismissively. "Of course we're coming in, woman. We'll be a minute."

"I want to go in now," I said. "It's getting cold."

"Don't be a sap, Neil."

My eyes were prickling with tears. I thought of Gran next Saturday, moving round the big house on her own. There was Archie McLeish, of course, but he might stay in his room. I wondered about his chair. He should have a chair to sit on.

"Neil – "

"What?"

"Neil, I don't want to have to get angry."

"You do. You're always shouting."

"I am not always shouting!" Dad's voice wobbled towards a crescendo, and a blob of spit hit the windscreen. "I am not always shouting," he continued in a measured tone, "I am just trying to make you see reason."

The truth of it was, my father was at least moderately angry for much of the time. Anger was a state to which he defaulted naturally, because it conveniently excused him from the social complexities of politeness.

"Neil, I want to know if you were overly friendly to this lodger fellow. For instance, was there any – embracing?"

I was by now too tired to argue or parry his questions. "No, Dad," I said, speaking in a low monotone, "there was no embracing. We just talked. Okay?"

"That's not what you told me before. Which story am I expected to believe?"

I rested my face in my cupped hands. "Dad, there is no story." I could feel wet on my palms. "He's a nice man. You'd know if you met him."

"Thank you, Neil, I have no desire to meet a child-molester."

I uncovered my face. "He is not a – what you said. I like him. And Gran trusts him to be in her house."

Dad sniffed contemptuously. "Oh, does she now? Your gran has a lot to answer for."

"How? What do you mean?"

"I mean, Neil, that your gran has plainly been irresponsibly negligent in this affair. When you are supposed to be with her, reading your comics or helping her to prepare the potatoes, she allows you to be off upstairs with this damned lodger fellow, and him pawing you with his small hands, reeking of after-shave, all the while just biding his time until, once he has gained your confidence, he feels it opportune to interfere with your trousers. The whole business makes me sick to my stomach."

I could stand it no more. I yanked open the car door and ran in through the back of the house. My mother's anxiously upturned face flickered through the banisters as I ran upstairs to my room and slammed the door behind me. Stripping to my underpants, I slipped quickly into bed, pulling the blankets over my head. For a while I lay still in the musky darkness, listening to my panting breath. Then I tipped my head to one side, straining to hear, as my parents' voices sounded in the hall below. I could not make out the conversation. It was just a distant echo in a dark tunnel. Moments passed, and I heard my mother's footsteps approaching. With a single tap, she opened the door, and I could feel her presence beside the bed.

"I know you aren't asleep, Neil."

I waited.

"Neil, I need to ask you something."

Slowly, I folded the bedclothes down to my neck. "What is it?"

"Dad says there's a strange man at Gran's."

"How does Dad know," I said, wearily. "He didn't see him."

"Dad says there's something funny about him."

"You mean, like a comedian?"

Mum sighed, looking perplexed. "Come on, Neil. Don't be silly."

"I'm not. It's everyone else who's being silly."

"No, no, it's only that we're concerned."

"What about?"

Mum squeezed her hands together and looked awkward. "Well, it's this man."

"What man?"

"Please, Neil. You know what man."

"He's got a name, Mum. He's called Archie."

Mum nodded thoughtfully, eyes downcast. "Archie," she repeated. "Listen, Neil." She suddenly fixed me with an icy stare. "This lodger man – he didn't try to – to touch you, did he?"

I pressed my head into the pillow and closed my eyes. "Gran introduced us. Of course he touched me. That's normal when you're introduced."

"Well, I suppose." She curled her lips doubtfully. "Why does she want a lodger?"

"I don't know. She's your mother. Why don't you ask her?"

"Yes. Yes, I think I will. So he's paying her money, this Archie?"

"That's right."

"What's he like?"

"I'm tired, Mum," I said, sighing. "Dad shouted at me."

"Oh, I'm sure he didn't mean to, dear."

"Of course he meant to," I said, screwing up my fists under the blankets. "How can you shout at someone accidentally?"

My mother nodded silently for a moment, gazing at the carpet. I could hear sparrows chattering in the eaves outside my window as they settled in for the night.

"Perhaps we'll talk about it in the morning," she said. She bent down and kissed me lightly on the cheek. Her face smelled of talcum powder.

I felt myself drifting towards sleep. A bead of dribble oozed from one corner of my mouth and slid slowly down my chin. I wiped it away with my finger, and when I looked, Mum was gone. Through the half-open window came the mingled summer scents of woodsmoke and mown grass. I heard a car backfire, and a dog bark a warning. But these were small, sweet reminders of the normal world, and right now I had no taste for them. I was not in the mood. I ducked back under the covers and waited for my eyes to adjust to the dark. After a minute, I could look down and almost see my bare knees. I fumbled through the hole in the front of my pants and pulled my penis out and held it gently in the palm of my hand. It was warm and slightly moist. I felt comforted.

My mind ranged back to my meeting with Archie McLeish.

Then it seemed to spin forwards, into the future, and that warm, dark cave was a screen on which flickering images were projected, soundless pulses of strobic light in shifting chiaroscuro. I saw the black prow of a boat, nosing through grey wraiths of coiling mist. A pale hand plunged into the water and withdrew the flexing, iridescent wedge of a fat black fish. Around the boat's silhouette, a million needlepoints of white light danced in cascading sparks. Down through the overhanging branches of the black trees, the sun poured in a torrent of molten silver.

There, hanging on the brink of sleep, I made up my mind. As soon as I was old enough, I would go to Kinlochrannoch with Archie McLeish. We would go fishing on the loch. He would be my friend. We would have secrets, but not from each other. In our shared private world, there would be no animosity, no rage, no dark suspicions.

The dream-like images began to fragment and fade. Archie's boat swung broadside across the frame until it was just a formless black blade cutting slowly through the water. It sliced noiselessly out of my vision, a dagger in mercury.

Chapter II

Nurse

Now I must introduce you to Nurse. I don't know how it came to be that, in my grandmother's house, she was always called Nurse, as though that were her actual name. I suppose it was just a habit that no-one ever bothered to shake off. It was years after I first saw her in the kitchen that I discovered her real name, which was Sally Melksham. I never heard anyone – my grandparents, my parents or any visitor to the house, until the time of Archie McLeish's arrival – refer to Nurse as Sally or Miss Melksham. It was always 'Good afternoon, Nurse' or 'Thank you, Nurse' or 'Nurse will be coming shortly'.

Even in the early days, when I hardly knew her, I always liked Nurse. Sometimes, if Gran or Granddad were ill, she would turn up in her pale blue uniform, with a navy blue cardigan over the top. On other days she might come to tea, wearing a grey pleated skirt and a white blouse with a ruffle neck. She invariably dressed neatly and conservatively, with the merest dab of colour applied to her cheeks and a thin pink stroke of lipstick.

I did know, from quite an early age, how old Nurse was, because she liked to chat to my grandfather, who had been gassed in the First World War, and I had heard her remark to him that she had been born in 1918, the year the war ended. So, when I first met Nurse in 1959, she was 41 years old, though to me she looked much younger, particularly as I was only fourteen and naturally thought of people over forty as being very old indeed. On reflection, Nurse appeared about ten years younger than her real age. Perhaps, being single, she simply had more time to take care of herself.

There is a touch of irony here, for I am introducing you to Nurse, when I do not recall ever being introduced to her myself. I just began to notice that she was occasionally there, sometimes in uniform and frequently not. She used to sit in the *Parker Knoll* chair in front of the small table supporting Gran's *Singer* sewing machine in its domed wooden case. If I peered at her over the top of my comic, she might glance at me and smile briefly. In time, I came to notice the tautness of her dress or blouse over the swell of her bosom, and the slightly boyish way she wore her honey-coloured hair flicked backwards above her ears. I wished she would befriend me, for there was about her a kind of warm, mature loveliness that made me gulp with hollow pleasure even as I thought of her.

Listening to her chat to the grown-ups, it soon struck me that one of Nurse's more distinctive physical features, and a gratingly unattractive one, was her curious voice. She spoke in a kind of metallic gargle, the sound emerging in a glottal double-tone which I found both fascinating and infuriating. I never heard anyone remark upon this defect, and so I resisted the urge to question Gran about it. Whether the phenomenon was the result of a childhood infection or throat surgery, I could only speculate. I was put in mind of a briefly fashionable recording technique, whereby singers of some popular ballads – I believe Connie Francis and Rosemary Clooney may have allowed their voices to be strangulated in this way – were recorded in double-track, sounding like two of themselves. So, when Nurse spoke, it was as if another Nurse echoed her every word.

My first close encounter with Nurse came quite unexpectedly, on one of the rather special days when, if the weather was fine and my parents in good humour, I was allowed to ride the five miles to my grandparents' house on my bike. I always relished the freedom of this concession, for it meant that I could travel at times to suit myself, without having to wait for the bus or endure the sullen claustrophobia of a car journey with my father.

As I pulled up at the kerb, I saw my grandmother peering anxiously over the gate. She looked pale and distracted.

"I tried to ring from Mrs Cooper's," she said, "but you'd already gone."

"Why? What's the matter?"

She opened the gate and I pushed my bike through. Old Mrs Cooper, the next-door neighbour, was standing in her front garden with her mouth open.

"It's Granddad," my gran said, her voice quavering. "He's been taken poorly. The doctor came. He sent him straight to the hospital."

I was struggling to remove my cycle clips. "When was this?"

"Breakfast time. He couldn't catch his breath." She put one hand to her mouth. "Oh dear."

"Well – what shall we do?" I asked.

"Gorn to the orspiddle," Mrs Cooper shouted over the fence.

"You can't do anything," Gran said. "Put your bike round the back and come indoors."

I went through the side gate and leaned my bike against the back wall, next to the old wooden bench. I remember there was a large cauliflower under the seat, freshly cut from the vegetable patch for Sunday's lunch.

In the kitchen, Gran was staring out of the window, grey-faced and distraught. "I'm going to the hospital," she said. "Mrs Cooper's boy's taking me in the car."

I nodded thoughtfully. "Will Granddad be all right?"

Gran touched my arm. "I hope so, Neil. He's not been well all week."

"Shall I come with you?"

"No, you stay here. I don't know how long I'll be. Look, I've asked Nurse to come over and sit with you."

"Nurse?" I queried, frowning.

"Yes. You'll be all right. You know Nurse."

"Sort of," I said, with a shrug.

A car horn sounded outside. Gran picked up her bag from the chair.

"Give Granddad my love," I said.

She touched my arm again and went out through the hall,

leaving me alone in the big house. I sat down at the kitchen table and wondered what I would say to Nurse when she arrived, for I had hardly spoken to her directly before, much less spent time alone in her company. The prospect alarmed and intrigued me, appalled and enthralled me. If I wanted, I could still avoid it. I could catch the bus to the hospital and find Gran. She would be cross, but she would forgive me. I sat quietly on the hard wooden chair with the squeaky back and listened to my heart beating. Perhaps Nurse had misunderstood the message and would not come. I hoped she would come. I imagined my relief if she did not arrive. I prayed she would come. I felt a little bit sick. ! was sure she would come. Supposing she forgot or was too busy. I so wanted her to come. What if I was to be sick? I knew she would come.

I went to the toilet, and as I came back into the kitchen I saw Nurse wheeling her bicycle past the window. It was a big black-and-white *Hercules* with a wicker basket on the front and a red plastic bulb horn. I heard her chaining it to the bench. I sat down at the table and then stood up again, not certain what to do.

Nurse opened the back door and beamed at me cheerily. "Hello, young man. Going somewhere?"

Her voice was a soft trill, a bird-like warble.

"N-no. I was just sort of stretching my legs."

"Oh, right." She pushed a canvas bag across the table. "I brought you some comics and a magazine. I wasn't sure what you liked."

"Thank you. I'll read them later."

She smiled. "Well, you don't have to stand up."

I subsided into the chair, while Nurse peeled off her red windcheater and mopped her brow with the palm of her hand. "Hot day for cycling," she gargled. "Uphill all the way from home."

"I hope Granddad'll be all right," I said, timorously.

Nurse slid into the opposite chair and clasped her hands together on the table. "You mustn't fret," she said. "Your granddad's not been well for a long time. His lungs were damaged all those years ago." She shook her head, eyes downcast. "Bad business."

"Do you think I'll ever have to fight in a war?" I asked her. I thought this an unlikely event, but the question was designed less for a definitive answer than to divert attention from my obvious awkwardness.

To my surprise, Nurse reached across the table and touched my hand, gently caressing the back of my fingers. "I pray to the Lord that you won't," she replied, her voice lowered to a quiet burble.

I blinked and stared at her. It had not occurred to me that Nurse might be religious. This was an unfamiliar concept. In our family, to the best of my knowledge, there had never been a serious outbreak of religion. My mother's social icons were always the Conservatives and the monarchy; God had carelessly allowed himself to become firmly aligned with the Labour Party.

With a smart clap of her hands, Nurse seemed to jump to attention. "Right, that's enough gloomy talk! Your gran asked me to look after you for the day – so what shall we do?"

"Um. Whatever you like."

"Well, what do you usually do with Gran?"

"I locked her in the pantry once," I said, brightly.

She laughed and pretended to slap my hands. "I mean things you do together. I don't want to be locked in the pantry."

"Right. Well, in the morning I read comics and talk to Gran and I might do something like shelling peas. Or sometimes we listen to the wireless, if there's comedy on."

Nurse tugged thoughtfully at the lobe of her left ear. "I see. And what happens about lunch?"

"We have fishcakes and beans, with pancakes after."

"What, every Saturday?"

I nodded enthusiastically. "Most Saturdays. I like fishcakes."

"Hmm, so I gather. These fishcakes – does Gran buy them or does she make her own?"

I clasped one hand over my mouth to ponder the question. "I'm not sure," I replied, at length. "I think maybe she makes them. Sometimes they have lumps in."

"Oh, do they?" Nurse sighed and her brow furrowed. "Long way to cycle for a lumpy fishcake."

I shrugged. "I really like fishcakes."

She rose to her feet and stood gazing down at me. "Well, young master Neil, I think it's high time you had a change of diet. Because, I tell you, I'm not about to be chopping up fish and potatoes. I'll look in the pantry; maybe there's something else you like."

"But fishcakes are my favourite," I assured her.

Nurse was already in the pantry doorway, peering sternly back at me. "I've heard quite enough about fishcakes for one day, thank you." She moved inside and began rummaging on the stone shelves. Her face appeared once more out of the gloom. "And don't you lock me in!"

As I remember it, we had fish fingers on toast, and there were no pancakes to follow, suggesting to me that, whatever her patient-care or child-minding skills, Nurse was not well versed in the culinary arts. We ate sparingly, mostly with our fingers. She asked me about my bike and how long I had had it, and about my best subjects at school, and where I was going on holiday. Rather quaintly, she asked me if I was 'courting', and I blushed and said 'no'. By the end of our lunch, I had almost begun to forget Nurse's strange voice and my own self-consciousness, and I was warming to her direct, easy-going nature. I even dared to hope that Gran would not return too soon.

"What do you like to do in the afternoon?" she asked, as I helped her clear the table.

"Er. Sometimes we go to the rec."

"I see. Bit old for swings, aren't you?"

"Granddad used to take me to them when I was little," I explained. "Now I like to walk under the trees and pick up fir cones. You can watch the trains from there. Some of the drivers wave. And I found a slow worm once.

She shuddered. "Ooh, I hate snakes. I hope you didn't touch it."

"Oh yes," I told her, proudly, "I picked it up to show Gran."

Nurse curled her lip distastefully. "Really? I bet she was pleased."

"I wanted to keep it as a pet, only she wouldn't let me."

"Hmm. Sensible lady, your gran." She suddenly slapped her

hands together in that sparky way she had, and her eyes brightened. "Come on then!"

"What?"

"We're going to the rec. Have you had your pocket-money?"

"Why?"

"Don't answer a question with a question."

"I got it this morning."

"Excellent! If Mr Icecool's there, you can buy me an ice-cream."

I smiled and Nurse smiled back, and her teeth were a vivid white, and her eyes were cornflower-blue and full of fun, and something seemed to be happening deep inside me, like a swelling kind of sweet pain that you never want to go away. I was happy and confused, and regretful for the past, for this was not the dour Nurse I had viewed from the corner of my eye for so many wasted years and thought untouchable. This was somebody else, somebody different, not the starched and tightly-wrapped chrysalis of the old Nurse, but the bright butterfly of a new-found friend who would take my hand and dance me into the light.

Walking behind me into the park, she guided me with her hands on both my shoulders, firm fingers kneading the muscles. My heart thumped at the closeness of her, drumming until I was sure she must hear it above the squeal of children playing and the rushing wind in the trees. In the copse beside the railway line, I picked up a stick and, stepping back, showed Nurse a trick taught us by our geography master, Mr Carlin, a rule-of-thumb method of measuring the height of a tree by squinting past the stick and aligning it vertically with the tree-trunk, then rotating it through ninety degrees to a perceived point on the ground to which you could pace, counting the steps.

Nurse stood some distance off, watching me intently. I strode back from completing my first measurement and called to her that a plane tree was forty-two feet high.

"But will that knowledge help you, the rest of your life?" she asked me, tossing her head.

I flicked some bark off the stick and smiled vacantly. "I'll just do one more."

"Mind you don't put your eye out with that stick," she yelled, and when I looked at her I saw the mirthful bulge of her tongue in her cheek and her face quivering with suppressed laughter.

Soon I heard the rails rattling and the self-important roar of the steam-hauled *Master Cutler* hurtling north to Sheffield. Nurse stood behind me, and we both waved at the locomotive cab, but the driver was busy and made no response. I watched until the blunt end of the last carriage was out of sight.

"Next Saturday, perhaps he'll see you," she said, and squeezed my shoulder.

As we strolled over towards the sandy path that ran around the bowling green, a vision of Granddad lying, gasping for breath in his hospital bed, flashed in my brain, and then I felt guilty, because in my haste to enjoy myself with Nurse, I seemed to have forgotten him. But for his misfortune, I should not now be out with her at all. Perhaps I should have followed my first instinct and gone to the hospital. What if Granddad died? What if I never saw him again? All of a sudden, my fleeting pleasures threatened to become a painful burden.

I stopped for a moment and clutched the iron railings at the edge of the green. Men dressed in white stooped and grunted, solemnly offering up their polished woods to the jade-striped turf, then slowly withdrawing to await the murmurs of approval or consolation amid the soft *clickclick* of harmless collisions.

Beside me, Nurse slitted her eyes critically against the light. "Old men playing with their balls," she pronounced. Then she half turned towards me with an impish grin. "Ooh, what am I saying, Neil? Whatever must you think of me?"

I scratched the side of my nose, gazing at the sky. "Actually," I said, "I think you're rather nice," and I hoped my feeble attempt at a casual compliment would mask my surprised embarrassment. In truth, I was quietly delighted that Nurse had made a risqué comment in my presence, for it told me that, when the moment was right, she was prepared to treat me as an adult. I knew that to appear alarmed at this development would be a retrograde step in our relationship.

Nurse punched me playfully on the arm. "Oh, you're not so bad yourself," she said, smiling, "apart from when you're poking sticks in your eyes or chasing snakes about." She pointed across the bowling green to the children's playground. "Let's go on the swings!"

"What?"

"You can push me."

We waited for some small children to move away, their mothers watching us in puzzlement. I felt awkward standing there, but I did not want to seem a spoilsport.

Nurse sat on the swing and jiggled her legs. "Push, Neil! Push my back, not the swing."

I did as she asked. At first, she was heavy to push, but soon she gained momentum and soared higher and higher, kicking out her legs girlishly into space.

"Push harder, Neil!" she cried over her shoulder, and the double-tone in her voice was all but masked by the rush of air in her face.

With each thrust of my outstretched hands, I felt the imprint of Nurse's brassiere on my sweating palms. I could hardly believe that, but for the thin cotton of her blouse, I was repeatedly pressing against Nurse's bra.

After a while she called out, "Getting hot?"

I grinned and nodded, swallowing hard. Nurse's underwear was stencilled on my hands.

Later, she asked me, "Something the matter with your hand? You keep staring at it."

We were sitting on a grassy slope of Haste Hill, above the cemetery. There was a refreshing breeze up there, and the shade of some bushes.

"What? No, it's all right."

"Thought you had a splinter."

I shook my head.

"That's all right then." She nodded towards the rec. "It was good on the swings, wasn't it?"

"Yeah, it was fun."

"I love it up here. It's so peaceful."

I pretended to be admiring the view, but out of the corner of my eye I could see that Nurse had unfastened three of her blouse buttons, and the sunlight was tinting a dark valley in the cleft of her cleavage. If she suggested moving on now, I would probably have to walk with an erection, so I began searching the sky for diversion, shielding my eyes against the glare.

"There's not a cloud in the sky," I pointed out.

"I know. Beautiful day. What about that ice-cream you were going to buy me?"

"I hadn't forgotten. I've got a ten shilling note."

Nurse arched her eyebrows. "Have you now? A man of substance."

"When do you think we'll hear about Granddad?"

She lowered her eyes and slowly shook her head. "I really don't know, Neil. I'll wait with you till your gran comes back. She'll have some news."

She stood up, brushing the grass from her skirt. From my sitting position, I could look up and see the insides of her thighs. I wondered what kind of knickers she wore. I had a strange, sick feeling in my tummy, a sort of forbidden excitement.

"Come on, moneybags!" She reached down for my hand and pulled me up. "I'm hot. I think we should go back."

The Mr Icecool van was parked at the rec gate, its generator throbbing noisily. I bought us two cornets, and we walked slowly along the road, licking hungrily at the soft ice-cream before it melted. Soon Nurse had a white tip to her nose, and sticky trickles were running down my fist. I looked at my hand, and it reminded me of Peter Jessops in 3B, who had shown us how to jerk off, and it had all run down his fingers.

For once, the cool gloom of Gran's hallway was positively welcoming as we stepped inside. The house was silent. A floorboard creaked above me, but there was no sign of Gran.

"I'll make us some tea," Nurse said, moving towards the kitchen.

I inspected my hands. "I think I should have a wash," I said.

In the bathroom, I ran a basin of warm water and sponged my face and hands. There was a smear of pink ice-cream on my shirt sleeve, and I dabbed at it with a wet flannel. Then I heard footsteps on the stairs. I turned to see Nurse coming into the room, blowing hair away from her forehead. She moved behind me, reached round and put her hands in the water.

"I'm nearly finished," I told her.

"Are you going to use the toilet, Neil?"

"No."

"Well then, you won't mind me. I'm all sweaty. I must just splash some cool water on myself."

"I can run some more. This is – "

"It doesn't matter, Neil. Wait for me."

And Nurse began to unbutton her blouse right down to the waist. I felt my mouth drop open, and there was that funny feeling again in the pit of my stomach. With a swift white flash, the blouse was on the floor. Nurse had her arms tucked up tightly behind her, then she drew them forward and peeled off her white bra. For a second, she dangled it by one strap, then dropped it on top of her blouse. I looked away, excitement and panic mingling in a blood-bubbling turbulence in my brain. I could taste sick in my mouth, and it felt as if I had been punched in the belly. When I turned back, Nurse was calmly massaging her breasts with the flannel, sighing and emitting little puffs of air through pursed lips. As she washed, her heaving breasts were like two squirming, furless, one-eyed animals, rolling playfully around in her arms. I stared, licking my lips, for my mouth was dry with shock.

She was watching me intently, a slightly sardonic smile on her face. "What's the matter, Neil? Have you never seen bosoms before?"

"Course I have," I said, boldly. "My mum's got them."

Nurse burst out laughing. "Well, Neil, I'm amazed to hear that! And you don't have to make them sound like a disease. They're not carbuncles, you know."

I grinned sheepishly and tried not to blush, which of course only made me turn redder.

She threw a towel at me and, clumsily, I caught it. Like the full-figured statue of some half-naked goddess, she stood there with her arms outstretched at her sides, taunting me gently with her eyes.

"It's the only towel, Neil. Dry your hands and then you can dry me."

"Pardon?"

"Don't say 'pardon', Neil; you sound priggish."

"Oh, right."

"Come on then." She wiggled her hips, and the pale, magnificently rounded globes of her breasts trembled as though an electric pulse had passed through them. "Under the arms first, then in-between."

I stepped cautiously towards her. My hands were shaking with nervousness, but I knew that I was aroused as well, and there seemed to be a torch in my pocket. I had scrunched the towel into a ball, with which I dabbed ineffectually at her left armpit, noting as I did so that there were a few stray wisps of brown hair nestling moistly there. This, too, I found exciting, for it suggested a kind of wantonness.

"Are you feeling all right, Neil? You've gone quite pale."

"I'm okay, thank you," I said, in a small voice.

I dried her right armpit. She nodded and lowered her arms.

"There's wet between, Neil. Find a dry part of the towel."

I made a fresh ball and slowly reached towards the mid-point of Nurse's ribs. I was trying not to look at her nipples. I moved closer. It was impossible not to look at her nipples. Nurse had wonderful nipples. They were a tawny reddish-brown, with broad, dark aureolae. The stubby tubes protruded thick and rubbery as door-stops. I hoped that one day, before I died, I would be allowed to kiss them.

Despite her forwardness, I felt anxious about touching any part of Nurse's body, and so I bunched the towel into as big a ball as possible before pushing it between her breasts. I glanced up, and Nurse had fixed me with a sly, knowing smile, which unnerved me all the more. As I rubbed the crumpled towel up and down, her ample swellings rolled and swayed, occasionally thwacking my wrists. Then, and for many weeks after, the moment seemed frozen in time.

"Thank you, Neil," Nurse said, stiffly, taking the towel from me. "Do you appreciate the importance?"

"What of?"

"The in-betweens, Neil, the in-betweens."

"The in-betweens?"

"I always tell people to remember Dip," and she nodded seriously.

"Who's Dip?"

"Not who, what. D-I-P. Dip. That stands for Danger-Infection-Pleasure. I know you can remember that."

"Aren't you going to put your top back on?" I asked, for I was becoming mesmerized by her quivering nipples.

"In a minute, Neil, there's really no hurry. We should let the air get to our bodies."

"I suppose."

"Now, tell me what Dip is?"

"Dip – umm? Dip is Danger, Infection and Pleasure."

"That's right."

"But what does it mean?"

"The three in-betweens, Neil. Danger between: supposing you try to cross the road between two parked cars." She wagged a finger in mock admonishment. "Infection between: if you don't clean or dry properly in your special places. Tut-tut. And then, number three. Pleasure between." She smiled and winked at me.

"What's number three about?" I enquired.

She gave that little hand-clap again. "You'll find out soon enough, lad."

"Right. Okay. Are – are you dry now?"

"Quite dry, thank you, Neil."

"Perhaps we ought to go downstairs now."

"Yes, we should have some tea." She raised a finger to her cheek. "But one last thing I must ask you..."

"W-what is it?"

A broad, mischievous grin rippled across Nurse's face. "Please can I have one of your Rolos?"

"No. I mean, I haven't got any Rolos."

"Are you sure? Do my eyes deceive me?" She seemed to be peering down her nose at my legs. "What's in that tube I can see in your trousers?"

I hung my head, studying the floor. If only she would cover herself up, I thought. When I looked up again, she was smiling at me generously, blue eyes sparkling with mirth.

"It's nothing to be ashamed of, Neil. You're a healthy young man." She clapped her hands briskly. "Come on, let's go for some tea!"

"Aren't you going to – ?" I pointed at her naked breasts.

She glanced down and then rolled her eyes to the ceiling. "Of course. Silly me!"

"I could put the kettle on," I offered.

"You're a good boy, Neil. I dare say you've had quite enough excitement for one day," and she winked at me.

In the kitchen, I filled the big blue kettle and set it to boil. Supposing that Gran might return at any moment, I went into the living room, took a freshly-laundered tablecloth from the dresser drawer and spread it carefully over the dining table. Gran always liked to set a proper table at tea-time.

When Nurse came down, her face looked warm and pink and she had buttoned her blouse to the throat. I gazed at her, wondering if perhaps the interlude upstairs had all been a dream. Surreptitiously, I pinched the loose skin at the base of my thumb, squeezed it until it hurt, but the room did not spin or dissolve and I did not wake up.

"Something the matter, Neil?" she asked, perkily.

I shook my head as I smoothed out the wrinkles in the tablecloth.

Nurse left the room, returning a few minutes later with a tray bearing a teapot, crockery and boiled eggs with toast soldiers.

"I'll set this out, Neil, if you could fetch the sugar and milk and some cutlery. Then we shall eat. I expect you've an appetite."

I wondered what we would talk about during tea. The times of the steam trains to Sheffield, perhaps? The probable height of the trees visible from the window? The gorgeous amplitude of Nurse's bosoms? In fact, we ate in almost total silence, though with each scoop of my egg, I could feel my companion's eyes on me.

As we were finishing, I heard the rasp of Gran's key in the latch. We dabbed our mouths and waited for her to appear in the doorway. She looked tired and drawn. Nurse offered her some tea, but she shook her head.

"Are you all right, Neil?" she asked me, quietly.

"Thanks, Gran. How's Granddad?"

She paused before answering. "I think – I don't know. I just don't know."

"Was he conscious?" Nurse asked.

"Yes, but dazed. He's in a special room. I don't know what they call it."

"You ought to sit down," Nurse said.

Gran frowned at her. "That's what I've been doing all afternoon."

She smiled at me quickly and went out. I heard her crying in the hall. I knew then that my Granddad was going to die. I tried to remember his face, for I believed that I would not see it again. You have to remember people's faces, for they are the windows that show the way to their hearts.

Nurse helped me to clear the table. I could hear Gran moving about upstairs. "You should talk to your gran," Nurse said. "In any case, I have to go. I'm on duty tonight."

We put everything in the sink. Nurse looked at her watch. "Will you do these?" she asked. "Don't leave it for your gran."

She picked up her jacket and bag and went into the hall. I followed her, feeling oddly nervous. She called up the stairs. "I have to go now, Mrs Blaney. I'll call on you during the week." The gargle of her raised voice rang out with unexpected harshness in the stair-creaking, clock-ticking gloom of the hall.

"I'll tell her," I said.

"Be kind to her. She's very fond of you."

I walked with Nurse as she wheeled her bicycle to the front gate. For a delicious moment, I looked at the saddle and thought about where it went.

She turned to me. "Now what must you remember, Neil?"

I pulled a face. "I don't know."

"Dear me. You must remember – Dip. Yes?"

"The in-betweens," I said, smiling shyly.

"Right. And Dip is – ?"

I counted them off, wagging my finger in the air. "Danger-Infection-Pleasure."

"Well done!" She patted my shoulder. "You're a fast learner."

"Does everyone know about Dip?"

"They should do. But – who knows? – maybe you're one of the privileged few. Eh, Neil?"

I thought about this. I thought about quite a lot. I wanted to kiss her, but I didn't know how to ask, if there was a proper way.

"You still haven't told me about pleasure," I reminded her.

There was the briefest flash of pale thigh as she mounted her bike and began wheeling it through the gate. "Don't be in such a hurry," she said. "It'll come, all in good time."

She leaned on to the pedals and, the next I knew, she was in the road. I waved, but she didn't look back.

I was going to sit in the kitchen and wait for Gran to come down, but then I remembered the washing-up. I ran some hot water into the sink and found a cloth. Then I remembered something else.

I had never even asked Nurse for her name.

Chapter III

A Bad Boy

My grandfather died in Northdene Cottage Hospital five days after that quietly unforgettable Saturday when he had been taken ill. My father broke the news to me when I came home from school. I had gone straight into the garden to feed my rabbit, which lived in a home-made hutch behind the garage. As I was pushing dandelion leaves through the wire netting, stalks first, I heard Dad's feet on the gravel path, and I turned to see him shuffling diffidently towards me, head down.

"I'm afraid you won't be seeing Granddad Blaney any more," he said. "He died this morning. Anyway, there it is."

I let a handful of leaves fall to the ground. The rabbit didn't seem important any longer. "What was it?" I asked. "What did he die of?"

Dad was still looking at the path, not at me. "Oh, I don't know. Broncho-something or other. His bloomin' lungs."

"Do you know how Gran is?"

"I do not," he replied. "She'll manage. It wasn't unexpected."

I waited for a moment before walking past him, hurrying towards the house. As I reached the back door, I was biting my top lip. My mother was in the kitchen, peering critically at a pan of potatoes. The wireless was on, a man yelling incoherently and people laughing.

I touched my mother's arm. "I'm sorry, Mum," I said, my voice trembling. I didn't want to cry, not yet.

"I hope I've put enough salt in these," she said.

I went upstairs and sat on my bed. Tears began to roll down my face. They trickled into the corners of my mouth, and I licked at the saltiness. I wiped my eyes with my fingers, blurring my vision. My school satchel was still on my back, and I shrugged it off and tipped the contents on to the bed. For a while I stayed there, wondering how long I should wait before I went down to see if Mum was all right.

Shortly, Dad's face, anxious and uncertain, appeared in the doorway. "Your tea'll be ready in ten minutes."

"Okay."

I removed my tie and draped it round the neck of my old teddy bear. Checking in the mirror, I dried my eyes with my handkerchief.

When I went down, Dad was already sitting at the table, fiddling with the cutlery. He didn't look at me. Mum brought in three steaming plates and set them out.

"I'm really sorry about Granddad," I said.

She curled her lip crookedly. "Well, he was an old man," she said. "He came through that war; thousands didn't. Now his time's come."

In those few words, it seemed to me, was encapsulated my mother's entire, uncompromising attitude to life and death. Life was but a shallow distraction, the briefest glimpse of scenery, along the short road from birth to dying. That her father had fought heroically on the battlefields of France, and miraculously survived, was to her no more remarkable than his eventual death was noteworthy. Mum – to coin a phrase – had no truck with honourable endeavour, still less with dying. Friends and relatives came and went, as apparently insignificant as puffs of their own dust, and I never recall a single occasion when she displayed any real sadness at their passing. She acknowledged no life after death except the sentimental memories that lingered on in other people's hearts, and grief in bereavement was but a weakness to be admonished. Because my grandfather was old and consequently frail, Mum had already shielded herself from the emotional inconvenience of his loss by perceiving its inevitability as suitable mitigation. Call it callousness, call it self-protection; I think I looked upon it as a kind of selfish efficiency, a quality you could almost, but not quite, admire.

I remember, on more than one occasion, my father dryly observing that there were "no flies on your mother." The veracity of the judgment was beyond dispute – even though, as I now ruefully reflected, there would soon be a few on Granddad Blaney.

"Have you seen Gran?" I asked, of no-one in particular.

"We shall see her tomorrow," my father replied. "Don't you worry about her."

"Eat your mince," my mother said.

I poked my fork at the boiled, greyish curds, appetising as the stewed mop-head they resembled. "I hate mince," I grumbled.

Mum sighed impatiently. "I'll take it away if you don't want it. There's nothing else."

"Can I go to Granddad's funeral?" I asked.

"You'll be at school," Dad said. "Anyway, there'll be nothing to see."

"Doesn't matter," I persisted. "Otherwise why would anyone ever go to a funeral?"

"When you're dead, you're dead," Mum snapped.

"Are you going, Mum?"

"I suppose I'll have to."

I ate some potato. "Poor Gran," I murmured.

Mum bridled at my sympathy. "Never mind about 'poor Gran'. She'll get everything."

I was tempted to say that she had, in fact, *lost* everything, but I kept quiet. In any case, I was well used to Mum's dismissive judgments at times like these, and I no longer flinched at them. She believed that the bereaved could be succoured in their pain by the simple availability of adequate funding, and I knew from past experience that it was futile to attempt to disabuse her of the notion.

In any event, I could see no reasonable prospect of Gran reaping a bountiful harvest from her husband's death. He was a pensioner who had previously done a manual job in a factory where they made cardboard boxes. How could he have amassed a fortune? She could sell the house, but then she would have nothing to live in. As usual, Mum had cultivated a wildly exaggerated impression of other people's wealth.

"Can I still go to Gran's this Saturday?" I asked.

"That would not be advisable," Dad said, jutting his jaw. "The week after, possibly."

I was in no mood to argue. I thought of my soft-spoken, gentle, agreeable grandfather lying pale and cold and unbelievably dead, and argument seemed pointless and disrespectful.

"I've got a lot of homework," I said, pushing my nearly full plate aside. "I'm going up."

In fact, I had very little homework that day, but it was a good excuse to be alone. I did some French exercises and some arithmetic, pausing occasionally to gaze out of the window into the garden, where a vomit-coloured splash on the lawn showed that Mum had thrown my meal out for the birds.

I repacked my satchel, undressed and climbed naked into bed. It had been a warm day, and the cool sheets felt freshly tactile against my skin. Turning over, I began to cry softly into my pillow, struggling to smother any sound, for there was a family protocol to be observed. You cried if your house burned down or a bully knocked your teeth out, but not when someone had only died. I sobbed until my cheeks stung and my nose bubbled, and then I lay on my back again and closed my eyes.

In my mind's eye I could see Nurse, and she was smiling that smile again, that mysterious, unspoken invitation to the land of dreams. My hand crept down in the musty darkness to nestle damply in the virgin scrublands below my navel, and soon I was a growing boy and, if I squeezed my eyes tightly shut, it was Nurse's hand that held me there, and she was whispering in my ear with wet lips, telling me not to worry, she would make it all right, it wouldn't matter, nothing would matter any more.

When finally I returned to the big brown house, something strange happened. Over the great many years that have elapsed since those childhood days, I have learned to accept it philosophically as a trivial, meaningless incident; but, in the manner of repeatedly picking at a sore, I keep revisiting that afternoon in my mind, as though by – as it were – returning to the scene of the crime, I might somehow alter that small nugget of history and render it more palatable.

It was a hot Saturday, the sun-splashed streets daubed with the bright primary colours of summer in suburbia: green grass, blue sky, yellow sun in your face, red splotches of bumbling buses. On good days, summer can be as vivid as a child's improbable painting.

I had spent most of the morning talking to Gran about my granddad and how, each in our own way, we would cope without him. I suppose it was less a conversation than an exercise, part of the process of learning not to be sad. We thought we understood, or tried to convince ourselves, that departed loved ones continue to live with us in spirit, and that spirit is borne on the air we breathe. If the burden of our grief is too great, the oppressive density of that trauma is more than the spirit's flight can sustain, and it becomes as a meteor falling through space into the earth's atmosphere, something light and brave and everlasting that is made ephemeral by unseen forces, and burns to death.

"Shall we go to the rec this afternoon?" Gran asked me, as we cleared the table after our fishcakes.

"That would be nice," I said. "We might see the *Master Cutler,* and I could watch the old men playing bowls."

"I didn't know you were interested in bowls."

"Well, sort of."

We walked slowly down to the little gateway under the trees. It was cool there in the dappled shade, and the breeze in the leaves pattered like falling rain.

"Gran?" I had to raise my voice to be heard above the snorting rattle of a passing train. "Would you ever marry somebody else?"

Gran laughed, shaking her head. "Goodness, no! I'm too long in the tooth for all that. I'll stay as I am."

"Could you sell your house and get lots of money?"

"I'd get a fair price. Then where would I live?"

I thought about this, kicking idly at twigs blown down by the wind. "You could come and live with us."

Gran tossed her head and made a funny whooping noise, which I took to be derisory. "Oh yes. Your mum'd love that."

"I think it would be all right. Then you could show me how to make fishcakes."

"There's more to life than fishcakes, Neil."

"I know. Gran?"

"Not another question, boy."

"You know Nurse?"

"Of course I know Nurse. What about her?"

"Well, I – she – "

"Spit it out, boy!"

"Well, she can't really be called Nurse, can she?"

Gran stopped in her tracks, took off her glasses, peered at me and put them back on again. We carried on walking in silence for a few seconds. "Her name is Miss Melksham," she said. "Sally Melksham." She stared at me again. "Why do you want to know?"

I shrugged. "I wanted to know what to call her."

"You should call her Nurse," she said, tersely, "like the rest of us."

We stood in the long grass, waiting for the express to Sheffield, but there were only a few electrics. Probably it had already gone through. I picked some toadstools, but Gran told me to drop them on the ground because they were poisonous. She warned me not to lick my fingers. When we reached the bowling green, I found myself thinking of Nurse. There were only a few elderly ladies playing, uniformly identified by their tight, white perms, cream linen skirts and flat-soled shoes. They spoke in clipped, educated accents and occasionally bent over to inspect the turf, displaying backsides the size of small pianos.

I murmured her name under my breath. "Sally. Sally Melksham. Sally Melksham."

"You talking to yourself?" Gran offered up a withering smile.

"I was thinking aloud," I told her, which was perfectly true, for I was thinking of Nurse, thinking how I might get to see her again soon, see her sunny face and shiny hair and that tantalizing secret chasm beneath her pale throat, where my trembling hand had oh so briefly roamed in delirious torment.

"I'm hot, Neil. Shall we have a lolly, perhaps?"

"Sally Melksham...Sally Melksham...Sally Melksham...Sa-"

"Neil!"

"Sorry, Gran. What did you say?"

"I asked you if you would like an ice-cream," Gran said, frowning. "A lolly, maybe."

Looking over the hedge, I could see that Mr Icecool had not yet arrived, and I pointed this out to Gran.

"Doesn't matter," she said. "We can walk up to the top gate. There's the paper shop in the main road."

I nodded in careless agreement, still lost in the reverie that came from knowing Nurse's name. As we turned towards the upper level of the rec, beyond the playing fields, I walked with my head down, eschewing all distractions, the better to concentrate on the novel discovery of Sally Melksham. Whatever my limited knowledge, of her or of the world, I certainly knew that, come what may, I had to see her again. She had become the sum of all my parts.

Yet something troubled me. For all that she had warmed to me, as I to her, and had appeared to enjoy my company, there lingered the suspicion that Nurse, recognizing my immaturity, would not take me seriously as a constant friend. Had she not told me I was a 'good boy'? I may have accepted that commendation as a compliment, but now I could see it as an oblique reference to my juvenile unworldliness, a perception of me which would surely prove an impediment to any meaningful development of our relationship. The great disparity in our ages aside, my innate 'goodness', if such it truly was, would not sit comfortably alongside any romantic intention. This was a time when I could not afford to be too good.

"You're very quiet, Neil. You're not unhappy, are you?"

"It's all right, Gran. I'm just thinking."

"About Granddad?"

"Sort of."

I could hardly tell her I was thinking about Nurse. My preoccupation with Nurse was a private matter between me and my inflamed hormones.

"I meant to tell you. Granddad said he wanted you to have his encyclopaedias. You know, the ones in the spare bedroom. He knew how much they fascinated you. They're yours to take whenever you want."

I looked up and smiled at her, a frail figure in her thin cotton dress and plain grey knitted cardigan. "Thanks, Gran. That was really kind of him."

I wondered: would it significantly advance my cause if I were to confide to Nurse – to Sally Melksham – that, as a mere child, I had pulled the wings off butterflies, fired stones at sparrows with my catapult and urinated high over our neighbours' fence while the lady of the house lay sunbathing on the lawn? Were these not acts of unpardonable badness? I plodded ahead, considering the matter. Upon further reflection, I decided, somewhat reluctantly, that these incidents were childish misdemeanours which could not be classified as bad deeds because they were not actually mean-spirited. There lay the key.

At the top of a sloping greensward, the rec's upper gate opened on to a quiet area of residential streets. I remember we came out on to Mandalay Avenue, which curved in a half-crescent and ran downhill to the main road. The houses here were mostly large 1930s semi-detached, standing well back from the road, with spacious front gardens set about with monkey puzzle trees. The people inside, you would guess, voted Conservative out of social necessity, attended church on Sunday and never allowed their children to be seen in the front garden, let alone play in the street. Mandalay Avenue stood quiet and immaculate, spotless house windows glinting self- importantly in the sun.

For no reason I can recall, somewhat unchivalrously, I was walking on the inside of the pavement, close to the front gardens. The steady uphill tramp across the rec had made us hot; now Gran looked tired, and occasionally her feet scuffed against the flagstones.

What I did next was, I now think, a misjudgment. That is the least that can be said of it. With the benefit of hindsight, I would say that it was a bad idea, even if the act itself was stupid rather than immoral.

"You look tired, Gran," I said, delicately touching her arm. "Can I carry your bag for you?"

It was the usual battered black leather holdall she took with her everywhere. The top zipped right across, but she always left it open. She smiled vaguely and handed me the bag, and I fell into step a few paces behind her. Glancing inside the holdall, I saw a headscarf, a spectacle case, a paperback book, a bulging paper bag and, resting on the top, Gran's tan-coloured purse. Ahead of us, a long box hedge at the foot of a lawn was bounded by a low brick wall, with a fire hydrant pillar halfway along its gentle curve. With my heart thumping, I edged closer to the wall and slackened my pace. I checked that Gran was looking ahead, then I plucked the purse out with my left hand and dropped it into the gap between the hedge and the wall. Striding on, I caught up with Gran, and we walked downhill to the main road. My mouth was dry, and there was a funny taste in it, a mixture of cheese and vinegar. I could hear my heart beating like a drum.

"That's a long walk," Gran said. "We deserve a lolly," and she took my hand and led me across the busy road to the paper shop. It seemed almost dark in the shop after the glare of the street, and our confusion was heightened by the gabble of a bunch of teenaged girls, laughing together at the counter.

"What would you like?" Gran asked me.

"*Orange Maid,* please." I gave her back her bag.

The woman serving ignored the girls and waited for us. Gran asked her for two *Orange Maids* and began rummaging in her bag. Gradually a cloud of dismay spread across her face.

"What's the matter, Gran?" I asked, feigning innocent concern.

"My purse. It's gone. All my money."

"You – you're sure you brought it out?"

She was blinking back tears. "Of course I'm sure. I remember putting it in the bag."

The girls were nudging and jostling one another; I could even hear their clothes chafing and snagging as they played around.

"Are you taking these or not?" The shopkeeper was brandishing the lollies in a ludicrous semaphore.

"Wassup?" one girl yelped.

"I've got some money," I said, as if this mattered.

"Daft ol' bat an't got no money," another girl sang out.

"No, put them back," Gran told the woman, without looking at her. With the fingers of one hand she stroked her forehead, as though this might help her to understand what had happened.

The girls were laughing again, punching one another, then bumping against the counter and rebounding on to Gran's arm. I put my hand on her waist and tried to steer her to the door, but she rounded on the kids, turning her back on me. "Have one of you taken my purse?"

The nearest girl glared up at her, eyes flashing. "I an't touched your bleedin' purse!"

"Bloody cheek!" her friend yelled.

I pulled harder on Gran's waist. "Come on, Gran. I don't think it was them."

"How do you know?" she moaned.

Reluctantly, she allowed me to manoeuvre her outside. A single tear ran slowly down her wrinkled cheek. "What am I going to do, Neil?" she asked me, her voice hardly more than a whisper. "All my money."

"We can walk back the way we came," I suggested. "We might see it if it's fallen out."

"Yes, and what if someone's picked it up?"

"Come on, Gran."

I led her across the road and into Mandalay Avenue. Her query had set me thinking. What if somebody *had* picked up the purse? Supposing they took it to the police station. Supposing they walked off with it. What if they removed the money and threw the empty purse over the next hedge? Too late, I realised that I had foolishly conceived the act in a kind of vacuum, something that made its own moment in time and space and was without consequence. It would be but a fleeting pulse of badness that only I would know about. Now, though the incident was no surprise to me, I found myself shocked by it, because it had caused pain to someone I loved.

"You were carrying my bag," Gran said. There was no note of accusation in her voice.

"I know. Perhaps – "

"Perhaps what? You didn't drop it, did you?"

"No. I think I sort of stumbled."

"You mean you fell over? I didn't see – "

"I didn't fall over. There was – like a jolt."

"Somebody jolted you?"

"No."

"Oh Neil! What then?"

I took a deep breath, and hoped I wasn't going red. Sometimes I was not very good at not going red. "Up there," I said, pointing ahead. "I think I can remember the place."

We walked on up the hill. I could see the bend and the yellow patch on the fire hydrant. You already know that I am not from a religious family; but now I prayed. I walked with my head bowed, my lips moving silently in blasphemously unmerited imploration: *Dear God, Please let it be there. Please let it still be there.* As I neared the hydrant I slowed almost to a halt, then turned to face downhill. My heart was racing, and a sour bile rose in my throat.

Gran moved up to face me. "Did something happen here?"

I hung my head. "Might've done."

"What? I can't hear if you talk to your boots."

"I think this might be the place," I said, looking up but avoiding her eyes.

"But where's my purse, Neil?"

For several seconds I stood there, chewing my top lip, hardly daring to move, then I stepped aside and began feeling my way along the top of the wall like a blind man, hand over hand, eyes straining into the shadowy tangle of roots behind the brickwork.

Supposing.

Please God.

My heart leapt. My unworthy prayers were answered. There, wedged in a fork low down in the hedge, I could see Gran's purse. I reached into the undergrowth and, straightening up, clutched it gratefully to my chest.

"Oh, thank Goodness!" Gran closed her eyes as she spoke the words, as though she, too, uttered a prayer.

"Here!" I held the purse out to her. "I thought I'd find it. I just sort of had this feeling."

Gran snapped the catch open, and I saw her pale lips moving slightly as she checked the contents.

"Is everything there?" I ventured.

Supposing.

She shut the purse and pushed it down into her bag. "As far as I can remember," she said, quietly.

I searched her face, but there was no sign of relief there, only a brooding thoughtfulness. A moment passed, and she looked directly at me for the first time since I had retrieved the purse. I tell you, as long as I live, I will never forget the look she gave me. It was a cold stare to constrict my throat and send a jagged wave of icy pain through my bowels, like the malignant onset of some dread disease. I stood stock-still, as though a bolt of lightning had fused me to the pavement. Reflected in my grandmother's eyes was a deep well of overwhelming disappointment, and I believed then that I had abused and betrayed her love and her trust. It was not until I thought to move that I realised I was holding my breath, and I choked noisily, tasting a sudden slap of acid on my tongue.

We began walking slowly down the hill. "I want to go home now," I said.

"How do you mean – home?"

"I mean to your house. We could get the bus."

Gran shook her head. "We'd have to wait, and it would be crowded. We'll walk. When we get to the shops, we can keep in the shade."

"Gran?"

"Let's just walk, Neil."

So we strolled down and turned along the main street. We walked in silence, and even the clamour of the traffic did not intrude upon our thoughts. I was hot and sticky, and there was a sickly-sour taste in my mouth, but I could not ask about the ice lolly now. It took us twenty minutes to get back to the house.

I told Gran to rest on the living room settee while I made a cool jug of lemonade. When I brought it in, she was slumped there with her eyes closed, but I could tell she wasn't asleep. I took two tumblers from the sideboard and put them next to the jug on a small rosewood occasional table which I had pulled from the nest of four that always stood beside the hearth in summer, when the fire would not be lit. These interlocking tables, I recall, had long been a contentious issue in the Blaney house, ever since the day when, checking the property during one of my grandparents' rare holidays, my father had taken it upon himself to undertake a little preventive maintenance. Mindful of an earlier accident, when hot soup had been spilled on one table top, imprinting the patina with what appeared to be the outline map of Madagascar, Dad had decided, without consultation, to seal the surface of each table with a sheet of *Formica*, a jaunty effort in pink gingham. When challenged by my mother as to the justification for this exercise, upon which even the Philistines themselves would not have embarked without reservation, Dad had replied simply that it would serve as protection against possible damage from future spills, obtusely ignoring the certain damage now inflicted by the application of *Formica*.

"Gran!" I roused her with a harsh whisper and indicated her glass.

She opened her eyes and squinted at me. "Mmm? Oh, thanks."

"Maybe you should go for a lie-down," I said.

"I'm all right. I'm just resting my head."

"Is it aching?"

"It's pounding something terrible."

"You could have an aspirin with your drink," I suggested, brightly.

Gran took a sip of lemonade, leaned back and closed her eyes again. "Haven't got any," she murmured.

I had an idea. "I could go to the chemist's and get some," I offered, though my idea had nothing to do with medication.

"Would you mind?" She peeked at me through one watery eye.

"Course."

"Take some money out of my purse," she said, wearily.

I patted the back of her hand, pale, curled and crisply veined, like a fallen dead leaf. "I won't be long," I said.

"Neil."

"Yes, Gran?"

"Go to Michaelson's for me. Get me a local paper, if there's one left. I want to put an advert in."

"What for?"

"Never you mind."

In next door's front garden, old Mrs Cooper was watering the dead flowers in her window box. I waved at her. "You goin' home, young Neil?" she croaked.

"No. My gran's got a bad headache. I'm going to get her something."

"Ah, you're a good boy, Neil."

I stared at her until she turned away. I seemed to be experiencing considerable difficulty in not being a good boy. The thought occurred to me that perhaps I was not designed for badness. That happens to people sometimes, like a gene missing or a group of brain cells subtly malformed.

I bought the aspirin and the newspaper, and then it was time to address the real reason for my keenness to run an errand that afternoon. Close to the newsagent's there was an alleyway, and a few yards down its privet-bordered length stood a telephone box. I stepped inside and felt the heavy door thud shut against my back, sealing me in silence. Thumbing through the directory, I found two people named Melksham, an L.T. Melksham and, yes, an S.J. Melksham. Sally Melksham. Standing there, butterflies skittering in my stomach, I spoke her name aloud: "Sally Melksham. Sally Melksham." It had to be.

Please God. Don't hate me too much.

I dialled the number. After just a few rings, somebody answered, a woman's voice. Or, almost, two women's voices in close, electronic harmony.

"Is this Sally Melksham?" came my plaintive enquiry.

"Who's there?"

"Sally?"

"Yes, this is Sally Melksham."

"This is Neil – Neil Robertson."

For one hollow, awful moment, I feared we had been cut off, for the ensuing pause, in which I clutched sweatily at a crude plastic shell filled with zinging nothingness, seemed to go on too long for sense or comfort.

When her voice returned, its suddenness made me jump. "Neil! This *is* a surprise!"

"I wanted to talk to you."

"Where are you, Neil?"

"In a phone box close to Gran's."

"I see. Is something wrong?"

"No. I just – I want to ask you something."

"I'm listening."

I took a deep breath. "I want you to tell me about the third in-between."

She made me wait through another silence. Was it my imagination, or did I hear stifled laughter seeping down the line?

"Neil, what's this all about?"

"What I said. I keep thinking about it. I keep thinking about you."

I heard a short, sharp sigh, an exclamation. "You're serious, aren't you?"

"I wouldn't have rung you, otherwise."

"Well, it's difficult. I mean, down the phone."

"I want to see you again."

"Right," and she stretched the word out – *Rrriiight* – in deliberate calculation. "Let's see. I – er – I could come to your gran's on a Saturday, but then you'd have to share me with her."

"I know," I said, sullenly.

I knew a better alternative, but it was important to me that she, and not I, suggested it.

"Maybe you'd like to come round to me."

I swallowed hard. The pips sounded, and I frantically punched in some more money.

"Neil? Are you still there?"

"Yes."

"Well?"

"Thanks. I'd like that," I said, trying not to sound too elated.

"Very well. But I'll have to work it out with my shifts. I'd need to look in my diary."

"Okay."

"Neil, how are you going to do this – with your mum and dad and everything?"

Crestfallen, I realised that the awkward logistics of the meeting had not occurred to me. I felt deflated and a little stupid. "I don't quite know," I admitted.

"All right, well don't worry for now. Perhaps I can think of something. If you're sure."

"Yes. Oh yes. I'm really sure."

"In that case – shall I ring you at home, say, on Monday evening?"

"No!"

"Oh, right. Then you ring me – about six o'clock? We'll fix something up."

I started to write down her number on the bag from the chemist's.

"That all right, Neil?"

"Yes! Yes!"

"Good. I'll hear from you, then?"

"Yes." I felt sick again. Supposing I was sick in the phone box. It would go on my shoes and everywhere. "Thank you."

"All right, Neil."

"Sally!"

"Yes?"

"I love you!" And I slammed down the receiver.

Grabbing the paper bag, I shouldered the door open and lunged out, past a man about to enter. As I reached the road, I heard footsteps behind me.

"Excuse me, son!"

I wheeled round, walking backwards.

The man thrust out a hand. "You forgot your paper."

"Oh. Right. Thanks. My gran asked for it specially."

He nodded, grinning. "Good boy!"

I crossed over and began striding back towards the house. In the distance I could see old Mrs Cooper leaning over her gate. I wrinkled my nose and poked my tongue out at her, but she was too far away to see me. Lifting my eyes to the scalding sky, I gazed into the impenetrable blue void until I felt I would be blinded. I expanded my chest importantly, and I smiled, for I was surely a man of the world.

Chapter IV

Food for Thought

My father's venomous indignation on learning of Gran's lodger was as short-lived as it was irrational. For three oppressive week-ends I moped about the house, before a natural preoccupation with more important issues, and my mother's gentle insistence, encouraged Dad towards a more relaxed attitude, and he suggested I cycle over to *Arcadia* next Saturday.

The school holidays had begun, and I was invigorated by the heady elixir of freedom.

"Dad, can I stay over?" I asked, as I pumped up my bike tyres.

Dad sniffed and jutted his jaw. "Better ask your mother."

As he habitually told my mother what to do, I was pleasantly surprised by this moment of deference, not to say reassured, for I knew that Mum would be pleased to have the house to herself for a few days. In fact, there was a precedent here, for at some stage during each holiday I would have an extended week-end at Gran's or perhaps go from Wednesday to Saturday. It was a carefree diversion to which I always looked forward.

Predictably, Mum agreed that I could go and stay longer. "What about that man?" she asked, guardedly.

"What about him?"

"Is he still there?"

"Don't know," I replied, vaguely, though I suspected that he was and hoped that he would be.

"Best not be friendly with him," she advised, a proposition so absurd that I could not be bothered to dignify it with a serious response. "I'll ring Mrs Cooper," she added, "and get a message to Gran."

"Why's she not got a phone, Mum?"

"Oh, that was Granddad," she said, wearily. "He wouldn't have it in the house." She shook her head in exasperation. "Old people!"

Going back into the garden, I met Dad coming up the path with a newspaper bundle in his hands. "Your rabbit died," he said, gruffly. "Stiff as a board."

I poked my finger into the paper and pressed it against the cold, unyielding fur. "Poor Monty. I always fed him, you know."

Dad squeezed the paper tightly together. "Ach, these wee animals. They pop off for no reason."

"Can I bury him in the gooseberry patch?"

"A garden's for living things, not dead things," he said, and he lifted the lid from the dustbin and stuffed the package inside.

Mum watched him from the open back door. "See you wash your hands," she told him.

"What for?"

She shuddered, screwing up her eyes. "Dead bodies – filthy."

I followed Dad towards the garage. "Do you think he was ill?" I asked him.

"Who?" he said, over his shoulder.

"Monty. Perhaps I should have noticed."

"Ah, it's like I said. Rabbits and things, you can never tell. Bloomin' nuisance." He turned and fixed me with a stern stare. "Don't worry about it. I'll get you a replacement rabbit. Problem solved."

"Pity it's not like that with people," I observed.

"What?" He tipped his head towards the garage door. "Your bike's all ready."

"Thanks."

"I was thinking about your visit," he said.

"Mum said it would be all right."

"Aha. But what about your clothes and things?"

I pursed my lips thoughtfully. "Put them in my saddlebag, I suppose. I don't know. Last time I stayed I didn't have a bike."

"That's right. My suggestion is, I drive over on the Sunday

with the rest of your stuff and then I can pick up those encyclopaedias and bring them back."

"Granddad said I should have them. Gran told me."

"I know, I know. It's all right, I'll put them in your room."

I nodded my agreement, privately reflecting that Dad's willingness to go to Gran's probably had more to do with satisfying his curiosity concerning her lodger than with the matter of the encyclopaedias. Though I was not convinced that a meeting, if such there should be, would necessarily bring about a harmonious relationship between Dad and Archie, I was generously disposed to gamble on the outcome, in case, as one Scot to another, the pair might find mutual favour.

That Saturday dawned heavily overcast, and I pedalled furiously all the way, anxious to arrive before the rain. As I rolled over the kerb, I saw Archie pushing the old red-and-green lawnmower round the front lawn.

"Hiya Archie! Remember me?"

He turned, pulling a well-used handkerchief from his pocket. "Neil lad!" He mopped his glazed brow. "Of course I remember you. To tell you the truth, I wondered what had happened to you."

"I can stay till Wednesday."

"Ah, it's good to see you again. Wednesday, you say?"

"We've broken up now."

"What? Oh, I see. You'll be pleased about that."

"Yes. I hate school."

He raised his eyebrows disapprovingly. "Hate's a vicious word, Neil. Hate's destructive."

"I know," I said, feeling suitably cowed.

"You know what my old daddy used to say to me? He told me, when you hate someone, a little part of them dies. Hate's that powerful."

"So if you hate someone, you could be a murderer?"

He nodded. "Maybe, maybe." He paused for a moment, as if to consider what he had just said, then he smacked the handles of the mower and leaned into it. "Got to get on, Neil. Your gran'll want this finished before the rain comes."

I wheeled my bicycle round the back and took the bulging

saddlebag indoors with me. Gran was talking to herself in the kitchen, one hand over her mouth, with her back to the open door. I couldn't hear what she was saying.

"Looks like it's going to rain, Gran."

She turned, with a sharp intake of breath. "Oh Neil! You made me jump."

"Sorry." I dropped my bag on the table. "I saw Archie."

"Yes." She tipped her head towards the bag. "Is that all your things?"

"Dad's bringing the rest tomorrow. He said he'd collect the encyclopaedias."

"Oh, right. I've changed the rooms round, by the way. Archie's got the big front bedroom, there's more room in there for his bits and pieces."

"I see. So where am I?"

"You can have your granddad's old room. It's plenty big enough for one. I've put you a chair in there."

"A chair?"

"Yes, a chair, a wooden one. You know what a chair is. Archie said there ought to be a chair in there."

"Is it that broken one from your room?"

"Of course not. Would I give you a broken chair to sit on? It's the old green one from the other room."

"From the front room?"

"Yes. I'm not about to go carrying chairs upstairs."

"No. So is there no chair in Archie's room?"

Gran treated me to one of her patronising smiles. "What, are you daft, boy? Haven't I just told you? I've put it in Granddad's room."

"But Archie wanted a chair, Gran."

"Well, the chair can't be in two places at once," said Gran, rolling her eyes. "I can't make two chairs out of one."

"But – what about Archie?" I persisted.

"What about him?"

Absurdly, I felt myself beginning to cry. Why did grown-ups insist upon complicating everything? "Shall I give him his chair back?"

"It's not his chair, Neil, it's my chair. The chair is nothing to do with Archie."

"It's not fair!" I cried, my voice quavering, "Archie's given up his room and now he's lost his chair."

"Now – will you stop this, Neil? Archie asked for the bigger room because he wanted the space. He never had a chair, so he can't have lost one. You can't lose something you haven't got."

"But what if I put my chair back? I – I – "

"Stop that grizzling!" Gran warned me, over a raised forefinger. "Otherwise you'll go straight home. And don't you go messing with the furniture!"

I stood there, blinking back tears of frustration. Behind me, I could hear the whirr and rasp of the mower, an irregular metallic respiration, as Archie struggled to finish the lawn. "I'll take my things up then," I said, coldly.

I went upstairs to the small back bedroom, closed the door behind me and began to unpack my somewhat crumpled clothes. Gran had put the chair next to the bed. I picked it up and moved it nearer the door, banging it down hard on the floor. Then I decided it might be in the way there, so I lifted it back a couple of feet and thumped it down on the floor again. I sat on the bed and stared malevolently at the chair, and it still looked to me as if it was in the wrong place, so I gave it a spiteful kick, and it fell over with a loud bang. After some consideration, I decided against picking it up, at least for the time being, and left it lying dead on its back on the rug, its spindly legs thrust out in helpless rigor mortis.

The cycle ride and my argument with Gran had tired me, and I lay down on the bed with my hands clasped behind my head. There was a ragged ochre-coloured stain on the ceiling, and I tried to imagine what country it resembled. By drawing my elbows in, one at a time, I could sniff my armpits, in case they smelled of tomato soup. They seemed to be all right. I thought of getting my penis out, but there was no lock on the door, and a discovery would be hard to legitimise.

Below the window, a sudden clanking noise told me that Archie was putting the lawnmower back in the shed. I carried on staring at the ceiling, supposing that the brown stain could be

Australia. The bed felt lumpy, but its firmness suited me, offering surer support than the huge, squashy double bed in Gran's room, where I had last slept in the spring. Now I was fifteen, I was too old to sleep next to my Gran, although the change of arrangement had never been discussed. It was something tacitly agreed between us, a mute acknowledgment that I was growing up.

In my recollection, then as now, the big bed, in what had long since ceased to be a marital bedroom, was a grand brass bedstead bearing a thick, marshmallow mattress, overlaid with a hotchpotch of blankets and a pink floral counterpane. The underside of the frame was fashioned from a series of U-shaped girders, stove-enamelled in grey, swooping halfway to the floor. It was a bed of whose construction Isambard Kingdom Brunel himself would have approved. Invariably, when I slept there, I was sent up alone no later than half past nine, to find the heavy curtains drawn and the room in near-darkness. When I turned on the bedside lamp, I could see on the wall facing me, to the left of the chimney breast, a moodily evocative painting, inscribed at the bottom of the frame: *The Welcome Light of Home.* The picture showed, in blending tones of sepia, grey and yellow, a weary shepherd and his dog driving a flock of sheep home on a winter's evening, along a snowbound lane towards a distant thatched cottage, where smoke curled from the chimney and a pale golden glow filled the window. I was sure that, as soon as the old shepherd had penned his sheep for the night and pushed open the front door, his smiling wife would be waiting for him with a bowl of soup, some warm bread and a consoling hug. With its aura of stark simplicity and gentle hope, the painting has somehow left an indelible impression in my mind, and whenever I gazed upon that scene I felt happy and sad at the same time. Perversely – for I loved my gran and treasured my visits to her house – I not infrequently lay in bed on the first night and grew morosely homesick at the sight of the ragged shepherd plodding to his warm cottage, until tears started in my eyes and I would have given anything for my mother's reassuring arm around me. *The Welcome Light of Home.* The calmness of the scene belied its power.

Hiding under the bed was a capacious china chamber pot. It was uncompromisingly white, and might almost have glowed in the dark. Gran was concerned that I should not have to traipse across to the bathroom during the night, and so I was allowed to use the potty instead. At fourteen, I was still on the potty. Whilst I would retreat from suggesting that there is an art to successful use of the chamber pot, I must say that, bleary-eyed from sleep and fumbling in the dark, I generally found the exercise rather more hazardous than stumbling to the toilet. Urinating from a standing position was ill-advised, as the pot then presented too distant a target to be reliably located, with potentially disastrous consequences. Also, the impact speed of my fountain as it hurtled downwards from a yard away tended to send a fine spray sideways on to my bare feet, which made them cold and sticky. Thus, I preferred to kneel before the pot, dramatically reducing the range-finding risk, but introducing the serious possibility, if not the inevitable likelihood, of hosing down the front of my pyjama trousers. Yet I remember the big potty with something approaching affection. I loved the chunky, solid feel of the curved, ornamental handle in my hand as I dragged the heavy crock out from beneath the bed, loved the melodic chime of my water as it rose, softly effervescing, in the bowl, and the humid, nutty fragrance that clouded my nostrils as I emptied myself to the last drop.

Another sound drew me back to present reality, this time from inside the house. Music. I could definitely hear music. It was coming from across the landing. I went to the door and listened, holding my breath. From the open door of the front bedroom, pulses of pounding music swelled into the corridor. Quietly, almost stealthily, I crept along to Archie's room and peered round the door. Archie was lying on his back on the bed in his vest and trousers, waving one arm in the air. The music was coming from a red-and-cream *Dansette* record player perched on a small table under the window, and Archie was too engrossed to notice me. I waited, smiling and nodding my head in time to the dark chords reverberating in the room. Then my shoulder made the door squeak, and Archie looked up and saw me.

"Neil! I didn't – did I disturb you?" He sat up and reached over to the table.

"No – please!" I waved his arm away. "Leave it. I like music."

"Well, maybe it's a wee bit loud." He fiddled with the volume knob. "There!"

"Do you mind if I listen?"

"Mind? Certainly not, lad. Of course, it may not be your choice of music."

"It's *The Planets,* isn't it?"

He grinned broadly. "Why, that's right! Well now. A youngster that enjoys orchestral music – that's a rarity!"

"I like all kinds of music. But I think I like this kind best."

"Really? That's tremendous!"

"This is *Mars,* isn't it?"

He nodded happily. "So it is. The Bringer of War." He raised his eyebrows and fixed me with a penetrating stare. "You're a bright lad, and no mistake."

I sat on the edge of the bed and listened with him until *Mars* had finished. When the last great outburst had died away, he carefully lifted off the pickup arm and set it aside.

"Now I'm interrupting you," I said.

"Oh no, it's all right. I can play it any time." He patted me lightly on the thigh. "It's good to talk, when you've like-minded company."

"Yes. Do you have lots of records, Archie?"

"Aye, I do. But most of them are back home in Scotland. I just keep a few favourites with me." He lowered his eyes and nodded slowly, thoughtfully. "Aye, just a few special ones."

I wanted to know about Scotland. I wondered why he was down in the south and whether he was really alone. Why would he leave Kinlochrannoch? There were golden hairs sprouting from the backs of his fingers, but he wore no rings. I thought that he might be embarrassed if I asked him about his home and his family, for these were private matters. All that might come later.

Rising from the bed, he took the record from the turntable and carefully slid it into its sleeve. "Vienna Philharmonic," he told me. "Finest orchestra in the world."

"I bet you know a whole lot about music and things," I said.

"Oh, a bit. That's the point about music; one man can only ever know a bit, even if he were to devote his lifetime to the learning." He shook his head, as if to make room for a new idea. "Now here's a thought for you. I expect you like your food, hmm?"

"My food?"

"Aha."

"I like most things, except cauliflower and cabbage."

He laughed. "Okay, we'll leave them out of the equation."

"But what's that got to do with music?" I asked.

"Ah," and he waved a forefinger authoritatively in the air, "that I am about to explain. I shall, as they say, draw an analogy."

Smiling in anticipation, I jiggled sideways until my feet were off the floor. But for me, I reflected, Archie would now have a chair in his room, and at least one of us would not have to sit on the bed. Perhaps the broken chair in Gran's room could be repaired. Archie looked to me as if he would know how to repair things.

"Now tell me, Neil: have you ever been to a banquet?"

"What, like in medieval times?"

"Yes, that's what I had in mind. A gargantuan feast."

I shook my head.

"Very well," Archie continued. "Then you must use your imagination. Right?"

"Okay."

"Good lad. So you're in a grand baronial mansion, maybe even a castle."

"I've been in a castle. In Scotland."

"Aha. That's good. So you can picture the scene. You are ushered through a grand hall with polished floors, lofty ceilings hung with huge chandeliers and all the walls resplendent with gilt-framed paintings by the great masters." He turned from this reverie to look directly at me. "Are you with me, Neil? Are you there?"

"Oh yes, Archie. Go on."

"Fine. An unseen figure places a gentle hand at your back and guides you to a pair of tall wooden doors, which mysteriously swing open at your approach. Within the room beyond is a sight to delight the eye. Stretching the full length of the long room is a beautifully veneered dining table spread with every conceivable delicacy – dishes piled high with – with fragrant seafood, plates bearing great hams and sides of beef – you're not a vegetarian, are you?"

"No."

"Thank God for that. I'd have been wasting my time here. Where was I?"

"Sides of beef."

"Oh yes. And a whole roast hog, sizzling and gleaming under the sparkling chandeliers. More plates with golden turkey and chicken, and cold meats, too, and cuts of exotic pate from around Europe, and – yes – there'd have to be vegetables, vast tureens of steaming potatoes and carrots and parsnips and broccoli, every imaginable vegetable, pulled fresh from the kitchen garden, and – and the fruit, Neil, you should see the wonderful mounds of brightly-coloured fruits from all over the world; you've never seen such fruits! Do you like fruit, Neil, hmm?"

"I ate a whole bag of plums once. I was sick."

"Aye, very likely. Well then. You walk slowly down the length of the magnificent table, a table positively groaning under the weight of so much glorious food, and you come to the end of the long room – and again there's this hand in the small of your back, easing you towards another set of doors, doors that open magically before you – and guess what?"

"Um? Is it more food?"

"Correct." Archie's right hand wafted the air, the better to emphasize his description. "Extending for yard upon yard ahead of you stands a mighty table set about with venison, game birds, rabbit, goose...incredible. You're in Heaven, Neil. All this is yours, you see. And look at the bread, Neil, all the different shapes of fresh-baked bread lying warm in wicker baskets, too many to count." He paused for breath.

"Do you think I'll ever see anything like that, Archie? I mean, really?"

He tipped his head on one side and gazed at me thoughtfully. "I think you probably will," he said. "Because I think you will listen and learn and accept the guidance to get you there. You will ask for the way towards wisdom."

"Is there another room in the castle?"

"Neil, there are rooms beyond counting. As the next set of doors swing open, you can see a table as rich and full as the ones before it, a table bedecked with all manner of colourful sweets and confections, and bottles of wine, and there are tempting pastries and strange jugs and bowls with lids on, full of – full of – I don't know, Neil." He shrugged his shoulders and leaned back against the headboard, as though the journey had exhausted him. "I just don't know, Neil; but what I do know is, those doors just keep on opening before you, and there's another room, another banquet, and another, and another, and there's no end to it. As long as you keep searching, Neil, it's there for the taking, like an infinity of mirrors."

He fell silent for a while, then he jabbed a finger at me, not an aggressive or intimidating gesture, but one that told me I should listen and understand. "Tell me, do you think I've been talking about food and feasting?"

I pulled a querulous face. "I suppose."

"You sure?"

"Well, maybe not. You said about an anagram."

"An analogy."

"Sorry. An analogy."

"That's right. And don't go being sorry. There's nothing to be sorry about. Now then."

"We were talking about music. Is the banquet to do with the music?"

"Not directly. But you're getting there, just like I knew you would." He looked up and gazed out of the window, as though addressing an invisible audience. "I'm talking about excess. Not a gross, ugly excess, but something rich and varied and sustaining that is so plentiful, it seems to go on for ever, so that it can never be used up. Something exciting and fulfilling that you can never get enough of, and however much you try, there's always more, like a magic pot that constantly refills itself as you drink from it." He turned back to study my face once more. "I'm talking about music, Neil, the power that goes on for ever and ever." Reaching out, he squeezed my shoulder. "Enjoy your great journey, Neil. You're on your way."

For what felt like several minutes, we sat side by side on the bed, leaning back against the scarred wooden headboard. I couldn't help but think of Dad, and what he would say if he could see us now. When Archie touched me, it was as if a searing current of knowledge and maturity flowed into me. My parents and grandparents seldom touched me. I remembered when Nurse touched me, only that was different, that was like my blood fizzing, like creatures moving inside me.

"Your gran'll wonder where you are," Archie said.

"She'll be making lunch. Fishcakes."

He laughed lightly. "She's always making those bloody fishcakes. She gave me a whole plateful the other day. Does she never make anything else?"

"She makes nice pancakes. Archie?"

"Aha."

"Will you really take me fishing on the loch?"

"Sure I will. Not yet a while, but when I can organize it. I'll take you out at night, with the fish below and the stars above. There's nothing in this world like fishing by moonlight. The greatest peace a man can know."

"It must be incredibly dark. How can you see to do anything?"

"I've a lamp. And if there's a full moon..."

I nodded, making the bed shake. "I expect you could see planets, too. Some stars are really planets, aren't they?"

"Oh aye. Are you interested in planets?"

"Sort of. That's why I like that music."

"Is that so?" He put his hands behind his neck, fingers interlocked, and leaned back, gazing at the opposite wall. "I see. Then here's a test question for you, Neil. Let's see how bright you really are. The music we just heard – tell me who wrote it."

"That's easy. Holst. He sounds German, but he was English."

"Very good. I can see I'll have to make it harder if I want to catch you out." Archie blew out his cheeks, making little popping noises with his lips. "Okay, try this one. Think very carefully. What's missing from the whole suite?"

"Missing?"

"Aye, missing. What's he left out?"

"Er...Earth. There's no Earth."

Archie coughed politely. "Well, all right, I'll give you one point for that. There's something else, though. Know what it is?"

I sat upright. "I know. It's Neptune!"

"Try again, lad. Neptune's in it. I'll give you another chance."

"Pluto!" I smacked the eiderdown in my excitement. "He forgot Pluto!"

"Well done, lad!" He nudged me in the ribs with his elbow. "You're right, there's no Pluto. He didn't forget it, mind; he didn't know it was there, so it was an innocent omission."

"But if he knew about the planets – ?"

"Ah, but he composed the music in 1914. Pluto was only discovered in 1930. Chap in Arizona called Clyde Tombaugh. Pluto's the outermost planet in our solar system, so far distant that no-one had ever noticed it. Poor, lonely Pluto, eh?"

I hid behind my fingers, thinking. I wondered what Holst's Pluto would have sounded like. I wondered if Holst, lying asleep, knew about this man in America spoiling his achievement, rendering his great manuscript incomplete. Did that make him sad? Perhaps it made him angry.

A shout came from below. I turned towards the sound, blinking to clear my fogged eyes.

"Neil! Are you up there? Someone to see you!"

"Sounds like your gran wants you," said Archie.

"Bet it's only that daft Mrs Cooper," I said.

"Better go down, lad."

"In a minute. Tell me some more about Pluto."

"Well," he chuckled, "there's not a lot to tell. It's more than three thousand million miles from here to Pluto, so you can appreciate information is in short supply. Even the most powerful telescopes are practically useless."

"Cor! That man must have had a good telescope."

"Tombaugh? He worked at the observatory. Even then, he could hardly see anything."

"So – if it's so far away...there could be people there we might never know about. Don't you think?"

"People living on Pluto?" He rubbed his neck, ruminatively. "I don't know. It's a long shot. One thing's for sure; when we're dead, scientists'll still be trying to find out. Too damned far."

"We watched this programme on television. It was about UFOs. My dad said there couldn't be life on other planets, because – well – they would have come here by now."

"Your dad said that?" Archie stared at me, then he shook his head in disbelief. "Where's the logic in that? Oh, I've heard it said before, of course. It's hardly a sensible argument, though."

"How do you mean?"

"Well, if we can't get there, why should we expect them to be able to get here, hmm?"

"But if they had brilliant rockets..."

"Brilliant rockets," Archie repeated, slowly. "Why should they have brilliant rockets – or brilliant anything? Just because they live on a faraway planet, there's no reason to suppose that their technology is superior to our own. They could even be a lot less advanced than we are. I mean, they might have no transport system of any kind. Why must they know Earth even exists? Eh?"

"I hadn't really thought of that," I confessed.

"No," Archie said, moodily, "no-one ever does."

"Still, if there's – "

"Did you hear me, Neil? It's the last time I'll call you!" Gran's voice rang out like a cracked bell in the deep vault of the stairwell.

"Best go down. You'll only get her all annoyed," Archie said, quietly.

"If you come too. You can tell me more stuff."

He smiled. "More stuff, eh? I'll say this for you, lad; you certainly like to know things."

"I was going to ask you about something – something else."

"Oh, and what's that?"

"If there's no air on Pluto – I mean, like on Earth – "

"Which there can't be."

"Then, it must be freezing cold and no oxygen to breathe. So, how can anyone live there, Archie?"

Archie shrugged, casting out his hands, defensively. "Did I say there were people walking about on Pluto? Did I? I think it was you said there might be people there."

"You said it was a long shot."

"Well then. So it is. It's what they call a hostile environment."

I could hear Gran clattering plates downstairs. It seemed to me she was making more noise than was absolutely necessary. Archie cocked his head to listen. "It'll be a hostile environment down in the kitchen in a moment," he warned me.

"I know. You could eat with us."

"Isn't that up to your gran?"

"She won't mind."

Sighing, he stood up and moved towards the wardrobe. "I'll have to put a shirt on."

"We can carry on talking about the planets while we're having our lunch," I suggested.

He glanced back at me. "I'm not so sure about that. Your gran doesn't look to me like a woman who wants to discuss the possibility of life in outer space, Neil."

"She might be interested," I said, doubtfully.

"Face it, Neil," said Archie, buttoning a cream cotton shirt, "most folk don't want to know. They've swallowed the propaganda. They like to feel their exclusivity protected. 'We are Lords of the Universe'."

"It'd be exciting if we weren't, though, wouldn't it? If there were other civilizations, I mean."

"Yes, and to the likes of you and me, Neil, it's the probability that makes the idea exciting. No point in thinking about it otherwise." He stood smartly to attention in front of me. "How do I look?"

"You look fine. On that film I watched, they said that life on other pl – "

"Don't tell me!" he barked. "They said something like, life cannot exist on other known planets because of extremes of temperature or a lack of breathable air. Am I right?"

"I don't know."

"No, I mean, is that what they claim?"

I nodded, somewhat taken aback by his vehemence.

"All right. But don't you see, Neil? That only applies if you stick rigidly to a fixed definition of life. We're looking for what we expect to see, because we're incapable of imagining anything else. If we don't know about something, we think that means it can't be there. All this pathetic drivel about blood and brain cells and oxygen. They'll have us worrying our heads over bicycles and bus tickets next."

"But I thought we were supposed to be clever."

Archie rubbed his nose between his thumb and forefinger. "Hmm. I think 'supposed' is the operative word there, Neil." He wagged a finger at me. "Okay, here's a wee test for you! Tell me a colour!"

"What?"

"Just shout out a colour, any colour."

"Red."

"Okay, another."

"Blue."

"Right. Give me three more."

"Yellow, black and white."

"Six more."

"Six?"

"Yes, go on, six more."

"Um. Green, purple, pink...brown..."

"Getting difficult, eh?"

"Yes, kind of."

"And do you know why? Because we don't know any other colours, so we can't think of them. We look around us, we don't see them, so they don't exist. That defines our ignorance."

"But surely, there can't be any other colours. Can there?"

"Not here, no. But out there," and he gestured towards the window, "there are other forms, other shapes, other colours, beyond the range of our dreams. We have to make some kind of allowance for that."

"But – that's amazing!"

"No, not really. It's amazing that we discount the possibility." He placed a firm hand on my shoulder and squeezed against the muscle. "Fear of the unknown, Neil. That's why we invented God, otherwise we'd spend our lives whistling in the dark."

He followed me to the head of the stairs. A thick smell of

cooking wafted up the stairwell. I could tell it was fishcakes again. I looked down through the banisters and saw Gran's face peering up at me.

Archie still had his hand on my shoulder. "I'm sorry, Mrs Blaney," he said. "I'm afraid I kept your grandson talking far too long."

"Yes, you did," Gran said, tersely. "Still, you're here now. Lunch is about ready. Archie, are you eating with us?"

I smiled inwardly at the thought of Archie politely confronting a mound of fishcakes; but I did want him to sit down with us. "Is it fishcakes, Gran?" I asked her.

"Fishcakes with minty peas," she informed us. "Or there's some soup, if you want, Archie."

I looked up at him, imploringly. "Thank you. A little soup with some bread would be nice," he said.

Gran turned towards the kitchen. "Did you say someone had called?" I asked.

"She's in the front room. She'll be out in a minute. Go in and sit down."

Archie took the chair opposite mine, and began adjusting the cutlery with quiet introspection. "Stand by for Cooper the snooper," he murmured.

"Sshh! She might hear you!"

"Then I shall placate her with the irresistible offer of a fishcake," he said, "the currency of the house." He poured himself a glass of lemonade. "So you're sleeping here tonight, Neil?"

"I'm in the room you had."

"Right. When you go up, before you sleep, give a few minutes' thought to our conversation. Hmm?"

"Okay."

"I want you to think up a new colour. Imagine what it might look like. Imagine – what objects or plants or animals might have that colour. Can you do that, d'you think?"

"I'll try."

"You can do no more. Then, when you've thought of a colour, think of a name for it. All right?"

I nodded.

"Tell me in the morning."

Gran appeared in the doorway with someone close behind her. The figure, obscured at first, slid past Gran's arched back as she served Archie his soup, and then my heart leapt into my mouth.

"Sally!"

"Hello, Neil. Long time, no see." Her voice was a warm, kittenish purr, and I imagined that it was tinged with affection. "Thought you might be here."

Gran went back to the kitchen, and a pregnant silence hung in the room. Archie, his head on one side, was regarding Sally with interest. I smiled at her, feeling slightly helpless. I had that funny sick sensation again.

Archie suddenly rose to his feet, the chair scraping back behind him, and thrust out his hand to Sally. "Archie McLeish," he said. "I'm lodging with Mrs Blaney for a while."

"I'm pleased to meet you, Archie," Sally said. "Now don't let me keep you from your dinner." I saw that she grasped his hand and squeezed it with her other hand, while their eyes seemed to meld and linger for a moment.

"It's no problem," Archie said. "It's good to meet you."

Gran returned with my meal. She gaped at Archie. "Don't let your soup get cold. It's home-made."

"Aye, and very fine it is, too," he pronounced, sitting down.

"I just brought your gran some knitting wool," Sally explained to me. "I get it cheap from the hospital."

"Gran's really good at knitting," I said to Archie. "She made me a pullover – turquoise. She does loads of things."

Archie was spooning his soup, his eyes flicking constantly between the bowl and Sally's face. I wondered if he had heard what I had said. "Turquoise is a beautiful colour," he said, at length.

Gran sat where she always did, at the window end of the rectangular table. She buttered herself some bread and cut it neatly into four squares. I watched Sally out of lowered eyes.

"You aren't eating much, Neil," Gran said, reprovingly. "Is it not all right?"

"It's fine. I'm not that hungry, that's all."

"I've put all your wool in the front room, Mrs Blaney," Sally said. "It's behind the armchair."

Gran nodded, nibbling bread.

Sally looked at me intently. "You should see the colours of that wool, Neil. Really vivid." She winked at me so blatantly, I thought perhaps she had something in her eye. "It's behind the armchair."

"You've just told us," Gran said.

My stomach was beginning to churn. "I could just have a quick look," I suggested.

Gran glowered at me. "After your lunch."

Sally darted a swift glance from me to Gran and back again. "It's time I was going," she said.

With no conscious effort, I stood up.

"Your food, Neil!"

"I won't be a minute," I muttered.

Sally turned to the door. "I'll see myself out, Mrs Blaney." She called out to Archie, as though he were deaf. "Nice to meet you, Mr McLeish. I expect I'll see you again."

Archie nodded to her, almost a bow. "I hope so, m'dear."

As I followed Sally out of the room, she waited in the hall and moved into the front room close behind me. Once inside, she pinioned me round the chest with one arm, pinning me against her, and leaned heavily on the door, slamming it shut.

"Thought you were going to ring me, you little bugger!"

"I was! I did!" I gasped, hardly able to breathe.

"You didn't!"

"I did! I had to ring off."

"What?"

"Before you answered, Dad came in."

"So?"

"I couldn't talk – with him in the room."

"Courage of conviction, Neil."

"I know. It's difficult. You're hurting me."

"Try to relax. Just lean back against me."

"What if someone comes in?"

"They'd have a hard job, with two people pressing the door shut."

I let her draw my body into hers, feeling her breasts imprint my back. I breathed with my mouth hanging open, panting rhythmically, slack-eyed.

"Now, do you want to see this wool?"

"No."

"Didn't think you did."

"I really wanted to ring you, Sally."

"Then why didn't you? You've had ages. No good being faint-hearted, Neil."

"I'm not."

"Okay, okay." She sighed elaborately, holding me tightly to her chest, and her hot breath on my ear was like a blowtorch. "I forgive you. Only don't let me down the next time, huh?"

"Will there be a next time then?"

I felt her shrug. "Up to you."

"Are you going to let me go?"

"No."

"I'm feeling a bit sick."

"In a minute. Just let yourself go." Slowly, Sally unlocked my chest and, lowering her right arm, freed the shirt button above my waistband. Her hand slid inside my shirt and found my navel, and my diaphragm suddenly jumped, in the kind of convulsion I'd felt once on first entering the swimming pool.

"What you doing?"

"Just playing. Don't worry."

I leaned hard against her and closed my eyes. My breathing was shallower now, though bubbles were forming on my lips. "You smell nice," I told her.

"Mmh? Am I nice, Neil? Am I? Do you want me to be nice to you?"

"Yes."

"Do you?"

"Yes. Do something nice."

She laughed softly in my ear. "Say 'please'."

"Please."

"Please what?"

"Please do something nice to me, Sally."

I heard the ripple of that low, burbling laugh again. "And what do you want me to do, Neil? Mmh?"

"Oh, Sally, don't."

"You want me to stop?"

"No."

"Well then. Let's see. Okay. How about..."

Someone banged loudly on the door. I heard Gran's voice. "Come on, Neil! It's only wool!"

I tried to reply, but Sally pulled her hand up and covered my mouth. "It's okay, Mrs Blaney," she called, arching her neck back, "we're just looking for something. Be out in a minute!"

I waited, licking my lips. Sally's explorations had started an erection, but in the interruption I had lost most of it.

"Come on, lean back. Be a good boy."

"Sally!"

Her cool hand was burrowing into my shirt once more. My whole body seemed to go rigid. The more I tried to relax, the more impossible it became. I felt the sweat pearling on my brow.

"Here we go, baby."

Sally's hand crawled, inch by inch, under my elastic, down, inexorably down, until, as another deep shudder rocked me, I felt her palm brush over my stirring penis with the lightest of caresses. Like a balloon instantly inflated, my cock sprang stiffly to attention, until it seemed to fill the whole of that fondling hand. My tender pink helmet jerked and quivered as Sally's fingers tickled it, dancing around its most sensitive contours.

"Remember the in-betweens, Neil. I'm there, Neil. Do I give you pleasure?"

"You know you do." I pressed the back of my head into her shoulder. "Go on, do it."

"Do what?" she asked, kissing my ear. "You want something else?"

"You know."

She laughed, a deep, knowing laugh. "I can't, not here, not now."

"Please."

"You'll mess your trousers."

"I don't care."

"You will if your gran sees."

She yanked her hand out and placed it on my shoulder. Her fingers bore the thin, snail-trail streaks of my youthful anticipation.

"Ohh-oow!" I sighed, relief and disappointment intermingled.

"Enough, young man!"

"You're teasing me."

"Let's say I'm teaching you a lesson. You have to learn to wait for things."

I buttoned my shirt with shaking, clumsy fingers. She gripped my shoulders and spun me round to face her. "How long are you here?"

"Wednesday."

"That's good. Is that your bike by the shed?"

"Yes."

"So you could ride over to see me, couldn't you?"

"When?"

"Monday. Come about twelve. We'll have lunch." She grinned mischievously. "You'll love the dessert."

"What'll I tell Gran?"

"Neil, that's up to you. That's your job." She pulled the door open. "Don't disappoint me. I won't disappoint you."

I went to bed early that night. As I set aside my dirty clothes, I kept one sock, stuffing it into the top pocket of my pyjama jacket. I lay on my back in the shadowy twilight, thinking again of the painting on the wall in Gran's room, the poor shepherd returning home with his flock, grateful for the warm sanctuary of his cottage and the good wife who would lie beside him and comfort him in the snow-hushed dark. I thought then of Sally and her softly fumbling hand in the front room, and I pulled the sock from my pocket, slipped it over my stiffening penis and slowly worked beneath the bedclothes to loose that surge of hot, sweet pain, making of my woollen condom a seeping poultice filled with the best and worst of me. That way, I came to be, however briefly, at peace with myself.

I had not forgotten Archie's instruction about conceiving another colour. I didn't want to let him down; but the task was not an easy one, and I was tired, for so much had happened to me that day. It was then that I remembered the people on Pluto, and I wondered if they were protected from the terrible cold. I worried about them, so alone and far away, mere specks on the edge of our imagination. Was their life merely a silent struggle for survival? Supposing their coats were hardly thick enough. Yes, surely that was it. The colour was in their coats. It had to be. I could see them now, the people of Pluto, hurrying across the petrified landscape in their oversized coats, sewn with coloured panels, like patchwork quilts. In the panels lay the secret of their endurance. The Plutonians had discovered a material which repelled extreme cold and would also generate heat, each thermal condition activated by applying the appropriate shade or intensity of a specific colour. Only, no matter how hard I tried, how fiercely I screwed up my eyes to aid my concentration, I could not see the colour; at least, not yet. Not yet. But I could give it a name, then Archie would be pleased, for he would know that I had tried. Perhaps, I thought, if I found the name before I knew the colour, the nature and appearance of the colour would, by some strange osmosis, filter into my sub-consciousness. So, what to call it? I thought of my mother, who often dressed in bright colours. Mum's birthday was in April. April was the first month of the bright part of the year, the awakening month. April. There I had it: Lirpa. The darkness on one side, the light on the other. And that would be my colour, Archie. Lirpa. The colour of magic.

Only then did I sleep.

Weaving on the walls behind my eyes were magic lantern figures who pranced like robots and uttered no sounds from their toothless mouths, people from far countries lost in the indigo sky, who were without blood or bones and moved among rocks of a different colour. From their coats came great plumes of steam like the breath of dragons.

Chapter V

Lunch

The tail of the car dipped perceptibly as we dropped in the last two boxes. There were five boxes altogether. Some of the encyclopaedias still wore their original coloured jackets. They all smelled of dust and age.

"Heavy old things," my father said, puffing from his exertions. "I don't know where you're going to put them all."

"I'll find somewhere."

"They'll need a good dusting. There's a spider, look!"

"It's all right. I'll look after them."

"Ah well. Maybe they'll be useful for your homework." He stood back and slammed the rear door. "That's it then."

"You could come in for some coffee," I said. "Archie might like to meet you. He's in the garden."

Dad sucked in his cheeks and gazed non-committally up the road. "I – er – suppose I might."

There was no sign of Gran when we went in, but I could hear her moving about upstairs. I guessed she was making the beds. Dad sat at the kitchen table with his back to the boiler, which was where he always sat when he went to Gran's. In all the years we had visited the house, I could scarcely remember my father sitting in the living room – once or twice maybe. On those rare occasions, he perched on the edge of the settee, sitting uncomfortably upright, reminding me of the fathers I sometimes saw shoehorned into miniature trains in the park, looking overgrown and ludicrously pompous as they chugged through the shrubbery.

I looked up and saw Archie coming up the cinder path, a pair of secateurs in his hand.

Dad followed my gaze. "Is this him?" he asked, as if it could be anybody else.

"Yes."

He grunted ambiguously. "Where's your Gran got to?"

"Doing the beds, I think."

"The beds? Can't you and this Archie make your own beds. Do you have to be waited on?"

"Gran likes to do them herself. She does them best."

"Hmmh. You wait till you're in digs."

Archie's florid, smiling face appeared in the doorway. "Morning, Neil! Missed you at breakfast."

"I slept in. Archie, this is my dad. He's come to bring my things and collect Granddad's encyclopaedias."

Archie leaned across the table, extending his right hand. "Well, I'm very pleased to meet you at last, Mr Robertson." Dad held out his hand perfunctorily, not rising from his seat. "Excuse my grubby hand," Archie continued, "but I've been cutting back some bushes. I seem to be all scratches."

Dad nodded in a manner suggesting disinterest. He turned as Gran walked into the room. Archie put the secateurs on the draining board and began rinsing his hands at the sink.

"Have you met Archie?" Gran asked, peering at Dad.

My father made no audible reply, but nodded slowly, his head bowed, as though he had been spoken to by the table itself.

I caught Archie's eye and attempted a smile, as if to reassure him that, despite all appearances to the contrary, this graceless reticence was actually quite normal. Archie winked at me as he shook the water from his hands, and I saw that his lips were pursed in a soundless whistle.

"I was going to make Dad some coffee, Gran," I said.

"All right, Neil. I've made a batch of scones. You can help me set them out."

"Nothing to eat for me," Dad said, sternly.

"Oh, but Mrs Blaney's home-baked scones are truly wonderful," Archie told him. "You'll not want to miss the treat."

"Thank you, I will retain control of my own stomach," Dad

assured him. He produced a large handkerchief, its condition bordering on the industrial, and blew his nose loudly.

Having dried his hands, Archie slid into the chair next to Dad. Gran had gone into the pantry, and I went to stand at her side while she emptied the scones from an airtight tin and began arranging them on plates. I liked helping Gran prepare food; there was something calm and comforting about the task. I found a butter dish and a china pot with strawberry jam in it, and a shallow bowl containing half a honeycomb. Gran reached up to the top shelf and handed me down a wicker tray. "Now go and see to the kettle," she said.

Returning to the glare of daylight, I filled the old blue enamel kettle and set it to boil. Behind me, I could hear Dad talking to Archie about Scotland. That, I thought, was quietly significant. Dad was talking to Archie, rather than the other way about. Very well, Dad's voice was a low monotone, without animation, but at least he was communicating, and for the present Archie seemed content to listen, offering just the occasional soft interjection. Dad was telling him about his childhood in Aberfeldy, and his brother Graham, who had died of scarlet fever at the age of six, leaving him an only child. His mind ranged on to embrace his schooldays, the war, the way the Perthshire valleys, where he had cycled, played and fished as a youth, had been changed for ever by the inception of the North of Scotland Hydro-Electric Scheme and subsequently by huge reforestation programmes. Much of this, I felt sure, Archie already knew, but the pair of them plainly found pleasure and perhaps a small degree of solace in discussing it. I felt an inner warmth myself, for I was heartened by the notion that animosity and suspicion might yet be sublimated to some modest friendship.

"Come on you two, make some room!" Gran edged a tray of scones and preserves on to the table, while I laid out the crockery, milk and sugar.

"Looks very nice," Dad said.

"Help yourselves," Gran urged, "I've warmed them in the oven."

Archie reached out for a plate and a scone. Dad waited, his eyes following the lodger's hand. "Tell me, Mister...uh..."

"Please. Archie."

"Ah. Archie. I was wondering what line of work you'd be in."

Halfway across the table, Archie's scone hung motionless in mid-air. His eyes registered surprise and confusion, though for no reason obvious to me, for my father's question seemed reasonable, if unadventurous, and I was only regretful that I had been too apathetic to ask it myself.

Archie placed the scone carefully on his plate and began to butter it. "Why do you ask?" he said, quietly.

"Because I'd like to know," Dad replied, with a brief snort of laughter. "As a responsible father, I take a natural interest in the man whom my son has apparently befriended."

"Archie's not been here long," I commented, hoping to mitigate any tension.

Gran pointed her teaspoon at me. "Let the grown-ups speak, Neil."

"Yes, Gran."

"Since you ask," Archie said, "I was a piano tuner."

"A piano tuner?"

"Aye. It's a living."

Dad choked up that laugh again, a kind of contemptuous snigger. "Not much of one. Anyway, you've not been here five minutes. You can't have many customers this far from home."

Archie took a sip of coffee and stared at Dad over the rim of his cup. "Well, of course, you have to advertise," he said.

"Advertise? What, from a house with no phone?"

"I did say, I *was* a piano tuner."

"Ah. I see. So you're an out-of-work piano tuner?" Dad somehow made this status sound reprehensible, as though piano tuning were socially corrupt.

Archie bit into his scone and sighed. "I am actively looking for openings," he said. He turned to Gran. "Delicious scones, Mrs Blaney."

Dad worked his lips in and out thoughtfully. "I couldn't help noticing your hands," he said. "They are not labourer's hands."

"Quite right," Archie said, putting his hands in his lap.

"Your hands are not large," Dad continued, "neither are they calloused. They are quite pink for a man of your age."

"Aye well," said Archie.

"But then, of course" – Dad lifted his hands and held them a few inches above the table, palms upturned – "I myself have neat hands, or so I have been told." He inspected first one hand and then the other. "It's just the way we're made, I think. Someone once told me that I have dainty feet."

"Aye, perhaps you should ha' been a ballet dancer," Archie remarked.

Gran laughed, then put her hand to her mouth.

Dad went on staring at his hands, turning them over and back again. "Pity we've no pianos in the family," he said, absently.

"You're not going to take your socks off, are you, Dad?"

"I'd like some more coffee please, Neil," Gran said, stiffly.

Dad was curling his fingers in and out. Slowly, silently, Archie brought up his hands and held them alongside my father's. Nobody spoke. They both continued to gaze at their hands, and at each other's hands, turning them this way and that and wiggling their fingers like waving tentacles. My abiding memory from that first meeting between Dad and Archie is of the two men seated side by side at the kitchen table, heads down as if in silent prayer, solemnly contemplating their outstretched hands.

As I followed Dad back to the car, to see him off, I pretended to myself that the gesture was nothing more than a moment's courtesy. In truth, I was anxious to hear some brief assessment of my new-found friend from the man who, not long ago, had so unfairly vilified him. At the same time, I was determined not to solicit his opinion, for I felt that an observation volunteered would be more meaningful. Thus, we walked in silence to the front gate.

"Interesting fellow, that Archie," Dad said, at last.

"Yes. I don't know him that well," I said, cautiously.

He opened the gate and paused halfway through. "Well, these things take time, you know." He placed a firm hand on my shoulder. "I always say, you mustn't pre-judge people. And you have to be prepared to give them the benefit of the doubt."

I wondered whose doubt he was referring to; his or mine. So far I perceived no cause to doubt Archie's integrity, although I allowed that I knew little of his background. By the same token,

Archie had scant reason to confide in me, and he had never enquired about my family or my upbringing.

I waited while he started the car and fiddled with something under the dashboard. He wound down the window. "Okay. Be careful now."

"Look after my books. Don't leave them in the car; they'll get damp."

That derisory laugh again. "Damp? They've been damp for years."

"Give my love to Mum."

"Aha." The car jolted as he banged it into gear. "Be good."

Amid an ominous rattle of tappets and a pungent blue cloud of carbon monoxide, Dad veered across the road and was gone.

Oh, I know what you're thinking comes next. You picture me pedalling furiously over to Sally Melksham's, arriving in a breathless lather of repressed desire, ready to tumble into bed with this voluptuous woman almost before I have become detached from my bicycle.

In the event, that was not quite how the day turned out. It began harmlessly enough, if a shade deceitfully, as I stuffed balls of wool into my saddlebag. These were the unwanted ones from the collection in the front room, now bundled into a large white paper bag. I can no longer remember whether I was doing this because the original supply was on approval, or if it was a matter of Gran's order having been wrongly filled. Either way, the situation was a fortuitous one, for it presented me with the perfect opportunity to appear helpful to Gran, by offering to return the wool to Sally, whilst fabricating a plausible reason for riding over to spend time with someone of whose avowed intentions my grandmother would certainly not have approved.

Gran also handed me a sealed envelope. "That's the money for what I've kept," she told me. I put it in my pocket. "You see she gets it," she added, perhaps recalling the incident with the purse.

I set off unusually slowly. The pedals felt leaden under my feet and every road seemed to rise steeply uphill. I had no appetite for the lunch Sally had promised me, much less for any sexual activities, and I rode with my heart in my mouth. Beset by the libido depressants of anxiety and self-doubt, I considered turning round after half a mile and hurrying back to Gran's; but then I would have other problems to face. For a start, I would still have the wool and the money. Sally, for sure, would not forgive me a second time, and so our friendship would perish. I would never see her nipples again.

I pulled in to the kerb and stopped, leaning almost drunkenly on the handlebars. I felt in my pocket. The envelope was still there. My heart pounded, the blood thumping in my head. Fear and regret overwhelmed anticipation and excitement. The idea of dismounting at the other end and shortly achieving an erection seemed impossibly preposterous. What had Sally meant when she assured me I would "love the dessert"? What could be so special about a pudding?

My mind raced ahead in several directions. I could pretend I had had a puncture. I could even find a nail and stick it through my own tyre; then the decision to abandon the appointment would be forced upon me, because I would lose so much time. I might invent a terrible stomach-ache, requiring my immediate return for remedial treatment. I could say I had turned a corner and had some kind of seizure and gone unaccountably blind. If I persisted with the original plan, blindness suggested itself as a not improbable consequence.

A petrol tanker swept past me, its backdraught jarring me back to reality. I slowly hooked the toe of my right foot under the pedal and brought it up, so that I could rest against it. If I aborted the mission now, I reasoned, all my efforts to condition myself would have been in vain; there was no point in striving for badness and then behaving impeccably. I had to see it through.

In another five minutes, I was lurching to a halt outside the house. I couldn't see the number, but as I was counting the front doors, Sally appeared on the path, waving cheerily. That took some of the tension out of the moment, for the openness of her greeting seemed to diffuse the clandestine nature of my visit.

"Hi!" I called, returning her wave.

"Hello, Neil," Sally said, rather formally, as I approached the gate. "Put your bike round the back." She indicated an alley at the side of the wall. "The back door's open."

I went round and emptied the saddlebag. Sally met me with a smile, standing aside as I came through the door, which opened into a narrow passageway. I walked ahead of her into a cool, bright kitchen, a yellow-painted table at its centre reflecting the sunlight falling in vivid panels through the window. There was a humid smell of cooking.

I gave her the bag of wool and the envelope. "From Gran," I said, not wanting to say too much yet, in case my voice should wobble and betray my nervousness.

"Thank you. Would you like a cold drink?"

"Yes please."

"What can I get you? There's orange, lemon, Pepsi..."

"Orange, please."

"Okay. I expect you're hot after your ride."

"I'm all right."

She trailed a hand over one of the chairs. "Sit down. We'll go in the other room in a minute."

I sat, feeling acutely uncomfortable. For all that she had come out to welcome me, I now felt her to be disappointingly restrained, her speech clipped and undemonstrative. I wanted her to put me at my ease, but she seemed to be holding back from me. I wondered if this was all a dreadful mistake.

"Here!" She placed a tall tumbler of orange in front of me; and then she bent down and, taking my face gently between the palms of her hands, turned me towards her. "It's lovely to see you, Neil." My mouth was opening to respond, but this proved a futile gesture, as Sally leaned forward and I felt the instantaneous soft-fruit crush of her wet lips on mine, dilating, sucking, nibbling, then the liquid thrust of her quick tongue raking my teeth and the smell of her breath like chocolate and tangerines.

When she pulled away, I was almost glad, for I had to catch my breath. The tumbler shook in my hands as I took a long drink, sweat beading my brow. My chest heaved in and out, and my eyes stubbornly refused to focus.

She touched my cheek. "Did you like that, Neil?"

I nodded and swallowed, playing for time.

"Talk to me, Neil."

"You know I did," I whispered.

"That's good." She passed a hand across my forehead, brushing back my hair. "You look very tense, Neil. Are you unhappy?"

"No. I said I wanted to see you again."

"I remember. I'm flattered I made such an impression on you."

"I keep thinking about you."

"Oh? Is that me as a person, or just – ? Well, you know."

There was an acid taste in my mouth, a scouring cocktail of fear and excitement. "I really like you, Sally," I said, and I cursed myself for the tears that swam in my eyes.

"I know." She touched my arm. "I believe you – only you mustn't get yourself in such a state about it." A shrill chirruping distracted her. "That's the oven timer. I hope you're hungry." With a sly grin, she added, "For food, I mean."

"Smells nice," I said, as she opened the oven door.

"Home-made chicken pie," she said, over her shoulder. "If I say so myself, you won't taste better. See, I'm spoiling you." She stood up, clutching the dish in a towel. "Neil, why don't you sit in the back room and relax?"

"I could lay the table."

"All done. Don't worry about it. Go in and make yourself comfortable. Talk to Rupert."

My heart skipped a beat. She hadn't told me there would be anyone else in the house. Suddenly, I felt cheated, taunted with a slap in the face. "Who's Rupert?" I asked, in a tiny voice.

Sally stared at me, before erupting into laughter. "Oh Neil! Don't look so down in the mouth! Rupert's only six. He's my cat!"

I went into the living room, which was as bright and airy as the kitchen, a room whose mood suggested contentment and optimism, its leaded bay windows looking out on to a pink-paved patio and a generous lawn shaded by apple trees. In the middle of the polished wood floor stood a round dining table laid with a cream linen tablecloth and green napkins. I smiled to myself, for Sally's preparations made me feel important again.

Curled up in the armchair next to the fireplace, Sally's black-and-white cat dozed with his chin balanced on his front paws. I stroked behind his twitching ear with my forefinger, and he opened one eye, gazed at me blearily, and resumed his nap, dismissing me with a self-satisfied yawn.

I sat in the opposite armchair and waited. A wooden-cased clock on the mantelpiece ticked like a dripping tap, and my stomach whined and gurgled, surely more from nervousness than hunger, emphasizing the aura of surrounding calm.

Sally called out from the kitchen. "Sit at the table, Neil. I'm bringing it through."

I pulled out a chair and sat down. From here I could see a bird-table on the lawn, where sparrows were squabbling over nuts and bread crusts. Rupert lazily craned his neck towards the commotion, flicked the pink leaf of his tongue in and out, and settled down again.

I wondered: should I have brought one of those things with me? Could it be possible that I might need one? Peter Jessops in 3B frequently supplemented his pocket money by selling them at school, at what we were assured were advantageous prices. Well, presumably they were advantageous to Peter Jessops, anyway. *Johnnies*, he called them. I suspected that most of his sales were in the interests of bravado rather than contraception, but it remained a trade that quietly impressed me.

"Wanninyjohnnies, Robertson, eh?"

"Er-no thank you," I would reply, my face turning an attractive shade of magenta.

"Antchergottagirlfren'?"

"Well, not just at the moment."

No sale. That, of course, was part of the problem. If I had approached him for a *Johnny*, the game would be up, his salacious curiosity aroused. Since I was never seen around the school with a female companion, and the boys I mixed with who were sexually active – or claimed to be – almost invariably had girlfriends on the premises, Jessops would torment me with a barrage of impertinent questions, designed to establish the identity of the person with whom I was to consummate my passion. That was the trouble with sex: it was impossibly complicated.

I was still turning these emotive matters over in my mind when Sally entered the room, wheeling a trolley laden with food. "Help yourself to vegetables," she said, as she leaned over me, standing so close that I could smell her perfume and feel the honeyed warmth of her against my shoulder, while she arranged my meal in front of me. She asked me if I would like some wine, and I read in the delicate manner of her enquiry a mute acknowledgment that she should respect my age and inexperience.

"I could try some," I said.

She poured me half a glass. "It might relax you," she suggested. "Of course, I don't want to get you drunk."

"Don't you?" Immediately I wondered why I'd said this.

She appeared to bridle at my response. "What do you mean, 'Don't you?'?"

I felt my face heating up. "I'm sorry. I just – I don't know."

"Sounds like you don't trust me, Neil," she said, petulantly.

"No. I mean, I do." Suddenly my mouth had gone very dry. "I'm not very good at this," I muttered, studying my plate.

Sally reached out for my left hand, covering it with her own. For perhaps ten seconds she didn't speak, just looked at me. "You're shutting me out, Neil," she said, at length.

"What?"

"You're always hiding behind the door. Come into the light so I can see you." She pushed the wine glass towards me. "Here, drink some of your wine!"

I lifted the glass and held it under my nose. "I'm sorry."

She shook her head, reprimanding me with a loud sigh of exasperation. "And don't keep being sorry! There's nothing to be sorry about."

I took a sip of wine, screwing up my eyes. "Okay."

"There's nothing to be nervous about, either. I won't eat you – at least, not yet." She picked up her knife and fork with an air of finality. "Come on, lunch is getting cold!"

For what seemed a long time, only the ticking of the clock and the clink of our cutlery lightly invaded the silence as we ate. The chicken pie was wonderful. I recalled Sally's half-hearted attempt at lunch that day at Gran's, and wondered how her inspiration had so deserted her then. I told myself, because I wanted it to be so, that today's meal represented a turning point in our relationship, a commitment, even an act of love. She had taken the trouble to create something specially for me, had used her time with me in mind. It made a vital difference that she had been thinking about me when I was not there.

"This is really good," I told her.

"Don't speak with your mouth full," she said, with a grin.

"Sorry."

"Neil!"

"So-"

We both burst out laughing, and I drank more wine, and then some more, until the glass was empty.

"Here, I'll pour you another one." This time she filled the glass. "You look more relaxed now. You know, you're a good-looking boy when you let yourself go a little."

"Thanks."

"My pleasure."

"Am I?"

"Ooh. Getting very forward, Neil." She hadn't looked up from her plate. "I hope I haven't misjudged you."

"Depends. I don't know how you see me. I don't know..."

"Don't know why you're here? Is that it? Is that what makes you nervous?"

I shrugged. "Sort of."

Now she was talking with her mouth full, even pointing her fork at me. "Right. You think I have a – a hidden agenda. An ulterior motive. Hmmh?"

"Not necessarily," I replied, without much conviction.

"But you rang me – remember? You said you wanted to see me."

I took another drink. In the armchair, Rupert yawned, showing two white incisors, and stretched out his front legs until they quivered with the effort. Watching Sally's lips, shiny from the wine and with crumbs of pastry adhering to them, I knew I wanted to kiss them, wanted to be close to her and taste her mouth. My vision began to waver and drift in and out of focus, the face across the table appearing as seen through the wrong end of a telescope. Pushing the plate away, I rested my elbows on the table and held my fingertips against my temples.

"Are you all right, Neil? You look a little pale."

"I'm fine," I said, not lifting my eyes.

"So long as you're sure. No more wine, perhaps."

"Maybe," I said, breathing deeply.

She reached across and placed the back of her hand on my forehead. "A bit sweaty."

"The pie was very nice," I said, "but I don't think I can eat any more."

"That's all right. We'll have a rest. Remember, I promised you dessert later."

"Yes. Is it a special one?"

"Very special. You'll never have had a dessert like it."

"I'm rather full up."

"You look as if you're in pain, Neil. Is there something I can do for you?"

"I told you. I'll be all right."

She nodded slowly, thoughtfully. "You are glad you came, aren't you, Neil?"

"Course." I realised I didn't want her to get up and leave me. I wanted to keep her there, to keep her talking. I took another deep breath. "Sally?"

"Yes?"

"Why – how come you didn't get married?"

She raised her eyebrows. "Well, that's a direct question."

"Would you like to be married?"

"What's this, Neil? A proposal?"

I smiled nervously. "No. I just wondered."

"I see. And how do you know I'm not married?"

"I – I just assumed. It just sort of seemed that way."

"Never make assumptions, Neil; they can be dangerous."

"I know. I suppose I shouldn't have asked."

"Well, if you wanted to know..." She lowered her head and peered at me critically. "I think your colour's coming back."

"That's because I'm embarrassed."

She suppressed a snigger of laughter. "You can be funny, Neil, when you let yourself go."

"So long as you don't make fun of me."

"We could have fun together," she said, and my heart skipped.

"I expect you think I'm prying," I persisted.

"Prying? Into what?"

"Your past."

"Well, when you become friends with people, it's only natural that you want to know something about their background. I wouldn't blame you for that."

"I really want to be friends with you. I think you-"

"You think I'm nice. I know, you told me. Only maybe I'm not as nice as you imagine."

Gazing at her soft, open face, I considered the possibility. In reality, I knew nothing about this woman, yet I believed I loved her. I was blinded, then, by the emotional chemistry of the moment, but I can see now that I had no idea who she was and as little conception of what love was. I was suffering from a painful disease; I had no notion of how I had contracted it, and no knowledge or experience from which to construct an accurate diagnosis.

"You're staring at me," she said, pleasantly.

"I can look, can't I? You let me look that time before."

"I did, didn't I?" She took my hand and squeezed it. "Is that what you want?"

"What?"

"Faint heart never won fair lady, Neil."

I rescued my hand and gazed abstractedly out of the window. A fresh breeze had sprung up, and the leaves on the big willow tree at the end of the garden shimmered green and silver as the branches dipped and swayed, like the skirts of an elegant lady as she coyly displayed her petticoats.

When I turned my head, Sally was at my side. "Come on," she said, "I promised you dessert."

"I don't know if I'm hungry yet."

"I'll make you hungry, don't you worry."

"Are you going to bring it?"

"Not here. Come with me."

"Where are we going?"

"Upstairs of course."

"What for?"

"Don't ask so many bloody questions."

"But you said we would ha-" Sally put her hand over my mouth, silencing my protest. We stood there motionless. Cautiously, I slipped out my tongue and licked the soft edge of her palm, tasting the salt tang.

"Ooh, that tickles," she whispered, holding herself against me.

I waited for her to take her hand away. "I don't know what to do next," I confessed.

She nodded sympathetically. "You're all hot and bothered, aren't you?"

"A little bit."

"Then it's time to cool down. I'll run you a bath – not too hot." She kneaded the muscles in my shoulders. "Dear me, all that tension!"

"But – what about the dessert?"

"I'll see to that."

"Shall I wait here?"

"Yes. Talk to Rupert. He likes men. I'll call you." At the door, she turned back, her head tipped interrogatively to one side. "Neil, do you like pineapple?"

"Yes."

Rupert had hardly moved since before lunch. He looked asleep, but his lime-yellow eyes were slightly open. I gently pressed the tip of one finger into the pads of his right paw, and he purred softly and gripped the flesh the way a small baby does. With my other hand, I stroked the top of his glossy head, working my fingers down behind his ears, and he arched his neck and purred busily, like a sewing machine.

Overhead, I could hear water running, and Sally's footsteps as she moved from room to room. I poured myself another glass of wine. I was beginning to enjoy the taste, and the musky feel it gave me.

"What do you think, Rupert? Am I wrong to be here? Should I go back to Gran's?"

Rupert yawned, his teeth chattering as if in reply.

"I didn't quite get that, Rupert. You'll have to speak more clearly."

He opened his eyes and looked at me, offering a small, reedy *miaow.*

"Okay, Rupert, I get the message."

Crossing to the window, I saw that there was a glass-fronted bookcase in the alcove, and I peered inside at the tidily upright spines, using one hand to shield the reflective glare from the garden. Mum always said that you could tell a lot about people by looking at the books they kept, for their collections reflected their backgrounds, passions and interests. In a well-planned bookcase, you could see a lifetime. There were four shelves in Sally's display, and the top one was devoted entirely to medical and nursing titles, which was merely what I would have expected. On the next shelf were a number of gardening books – *How To Design & Build A Rockery...Guide To A Perfect Lawn...Arthur Gallicott's Gardening Diary* – showing signs of wear and tear, presumably from having been put to practical use outdoors. The third shelf was more interesting, for some of the books were familiar to me from school, such as *Swallows and Amazons, The Cruel Sea* and *David Copperfield.* Standing somewhat uncomfortably, my head to one side and my hand in salute, I worked my way along the last row. Joyce's *Ulysses* stood next to the *Penguin* paperback of *Lady Chatterley's Lover,* and there was something called *Karma Sutra,* and a very large volume apparently bound in red leather, entitled *Fruits and Spices as Aphrodisiacs: A World Exploration.* With a quick glance over my shoulder, I fumbled at the door latch, but it was locked.

Sally's voice rang out from the landing above. "You there? You can come up for your *dip*!"

Did I imagine the emphasis on that last word? The sound of it made me tingle.

She was waiting for me at the top of the stairs, wearing a smile which seemed at once friendly and slightly challenging. It was a smile that said, "I want us to be friends, but I need to be in control." The import of this signal may have eluded me then, but now I realise that I should have interpreted it as a potential threat, a destabilizing dynamic in our relationship.

"Bathroom's on the left," she told me. "I've put you some bubbles in."

I went in and closed the door. There was no lock. As I undressed, I folded my clothes neatly and placed them in a pile on the lid of the lavatory seat. I glanced down and inspected myself. It felt very strange to be standing naked in an unfamiliar house, somehow improper and vaguely ridiculous. I had come for lunch and ended up with no clothes on. One moment I was sipping wine, impeccably mannered, at a table for two, and then I was alone with my smooth, white, quaking body, surrounded by scented steam, mesmerized in contemplation of the viscous dewdrop that bejewelled the tip of my inadequately dangling boyhood.

With one rigid big toe, I tested the bath. It felt fine, hot but safely bearable. Under the froth, the water was pale green and smelt of pine. I climbed in and sat down facing the taps. I stretched my legs out and moved them up and down, watching the water cascade over them. There was a yellow sponge in the metal rack suspended in front of me, and I soaked it and squeezed the water out over my chest. My skin bloomed to a mottled pink and was instantly cool to the touch, glassy as latex.

I stopped splashing when I heard the knock at the door. "You all right, Neil?"

"Thanks."

Slowly, the door swung open. Sally stood before me, holding a tray on which she had arranged glass dishes and some spoons.

I stared at her in disbelief.

She held the tray across her chest.

She was completely naked.

In the glasses was some kind of syllabub, and Sally's left nipple, visible against the pale cream, appeared as a decorative cherry.

Beneath the tray, the dark puncture of her navel drew my gaze down to a greyish-blonde fern of pubic hair. The slender submarine of my penis launched itself to the surface and lay, glistening and supercharged, amid the foaming waves.

"Dessert!" she announced, with an air of triumph.

My eyes flitted from the tray to her face, then to her crotch and back to her face again, in a breathless, unstoppable cycle of confusion.

Sally stepped forward and placed the contents of the tray in the bath rack. She leaned the empty tray against the sink pedestal. Then, carefully sliding the rack along, she stepped in and sat facing me.

I swallowed hard. "Sally!"

"Something the matter, Neil?" she asked, casually.

"I – I don't believe this. I can't believe it's happening."

"Nothing's happened yet," she said, fiddling with the dishes. "Here." She handed me a spoon and a dish of pale yellow whip. "This is home-made banana syllabub. There's fresh cream in it, and *Tia Maria*. It's very rich."

I took a few spoonfuls, licked my lips and replaced the dish in the rack.

"What's wrong? Don't you like it?"

"I love it. I just can't concentrate."

White coronas of foam clung to the undersides of Sally's breasts like small, silvery beards. "Best eat up," she said, between mouthfuls, "else the water'll get cold."

"I love you, Sally."

"Mmm, I know," she murmured, licking her spoon. "Though I say it myself, this is really good."

I could resist the temptation no longer. I reached out and caressed the pale, steam-blotched globe of her left breast, wiping away the froth.

She put down her dish. "I see. We're into touching now, are we?"

"You're lovely."

"Am I?" She pretended to shiver, making her breasts jiggle up and down. "Do I excite you, Neil?"

"You know you do."

She studied the water lapping around my belly. "Well, I don't see any evidence of it."

"No. Perhaps I should finish my banana."

"Perhaps you should be quiet and let me sort out your banana."

"Pardon?"

She tossed her head with a peal of laughter. "This is hardly the time for formality, Neil. We're sat here naked, for God's sake."

I started breathing deeply through my mouth. My hand seemed to go forward of its own accord, reaching for her again, but she caught it and held my wrist.

"Come closer to me, Neil."

"What?"

"Come on, you're not deaf. Just – squidge yourself forward."

Sally moved to meet me, until our chins were almost over the bath rack. Her free hand slid under the water, and then I felt it crawling between my legs, a baby octopus, probing and slippery. I let my head tilt back, and I didn't look down.

"That's better," she said. "From here, through the fog, I can see the Eddystone Light."

With half-closed eyes, I sat quite still in the cooling water and let the octopus play. My strength seemed to have drained out of me, as though it had condensed and evaporated into the humid atmosphere.

"Well done, Neil. Look down and be proud of yourself."

I did as I was told. Several inches of pink periscope protruded hopefully above the green algae. I stared gravely, as though I had never seen it before.

"Why so serious, Neil? Why so sensitive?" Suddenly she scooped up a handful of water and threw it at me. Soap stung my eyes. "Don't you ever laugh, Neil?"

"Course I do," I told her, spluttering, rubbing my eyes.

"Private laughter, Neil. You want to share yourself more. Don't be greedy."

"Yeah, okay."

"And now what's happened?" She nodded towards my shrinking penis. "Disaster. The Eddystone Light has become the Leaning Tower of Pisa."

"I don't know how to take you, sometimes," I said, covering myself with my hand.

She shrugged, pulling a face. "Take me any way you want."

"Trouble is," I said, lowering my eyes, "I don't know what I do want."

"You don't know much, do you, mate?"

"I know some things," I said, ineffectually.

"You know you like it when I touch you. Isn't that right?"

I nodded. "No-one's ever done that to me before."

"Give it time, Neil, give it time."

"What *is* the time?"

"Why? Are you going somewhere?"

"Well, not exactly."

"You're not worried about your gran, are you?" She gave me one of her calculating smiles. "Wonder what she'd say if she saw you now."

"Don't."

With a sudden intake of breath, Sally smacked the water with the flat of her hand, sending a miniature tsunami over my chest. "Dear me! It quite slipped my mind!"

"What?"

"The pineapple. I completely forgot."

She took the lid from a china pot balanced behind her on the corner of the bath, and held out a pineapple ring. I pinched it between my thumb and forefinger and nibbled at the corded flesh, until the juice dribbled down my chin.

Sally watched me. "Was that good?"

"Aha. Nice and sweet."

"Is that me or the pineapple?"

I chuckled and made no reply. I still felt awkward, telling her how I felt about her. I knew what I wanted to say, but the words wouldn't come out, at least, not when I was face to face with her.

"Right. Next one's even better." She held another piece in front of me. "This one's unforgettable."

I reached out, but she pulled back her hand. "Ah-ah-ah. Not yet."

The water surged and hissed as she scrambled on to her knees, still holding the fruit, and told me to lift the bath rack on to the floor.

"What for?"

"It's in the way, Neil. Just do it."

I lowered the rack over the side.

"Now then." She leaned towards me and gently lifted my penis out of the water. My mouth fell open. Slowly, methodically, inch by stickily sliding inch, she drew the pineapple ring down over the stiffening length of me, until I wore it like a golden bangle. "A perfect fit," she declared, "a one-eyed sailor in a yellow lifebelt."

I clutched the handles at either side of the bath, gasping for breath. "You're – you're crazy!"

"Shut up! You don't need to talk now. Close your eyes and enjoy your dessert."

Just for a moment, I shut my eyes, but I opened them again when I felt her head bump my chin. Then she was over me, and her lips were nuzzling me there, her hand holding me upright, while her teeth found the disc that gripped me ever more tightly, and began to peck and tug and tear at the softening fruit. Looking down upon her bobbing head, I tried to believe that this was actually happening to me, that this was not just a film scene of someone else's secret life invading my imagination. But in a film there were no sweet, tantalizing points of pummelling pain as fierce as these, no smell or sting of soap and hair, no rub or chafe of incisors and gums on tender, twitching flesh.

I hawked up some thin, rattling shards of breath. "Please Sally!"

She mumbled something I couldn't hear, her mouth almost under water.

"Sally! It's going to come out of me!"

One last jagged cube of pineapple jammed in her teeth, she brought her head up just in time, as a warm stickiness slapped the inside of my knee. Grey tendrils of phlegm-like weed trailed dead in the water.

While I chewed anxiously at my top lip, Sally sat back on her heels, a thin, thoughtful smile lighting her face. "Better now?"

"I'm sorry. I couldn't help it."

Her eyes danced to the ceiling and back to me. "Haven't I told you before? Don't be sorry. There's nothing to be sorry about. It's all perfectly natural."

"I liked the pineapple," I said, sheepishly.

"Good. I told you it would be special."

"Only I didn't mean that to happen."

"Well I'm sure it's not the first time, eh?"

"No. Except, normally I'm on my own. It's the first time with anybody else." I could feel myself flushing, my hands beginning to shake. "You probably think I'm daft."

"Nothing of the kind. I'm just relieved to know all your parts are working normally."

I reached down to move a dish that had tipped over when I laid the rack on the floor, and as I looked up again I thought I saw a red floater, swimming like a microscopic amoeba, in the corner of my eye. I tried to blink it away, but it stuck there, a bright jewel on the edge of my vision. It was a carmine bead, sliding slowly towards me. The bead trailed a pink tail. It was running down Sally's left thigh.

She must have seen the change in my expression. "Okay, now what's the matter?"

"You-you're bleeding," I said.

She glanced down. "Jesus, so I am! All this warm water...I thought I might start."

A second drop came. There was reddish-brown smoke in the water. I stared at her, wondering what she would do, but she just sat there, staring back at me.

"Should we do something?" I asked her.

"Such as?"

"I don't know."

"Apply a tourniquet, perhaps?"

I shivered. The water was getting cold. "I think you're making fun of me."

She shook her head. "Poor Neil. Still so sensitive."

"I suppose I can't help how I am."

"No, maybe not." She stirred the discoloured water with one hand. "Once we're out of this bath, we'll be dirtier than when we got in."

"You're funny," I told her, only I didn't smile.

"You mean, I'm odd. I unnerve you."

I carried on staring at her. The blood seemed to have stopped.

I could see a pink pip, like a rosebud, showing between her legs. Then, still gazing at me, she flicked a finger inside herself and brought the scarlet tip towards me. I seemed to freeze with surprise. She leaned over and painted a red cross on my chest.

I hung my head, peering at the bloody tattoo. "What're you doing?" I whispered.

"A small gift," she said. "Bless you for loving me."

I could feel the pulse behind my eyeballs, as if my eyes were adjusting to a change in light. Reaching down, I found the sponge, dunked it in the water and pressed it to my chest.

Rockets seemed to explode in her eyes. "What the Hell are you doing?"

"I've got blood on me," I said, plaintively.

"I know, I put it there! That's the purest part of me, and you –"

"I'm only washing it off, Sally."

"'I'm only washing it off, Sally'" she mimicked, in a nasal twang. "Well don't! How dare you!" She grabbed the sponge and flung it at my face. "Washing me off you like I was a piece of dirt!"

I shrank away from her, sensing the blood draining out of my face, my bowels expanding and contracting, a fleshy clam opening and closing under water. "I want to get out," I said, clutching the chrome handles, but she sat down hard in a whoosh of grey water and kicked at my chest, hurling me against the sloping end of the bath. Instinctively, I lunged forward once more, but as I did so I met her hand flailing up at me, and something sharp, a fingernail or a ring, cut the side of my lip. Through the spray I saw her face, contorted with rage, and as her teeth clenched and flashed, her foot was coming at me again, and in that small space there was nowhere to go, so I ducked aside, closing my eyes, but her heel caught the bony corner of my right eye-socket in a thudding percussion of pain.

Believe me, somewhere hidden inside me, I can still feel the sickening shock of that blow today, a trauma buried deep but not forgotten, like a nugget of simmering, livid fire.

My stomach churning, I jumped up and almost threw myself over the side of the bath.

"That's it, go! Get out of here!" Sally was screeching at me, her fractured voice now the high, atonal blare of a trumpet blown out of key.

I scooped up my clothes and shoes, my whole body shaking, terrified I would vomit or urinate on the floor.

"Go on, sod off back to your gran's!"

"I'm going! I'm all wet!"

"Too bloody right you are!"

"I've got to put my clothes on!" I yelled, and my eyes and my voice were full of the frailty of tears.

"Get out of my sight, cry-baby!" she screamed. "On your bike and *go*! Filthy little tike!"

I ran down the stairs and dressed quickly in the hall, yanking my clothes on frantically over my wet body, hopping madly from one leg to the other. Rupert wandered out to look at me, and I bent down to stroke him, to thank him for his trusting gentleness, and he sniffed my hand and peered up the stairs, then back at my frightened face, as if, in some small, secret way, he understood.

I must have pushed my bike along the pavement for about half a mile, feeling too unsteady to ride it. The sun's warmth on my back was softly reassuring, a moistly gentle poultice, and I tried to ignore the ache in my swollen eye and the salt-sting that marked the red eruption in my lip.

A man approached, towed energetically by a small dog. "You all right, son?" the man asked me, hauling the dog to a halt.

"Thanks."

"Come off, did you?"

"What?"

"Fall off your bike?"

"Oh. Yes, yes I did."

"Got far to go, have you?"

"No. I'll be all right."

"That's the ticket. Good lad!"

I bumped the bike into the gutter and swung my leg over. "I think I'll ride from here."

"Gonna have a shiner there," the man said, nodding at my eye. "Cruel old world, eh?"

"You are so right," I said, emphatically, and I wobbled out into the road. At first I pedalled along quite slowly, feeling strangely disorientated, as though the past half hour had not really happened at all, except in my tangled imagination. Then I pressed on, head down over the handlebars, eyes slitted against the rush of air in my face, and the faster I went, the less I could see, for my vision was a kaleidoscopic blur of flooding tears. I told myself that the wind tugging at the roots of my hair was making my eyes water, and then there was the inflammation below my right temple, and the delayed-reaction shock of it all; yet I knew in my heart that I wept not from physical distress or even from the humiliation of rejection, but because I had discovered the brutal truth of consuming affection unreturned, and learned also that in all the world's infinitely prolific alchemy of the human spirit, there is no formula for the manufacture of love.

Chapter VI

The Truth

I teetered out of bed and examined my right eye in the wardrobe mirror. At the outer corner and in a half-crescent underneath, the skin had thickened and turned a deep, mottled pink, the colour of blackberry juice. The eye was slightly bloodshot, but I could see normally. I touched the socket with two fingers, which I then trailed down to the crack in my lower lip, a slanting split where the blood had crusted.

None of this mattered. It even struck me as faintly amusing. Inside me, there was a worse disfigurement, a malignant, gnawing pain that felt like a blunt knife-blade being twisted in my heart.

I went to the bathroom. My urine fountained out in a golden bow, filling the bowl with a dense, tawny brew redolent of oatmeal and iron filings. Gingerly, I sponged my face with warm water. I soaped my armpits and then moved down to my genitals, half expecting, upon minute inspection, to find a portion of pineapple stubbornly adhering to my penis.

I was about to sit down on the lavatory when I heard voices downstairs, followed by footsteps approaching, and a knock at the door.

"Can you hear me, Neil?"

"Hello, Gran."

"Mrs Cooper says there's a telephone call for you."

I opened the door a few inches. "Who is it?"

Gran looked flustered. "I don't know. You'll have to go and see. Put your dressing gown on."

Sighing irritably, I grabbed my green paisley dressing gown from the hook on the bedroom door and hurried downstairs. Old Mrs Cooper was waiting by her side gate. She showed me into the dingy hall and pointed to the telephone. "I think it might be your mum wants you," she said, squinting up at me. "'Ere, what 'appened to your face?"

I couldn't imagine what my mother would want so urgently. That is, I could *imagine.* Perhaps there had been a terrible fire. Mum was standing in the scorched remnants of her nightdress, a few remaining coils of singed hair protruding bravely from the smoke-blackened dome of her skull. Or maybe it was a car crash. Dad had inverted the Hillman Husky. He was in hospital, plastered arms and legs splayed in all directions, his bandage-swathed head a caricature of an irascible sikh, tormenting the nurses with a catalogue of unreasonable demands.

The receiver smelled of fish, and I attached it reluctantly to my face. "Hello. This is Neil."

"Hello, Neil."

There was no mistaking the voice.

"Oh, it's you. What do you want?" All I could manage was a flat monotone. "It's very early."

"Don't be sulky, Neil."

"How do you expect me to be?"

"Of course you're upset. I behaved abominably. That's why I'm ringing."

"You shouldn't use this phone, except for emergencies."

"This is an emergency. It's a crisis in our relationship."

"Sally, I don't think we have a relationship, not any more."

"Oh, Neil, don't say that, please." She emphasized the last word, almost as if she meant it. "Don't let's be melodramatic."

I decided I could allow myself a brief flight of self-pity. "I can't believe you called me those things, and did what you did."

A silence. "Neil, you've no idea how bad I feel about this. Did I hurt you a lot?"

"Depends what you mean. My face'll get better," I said, meaning her to infer that the rest of me might never recover, that forgiveness could be impossible. I loved her fiercely, but I wanted her to be hurt. It would make me feel better, if only superficially.

"Neil, I am just so sorry. This – look, I can't do this over the phone. I have to see you."

I was aware of Mrs Cooper hovering behind me, breathing noisily through her mouth. "I'm not even dressed, Sally," I said, quietly.

"I'm sorry. I had to speak to you. I've been worrying about this all night."

"This is someone else's phone, Sally. I'm in my pyjamas in someone else's house."

"Yesterday you were stark naked in someone else's house."

I closed my eyes and sighed. "What do you want, Sally?"

"To be friends again."

"I don't know about that."

"You said you loved me, remember? Does that just finish, like switching off a light? Don't cut off your nose to spite your face, Neil. You'll wake up in the dark and think of me, and it'll hurt far more than your sore face, believe me."

I thought about this warning. It sounded rather imperious, but I couldn't bring myself to ignore it. I wasn't that strong. "So what do you want to do?"

"Like I said, I need to see you. I'll come over."

"I don't know," I said, unhappily.

"Tuesday…does your gran still go to WI on Tuesday? If so, I – "

"I'm not sure. She might not, 'cause I'm here."

"Hmm. I'll take a chance on that. Oh, Neil." She sniffed several times, and for a moment I wondered if she was crying. "I'll be over. Wait for me."

That was it. I was spared the inner turmoil of constructing further protest, for there was a click at the end of the line, and she was gone. I replaced the receiver and wrapped my dressing gown tightly about me.

Mrs Cooper was standing at the kitchen door. "Your mum, was it?"

"Uh – no, no, it was my aunt."

"Oh, right. You got problems?"

"No, we've sorted it out. I better get back. Sorry for the inconvenience."

"That's all right, Neil. You're a good boy."

I pushed past with my head down, not looking at her.

"I say!" she called after me. "Best get Doctor Linder to 'ave a look at that eye."

I dressed and hurried down to the kitchen, where Gran was applying thick layers of butter to the morning toast. Gran's toast was always served up in triangular slices, complete with crusts. At home, toast was invariably rectangular, the crusts sliced off because Dad refused to eat them.

"Eat your crusts, they'll make your hair curl," Gran would say to me.

I did as I was told, speculating meanwhile as to the likely cause of my father's baldness.

Today, though, I was not hungry. I bit a moon-shaped edge out of a piece of toast, drank half a mug of tea, and got up to go to the shed, where I saw Archie standing with his head bowed over the workbench. Gran watched me go, and I heard her sigh and *tut-tut* as I opened the door. "You be careful of that eye," she called after me. "I'll have your mum complaining I'm not taking care of you."

I had noticed that she was dressed quite smartly, wearing a pleated heather-mixture skirt and a row of glass beads with the grey-and-white Wedgwood brooch which my mother had given her for her seventieth birthday. Plainly, she was not intending to do any housework.

Archie was poking around in an old tobacco tin, searching for screws. As he found a screw of the right size, he took it out and placed it on the window ledge, where the early sun glittered on a neat row of self-tappers. He looked up brightly as I came in. "Morning, Neil. It's a beautif- God! What happened to you?"

"Don't ask," I groaned.

He dipped his chin to peer at me. "Been in a fight?"

"No, course not." I hated the idea of lying to him. "I fell off my bike."

"I see. Well now. How's the bike?"

"It's okay. It sort of fell on top of me."

"Hmm. Want me to take a look at it?"

"What, me or the bike?"

"I meant the bike. I'm not a doctor."

"No, honestly, it's fine. Don't bother about it."

"If you ride it, and it's damaged, you – "

"Archie! Please, it's perfectly all right. Don't worry about it," and my voice tailed off into an uncomfortable silence.

"Okay, okay, whatever you say." He snapped the lid back on the tobacco tin. "I think there's enough," he said to himself.

"What are you doing?"

"Oh, Mrs Blaney wants a shelf putting up. Won't take long." He pointed through the window. "Here, did you see the sky last night? Jupiter, bright as a street light!"

Really? No, I was – well, I didn't feel all that good. Anyway, I didn't know to look."

"Never mind. I'll look again tonight, if it's clear. If Jupiter's there, I'll call you. About eight o'clock, under the moon. My telescope's in Scotland, but we can use my binoculars."

I frowned. "Surely it's not dark at eight o'clock?"

"No," he said, chuckling, "I mean in the position of eight o'clock. Down and to the left. Okay?"

"Oh, right."

"No, I said left." Then he started laughing again, and tweaked me under the chin. "It's all right, Neil. I think we understand each other, eh?" He turned back to the window and counted the screws into the palm of his hand, before facing me once more. "Something else I meant to tell you. Did you know they've opened the new library? It's just the other side of the railway bridge."

I shook my head.

"I was in there yesterday. It's a grand place, Neil. You'd love it; there's a whole section on astronomy. I even saw a wee book about the discovery of Pluto."

I considered the matter. Would Sally come? Was Gran going out? Should I just stay and talk to my friend Archie? "Is it the new brick building on the right, with the bushes outside?" I asked.

"Aye, that's the one. It's no distance. You could ride down there in three minutes."

"Well, maybe. I'm going home tomorrow, so I'd have to go today." I rubbed my chin, thoughtfully. "Trouble is, I think my friend's coming round shortly."

"Up to you, lad. Just seems like a good opportunity. While you're here, I mean." Archie dropped the screws into the breast pocket of his shirt. "Anyway, your gran's away out."

"Where's she going?"

"WI. Fat chappie in a Fiat bus picks her up. Scruffy looking individual."

He meant Sam Wicken. I had met the fat man before – or, more specifically, I had encountered him. He must have weighed twenty stone, maybe more, and his thick, black hair was always swept back in a sleek, oiled helmet over the crown of his huge head. His lardy face, deformed by several chins, was decorated with pink pustules, greasy inflorescences that both fascinated and repelled me. I remember he invariably wore pale, baggy trousers, either green or beige, with some unsavoury menu on the fly, evidence of where he had dropped his tea or his food, or sometimes a cloud-shaped stain of old urine from a fumbling misjudgment or a helpless moment of stress incontinence. Sam Wicken was big and gruff, with a sour face and no life in his eyes, and I never saw him smile.

Strangely, I think Gran quite liked him. I suppose he was occasionally useful to her. He ran a chicken farm just over the county border, a ramshackle collection of wooden sheds and barns accessed by a rutted track which was always puddled and potholed in summer or winter. You could buy chickens or eggs, either from Sam or his wife, a large, square woman who waddled about in a floral-print housedress and gumboots. The place was a complete shambles, with loose chickens strutting everywhere and the ground littered with broken eggs. Approaching the farm buildings, visitors were greeted by a hand-painted wooden sign, sawn from a plank: *Wickens Chickens. Ets. 1956.* He meant 'Established', obviously, but the mistake there was his, not mine; that's what the sign said.

Anyhow, from time to time Gran would buy some eggs or a chicken from the farm. The bus stopped in the main road at the bottom of the track, or she might persuade someone to give her a lift. The first time she went by bus, I went with her to help her carry the bags. Mrs Wicken served us, and we noticed several dilapidated Volkswagen buses standing about, some with broken windows, others without wheels, and all in a state of obvious neglect. As we were leaving, Gran asked Mrs Wicken if her husband had any serviceable buses, something that might provide suitable transport for occasional WI outings.

"I'm a new member," she said. "I'd like to do something to help them if I can. Sort of make my mark, you know."

Mrs Wicken regarded her doubtfully. "What, you wanna buy one?"

"That would depend on the price," Gran replied.

"I see." The farmer's wife gathered up the front of her dress and wiped her hands in the folds. "There's a Fiat in the big barn. Seats about a dozen."

"Does it go?" Gran enquired.

Mrs Wicken looked affronted. "Does it go? Course it goes. Nice little runner, that."

"I'd have to have some idea of price. I'd have to tell them."

"Why don't you just hire it out when you need it? Be cheaper. Let Sam know when you're going out, and he'll come and drive you. He could do with a bit of pocket-money." She kicked at a crushed egg, congealing in the mud. "Tell you the truth, be glad to get him outa my hair for a day."

That was how Sam Wicken got the job of part-time bus driver for the Women's Institute. He was a volunteer by proxy, albeit a paid one. My recollection of the inaugural excursion, to Ruislip Lido, is by now a little hazy, but the event had its defining moments, a foggy flotsam of inconsequential memorabilia from the wrenching journey of those years.

Four of us went along: Mum, Dad, Gran and I. It was a fine, sunny day. There were about six others on board, apart from Sam Wicken, including the local WI secretary, Rona Markevitch, who brought her daughter, Janna, "to bring her out of herself by helping others", as she rather grandly put it. The girl was to assist people in and out of the bus, make sure they were comfortable and dispense refreshments at the afternoon picnic. I was too young to understand exactly what Janna's handicap was, but she was thirteen, with a seventeen year-old's body and, trapped desperately inside it, a six year-old's mind. For some reason, she called me Nell. I told myself repeatedly not to stare, bemused, at her chicken-white skin, her lolling breasts and circular, crust-rimmed eyes; it was rude to stare, the more so when the stimulus was vicarious satisfaction that I had unwittingly avoided the physical plight displayed to me by other children.

Mum took an instant dislike to Sam Wicken. He was rumoured to be of Romany stock, a social disadvantage which my mother at once converted to the darkest opprobrium. "That man is just a dirty *gyppo,*" she informed my father, as the bus pulled away. Dad, affording Sam the briefest of summary glances, was quick to counsel her against the incautious use of this charmless sobriquet, but I could tell that Mum's mind was made up. Once that had happened, there was latitude for neither compromise nor negotiation.

While Sam drove, Mrs Markevitch's daughter shuffled to and fro, occasionally toppling into an unsuspecting passenger's lap, as she did her ponderous best to please her mother with her ministrations. Our progress, as I recall, was largely uneventful, and Sam's attention to the road ahead seldom wavered, save for the odd furtive glance at Janna as she lumbered around behind him. Every so often, as he hauled on the wheel of the fully-laden bus, a tuneful stress fart would ripple from the fat man's jouncing rear, its burbling trill clearly audible above the boom of the engine.

Dad cocked his head at me across the gangway. "These squeaks – are they in the bus or in the driver?"

I smiled, answering with my eyes, as a fusty sulphuric odour wafted back between the seats.

Summer days from childhood meld together in the mind's eye to form a series of loosely interlinked snapshots, mirroring memories in swiftly unfolding scenes infused with a fragile, actinic light, like a faded concertina postcard unearthed from a pile of dusty treasures. Archie's eyes were on me, searching for some small resolution, but I was busy, toying with the postcard pictures of the Lido flickering in my head – the red double-deckers pulled up outside the gates while the drivers and conductors sprawled full-length along the inside bench seats, drinking from their *Thermos* flasks and reading *Titbits* or *Reveille*...the shallow, sandy pools at the water's edge where we dipped our spindly nets, chasing the darting grey needles of myriad minnows, to be scooped out in triumph and clumsily decanted into jamjars full of brackish water...slow, grinding rides on the miniature railway, laughing faces full of the sweet-oil stink of the polished locomotive's wheezing breath...the lazy picnics under the trees where grown-ups distributed paper cups of *Tizer* and buttered baps and bruised bananas and fish-paste sandwiches and fairy cakes and, if you were good, chewy caramel bars in shiny red-and-gold wrappers that glinted in the sun...and, hauntingly unforgettable from that first trip, the cosy pleasure of the half-crown, nestled in the palm of my hand, given me by Dad to buy ice-creams, the quiet, private thrill of it, turning suddenly to shadowy madness as I passed the clump of rustling bushes by the boggy hollow, and looked over to see if there might be a frightened rabbit or an injured bird, and down in the green gloom I saw them, could smell them too, Sam Wicken sitting with his trousers in a bundle and Janna Markevitch facing him, her legs on his shoulders, one shoe off, her pink knickers flapping from his shirt pocket, and Sam with his long red thing half inside her, his massive scrotum dragging in the dirt as he pumped, making his face a burst tomato, and Janna the first to see me, yelping gleefully, "Look at us, Nell! We're playing monkeys!" and fat Sam jumping, sliding out of her like a snake, and the way he seized my shirt fiercely under my chin, nearly pulling me over, and the rancid smell of his breath as he snarled in my face, "Piss off, Robertson! Snoopin' around!" and the hot rain of his spit on my cheeks, his eyes blue flames of cold fire, while Janna squealed and kicked her legs, knocking his hand away, so I ran, ran as fast as I could, with the fat man's curses bludgeoning my ears and my heart pounding in my shock-dry mouth like a chunk of my insides sicked up and wedged there, rattling in frenzied convulsions of fear.

I shook my head, meeting Archie's enquiring gaze. "Are you okay?" he asked.

"What? Oh, yes."

"Seems like you were miles away there, for a minute."

"I was just remembering something."

"Ah, right."

"Archie, I think I will go to the library. I could walk – to sort of clear my head."

"Up to you. I can look after your friend."

"The only problem is..."

"You've no ticket."

"That's right. How did you know?"

He grinned. "Oh, I think I'm getting to know you, Neil." His strong fingers gripped my shoulder. "Don't worry; you can borrow mine. You can be Archie McLeish for the day."

He fetched me his library ticket, then disappeared into the kitchen to fix the shelf. I looked towards the gate and thought about traipsing nearly a mile to the library – almost two miles, there and back. The sun was gathering strength, and my head was starting to hurt. It seemed only sensible to change my mind, so I wheeled my bike to the road and pedalled steadily towards the railway bridge.

I wasn't in the library for long. It was hot and airless in there, blinding ladders of sunlight slanting through the tall windows, painting searing parallelograms on the floor, and soon my head was stuffed with a thick humus of pain. By the time I had located the astronomy section, I was aware of the soupy smell of my own sweat, gathering in ragged moons under my arms, and my only focused thought was to escape into the fresh air. The book on Pluto, which Archie had mentioned, was still there, so I took it down, and I also chose an encyclopaedia of the universe and a glossy paperback, speculating on how long and arduous would be the journey to Mars.

When I came out, I saw the WI bus parked under a tree. Sam Wicken was sitting on the rear step, puffing at the stub of a cigarette. The clatter of my bike chain, as I unlocked it, drew his attention, and he nodded sullenly in my direction and gave a little jerk of recognition with his clenched thumb and forefinger, before re-inserting the dog-end between his chubby lips. With the books secured in my saddlebag, I climbed up and rode quickly past him without acknowledgment.

As soon as I entered the house, I felt that something was not as it should be. I knew that Gran would be out, but still the silence seemed unnerving. The feeling of the place was...wrong. In a heap on the kitchen table lay a wooden shelf, some brackets and screws, and the battered box containing Granddad's tools. Archie's job had not even been started.

I thought I would find Archie and show him the books I had borrowed. As I reached the corner in the stairs, I heard from above me the low grumble of voices and a peal of soft laughter. It didn't sound like a man laughing. Clasping the books tightly to my chest, I carried on very slowly to the top of the staircase.

The door to Archie's room stood partly open. I could see the wardrobe to the right of the doorway, with the tall mirror on the front. Taking a few silent steps forward, I narrowed my eyes and looked at the reflection. Archie was lying on his side in bed. The blankets were pulled up, but I could see his hairy chest. His face was obscured by the person lying in front of him. There was a bob of blonde hair, catching the light, and a pale, smooth leg tucked up on the bedclothes. I stared, frozen in disbelief. I was there, and I was not mistaken. I was not mistaken.

It didn't matter to me that the books thumped loudly on the floor as I let them fall. There was no secrecy now, and I didn't care. In that brief moment, I didn't care about anything. I hurried downstairs and sat at the kitchen table. My eyes began to flood, and a sour milk taste seeped into my mouth. A minute passed, maybe two, and I heard light footsteps on the stairs. She came in, wearing Archie's dressing gown, and sat in the chair facing me.

"Hello," I said, flatly.

She sighed and tucked each hand into the opposite sleeve, as if she were cold. "We didn't expect you back so soon," she murmured.

"Obviously."

Another sigh. "Oh Neil. What a mess, eh?"

I turned down my mouth in a kind of careless pout. "I don't know. It all seems quite straightforward to me. I mean, it's not complicated, is it?"

She nodded, looking more relieved than embarrassed. "You're a brave lad, Neil."

I bristled. "Please. Don't say that. Don't – "

"Don't patronise you, you mean." She arched her neck, twisting her head around, and her eyes shone with tears. "No, you're right. I've hurt you enough already."

"It's all right, you know." I reached out and touched her arm. "I never thought it would be for ever. Things don't last. They never last." That was the most I could manage. I started to cry.

I could hear Archie bumping around upstairs, but he didn't come down.

She sniffed, and wiped her eyes with her fingers. "Look at your poor face," she said, shaking her head. "What a cow I am! How could you even think of loving me?"

"I didn't think. It just happened. I crawled into a trap and I couldn't get out again."

"Is that how you see it – that I trapped you?"

"I didn't say that."

Sally stood up, gazed out of the window and sat down again. "Neil, there's something you should know."

I allowed myself a stutter of ironic laughter. "I don't think I need to know any more," I said, staring morosely at the table top.

"Believe me, Neil, you don't know the half of it."

"Really," I said, affecting disinterest. "Go on then."

She lowered her eyes and shifted awkwardly in the chair. "Oh God," she whispered. "Neil, there is really no easy way of telling you this."

"Tell me anyway. It can't be worse than what I've just found out."

"It's about Archie," she said, looking up at me once more.

"Oh? What about him?"

"Well, you see, he..."

"What is it, Sally?"

"I'm very sorry, Neil. He's my husband."

Chapter VII

Night Fears

It was raining hard, and Dad drove slowly, the windscreen wipers juddering and squeaking on the dirty glass. Through the imperfect seal of the door, I heard the squelching hiss of the tyres on the wet road and an occasional muted rasp from the rusty exhaust silencer. Behind us, the detached front wheel of my bike drummed on the bare metal of the flattened rear seat, while the rest of the machine lay capsized against the back window, like some giant dead insect.

"Just as well I decided to pick you up," Dad said, glancing quickly towards me. "You'd have got drenched, riding in this."

I grunted, almost inaudibly, and stared grimly ahead through the streaked and splattered screen.

He glanced at me again, a quick flick of the head. "So you had a crash?"

"Not exactly," I said, without looking at him. "I just skidded and came off."

"Going too fast, I suppose."

"No. Something distracted me."

We continued in silence for a mile or so. I was grateful for the lift, but I didn't feel like talking.

He sniffed fiercely and opened his mouth with a loud click. "Your friend Archie has nothing to do with this, I take it."

I turned to him incredulously. "What?"

"I mean these – these facial injuries."

"For goodness' sake, Dad." I slumped down in my seat. "I told you. I fell off my bike. It's nothing, it happens all the time."

"You've fallen off before, then?"

"No, I mean other people. They fall off their bikes. It's not unusual."

"Ach, I'm not interested in other people."

I shut my eyes and wondered if, by staying quiet, I might lead my father to suppose that I had fallen asleep. It was warm in the car, and with nothing to see but a field of reddish darkness behind my quivering eyelids, I soon found the drone of the exhaust and the swish of the tyres pleasantly soporific.

At the next roundabout, one of Dad's particularly ham-fisted gear-changes jolted me back to wakefulness. When he spoke, he had to raise his voice to be heard over the metallic screaming of the tortured engine. "I expect you're tired."

"A bit," I mumbled.

"Keep you awake at night?"

"What?"

"Your face. Does it ache at night?"

"Not much."

"Ah. So what else did you get up to in your break?"

"Oh, this and that, you know."

"No, I don't know. Why else would I be asking?"

In my mind, I constructed an imaginary reply, one that would seal the matter once and for all. 'On Saturday Nurse came round and shoved her hand down my trousers. She invited me over for lunch on Monday, so we stripped naked and jumped in the bath and she decorated my privates with fruit. Then she got mad and tried to punch my teeth out. Next day I went out on my bike and when I came back Nurse was upstairs, in bed with the lodger. Good, it was. It all happens at Gran's.'

For the first time that day, I found myself beginning to laugh. Dad couldn't hear me above the road noise, but he seemed to notice when I put a hand up to my right eye, reacting to a sudden twinge of pain. "Are you not well?" he asked.

"I'm all right," I said. "It'll be nice to be home."

"Oh, I forgot to tell you. There's a surprise for you at home."

I had had quite enough of surprises recently, but I let that pass. "What sort of surprise?"

"You'll find out," he said.

I smiled thinly, and pulled out my handkerchief to wipe the condensation from the windscreen. The rain was falling harder. Behind my head, my upturned bicycle rattled and graunched against the steel panels.

I was leafing through an encyclopaedia in my bedroom when Dad carried the box in. It was a large brown cardboard box with hand-holes cut at either end. The blue script on the side read, *Heinz Baked Beans – 57 Varieties.*

"Don't worry, it's not beans," Dad said, lowering the box gently on to the bed.

"I like beans, but not that much," I said, trying to keep the mood as light as possible.

There was a sudden scrabbling noise from beneath the flaps. I looked from the box to Dad and back at the box again.

He nodded at me. "Go ahead. Open it."

I prised the flaps apart and peered inside. A pleasant fruity musk filled my nostrils, and something moved under a pile of straw.

"It's a guinea pig," Dad said. "Thought he'd make up for Monty."

Carefully, I eased my hands into the box and lifted out the warm, vibrating body. "He's beautiful. Thank you." I held the softly protesting bundle against my cheek, cradled in the palms of both hands. "I shall call him Hector."

"Hector," Dad repeated, sounding pleased. "Any particular reason?"

"No, he just looks like a Hector."

Hector squirmed in my hands, squeaking softly. He was a short-haired pig, quite small, with dappled black and white fur and a butterscotch-coloured ruff around his neck. When I placed him gently on the bedspread, he immediately squeezed through the hole in the end of the box and hid himself inside once more.

"Seems like he's made up his mind," Dad said, laughing. He closed the flaps and picked up the box. "Anyway, he can have Monty's hutch. I've cleaned it out and moved it into the garage, so he won't get cold in the winter."

"Thanks, Dad." I watched him turn and go, and I felt grateful and sad and a little apprehensive, for my father was old enough to have forgotten the turmoil and confusion of growing up, the frantic, dangerous pursuit of formless dreams and a small, cold death in the morning.

If only he knew, I thought. If only he could remember about where childhood ended and people with long faces began. It somehow chilled my blood to contemplate this most palpable of delusions, his mistaken belief that a kiss from my gran and a new pet in a box would sublimate my desires and appease my youthful yearnings, when I had already nibbled the forbidden fruit from other, wilder orchards and my fiercest longing was for more. My father's innocent miscalculation reminded me how quickly we become strangers. Beyond the first few lightly brushing years of childhood, when all the days are sunny and we sleep with smiles, the darker mantle of a subtle estrangement settles over us, irremovable as a second skin. From that time forward, until there is no time, there is no completeness to our knowledge of anybody else, because we are all by nature secretive and egocentric, each of us moving quietly in a private island, a shadow-haunted place where even the concessions of family links or the most intimate friendships allow no border access. We hide behind doors that are closed for ever.

I went to bed early that night, the evening light pulsing strongly against the drawn curtains. A crimson universe shimmered behind my closed eyelids, pricked by the glittery silica of floating blood bubbles. I lay quite still and imagined I was landing on Mars. Yet the sounds filtering into my head were not from outer space, they were earthly sounds that fixed me stubbornly to the present time and place: the optimistic chimes of a last ice-cream van not bothering to stop; the unnerving burbling wail of two cats disputing their territorial rights; the thump of the fat kid next door kicking his football against our fence; the chilling metallic scrape as old Mr Krups two gardens away dragged shut his greenhouse door to keep out the night.

The last thing I wanted was to sleep. I wanted to think. I thought of the people on Pluto, trudging through the terrible, icy darkness in their thick, ankle-length coats, sewn with mysterious, life-saving panels of indescribable colours. I tried to find their faces in the gloom, to see if they looked human, but they had deep hoods, made of some fur material, pulled forward over their bowed heads, and all the facial features were obscured. In my heart, I wept for the silent, desperate people of that forgotten planet.

Then, inevitably, I thought of Archie. For all that had happened before and was said afterwards, I was glad that Archie had come downstairs that afternoon to join Sally and me in the kitchen. I might otherwise have thought him a coward, content to let Sally's faltering explanations speak for both of them.

I remember how he had hovered awkwardly in the doorway, apparently uncertain whether the moment was right for him to come in. He had put on a pair of trousers and a vest, and it struck me that my two friends were sufficiently anxious to unburden themselves of the truth that they were prepared to risk Gran's disapproval, and possible interrogation, if she were to return early and find them together, improperly dressed.

"Oh dear," he said, a little sadly, as he pulled out the chair opposite me and sat down next to Sally.

I stared balefully at the table.

"I'm sorry," Archie said, "I don't know how much Sally's told you."

I gazed at the barley-coloured hairs protruding from his armpits.

"I've barely started," Sally said. "I was hoping you would come down."

"Aye, well I'm here now."

There was a silence, as though neither of them could decide who was to do the talking. I coughed expectantly and, resting my elbows on the table, buried my nose in the tent of my clasped hands.

Archie sighed, wiping an imaginary sweat bead from one side of his brow. Sally tugged the dressing gown impatiently about her. I could still smell the book print on my hands.

"We'll be sat here all day, at this rate," Sally said, finally.

"Gran'll be home soon," I reminded them, gloomily.

Archie was peering at me with a nervous, pained expression on his face. "You know, Neil, we'd have done anything to avoid hurting you. This is not how we wanted you to find out."

"Perhaps you didn't want me to find out at all," I said. "It's made it all a bit inconvenient now, hasn't it?"

"The fact is, Neil, Sally and I were married in Scotland in 1957. We were – I think I can say we were very happy." He slipped one arm affectionately round Sally's shoulders, but she seemed to freeze at his touch, and shook herself free. "Well, anyway, maybe we didn't have a great deal, but at least we had each other, and a wee house with a bit of garden out the back." Archie's chin dropped for a few seconds. "I mean, how much do you need?" When he raised his head again, I saw tears glistening in his eyes.

Sally's eyes had acquired a steely glaze. "You know what we needed," she said, and it sounded as if she spoke through clenched teeth. "Don't start your philosophising."

"So what happened?" I asked. "What went wrong?"

Sally stared at me from narrowed eyes, almost pityingly. "Oh, look at your poor face," she said, as though noticing it for the first time. "Did I really do that?"

I saw Archie clench his jaw, the muscles in his face contracting. "What? You told me you fell off your bike."

"I told you a lie," I said, miserably.

"Why? Are you protecting her?"

"He's protecting both of us," Sally said.

Archie blinked, shaking his head. "I must be dumb," he said. "I don't follow."

She clasped her face in her hands, not looking at him. "If you must know, Neil and I have – have seen each other once or twice. I was with him the other day. Then I got cross about something, and lashed out." She sighed, biting her lip. "It was very bad of me, and I'm ashamed of it."

I searched Archie's face for a reaction. He looked more confused than before. I felt wretchedly sorry, as though I had betrayed him.

He stared at Sally incredulously. "Are you telling me in all seriousness that you and – no, no, I can't believe any of this stuff. This is madness."

It wasn't all Sally's fault. She deserved some help. "It's true, Archie," I told him. "I really like her. You know, really."

He opened his mouth to say something else, but Sally cut him short. "It's all right, Archie. It's not what you think. We haven't – well, you know," and her voice trailed away to a whisper.

"It's all right, is it? What d'you mean, woman, it's all right? Of course it's not all right. For Christ's sake, he's just a wee boy!"

I flew at him, so swiftly I took even myself by surprise. "I am not a little boy! I am not a child!"

The palms of Archie's outstretched hands pawed the air placatingly in front of me. "Okay, Neil, I'm sorry. I didn't mean to sound unkind."

"I don't want you to be kind to me. I just want people to treat me like a grown-up."

"Aye, it seems like you're growing up too fast for your own good, lad. Don't try to fly too high, not yet awhile."

Sally was leaning forward, one hand covering her face. The dressing gown was too big for her; it was gaping open at the front, revealing the dark-slotted curve of her cleavage. Underneath, I suspected that she was naked, and I thought once more about the in-betweens.

"I had no idea," Archie murmured, wearily.

I looked at him and tried not to feel sympathetic, for although there were no innocent parties here, their deceit was more deliberate, more artful, than mine. "Perhaps you should go on with your story," I said.

"Aye, maybe I should. Where was I?"

"I asked if something went wrong."

"Ah, right. Well, obviously it did, or we'd not be sitting here, fussing our heads about it."

"Did you argue about money?"

"What? Oh no, no. No, it wasn't about that. In any case, we didn't really argue."

"But you separated."

"Let's say we had some – disagreements. We had a technical difficulty – "

At this point, I heard Sally click her tongue irritably, as she rocked back and forth in her chair – gestures which Archie affected to ignore.

"As I say, we had a technical difficulty and, over a period of time, that put a strain on our relationship. It wasn't something we could have envisaged at the outset, you understand."

The trouble was, I didn't understand. It sounded to me as if Archie was reading from a script. I wondered why he didn't just tell me what the problem was.

Sally had evidently divined my thoughts. "Spare us the circumlocution," she said, testily. "Just tell the boy – just tell Neil where it all went wrong."

"Aye, I will. Well, we had a disappointment."

"What sort of a disappointment?" I asked him.

"From the day we were wed, we'd set our minds on – on the future. As a family, I mean. We knew we'd make good parents."

"Good parents, he says." Sally made a minute inspection of the table top. "Couldn't even get started."

"Okay, okay." Archie paused, working his lips, anxiously. "It was my fault. No, well, it wasn't my *fault* exactly, but it was me had the problem." He sighed and shook his head. "It was all very distressing."

"What he means is, his house keeps falling down," Sally told me.

"What?"

"Man to man, Neil." He winked at me, humourlessly. "You know about erections and all that."

"Oh, right."

"Yes, well, we had these damned tests and all. Waste of time."

I gazed earnestly into his blue eyes. "Maybe now there's something they can do," I said. "Some pills or something."

Sally sniffed frostily. "Scaffolding, more like."

Archie sensibly dismissed this remark with a fleeting sideways glance. "The damage is done now, Neil," he said, with an air of resignation.

"But I saw you together. You were in bed."

"Old times' sake, Neil." He laughed shortly. "A man needs a bit of company." With one forefinger, he traced an imaginary map on the table top. "I guess it doesn't mean much any more."

"Maybe it does," I said. "You bothered to find each other. That can't have been easy."

"I knew Sally had gone south to her sister. I telephoned, but she'd helped Sally find a place and she wouldn't say exactly where. But I found out from the hospital. There's always a way."

I looked at Sally. She seemed pale and fragile – shaken, almost. "Did you mind Archie coming after you?" I asked.

She gazed back at me, dreamily. "Not really. I didn't want rid of him. I love him, you see." She was speaking as though Archie wasn't there, not touching him or looking at him. "Oh, I don't expect you to understand any of this."

"But you left him. Why did you do that?"

"Because I loved him. I mean, I still do. It doesn't make any sense, does it?"

"It doesn't seem right," I said. "None of it seems right."

"I suppose, in a way, I wanted to hurt him."

"Why?"

"So he would notice me. Then he would come to me and ask what he'd done to upset me, and want to be forgiven. A reaffirmation of faith, I suppose you'd call it."

"Is that what people do when they love each other?"

"Sometimes, if they get frightened or they feel unhappy or insecure. If someone loves you, it means they need you, only maybe at times they forget to show it. Then you have to remind them, by pretending you don't really need them. You'll find out one day, Neil; it's one of the saddest things we do."

"What, hurting people because you love them?"

"Yes. It's hateful and it's spiteful."

"Then I would never want to do it."

"No, but you will, Neil. Everybody does. We aren't perfect, you see."

A small sound distracted me and, when I glanced at him, I saw that Archie was crying. His face was in his hands, and the tears were running down his fingers. I looked back at Sally, wanting her to comfort him, at least to touch him, but she sat quite still, staring ahead, as if in a trance.

I reached out and lightly squeezed one of Archie's wet hands. He tried to smile, stifling a moan. "It's all right, Archie," I said. "There's got to be a way we can all be friends."

"Why did she do it?" he pleaded, the tears coursing down his cheeks. "It wasn't my fault. I loved her all I could. The only thing I didn't give her was what I didn't have."

"Why don't you ask her? You're both talking to me. You should talk to each other. You're making it like a game."

"That's all it is," Sally said, "one long, tedious, never-ending game. And somewhere along the line you usually get into an argument about the score."

Was this wisdom or cynicism? I had no way of telling, because I lacked the experience. All I could see was that two people who claimed to love each other were making themselves unhappy, their relationship menaced by selfishness and despair. Growing up seemed a treacherous journey into fear and darkness.

"Now that you're – sort of together," I said, nodding from one to the other, "do you think you could be friends again? I mean, really friends?"

To my surprise, Sally took my hand and held it warmly, clasping her hands around it. "Is that what you want, Neil? Is that what you'd like?"

"It's not about what I want, is it?" I answered, with a shrug.

"Here." She pulled out a handkerchief and offered it to Archie. Tears were dripping from his chin, wetting the table. "Stop your crying. There's no need to cry."

He took the handkerchief and dabbed at his swollen eyes. Then he unfolded the cloth and peered into it. "Is it all right if I blow my nose?"

Sally stared at him. "Do you need my permission?"

"I mean, if it's your hanky."

"It was in the pocket. It's yours. It's got an 'A' in the corner."

Archie blew his nose extravagantly and held the handkerchief in his cupped hands, inspecting the results.

Sally frowned at him. "Why do men do that?" she asked, of no-one in particular.

"What, blow their noses?" I enquired.

"No," she said, her tone a disapproving whine. "Make an engineering operation of it. A woman always does it quickly and discreetly."

Archie stuffed the handkerchief in his pocket. "Ah, you're

very posh, you," he said. "Except when you're taking young boys to bed."

Sally stiffened at this remark, and the corners of her mouth turned down. "Excuse me," she said, haughtily, "what young boys are you referring to?"

Archie glanced at me but said nothing.

"We didn't go to bed, Archie," I told him. "Honestly."

"Oh? You hear that, Sally?" He threw her a reproving sidelong glance. "The boy says you never went to bed. So where did you do it then?"

She pulled an ugly face, grinding her teeth together. "Archie, please."

"No, no, I'd like to know. Did you do it on the floor in his room, then? I hope you didn't do it in my room."

"We didn't do it in your room. Archie, what's the point of this? What purpose is it serving?"

"The point, Sally, is that if we're to have any future at all, we have to be able to trust each other. We must be open and honest about our lives. I think a little more information wouldn't come amiss."

"It wasn't here," I blurted out.

He scowled at me, knitting his brows. "Not here? Where then?"

I looked at Sally, but she seemed lost for words. "Round Sally's house," I said.

"Neil!" Her eyes blazed at me.

"Round – so you've been to her house – you've visited my wife's house for sex?"

"I didn't know she was your wife!" I shouted.

"Oh, I see. And that makes it all right, I suppose."

"She asked me to lunch," I said, miserably.

"She asked you to lunch," he repeated slowly. "Ah well, that's a new name for it. A most civilised euphemism."

"Archie," Sally said quietly, "I really think we should stop this. It's upsetting Neil, and it's getting us nowhere."

"It's getting us nearer the truth," Archie said. He offered me a thin, withering smile. "I must say, Neil, you do surprise me. Here was I, believing you were keen to learn about the planets and great music, and all the while, what you were really interested in was having sex with my wife, committing filthy, adulterous acts behind my – "

"Archie! Stop it at once!" Sally pressed hard on the table, almost rising to her feet. "It's not fair!"

"That is precisely my point," Archie said, levelly. "It's all so very unfair."

Now my sadness and despair came seething to the surface, and overwhelmed me. I folded my arms in front of me, leaning heavily on the table, and let the tears flow until they blinded me. At first I wept silently, eyes downcast, my shoulders gently shuddering, but then my grief became something monstrous and uncontainable, and I laid back my head and cried open-mouthed, the deep, guttural sobs that racked my body drowning out the pacifying implorations issuing across the table from the friends who sought in vain to reassure me.

I felt a hand touch my arm and softly squeeze it – once, twice, three times. Then I heard a voice, Archie's voice. "Come on, Neil. We can get through this."

I peered at him through a liquid mist. I opened my mouth to ask, "How?" – but no sound came out, just a drooling breath, a crawling wetness.

Sally spoke with her eyes closed, as though this might help her to formulate the words. "Neil, can you still love us? Can you forgive us and be fond of us?"

I nodded.

"Then pick up your chair and move round here."

"Why?"

"Do it, Neil."

I did as I was told. I swung the chair around the end of the table and stood behind the two of them.

"Move up, Archie," Sally said.

I waited. They made room for me. I sat down between them. Archie slid his left arm around my shoulders, while Sally put her right arm around me, so that it rested on Archie's arm.

With her free hand, Sally drew her fingertips down my face, from my eye to my chin. "I love you, Neil," she said. "We both love you."

They each leaned towards me, strengthening their embrace.

Archie smiled and kissed the lobe of my ear.

"You can be our boy," Sally said. "Everything will be all right now."

I stared straight ahead of me. My heart was pounding, pounding. There was the taste of almonds in my mouth. I tried to relax, to let myself go so they could just draw me into themselves, but something was not right, there was the feeling of fear. I could taste the fear. They did not frighten me; it was the fear that frightened me.

Sally caressed my cheek again with the soft pads of her fingers. "Our boy," she murmured, "our special boy."

They held me close. They held me very close.

My eyes grew heavy, and I gave myself up to fitful sleep. I slept and woke, slept and woke, until the two alternating states became a senseless seesaw to which I clung in perspiring confusion, unable to determine at any one moment whether I was awake or asleep, seeing or dreaming. The encroaching night was a dark stain that crept across the ceiling and seeped down the walls to lie in black lakes on the carpet, where razored stencils of moonlight suggested phosphorescent holes into which I might fall to oblivion if I stepped from my bed. It was not a simple, juvenile night fear, for I have never been afraid of the dark; but something troubled and perplexed me as I recalled the conversation in the kitchen with Archie and Sally. Emotional disorientation, I suppose you could call it. I propped myself up on one elbow, studying the inky shadows on the floor, as if those formless shapes were an oversized Rorschach test, from whose interpretation I might somehow understand the mysteries of human relationships.

I wondered about Sally. If she was in love with Archie, why had she deserted him to live five hundred miles away? And what of Archie? What exactly was the matter with him? Could he be seriously ill? He was always very pale. Then I wondered, too, about the future of our triangular friendship. Perhaps reconciliation for Archie and Sally would only mean rejection and exclusion for me. Except – except that Sally had whispered to me a strange assurance: I was to be their boy. What did she mean? What would be the nature of the possession? *You can be our boy, our special boy.* Was she alluding to a close and enduring friendship, or something more compromising? Cold waves of panic washed over me, as crazy, irrational thoughts raced through my head like dancing demons. Suddenly the dark shadows were filled with menace.

Kidnap. That was it, of course. How foolish I was not to have seen the threat before. They had, and could have, no child of their own, so they would take me instead. They would overpower me, perhaps even bind my arms and legs, and spirit me away in the darkness. Never again would I feel my mother's talcum-powdered hand on my brow, or hear the gruff assertion of my father's stolid goodness.

Archie, as far as I knew, was unemployed. The plan was obvious. They needed the money, and so I would be held to ransom. Mum's Post Office book would be emptied to buy back her own son. They would find me in a sack, trussed up like a chicken, abandoned on waste ground beside the railway line. Dad's angry words, as he tore the ropes from my bruised body, already echoed in my brain: "What did I tell you? What did I tell you? Will you never listen?"

I buried my face in the pillow, compounding the darkness. Immersed, half-smothered, in a dreamless black morass, I finally subsided once more into sleep, tumbling headlong into a timeless void; until, like someone tapping on my skull, a familiar sound intruded, the impatient staccato of the rapping door knocker. My sleep was neutralised, fragmented, and I opened my eyes and clawed my way back to the changeless world of my bedroom, its features now freshly defined by a pale wash of early light, filtering through the curtains. I rolled over and sat up, hugging my knees in a manner that seemed to offer me some vague sense of self-protection. The knocking, a fierce double *rat-tat,* came again, and I felt my whole body beginning to tremble. Could it be them at the door? For sure, when they came for me, it would be early or late. They would not risk it at the height of the day, when people were about in the street. They were clever, and would take no chances.

Quickly, silently, I flung aside the bedclothes, crossed to the wardrobe and stepped inside. I squatted on a pile of blankets, holding the door an inch ajar. The flimsy wooden cabinet creaked as I quaked uncontrollably, breathing through my open mouth. Someone's feet thumped on the stairs. They were going to open the door, going to let them in. I tried to cry out – 'No!' – but I couldn't make the noise come out of my parched throat. All that came was a ragged hissing, and then, to my shame and dismay, another rustling hiss from lower down, as my pyjama bottoms heated and filled with my escaping urine. In the cramped space of the wardrobe, I smelled the thick ammoniac stink rise to engulf me as I soaked the neatly folded blankets, my spouting wee already stinging the insides of my thighs.

My mother was at the front door, and I heard voices. I opened the wardrobe door another inch. Somebody laughed, then there was a click, and silence. I winced as a trickle of urine ran back up the crack of my bum.

"Neil! Are you awake? There's a parcel for you!"

I ground my teeth together, feeling sick. It was all right, it was only the postman.

"Neil?"

When I heard Mum climbing the stairs, I scampered from my hiding place and wrapped my dressing gown around me. She found me sitting nervously on the edge of the bed. Something large seemed to follow her into the room.

"Oh, you're awake. I called you."

"I was just getting up."

"Right, well there's this come for you." She heaved a brown paper parcel, about two feet long, on to the bed, and stood staring at it. "Whatever do you think it is?"

"I don't know," I said.

"Have you sent off for anything?"

"No."

She peered at me critically. "Hmm. Smells like you could do with a bath, young man."

Now I saw that, in my breathless haste, I had left the wardrobe door hanging open. I dredged up some spit, trying to wet my mouth.

"Well, aren't you going to open it?" Mum asked.

I began to tear at the paper, not merely to reveal the contents, but also to distract Mum's attention from the open wardrobe. The wrapping came off easily, but underneath was a cardboard box, sealed with brown tape. As I picked at the tape with shaking fingers, Mum's head turned slowly away from me.

"Neil?"

"What?"

"Why is there water running out of your wardrobe?"

Chapter VIII

Inside the Box

Hector snuffled at my fingertips, the warm stub of his nose prodding and probing, as I threaded the lettuce leaf through the wire mesh. The chocolate-coloured buttons of his eyes shone jewel-bright, and he squeaked in gratitude.

I didn't hear Dad come in. He was suddenly there, standing at my shoulder, watching.

"He loves lettuce," I said, without turning round.

"Aha. You all right?"

"Yes thanks."

"Mum said she thought you might have a problem."

"How do you mean?"

"Something about going to the toilet."

"Oh, that." I hung my head awkwardly. "I-uh-had a bad dream."

"I see. Are you sleeping in the wardrobe now?"

"No. I'm really sorry. I can help with the washing if you want."

"That won't be necessary. I don't understand why you were in the wardrobe."

Upon reflection, neither did I. The whole incident seemed grotesque. I could think of no plausible explanation. "I was sort of hiding," I said.

"Oh. Is this a game?"

"No. I was frightened."

"So you hid in the wardrobe?"

"Yes. I know it sounds silly."

"Why did you go to the lavatory in there? You're supposed to do that in the bathroom, hang your clothes in the wardrobe and sleep in the bed. What are you going to do next? Sleep in the bath, put your clothes in the bed and use the wardrobe as a toilet, hmm?"

There was a scalding sensation behind my eyes. "I said I was sorry. I had this nightmare."

"What sort of nightmare? Are you worried about something?"

"Not really."

"Well, either you are or you aren't. Is it something to do with your school work?"

"No. I'm on holiday."

"I know perfectly well you're on holiday. Your school work is still important. There's the GCE soon, remember. By Christ, Neil, if your work's not up to standard, I'll have something to say about it!"

"I know it's important. I'm not worried about that."

"Okay. Is someone bullying you? A boy in the playground, perhaps, or one of the teachers?"

I turned and faced him squarely, feeling the blood draining from my cheeks. "Yes," I replied, "there's someone bullying me. I don't like it."

"I thought as much. Will you give me his name?"

"All right," I said, and I drew a deep breath. "It's – his name is Stanley Robertson." Tears flooded into my eyes. "And sometimes I don't like him very much."

I had no intention of waiting to gauge a reaction. I bolted into the house, meeting my mother at the foot of the stairs. She looked harassed, and her arms were full of dirty laundry. There was no room, or I would have pushed past her and run upstairs.

"What's the matter, love?" she asked.

"Nothing," I said, averting my eyes.

"Oh well. I've got those blankets and your pyjamas, and I've stripped your bed as well."

"But I didn't – there's nothing wrong with my bed."

"Best be on the safe side, eh?" She lowered her face into the washing and sniffed extravagantly. "Oh, and I've cleaned your wardrobe. All your clothes are on the bed, in case they smell of disinfectant."

It seemed that the incident and its repercussions clung to me – appropriately – like a bad smell. Perhaps I would never be rid of it. A small black cloud of shame would follow me, hovering just above my head, cartoon-like, wherever I went.

Mum had thrown open my bedroom window, and the net curtains ballooned gently into the room. I sat on the uncovered mattress and stared at the cardboard box, lying open on the floor.

"Oh, there you are! I was coming back to shut the window."

"I'll do it."

"It was just the smell of *Dettol.*"

"It's all right, I'll close it."

"Don't want your room smelling like a hospital, do we?"

"All right, don't keep on about it."

"No-one's keeping on. No-one's bothered."

"I'm bothered," I said. I knelt down and looked in the box.

"I was thinking," Mum said. "That man at Gran's – what was his name?"

"Archie."

"Yes. Well, I must say, he's really been most generous. It must have cost him a lot of money."

"I'll see him on Saturday. To thank him, I mean."

"No, I think you should write him one of your little notes. Like when you do your 'Thankyou' letters at Christmas." She ran a hand over my hair. "You always do them so nicely. You're a good boy, Neil."

I looked at her over my shoulder. "All right. I'll do it in a minute."

She nodded. "Dad can post it when he goes to work."

I pulled the packing aside and carefully lifted Archie's gift on to the floor. It was the most handsome telescope I had ever seen. The white script on the polished red barrel read, *Skygazer De Luxe Twin Lens Refractor Model SJ125.* Just to touch it, to run my hand over its glossy curves, made me feel proud. The day had hardly begun, yet I longed for the dark. I read the instruction booklet from cover to cover, and then I turned back to the beginning and read it again, until I could almost have recited it from memory. I took it with me to the bathroom to study as I sat on the lavatory, imagining the mysteries of the star-flecked heavens unfolding before my eyes as I strained and sweated amid the humid splashing of my turds.

I wondered if I might just be able to see the faintest glimmer of Pluto, where those poor, forgotten people crept quietly over frozen boulders, their eyes filled with shadows as dark as black blood. The night sky would be a kaleidoscopic dreamscape where I roamed in endless flight, an eagle questing between galaxies, a bringer of bright winds to dark canyons of terrible silence.

I had tucked the postcard into the back of the booklet. Now I pulled it out again to read Archie's note a second time. On the front was a picture of Schiehallion in winter, a pink iceberg rising above the dawn mist. On the back was written: 'To Neil, so that you may reach out to other worlds. Discover your dreams. Your friend, Archie'. I gazed at the picture for a while longer, the glassy waters of Loch Rannoch gleaming in the foreground, then I put the card away in my bottom drawer, pushing it under my socks, where I had hidden the magazines furtively handed me by Peter Jessops in 3B, featuring colour photographs of bare-breasted young women, incongruously depicted on the telephone, pegging out the washing or removing the family dinner from the oven.

There was always a rickety wooden table standing on the flagstones outside the French windows, its surface split and bleached by the sun until it resembled a jettisoned shipboard artifact washed up with the tide. It wobbled drunkenly when you leaned on it, but you could steady it with your knee. Sitting there, crouched over a ruled writing pad, the sunshine licking my back like a friendly dog, I composed a short letter to Archie, in fondness and in gratitude.

'Dear Archie,

I wanted to write and thank you for sending me the marvellous telescope. I think it is really impressive, and I am learning how to use it like an astronomer. I remember

you said you had a telescope, so I will ask you to show me the tricks and things.
Mum and Dad said it was very kind of you to spend your money on me. Now I expect they know we are special friends. Dad says to see the stars and planets clearly you need somewhere where there's not lots of street lights, so we will have to find a good place to go after dark to try it out.
Thank you very much, it is a brilliant present.
See you soon.
Love from Neil xxxx'

As I was shortly to discover, Archie's capacity to surprise was not confined to personal revelations and mysterious presents. When next we met, and the subject of the telescope naturally arose, he intrigued me by recounting a conversation he had recently had with someone whom I thought, to put it mildly, an unlikely *confidante.*

"You mean the bloke who runs the chicken farm?" I asked, uncomfortably suspending disbelief.

"I think that's him. Drives the women's bus."

"Sam Wicken – fat and scruffy."

"That's the fellow. I met him out in the road. Seems a decent enough chap when you talk to him."

With one hand clasped over my eyes, I sought brief refuge from the baffling eccentricity of this judgment. "So what did you say to him?"

"I had in mind getting a lift. You know, him with his transport and all."

"A lift? Where to?"

"Ah-hah." He smiled knowingly over a raised forefinger. "I was thinking of a place where it gets properly dark at night. This Sam – he suggested the big clearing in Croakers Woods. The tree-line falls away, and you can see the sky. Perfect."

I shook my head, as if this might help me to understand. "Archie, why do you want to go to the woods at night?"

"Not me. That is, not just me; the both of us. Don't you see? It'd be just the place to set up your telescope." He closed his eyes and laid back his head in a moment of reverie. "Ah, yes. The magic of darkness."

"That's amazing. And he'd take us there?"

Archie nodded. "For ten pounds. He's got an old van. He knows the place. He'd take us there and bring us back. Problem solved, Neil."

"You think Dad was right, then?" I could feel my heart beating with suppressed excitement. "About it being best in the real night, I mean."

"Oh yes. Your dad's right. All these street lights everywhere..."

"So what did he say, exactly?"

"Wicken? He offered to drive us up there after dark and let us set up the telescope in the back of the van. We'd park with the back doors open, see. Nice flat surface." He grinned at me enthusiastically. "What do you think?"

"Won't it get cold – if we've got the doors open?"

He laughed. "Are you a man or a mouse, Neil?" Pausing to think, he pinched the bridge of his nose, the vestige of a smile still clinging to his face. "I could ask him to bring some blankets and things. I'd get us something to eat."

"Cor! It sounds great! I'd really like that!"

He ruffled my hair. "Aye, I thought you might."

"It'd be like a real adventure – just you and me."

"And Sam Wicken. It won't work without him."

"Oh yeah. Okay."

"There's just one thing." All of a sudden, Archie looked serious. "We have to address the practicalities."

"What?"

"How we're going to do it."

"But you said we could use Sam's van."

"Think on, Neil. The three of us, going off in the middle of the night, when you should be in your bed." He tapped the side of his nose. "We have to have a plan."

Of course, he was right. As I digested this unpalatable truth, elation turned to sullen disappointment, a tedious complication that sank to the pit of my stomach and lay there festering, like tainted fruit. Grown-ups made everything awkward and unmanageable, as though they had stumbled upon a fourth dimension.

"I think it would have to be a Saturday night," I said.

"That's what I thought. Sam can do a Saturday night. What about your gran?"

I wrinkled my nose dubiously. "I don't think she'd want to come. She might get cold."

Archie flapped his fingers at me, a small gesture of exasperation. "No, no, that's not my point. What I mean is, how would she take to letting you go?"

"Oh. Umm..."

"We have to work all this out, Neil. There's no show, otherwise."

"I know. In any case – "

"What is it?

"I don't normally stay over till Sunday, except when I come for a sort of holiday, and I've just had one of those."

"Right. So first you'll need to ask your parents. None of us must get into trouble over this, or there's no fun in it. You understand me?"

"But what if they say 'no'? What if they won't let me do it?"

"I can't help you with that, Neil," Archie said, with a sigh. "I can advise you, but I can't interfere. I'll make the necessary arrangements with Wicken; the rest is up to you."

"I don't know," I muttered, gloomily.

"Look, Neil!" He took me by the shoulders and shook me, not roughly, but firmly, insistently. "You told me you want to be treated as an adult. Well, that means confronting other adults, it means making decisions and standing by them. This is not about doing anything wrong, Neil; it's about doing what's right."

"Yes. Okay, I'll do it." My voice was hardly more than a whisper.

"Good for you. We could go next Saturday. You'll let me know?"

"Yes."

When I manoeuvred my bike into the garage at home, I found Dad tinkering with the car. The bonnet was propped up, and I heard him grunting in the semi-darkness, one side of his face harshly lit by the glare of an inspection lamp.

"Something wrong?" I asked him, pulling off my trouser clips.

"Tappets," he said, without interrupting his work. "Bit of adjustment."

"I see. Is it not running well?"

"She's a bit breathless on hills. Not pulling properly."

I stood next to him for a while, waiting for an opportunity to ask my question. For a minute or more, neither of us spoke. I could hear Hector scrabbling and squeaking in his hutch.

When he pushed the lamp aside and turned towards me, I took a deep breath. "Dad, next week-end, can I stay at Gran's till Sunday?"

His face looked tired and strained. "Sunday? What for?"

"I – well, the thing is, we were wondering if I could take my telescope and then on Saturday night we'd set it up somewhere else, somewhere where it's really dark – you know?" I paused, hearing my voice about to crack. "I mean, you did say we ought to try it in the pitch-dark."

Dad sniffed and stared at me. "Who's this 'we'?"

"Umm. Actually, Archie said he'd help me."

"I see. And does he have a place?"

"Croakers Woods. A friend of Gran's'll give us a lift in his van and bring us back." My heart was pounding now, my mouth drying up. "It'd be all right."

"Hmm. Do you know this chap?"

"Sort of. He's got a chicken farm."

Dad sighed and reached out to switch off the inspection lamp. He unpropped the bonnet and lowered the lid carefully on to its catch. "So. The plan is this: you will get into a van with a man you hardly know, who spends most of his time with chickens, and allow him to drive you into the woods in the middle of the night." He puffed his cheeks in and out, making little popping noises. "Where does the telescope come into it?"

"We're going to look at the sky."

"The sky? Why are you hiding in the trees if you want to see the sky?"

"We aren't hiding." I gulped. "There's a big clearing. You can see all the sky."

"Ah, can you now?"

"Yes. Archie says you were right about the sky – about the dark."

"This Archie...he's going with you?"

"Yes. He's going to show me how to use the telescope to see the planets. He knows a lot about telescopes."

"Oh? I thought he was a piano-tuner."

"Well, he is. He was. I don't know."

"Sounds like a bizarre gathering. My son, a chicken-plucker, a piano-tuner and a whacking great telescope, holed up in the woods at the dead of night. Can you not find something useful to do with your time?" He picked up a rag and began wiping his hands. "And what'll you do to keep warm? Don't tell me; build a fire and dance round it, chanting, in mysterious clothing."

I decided to try a different tack. "It's all right," I snapped, "I won't go. I don't have to go. You're right, it'll be cold. I can see stars perfectly well from here. It was a stupid idea. I'll tell Archie." I turned away, so that he didn't see the tears in my eyes.

Dad ducked under the car bonnet and disconnected the lamp. He slammed the lid shut and carried on rubbing at his hands. "Are you sure about it?" he asked, speaking to the back of my neck.

I looked round at him. "You mean about going or not going?"

"Do you want to go or don't you?"

"I thought you wouldn't let me."

"I never said that." He glanced at his watch. "It's time for your tea. Let's go in and ask your mother. It'll be her decision."

Mum, predictably, was content to address the practicalities of the proposed expedition. How would I get my telescope over to Gran's? What if the weather was bad and there was nothing to see but clouds? Would I get tired and simply fall asleep in the van? Who was paying the ten pounds? The questions came thick and fast, but they did not worry or frustrate me, for I could tell by the tenor of her voice, by the sheer maternal *reasonableness* of the set of her head and shoulders as she faced me, that these enquiries were designed not to challenge me but to reassure her.

"What do you think, Stan?" she asked him, as the meal plates were removed.

"About what?" he retorted.

"Neil going out at night with Archie."

"Oh aye. I've told him I've no objection."

I opened my mouth to protest this statement, but then I bit my tongue and settled for the consolation of what appeared to be a satisfactory outcome. To do otherwise would surely plunge us into senseless argument, a verbal affray from which there could be no dignified escape for any of us.

"You'll need a lift," Dad said. "That thing won't go in your saddlebag."

"Thanks."

I loved him then, at least for a moment. I reminded myself constantly that he did not know the way to be different from how he was, and his love for me was never in the slightest doubt. You cannot blame people for being what they are once they have been conditioned by influences outside their control; you can slander or even despise them, but you cannot blame them.

Over the next few days the wind shifted, and a disappointing drizzle hung in the air as Archie came out to the gate to help us hurry the telescope into Gran's kitchen.

"Miserable morning," Dad called out, as Archie took the box.

"And a miserable morning to you too!" came the response.

Stony-faced, Dad did not see the joke. Raindrops pebbled his glasses, and the lenses steamed up as he reached the warmth of the kitchen.

Gran appeared from the pantry, brushing flour from her hands. She stared disapprovingly at the large cardboard box which Archie had placed on the table. "Is anyone wanting lunch today?"

"Not for me," Dad said.

"Can we have fishcakes with beans, Gran?" I asked.

"There'll be nothing for anyone if you don't move that box off my table."

I saw Archie roll his eyes as he carried the telescope into the hall.

Gran washed her hands, dried them on her apron and made

us coffee. Apprehensively, I watched the rain flecks streaking the window.

"This stuff'll pass over," Archie said, sensing my anxiety. "Barometric pressure's rising."

"I didn't know you had a barometer, Gran," I said.

We had a large teak-cased barometer hanging in the hall at home. No-one ever looked at it or had the slightest notion what it indicated. It might as well have been a banjo or a frying pan. Occasionally it was disturbed by dusting, fell on the floor and promptly threatened 'Rain', as in an act of retaliation.

"Oh, him and his wireless weather forecasts," Gran said, scathingly, by way of explanation.

"The depression in the south is moving away north-east towards Scandinavia," Archie assured us.

It seemed to me that a modest depression was centred over the kitchen table. Coffee was drunk with quiet slurps and sighs, and nobody spoke for several minutes. There were no biscuits offered. I wanted to do a fart, but I didn't dare. I gazed into my lap and thought about Sally, and I felt myself going stiff.

Dad chinked his empty cup and stood up. "Well," he said, pointlessly.

Archie looked up at him. "Thanks for bringing Neil over, Mr Robertson. And don't worry. He'll be well looked after."

"What? Oh, you mean tonight?"

"How many fishcakes for you, Archie?" Gran asked.

"Here." From his inside jacket pocket, Dad produced a ten-pound note and held it out to Archie. "I owe you this."

Archie stared at him blankly and waved his hand. "There'll be no need for that," he said, quietly.

Dad thrust the note under the lodger's nose. "On the contrary, there'll be every need. I pay for my son's outings, that's my responsibility."

Archie looked at the money but made no move to take it. "I invited him," he said.

"And I gave permission," Dad persisted. "You've been more than generous already. Neil's wee excursion is conditional upon your acceptance of my contribution." He shook the money emphatically. "Is that understood?"

"Perfectly," Archie replied, and he took the note, folded it in half and slipped it into his shirt pocket.

I saw Dad to the front door. "Thanks for paying the money," I said. "You didn't have to."

"That's my decision," he said. He patted his pockets, searching for the car keys. "When shall I pick you up? You'll be tired, remember."

"About twelve tomorrow?"

He nodded, and was gone. I could see the car roof over the hedge, and I waited until it moved and disappeared.

Archie had started laying the sitting room table for lunch. I went in to help him. "I like your father, Neil," he said. "He's a good man."

"Mmm." I tugged abstractedly at the tablecloth.

"Something the matter?"

"No, it's just..."

He tapped a knife handle on the table importantly. "What's wrong, Neil? You can tell me."

"Well, I wouldn't want to hurt him."

"Hurt him? Why should you hurt him?"

"I wouldn't mean to."

"Of course not." He put one arm around my shoulders and gave me a hug. "What's brought this on, hmm?"

I sank into the nearest chair. "Oh, I was just thinking."

"I see. Does this have anything to do with – er – a mutual friend?"

I nodded. "There's lots he doesn't know. I think about it sometimes."

Archie pulled out the opposite chair and sat down facing me. "Your father loves you as his son, Neil. But he knows you're growing up. He knows you'll have new problems to face, and a few secrets along the way."

"Archie, do you think it's wrong to have secrets from people you love – people who love you?"

He thought for a moment. "No. We all need our private places, Neil. We can't give away everything of ourselves." His fingers moved across the table and touched mine. "Bet there's things about your Dad you'll never know."

I couldn't help it. I had to think about all the times I'd spent with Sally – me, with another man's wife. I had to ask myself what Dad would think, would *feel*, if only he knew. I couldn't stop pricking myself with the pain of that question. I just knew in my heart how hurt he would be. He would be angry, too, but more hurt than angry; more sad than indignant. Supposing Dad were ever to find out that Gran's friend had exposed herself to me. What if he knew that she had touched me? What if he knew I had let her do that thing to me in the bath? And if he knew she had daubed me with her menstrual blood? And I hadn't really fallen off my bike at all?

Stop it, I had to stop it. I had to stop this now, this mad, roaring, going-nowhere train of manic thought. It was like self-mutilation. It was a way of making more and more pain, until it was unbearable.

Archie's hand was still touching mine. "I should let it go if I were you," he said. "It'll work out all right. Honestly."

Gran called out from the kitchen. "Bringing it through in a minute!"

We tidied the table and sat there, solemnly waiting for the food to arrive. Then, when the plates were set down, I realised I was no longer hungry. I took my fork in my right hand and picked listlessly at the crunchy brown flakes on the top of a fishcake. I scooped up some beans, letting most of them fall back on to the plate. What little went into my mouth seemed to have no taste, as if my senses were dulled by a bad cold.

"Don't fiddle with it, boy." Gran frowned at me. "It's what you asked for."

"I know. P'raps I'm not as hungry as I thought I was."

"Ah well." She smiled sympathetically. "I expect you're excited about tonight, eh?"

Archie leaned towards me. "You look a bit pale, Neil. You've a long night ahead of you. Maybe you should have a rest this afternoon, a lie-down."

I went on prodding my lunch morosely. When I looked up at the window, I saw that the rain had stopped and the sky was clearing. Archie had been right about the weather.

I put down my fork and let Gran take my plate away. "I think I will go up for a while," I said.

"You're not ill, are you?" she asked.

"No. I just want to be quiet for a bit."

She sighed. "Well, there you are. Take as long as you like."

Archie climbed the stairs behind me. I kicked off my shoes and lay down on the bed, while Archie hovered in the doorway.

"Can I get you anything, Neil?"

"No. Archie?"

"What is it?"

"Can we look at the moon tonight?"

"Aye, if it's clear we will."

"Archie?"

"I should try to get some sleep, Neil."

"Might we see a comet or a shooting star?"

"Well, you never know. That's part of the mystery."

"I expect we could see some planets, perhaps."

"Just close your eyes, Neil."

"Archie?"

"Go to sleep now."

"Do you think, when we're looking into space, someone on Pluto might be looking at us? Do you think?"

"They might very well be. There's more out there than you and I can ever know."

"That's right. Archie?"

"You need to rest, Neil."

"I am rather tired."

"Time for sleep now."

"Archie?"

"Sleep, Neil."

"Yes. I think so."

"I'll be close by."

"I love you, Archie."

"That's good, Neil. That's so good."

"Okay."

The stain on the ceiling was a great crater on Pluto. It gave me a funny feeling, like desolation.

Then I slept.

Chapter IX

In the Woods

"Like a sick old man with bad skin," said Archie, staring up at the full moon as it cruised over arctic hedgerows of broken cloud.

I followed his gaze, and shivered. It was a cold night for August, and I had not yet adjusted to the chill after sitting in the van, where Sam had kept the heater on. Even so, I was glad to be out in the fresh air, for Archie had sat me in the middle, next to Sam, and after a mile or so I noticed there was a bad smell about him, a thick, canine sourness, its intensity periodically amplified by one of his gaseous farts.

I pulled my jacket tightly around me and carried on gazing at the sky. There were stars visible now, as well, trembling pin-pricks of white light, like sequins sewn on black velvet. Nothing stirred, and the black branches of the trees, lit from behind by the pulsating brightness of the scudding moon, reminded me of prints of blood vessels in cancered lungs.

A metallic thumping from inside the van told me that Archie and Sam were setting up the telescope. The back doors stood wide open. I went over, and Archie thrust out a hand to haul me up.

"Smells sort of fatty in here," I said.

"Chickens," said Sam, and loosed a long, hissing fart.

Archie nodded to the corner by the spare wheel. "Fetch me some of that cardboard, Neil. We'll put it underneath."

Some flattened boxes made useful insulation between the telescope's tripod legs and the smooth steel floor, as well as providing a level surface. Archie reached this way and that, twiddling screws and cams, finally cranking the barrel up to the sky.

"You'll find a cushion in the front, Neil. If you'd like to bring it, please."

I reached into the cabin and tossed the cushion down to him.

"Thanks. A few more minor adjustments, and we'll be there."

Sam was squatting next to him. "Bit complicated, innit?" he grunted, and farted loudly.

"A little care now will bring its reward," Archie murmured, grimly preoccupied. "Can you shine that torch here, Sam?"

"I've got a lantern," Sam said. "Save batteries."

I was warming up now, and the thin yellow light from Wicken's lantern cast a comforting glow around the metal walls. Our shadows bobbed and weaved, changing size and shape as we moved in and out of the lamplight, but these were friendly ghosts, and I felt safe and secure among them.

"Hey! Come and have a look at this!" Archie's voice was bright with childish enthusiasm. "The Sea of Serenity."

I knelt on the cushion and peered through the eyepiece. Before me swam a wondrous vision, the moon filling my whole field of view. It was as if I looked down from a descending spacecraft, preparing to land among the mountains and craters of the lunar landscape. I was enthralled and speechless with excitement.

"Here, Sam, take a look!" Archie beckoned him over.

Reluctantly, I edged aside, while the fat man, puffing and snorting, lowered himself on to the cushion.

Archie waited for a response. "What do you reckon, Sam?"

"Guess one part of the moon looks much like another," Sam declared, wheezing as he straightened up.

Even in the dim light, I could see Archie's eyebrows twitch in amused resignation. Sam's curt dismissal rather pleased me, for it meant I could have another look without delay. On my knees again, I continued my awe-struck descent towards the surface of the moon.

I could feel Archie crouching next to me, breathing rhythmically in the silence. "See anyone you know?" he enquired, and I glanced briefly across at him and smiled. Something snapped softly out of sight, and my friend nudged me in the side. "Here, piece of chocolate. Keep your strength up."

"Thanks."

"You carry on. I'm just going outside for a leak."

Marvellous as the moon was, I wanted to see more, much more. I swung the telescope around, aiming for a patch of clear sky. Quivering white blobs of aeons-old starlight pulsed in my flickering right eye, as I travelled the heavens like a weightless spaceman, open-mouthed, frozen in wonderment.

Through the thin metal hull I heard the crisp rustle of Archie making water on the ground. The sound made me realise I wanted to go, too. I waited for him to return, then I passed the telescope to him and went outside into the night. I had expected it to be pitch-dark, but the moonlight cast an eerie silver glow over the woods and the forest floor, a frost-like filigree luminous as Saint Elmo's Fire. For a breathless moment, I stood motionless before the lofty trees, transfixed by the still beauty of the scene.

Remembering the reason for being out in the cold, I stepped into a clump of bracken, unzipped my trousers and stretched my penis towards a shadowy hollow. Despite the quiet, I never heard Sam Wicken moving behind me.

"Need any 'elp?"

I swung round, nearly spraying my shoes. "What? No. No, go away!"

"Okay. Only asking." He wiped his nose with his fingers, then checked his pockets. "I'm going for a smoke."

I watched as he made for the fringe of the clearing, stumbling slightly, and disappeared in the darkness. Somewhere behind me, an owl hooted.

When I got back to the van, Archie had moved the telescope closer to the doors, to gain a sharper angle against the sky. He helped me up, and I inhaled the mingled smells of paraffin and chicken fat, clogging my nostrils after the pure, sweet breath of the night.

"You okay, Neil? You look cold."

"I'm all right. I heard an owl."

"Isn't this a great place? The sky's almost completely clear now. Just a second." He lowered his eye to the cup again. "Right, I want you to look at this."

I did as he said. My sight took a few seconds to adjust, and then I saw it, a shimmering brownish-cream dot in the blue-black void. It vibrated so intensely, it might almost have hummed.

I felt Archie's breath on my ear as he leaned over me. "Now, do you know what you're looking at?"

"It looks like a planet."

"It is a planet. It's Jupiter."

"Yeah? That's tremendous! It's like a tiny spinning top."

"Isn't it beautiful?"

"Yes. It must be very far away."

"Nearly four hundred million miles. Sixteen hundred times as far as the moon."

"Gosh! You can't imagine it."

"Distances and creations beyond our wildest imaginings, Neil. Worlds so far away, no man will ever see them. He will be defeated by extinction." He stood up and stretched his back. "It's a sobering thought."

I looked up at him, his face craggy with shadows. "How long would it take us to get to Jupiter?"

"To get to Jupiter...well, that would depend on how fast we could travel. Never fast enough, I'm afraid, is the likely answer."

"No hope of ever getting to Pluto, then."

He shook his head, laughing. "No chance. Unless..."

"Unless what?"

Then he knelt down beside me and gazed earnestly into my eyes. "Neil, the whole key to interplanetary travel is speed. Speed will bring us time as well as space."

"Meaning?"

"Meaning, we need to be able to design and construct a spacecraft capable of carrying us into the solar system at the speed of light. Only then can we truly be free."

"The speed of light." I rolled the words around my tongue, repeating them like an incantation. "The speed of light."

"That's right. If we solve that problem, Neil, we can reach

Jupiter from Earth in less time than it takes us to fly to New York. Think about that."

I thought about it. "I'd really like to be a scientist," I said.

"Well then. That could be your ultimate challenge: to design a space vehicle with the potential for manned exploration of the universe. You'd be the most famous man in the world."

"Or in another world, eh?"

"Aye, right enough." He frowned, casting his eyes around the van's interior. "Is it my imagination, or are we losing the light?"

My eyes followed his around the steel panels. Sure enough, the pale light was dimming down, flaring and fading, feigning death. "Probably out of stuff," I said.

Archie looked anxious. "Paraffin. He must have more paraffin. He's quite organised."

"We've got a torch, remember."

"I don't want to use that all the time." He scratched his head. "Where did he go?"

"I saw him. He wandered off for a smoke."

"Did he now? I wonder how long he'll be." He picked up the lantern and shook it. "I don't want to go through his things."

"We'll be in the dark in a minute," I said.

"I know. Did you see which way he went?"

I nodded. "I could go and find him, if you like." I wanted to be helpful, though the idea of bumping into Sam Wicken in the dark unnerved me.

Archie stood at the very edge of the doorway and craned his neck into the gloom. "I wonder where the Hell he went," he growled.

The lantern sputtered and went out.

"What shall we do, Archie?"

"I'm not keen on you walking about the woods on your own in the dark," he said, moodily.

"But we can't both go. Someone has to look after our things."

"I know. Maybe I should leave you here."

I thought about this, and shivered. I imagined being entombed, alone, in a cold metal box in inky darkness, enveloped in the stink of dead chickens and stale oil. And what if Sam Wicken came back by another route and found me on my own? Supposing he shut us in… he would be so much stronger than me…supposing…

"I'd be quite safe," I told him, chirpily. "I might see that owl. I expect he knows exactly where Sam went."

Archie grinned, shaking his head. "You love it out here, don't you?"

"Course I do. I think it could be our special place."

"Right," and he aimed a playful mid-air kick at me, "off you go then. What your father would say, I hate to think. Now listen up." He stabbed a dark finger at my face. "No going off exploring. Understand?"

"I promise."

"I warn you, if you're not back here after five minutes, I'll be on your tail, and then there'll be trouble. Is that clear?"

"Yes, Archie." I jumped down to the ground. "I'll ask him for his lighter as well."

"Just make him come back with you," Archie called out, but I was already walking away, sucking in deep draughts of the sharp, ferny air. Twigs and dry bracken crunched under my feet. The cold nipped at the lobes of my ears. All the patches of undergrowth looked similar in the moonlight, but I managed to find what I thought was the hollow where I had urinated, and I stopped and looked around me, my eyes straining into the distant darkness.

The owl hooted behind me, sounding closer this time, making me jump. I spun round, but there were no trees visible there, only a tangle of bracken and brambles. What if it wasn't an owl at all? What if it was somebody pretending to be an owl? Someone could be watching me, hidden, crouching, in the black shadows. My mouth went bone-dry, and I heard the *boom boom* of my heartbeat.

Then, when I saw the spark in the distance, I felt relieved – thankful that, after all, I was not alone, and pleased to have found Sam Wicken, for the tiny red light was surely the glowing tip of his cigarette. I walked silently towards the burning speck.

I had never meant to alarm or surprise him. Perhaps, on reflection, I should have announced my presence, coughed or called out or stamped my feet. I just came up behind him, saying nothing. A yard from the fallen tree on which he sat, I stopped. It was very dark there, though a thin shaft of moonlight fell across Sam's hunched back. The cigarette, hardly more than a dying stub, was clamped in his mouth, a frail crimson ember suffocating in the blackness. Sam seemed to be doing something with a stick, scratching or whittling it, his head bowed. Only as I moved to his shoulder did I see that what he gripped in one hand and lightly supported with the other was not a stick, but his stiffened penis. It overhung the curled fingers of his left hand, a pale, fleshy rod, bulbous and grey-wrinkled.

Suddenly I was a looming shape in the corner of his eye. He wheeled round, cursing under his breath. "Shit! Little bastard!"

My heart was racing madly now. "I – I'm sorry, I didn't mean – I'm not spying!"

In a strange, wordless frenzy that unfolded before me in bizarre slow-motion, the scene distorted by my icy panic, Sam Wicken struggled in vain to compress his flapping member into his gaping trousers. It was a futile task; the snake was alert and thrashing, and would not be coaxed back into the basket. In that frozen moment, I had the briefest of chances to escape, but my legs refused to work, stranding me on that coldly spotlit patch of barren earth, inert as the dead tree before me.

For a big man, Sam moved with lightning speed, his right arm flailing out to grab my jacket sleeve. "Gotcha!"

I tried to pull free, but it was useless. "Let me go!" I may as well have hoped to blow him away.

"Shut your noise, Robertson!"

"I wasn't doing anything, honest!"

"Stop your squeakin'!" He dragged me down so he could leer closely into my face. "Now come and sit next to old Sam," and he patted the tree-trunk by his beefy thigh.

My bellowing breath tasted of sick. "No, I don't want to. I want t – "

"I don't give a sod what you want, sonny! Siddown!"

His vicious grip was hurting my arm, so I stumbled over the tree and sat there, my legs shaking uncontrollably. I stared desperately ahead, into the impenetrable forest, not daring to look at him.

"'S better! Nothin' to be scared of."

"W-what do you want?"

A gruff laugh spluttered from his lips. "Reckon I should be askin' you. Creepin' about in the dark."

"I-I came to get your lighter. And we need some more oil."

"Oil?"

"The lantern. It's gone out."

"Oh, 'as it now?"

"Please. Don't do anything." I turned to look at his lardy face. "I won't tell anyone, I promise."

"Too right you won't." His eyes, reflecting the moonlight, seared into me, wild and snake-like. "Else I'll tell 'em on yer."

"Tell 'em – tell them what?" I asked, my voice quavering.

"That I seen yer sneaking up on me." His huge cock was in his hand again, and he flapped it aimlessly up and down. "You was 'avin' a good old eyeful, lappin' it up, playin' wi' yerself an' all."

"But then they'd know you must have been doing something bad – else why would I be watching?"

"Don't get clever wi' me, Robertson. You're makin' your way in the world, remember. Me, I ain't gotta impress no-one. Who's gonna care?"

"Surely Mrs Wicken would care," I suggested, bravely.

"What, and you're gonna tell her? Don't make me laugh."

Although he had released his grip on me, I didn't dare try to run away, because if I tripped and he caught me, I was sure the big man would hurt me or even kill me. I felt trapped in a nightmare.

"I won't hurt you, you know," he said, quietly.

"I ought to go back," I said, looking behind me. I wondered where Archie was. Five minutes, he said. "What do you want me for?"

"This," and he lifted his penis until it shone in the moonlight like a grotesque magic wand. "Bet you've started, eh?"

"Started?"

"Tossin' off." He sniggered. "Can't bullshit me. All the schoolkids I know – wank their bleedin' brains out."

"I don't know about that," I told him, without much conviction.

"Oh, ay don't know about that sort of thing, Mister Wicken, no, no, not at all, Mister Wicken." He mimicked my voice, bobbing his head ridiculously from side to side as he spoke. "Bollocks!"

I knew now that the relief I had felt, when Sam told me he wouldn't hurt me, was to be short-lived. I understood perfectly well why he was keeping me there, what he wanted me to do. Everything inside me cried out for it to be over. A slow, crawling sickness seethed in my stomach.

"I could shout very loud," I warned him.

"Try it, Robertson. I'll break yer neck. It'd be a accident, of course."

"Just – tell me what you want, and let me go. Please."

"Easy job, Robertson." He jiggled himself closer to me. "Take a hold, son. Finish us off."

How many times since that haunting night have I been forced by my own conscience to relive that vile experience. Just when I believe I have driven the spectre from my mind, it comes swooping back before me, a sinister, squawking black bird, pecking at my brain. The sheer tactile obscenity of those few minutes somehow renders them morbidly ineradicable from the darkest recesses of my memory, a putrid grey sludge that no regenerative process can extract. You know, today I still stop what I am doing, as though briefly immobilised by some kind of spasm, and stare at my hand, where the sensory imprint seems to linger indelibly. All over again, I feel the warm wet leather tackiness of Wicken's thing, feel the steam engine chuff and judder of his trembling body against my shoulder, the hot crawl of his stuff on my wrist as he bucks and gasps, jetting his pale beads into the dark. The horror of it is that it is there for ever.

Do you want to know another secret, the worst confession of all? The shame that diminishes me comes not from the act itself, but from my instinctive reaction to it. As I brought the loathsome task to its inevitable conclusion, I realised that, by some monstrous biological mechanism, the nauseous disgust that chilled me to the marrow could not dispel my own feverish arousal. So, as I cursed Sam Wicken for his bestiality, I cursed myself for my weakness.

"Will you let me go now?" I asked, my voice a shuddering whisper.

He nodded at the ground. "You done good."

I stared at my hand, opening and closing it.

"Grass is wet," he said, "if you wanna wash."

"In a minute."

"You ain't a bad kid." He shook his head, as if acknowledging a misjudgment. "Nah, you're a good lad."

Despite the darkness, I wanted to hide my face. I leaned forward, bringing my hands up to shield my eyes. If I looked to one side, through the gaps in my fingers, I could see Sam twisting this way and that, putting himself away.

"What about the lantern?" I reminded him.

"Under the driver's seat. The floor lifts up. There's a wooden box with a bottle in." He sniffed fruitily. "Matches in the glovebox."

"Thanks."

Another sniff, a bubbling inhalation. "Tell McLeish I'm on me way."

"Right." I glanced at him. "You got a cold?"

"No," he replied, and the word sounded like a sigh. Then he turned to look at me, and his eyes were full of tears, his lips distorted and quivering.

"It's all right, Mr Wicken," I said, "I won't tell. I won't tell anyone."

"It's not all right," he moaned. "It'll never be all right. I'm a bad, bad man."

I touched him lightly on the arm. "No. You helped us. You brought us here."

"No. You mustn't praise me. It's livin' a lie."

"I'm not a liar. I just wa -"

I couldn't finish the sentence. With a swiftness that belied his blundering bulk, Sam hurled himself against me, flinging his huge arms around my shoulders until I feared he would crush the breath from me. I was too stunned to react or feel threatened. Unthinking in my suffocating shock, I let him hang from my neck, and his guttural screams, tearing at my eardrums, echoed as the cries of a wounded animal, racking sobs wrenched from the very heart of the night. I held him like a child, and his tears flowed down my neck, mingling with my own grief. We huddled at the forest's fringe and wept together, and clasped each other tightly, trembling in the silvery dark, and the moon raced above us, streaking our hair, painting white arrows on our faces.

I felt his body go limp, and I eased myself away from him and stood up. "Don't stay out here too long," I said. "You'll catch your death."

"I'd deserve that," he said, grimly. He pulled something from his pocket and held it out to me. "Here, take it."

I saw then that he had given me a ten-pound note. "What's this?" I asked.

"He gave it me. McLeish."

"It's for your petrol. I don't want it."

"Reckon you've earned it," he said. He shook the note irritably. "Go on, 'ave it!"

I sensed that this was not a time for argument. I took the money, though it seemed tainted. It would not benefit me, I would see to that. I walked off towards the van, and after a few steps I heard him crying helplessly in the darkness, but I didn't look back. My eyes were fogged with tears. When I made out the square bulk of the van in the distance, a blackened tooth against the pale yawning of the moon-flooded sky, I stopped beneath a tree and ripped the note into a hundred pieces. I tossed them into the air, letting them rain down around me like confetti.

Archie met me behind the van, looking stern and anxious. "Thank God," he said. "I was just coming to find you."

"Sorry. I was expecting you."

"I was delayed. We've a visitor."

"Who?"

"Look inside. What about Wicken?"

I told him that Sam Wicken would not be far behind me, and I repeated the fat man's instruction about the paraffin and matches. Archie listened, nodded and gave me a hug, before hoisting me up beside the telescope.

Instantly, I could smell her perfume, almost feel her warmth, as she moved towards me out of the darkness, like a figure resolving from a photographic negative. "Sally! How did you get here?"

"Easy. I caught the last bus to the bottom of the hill and walked up." She took gentle hold of my shoulders and bent to kiss me on the cheek. "You don't mind, do you?"

"Mind? Course not." The incident across the clearing had scared me, but in its aftermath I felt suddenly bolder, more focused, as though the rules of engagement had subtly changed. "I love you," I hissed in her ear, and part of me melted when she squeezed my arm.

Soon we had flickering light again, and Archie draped a blanket round my shoulders while I sat on the narrow platform over the wheel-arch. Sally knelt in front of me, opening a large shopping bag with a zip top. I remember it had a picture of a dancing elephant on the side, and the elephant held a trumpet in his flailing trunk. Sally smiled comfortably to herself as she burrowed into the depths of the bag.

"I bet you two have had nothing to eat," she said, producing a flask and an extra cup.

"We had some chocolate," I told her.

"Really. You need something hot." She filled two cups. "Here. Vegetable soup."

I took the cup, wrapping my cold hands around it. "This is like a real adventure."

"Hmm. Take yours, Archie." She gazed about her. "So where's old Wicken gone?"

"He went off for a smoke," I said.

"Oh, right. Gives me the creeps."

"Sam's all right," I said, cautiously. "I know he's married, but I think he's a bit lonely."

Sally screwed the top back on the flask. "He deserves his loneliness, if you ask me."

Archie raised his cup in a gesture of gratitude. "Are you not having any, love?"

His momentary endearment made me wince. It reminded me of who I was, and what I was. I looked into her face, but she was too busy with her bag to return my gaze. I wanted her so much.

"There's tea in the other one," she answered. "I'll have some of that."

She had brought jam doughnuts, too, and caramel wafer bars and some fruit. With the dancing lamplight on our faces and the moon's gaseous glow lacquering the sky outside, it was an unexpected midnight feast among friends, though never quite so heartening as to dispel the sour chill of what had gone before.

While I ate, Archie re-adjusted the telescope. "More cloud coming up," he murmured, searching for a patch of open sky. I watched him as he panned towards the west, just over the closer tree-line, and then slowly back again, a few degrees higher. His sudden whoop of delight made me choke on my food, while Sally slapped me obligingly on the back.

"What is it?" I gasped.

"Neil! Come and look!" He waggled his fingers vaguely at his coat and bag thrown carelessly on the floor. "Bring me that chart – in the bag! And the torch!"

I gave him the chart – a piece of dog-eared cardboard folded in two – and the heavy rubber torch, and he moved over to let me see what he had found in the inky darkness to the left of the cloud-scarred moon.

"You see it – the star-field?"

"Oh Archie, it's beautiful!"

"Isn't it just?"

"It's like I'm riding on a magic carpet."

His hand touched my neck, then he studied the star chart in the torch beam, patiently describing the spangled parchment unfurled before my eyes. He guided me through the dazzling star clouds of Sagittarius, up to the vivid red flare of Antares in Scorpius, and then he helped me find Ursa Major, the Great Bear, with Polaris keeping watch over it.

"Come back to Sagittarius, Neil. You got it? Right. There's the Milky Way, right in front of you. Just imagine: that light has been speeding towards us for over five thousand years."

"So – this is how those stars looked five thousand years ago?"

"That's right. They say exploring space is all about looking to the future; but it's also a window into the past."

For half an hour we roamed the infinite prairies of the night sky, flying among diamonds. We travelled to Lupus and Capella, cursed at the skeins of cloud obscuring Cassiopeia, and came looping back to the silvery shawl of Sagittarius and the bright white blade of the Corona Australis. I can see it all now, etched on my retinae, unfolding for ever in the darkened theatre of my brain. It was – and is – unforgettable.

Sally's voice cut through my reverie. "It's getting late," she said.

I ignored her, not wanting to interrupt my voyage, but Archie moved behind me and placed a gentle, insistent hand upon my back. "Come on. Sally's right. You'll be tired now."

Sighing, I turned away and stood up. Our three dark, misshapen shadows swarmed over the metal walls, brooding spectres that crowded the small space, yet seemed to offer only warmth and protection.

Archie laid a hand on my shoulder, smiling. "Glad we came?"

I nodded, eyes downcast, unable to speak.

"This is all very well," Sally declared, "but we need to find Wicken. Where the devil is he?"

"We don't know," Archie said, passing a hand wearily over his eyes. "I could go and look." He peered out into the darkness. "We're losing the moonlight"

"We can't go without him," I said.

"You're damned right we can't," said Archie, snapping his fingers. "And I'll tell you why; he's got the van keys."

Sally threw out her hands in frustration. "Oh, great! So we're stranded."

"He's got a watch," Archie said, defensively, "he must know the time." He switched on the torch and jumped to the ground. "You two stay here," he called. "Blankets and things in the corner if you get cold."

I wanted to do something useful to occupy my mind, so I started removing the telescope from its tripod. Sally watched me in silence. I asked her to bring me the box, and she helped me pack the instrument away securely. As we worked, we could hear Archie yelling Sam Wicken's name in the distance, a thin cry that was eventually swallowed up by the night.

"I hope he's all right," I said, as much to myself as to Sally.

"Which one?"

"Archie. But Sam as well. Why did he go off like that?"

"I don't know," she sighed. "I wasn't even here." She bent down in the dark corner by the spare wheel and pulled out a heap of blankets and a tattered sleeping bag. "I'm tired and I'm freezing. I'm going to get some rest."

"Sorry," I said, pointlessly.

"Don't you start being sorry again, Neil. None of this is your fault." She kicked off her shoes, threw her jacket on top of Archie's coat and wriggled into the sleeping bag. "There, that's better! This is what happens when you leave men to organize things."

"But if Sam hadn't just wandered off..."

"Yes, and if Archie, whose head is full of music and spaceships, had thought to check with Wicken about times and keys and practical matters, maybe we wouldn't be in this mess. Now, hand me my bag and we'll have some more soup."

Her remarks seemed to me rather unfair, but I knew better than to risk an argument. In any case, it was cosy there, just the two of us, and I was beginning to relax, despite the gathering chill.

I asked the question almost before I realised what I was saying. "Sally, can I come in there and keep warm? My toes are cold."

She pushed her cup away and smiled up at me. "I thought you'd never ask."

I took off my shoes and my woollen jacket and slid down next to her. It was a double bag, so there was plenty of room. It was deliciously warm inside. Instantly, I caught the scent of her perfume. I had never been so close to her, touching like that. I wanted to hold her, only I didn't know where to put my hands. They were shaking. In my tummy, there was that funny feeling again, a sort of pleasurable sickness.

"Warmer now?"

I nodded.

"I can't reach your toes, or I'd warm them in my hands. I hate cold toes."

"I had chilblains once," I said. "They really hurt. Sally?"

"Mmm?"

"What will we do if Sam doesn't come back?"

"Never mind that now. Lie down."

"But how will we get home?"

"The buses start again in the morning. We can walk down to the road."

"Is it far?"

"About a mile. The sun'll be up, and it's downhill."

"What about the van?"

"We'll go to Wicken's place. Get a spare key." She rolled over to face me. "Lie down, Neil."

I lay back and closed my eyes. There was no sound outside. I had a strange taste in my mouth; not sick, exactly, but a kind of *frightened* taste. I wondered what would happen if I tried to touch her breast. She had a red blouse on, buttoned almost to the neck. I was so close to her. I thought about her bra, what colour it was. Red? Red. Red. I remembered the red in the bath, smoke in the water. Red. A bead on her white thigh, running. Red. I loved the colour red. Red was like fire and blood and meat and roses and the insides of things you shouldn't know about, not yet, not quite yet.

Then I felt her hand moving. I thought perhaps if I imagined the stars, if I tried to see Sagittarius again in my head, or the orange smear of Jupiter, I might not have to get an erection; but I couldn't help myself, couldn't make it work, and quite soon she was holding my cool little man in her hand, coaxing him until he was bigger, and she was snuffling against me, all warm and soft like a cuddly animal, making a quiet *thupthup* of buttons undoing somewhere down there in the sweet dark, not my buttons, and next she was cradling me under her leg, her heel prodding the small of my back, so I felt the crisp tangle of her bush rasping my stiffness, squeezing, devouring, then the swift, electric, fire-and-ice charge of it all drilling out of me. Behind my eyes there was a red sky. Red as an inferno. Blood red. Mad red.

We lay on our backs. I had one hand thrown over my face. I could hear my watch ticking. I squinted at the dial and saw that it was half past one. There was a warm, wet worm asleep on my trousers.

"Should we go and find Archie?" I asked, because I was a little afraid of the silence.

"It's all right," she said, stroking my arm. "He'll be back soon."

"Supposing he's lost."

"Did you enjoy the in-betweens, Neil?"

"Yes. Like lighting a fire and putting it out."

"That's right. I think we should try to sleep now."

"Now the fire's gone out."

She chuckled, nestling closer. "You're a good boy, Neil."

We were both asleep when Archie returned. The stomp of his boots on the hollow floor woke us. He peered at us through critically narrowed eyes. "Like two peas in a pod," he said.

I waved one listless hand. "We're keeping warm," I whispered.

"Aye, so I see." He hopped from one leg to the other, pulling off his boots.

Sally propped herself up on her elbows. "Any sign?"

"Hopeless. It's pitch-black out there. I kept on calling, but – nothing."

"You ought to have a sleep, Archie," I told him.

"Aha. We'll join forces at daybreak. We have to find him." He was unfolding blankets, searching for a suitable patch of floor. "He could have met with an accident, anything."

He slammed the doors and blew out the lamp.

Birdsong. I freed my arm and peered myopically at the luminous green dabs on my watch face. It was ten to five. In the gloom, I saw Archie rolling over, emerging from a pile of blankets, yawning, scratching his armpits.

I slid out of the sleeping bag, trying not to disturb Sally. Archie coughed and tossed me my jacket. He broke off a piece of foil-wrapped chocolate and handed it to me. "Breakfast," he said.

As he flung open the doors, a watery grey light filtered into the van. The thin metal walls were pearled with moisture from the dream-sighs of our sleeping breath.

Archie said, "I'm going for a wee," and he dropped to the ground and disappeared into a thicket.

I stood in the doorway, inhaling the earthy smell of the morning. Sally came and leaned against me, smiling, speaking softly with her eyes, and in that moment we shared something different, something that had not been there before.

When Archie came back, we threw our bedding over the telescope box, helped one another down and shut the doors behind us.

In the scant dawn light, we found Sam Wicken quite quickly. He had not gone far from where I had left him. The van keys were in his back pocket. Archie gave them to me to keep safely. I felt very grown-up and important as I helped my friends look after Sam. The trouble was, he was very heavy. He wasn't up very high, but the buckle on the leather belt, which he had taken from his trousers and looped around his fat neck, had swivelled round under the strain, and the steel prong had pierced his windpipe.

"No good," Archie said, grunting, "I'm going back to the van. There's a hacksaw under the seat." Already his brow was sweat-glazed from the effort of tugging at the viciously tightened belt. "Will you wait with him?"

Sally smiled sympathetically. "Of course."

Neither of us spoke a word while he was gone. I stared up at the dangling figure. He had messed himself; there was brown stuff down his legs and on the grass beneath his feet. His shoes must have come off as he dropped, and his trousers, unsecured, had collapsed about his ankles. His head lolled to one side and downwards, the eyes bulging wide open. As I watched, a squirrel ran down from an upper branch and perched on Sam's head, like a Davy Crockett hat, its bushy tail swishing to and fro over his ashen face. I moved, and the creature scampered away, shitting in the fat man's hair as it sprang upwards. Since that day, I have always hated squirrels. In my mind, there lingers, too, the stubbornly indelible vision of that icily surreal interlude – a fat man hanging trouserless from a tree, tubby legs streaked with shit, a squirrel balanced on his head.

It took Archie only a few seconds to cut him down. I remember vividly how his body collapsed to the ground like a sack of foul-smelling potatoes, and how strangely small he looked, lying in the dewy grass. In death, Sam Wicken was nothing but a crumpled mess in the weeds.

I spread my fingers and closed his eyes.

Above our crouched forms, the sun rose in silent fury, igniting the spiked tree-tops in a corona of fire.

Chapter X

Revelation

As in a kind of homage, I knelt on the rug with an encyclopaedia on the bed, poring over the small, tightly-packed print and the grainy black-and-white photographs. The book before me was Volume One of the set, marked *A to Be,* and I was enthralled to find that there were sixteen pages on Astronomy.

I saw what Archie meant about our revolutionary spaceship being useless for a flight to the Sea of Serenity. The encyclopaedia told me that light travelled at a speed of 186,000 miles per second. Well, the moon was only 240,000 miles away, so you didn't have to be a scientist or a mathematician to appreciate that we would spectacularly overshoot our target. I tried to imagine what it would be like to hurtle through space at ten million miles a minute. What would it feel like? What would it sound like? What could we see from our porthole window? By its sheer enormity, the experience was something inconceivable, like dreaming you had five million pounds in the bank. These were absolutes so extreme, they defied both imagination and comprehension. Their frontiers lay at the boundaries of madness.

On the next page, there was something else, something that puzzled and disturbed me. According to the judgment of eminent physicists, there was the serious risk that a three-dimensional body attempting to attain the speed of light would inexorably increase in physical size as it approached that ultimate velocity, until its growth became limitless, and it expanded to fill the entire world. The notion was as confusing as it was horrifying. For this phenomenon to occur, all the accepted laws of matter would have to be defied. How could there be such expansion without destruction? In any case, a craft moving at the speed of light would inevitably have left our world far behind it, so the reference to that extent of enlargement seemed, at best, irrelevant. Logically – if rational logic could even be applied here – an uncontrolled, uncontrollable process might as well continue until it occupied the universe. I stretched my hands out in front of me and tried to envisage what would happen when they began to grow bigger. Of course, it would feel strange. I wondered if it would hurt. What if the various parts of my body grew bigger at different rates or different times? If my eyes and brain became enlarged, perhaps this would cancel out all the normal parameters of perception, so I would notice no changes at all. And finally, at journey's end, when I wanted only to return to my home and my mother and eat steak-and-kidney pie instead of blue pellets, what guarantee would I have that, as a simple consequence of retardation, I should shortly be restored to my original size? On such vital points, the book was vexingly reticent. These matters I resolved to put to Archie at the earliest opportunity.

The door clicked open and my father stood at the other side of the bed. There was something brightly coloured in his hands, a neat fan of shiny magazines. In the space of two seconds I felt my heart leap to my throat and rebound into my bowels.

"One of your encyclopaedias?" He nodded at the bed.

"Yes. I'm reading about astronomy," I said, standing up.

"I see. Some intelligent matter."

"Yes, it's informative," I added, in a shrinking voice.

"Hmm. More than can be said for these," and he tossed the magazines on to the bedspread.

I stared at the lurid covers as though seeing them for the first time. "Where did you get them?" I enquired, not looking at him.

"I think I should be asking you that very question."

"Right. Okay."

"Your mother found them in your sock drawer."

"I didn't buy them," I said, hoping to achieve some palliative effect.

"Really? I'm glad to hear it. I'd be thinking I'm giving you too much pocket money."

Aimlessly, I picked up one of the magazines – "a portfolio of nature studies", Peter Jessops had called it, as he slid it into my satchel – and flicked quickly through it, noting that, mercifully, none of the pages were stuck together. Under my trembling thumb, a grinning gallery of young women, spectacularly underdressed, cavorted past, taunting me with the great pale hams of their thighs and the pendulous gourds of their breasts.

"A boy gave them to me," I explained, replacing the magazine with the others and dropping a pillow on top of them.

"Gave them to you? Very magnanimous of him."

"Well, he didn't exactly give them to me."

"Was money exchanged?"

"No. Actually, I gave him my lunch."

"You gave – let's get this straight. Your mother spends time and money making you a nourishing packed lunch so that you remain healthy and have no need of the unappetising school dinners, and you then proceed to trade them in for parcels of filth. Am I right?"

"Well no, actually I – "

"Don't answer me back!" he shouted, spittle frothing on his lips. "This whole affair is quite disgraceful."

"I only did it once," I whined.

"From now on, you'll be taking school dinners like your mates. There will, of course, be an adjustment to your pocket money to accommodate the expense."

I hunched my shoulders and threw the magazines on the floor. A centrefold spilled out, and a fat girl with buck teeth and huge mammaries sprang at me like a sideshow freak.

Dad's hand was on the doorknob. I willed him to go. I wanted to go myself, but I couldn't think of anywhere to go to. He turned towards me once more. "You may care to bear in mind, tinkering leads inevitably to thinning hair and impotence."

Only in the remotest outposts of my imagination did it occur to me to enquire whether this misadventure could account for his being practically bald and having a single child. There were avenues, I reflected, that were demonstrably not worth exploring. I was fifteen and just beginning my journey through life, and already the dark boulders of emotional turmoil were rumbling into my path. I did not need to go down rabbit-holes as well.

These considerations aside, Dad's reaction was both typical and predictable. My parents had never attempted to talk to me openly and reasonably about sex. It was something best brushed under the carpet. Matters would resolve themselves satisfactorily in the fullness of time. With the natural progression through puberty and adolescence to manhood, the various physical procedures would instinctively become apparent. There would be no morbid dalliance over details. With one bound, so to speak, I would be free.

Apart from the furtive experiments in which we naturally engaged at school, I relied upon Sally for my lessons in personal biology. She had become my guide and mentor. Archie, my other great friend, I looked up to as a source of inspiration in astronomy, music and literature. In educational terms, they were perfect foils for each other, and I considered myself fortunate, for although my parents were consistent in providing a loving, supportive and disciplinarian influence, and hence a framework within which I could comfortably control my life, I received from them no recreational encouragement. To express or pursue an interest in artistic, scientific or technical matters, beyond the limited bounds of the school curriculum, was to invite a weary derision, arising apparently from the precept that I would shortly be in mortal danger of 'getting above myself' and straying irresponsibly from the well-charted route to adulthood.

By now I realised, of course, that this deflection had already happened. There would be no going back, because I did not want to go back. My worldly explorations with Archie, and the more intimate ones with Sally, had invested my previously mundane existence with a new sense of excitement and discovery. I suppose, in a way, I loved my friends as much for what they represented as for who they were. That I did not really, truly know them, never occurred to me. I had no comprehension of how I should measure the worth of a friend. For a while, that blissful ignorance might protect me from the jagged edge of truth, but it would also cloud my vision of the future. I ran on blindly, arms outstretched, reaching zealously for something that, just possibly, would not be there when I arrived, menace disguised in a mirage.

So what of the future? To me, at fifteen years old, there was hardly any such thing. Do adolescent schoolboys consider the future? If I thought of the future, I looked ahead to the day after tomorrow or the coming week-end. I had no notion of the future on a scale of years. It was an entirely abstract concept. There, almost certainly, lay the problem obstructing my academic progress. The sixth form, university, career qualifications, the pathway to a successful and rewarding professional life...these were distant milestones around which a dense grey mist swirled, practically obscuring them from view. Ignorant of the route, I quietly resolved not to attempt the journey. At fifteen, a vital part of my imagination was already a closed book.

From time to time, as the summer days passed, I dabbled a toe in the murky waters of the future by wondering where my relationship with Archie and Sally might lead me. I had gradually come to accept that, as man and wife, rediscovering themselves, they would be driven to take a new perspective, individually and as a couple, on our triangular friendship. Part of me privately wanted nothing to change, but I also wanted them to be happy, and I felt that this contentment was most likely to grow from their togetherness. If I loved them, and wanted them to love me, our interests would best be served by my sympathy and encouragement, even though this concession would subtly alter the polarity of the situation. I understood that sometimes I might have to share my friends in order not to lose them. This was no time to be selfish.

I decided not to put the magazines back in the sock drawer. Mum would be bound to find them again – although perhaps that no longer mattered. If she looked, and they were gone, she would probably conclude that I had hidden them somewhere else, and not actually disposed of them. Now that my dark secret had been exposed, the matter of concealment became somewhat academic. It was hardly worth the bother. With one eye on the door, I riffled through one of the magazines, pausing to rotate the pages through ninety degrees whenever a full-length model appeared. The photographs were mostly black-and-white, and knickerless girls facing the camera had been cruelly doctored with an airbrush. With some dismay, I noticed that Peter Jessops had sought to repair this indignity by pencilling the hair back in on some of the pictures. The accuracy of his artistry left something to be desired, I felt, as I scanned the austere images, women overdosed on make-up, sitting anxiously astride hedgehogs. I wondered if Dad had seen the artless embellishments and, if he had, whether he supposed them to be my handiwork. His display of indignant anger, I reflected, was simply a reflex disciplinarian gesture rendered meaningless by its predictability. The threat to impose the punishment of school dinners had to be viewed within this context.

I knelt down beside the bed and dragged another encyclopaedia towards me. The gold-blocked spine read *Pa to Ra.* Now, at the speed of light, I was travelling to Pluto.

Then two traumatic events followed in quick succession. Mentioned glibly, without the detail, the first incident would surely seem the more disturbing; but you have to wait for the rest of the story.

Precisely. Allow me to emphasize the point – the matter of the rest of the story. Having come this far, I find myself acknowledging that, with the simple ringing of a telephone, my book of memories truly, materially begins. I am not asking you to forget or dismiss what has gone before, but to understand that it has to be viewed developmentally, in proper context. Let us, if you like, begin, or recommence, in the middle.

The first of these diversions, jarring but insignificant, involved a sudden death in the family. One sultry afternoon, for reasons known only to himself, Dad announced that he was to give Boris a bath. I have no idea of Boris' age, but we had enjoyed his cheerful, undemanding company for a couple of years. As budgies go, he was a perky little specimen, cerulean blue and white, with tiny black darts above his wings, rather as if a bored child wielding a black pen had drawn inky flecks on him for idle amusement. Most evenings, if encouraged politely, Boris would entertain us with a tinkling medley of song. His selections were generally difficult to identify, but I recall that he had one particular specialty in his repertoire, a neatly cadenced trill which sounded remarkably like the galloping theme from the *William Tell* Overture. His spirited rendition of this piece never failed to make us smile in affectionate endorsement of his simple pleasure.

In any case, I never knew why Boris needed a bath. His small, sweetly-rounded body was as flawlessly blue as the summer sky, while his immaculate bib was snowy-white. When the last of the sun touched his cage, before we covered him up for the night, he danced on his perch like a windblown blue flame.

Dad used the yellow china bowl from which I habitually ate my cornflakes. He filled it to the brim with water and placed it on the floor of Boris' cage. We watched nervously as Dad's pink hand, obscenely large as it moved to enfold the tiny body, rattled the frail cage in its monstrous pursuit of our squealing, terrified friend.

"Get in there, you stupid thing!" He had the budgie in his fist, cramming it into the bowl.

I pressed my hands over my ears to muffle the high, thin shrieks of frantic fear. It was all over very quickly. Boris let out a single burbling screech, a noise that seemed almost too loud to have come from so minute a body, a sickening half-human yelp that sounded like – "Why?" That was the end of it. Eyes closed, beak agape in the water like a split seed, Boris lay suddenly, horribly quiet, the flickering pulse of his tiny heart quelled, a candle flame snuffed out.

I ran from the room. The back door was open, and I sat on the step, my lungs pumping. Mum came into the kitchen behind me and poured herself a glass of water.

"Boris is dead, isn't he?" I asked her, in a quavering voice.

She peered at me irritably. "You know your dad," she said. "He insisted it would be all right. He always thinks he knows best."

"I loved Boris. Really."

"Yes, well." She was shaking her head in frustration. "We can get another one."

"Course we can't," I told her, fighting back the tears. "He was special."

I don't think I had ever seen my mother cry before. She stood there, gazing down at me, biting her bottom lip, while a single tear ran down each cheek. "He said it would be all right," she repeated. "He said, 'Birds go in bird baths. They don't drown.'" She wiped her eyes with her fingers. "Silly man."

I turned away from her, and she bent down to hug me. I clung to her, and the world dissolved into skeins of drifting mist.

Dad wanted to put Boris in the dustbin, but we talked him out of it. The little bird deserved better than that, after all those bright, brave songs and a tiny lifetime of selfless companionship. Mum searched the kitchen for a small box to fit him, without success. Instead, we used an empty custard tin, with a fluffy nest of cotton wool tamped down inside. I put some seed in for him, and the blue plastic-rimmed mirror from his cage. Boris loved his mirror. Mum said we could keep him until tomorrow, and then, if he was all right, I could bury him in the garden. I put the lid on the tin, just lightly, so there was a crack of air, and hid it under my bed. During the night, I got up and peeped at Boris with my torch. He looked comfortable and very peaceful. In the morning I looked at him once more, and a fine haze of custard powder had drifted down, as though, in final sleep, he had been sprinkled with pinkish-yellow fairy dust.

It was while I was putting the finishing touches to Boris' burial that the phone call came. The first I knew of it was when Dad came stalking up the garden, pursing his lips in a blend of puzzlement and disapproval. I patted the soft earth with the back of a trowel, making our budgie safe.

"Telephone for you," Dad said, gruffly.

"Who is it?" My friends hardly ever rang me.

"Female," and he walked away with his head down.

I went into the hall and picked the receiver off the window shelf. The voice on the other end was unmistakably Sally's. "You all right?" she said, curtly.

"Yes. This is unusual."

"What is?"

"You ringing me at home." I was careful not to say what was

in my mind, that I felt uneasy about her contacting me there, in case she took it as a rebuff. "Is something wrong?"

"Does something have to be wrong for me to want to talk to you?"

"No. Course not."

"Anyway, I don't think your dad knew it was me," she said, as if she had read my thoughts.

"Well, he hardly knows you." This was true, but I wondered about the distinctive voice. I also noted that Sally had not answered my question. There had to be a reason for this call.

"Neil, are you going to your gran's on Saturday?"

"I expect so."

"Will you be on your bike?"

"If it's not raining. Why?"

"After your lunch, can you ride to the library and meet me? There's some seats under the trees."

"I know. What time?"

"About two o'clock? Don't rush, I'll wait."

"What's it about?"

"Not on the phone, Neil. We can talk properly when I see you."

"Can't you give me a clue?"

There was a pause, as though she was considering the possibility. "Let's just wait till Saturday, Neil," she said, at length.

It would be an understatement of almost epic proportions to say that I was intrigued to know why Sally wanted to talk to me. Inevitably, the open skies of my next few days were patched with the cumulus of dreamy speculation. I wondered if my two best friends had finally decided to live together again and try to repair their relationship. In that case, where would they make their home? They could go to Sally's. Or they – no, it was too upsetting a prospect to imagine...but, yes, for sure, they might return to Scotland to live five hundred miles away from me. Probably I would never see them again. The mere thought of it was unbearable. Sally wanted to see me to say 'goodbye'. She would smile a thin smile and peck me on the cheek and that would be the end of it, the wrenching, scalding-throated, heart-lurching end of everything. I longed for Saturday to come, even as I tortured myself with the hungry fear of it.

A few fat spots of rain fell as I wheeled out my bicycle. It was an easy decision to ignore them. I was too morose and anxious to abandon my own transport and go by bus, mingling with faceless shoppers, and I felt still less like making small talk with Dad in the car. In a paper bag I had a box of chocolate Brazils for Sally, and I hid them in my saddlebag. At least the cloudy weather should prevent them from melting on the journey.

I rode slowly, with my head down, treading heavily and deliberately on either pedal, as though on a long, uphill grind – not because I was reluctant to reach my destination, but so that I might give myself more time to think about the day ahead. If Archie was there, should I tell him about Sally's invitation? Perhaps he knew she had called me. He might know exactly what she intended to say to me. And what if Gran was involved? Supposing she had found out about my relationship with Nurse – about our 'affair'. I said the word out loud, letting the wind snatch it from my lips: our *affair.* The thought of it frightened me, but it also made me feel grown-up and a little bit important. None of the boys at school, I suspected, had ever had an affair, and certainly not with a married lady. How impressed they would be – if only I could tell them of my worldly misdemeanour. Even Peter Jessops, I felt sure, had not yet done anything so seriously wonderful. With Sally, my life was moving inexorably into a new dimension, for she had led me on to the perilously swaying bridge that spanned the yawning chasm between childhood and the adult world I sought feverishly to embrace. I felt that I was poised with one foot in the air, halfway across the smouldering gorge, gripping the side ropes with a knuckle-whitening intensity, hardly daring to chance another step forward, yet too fearful to turn back. Whatever the outcome, no matter how sickening the dangers lurking in the mists ahead, there could be no turning back. The fear thrilled me.

Archie was out when I arrived. This presented me with a problem, for I had forgotten I would need to borrow his library ticket again. I asked Gran if she would go up to his room and find it for me.

"I think it's under his bedside lamp," she said. "I'll go up in a minute. You can lay the table for lunch."

"I'm not very hungry," I told her. My stomach felt as if it was full of jelly.

"All that cycling about. You must have something."

She went upstairs, returning with the ticket. "Here. You should get one of your own."

"I know."

"Is it more books about outer space?"

"Sort of. I want a book on people from other planets."

"Oh?" She fluttered her eyes with the briefest flicker of a smile. "Are there any?"

"What, books?"

"No, daft. People on other planets."

I shrugged. "Nobody knows. It's impossible to find out for sure."

"Hmmh. So you're looking for a book on something no-one knows anything about. That'd be a thin volume."

I loved my grandmother for her solid, indefatigable good sense, her unadorned directness and her tendency to remain slightly in the background of the lives of those she touched. Jean Blaney was placidly reliable, a quiet observer, and her undemanding simplicity invested her with a sweet and delicate warmth which gladdened my heart. She was not bright or intellectual, but she was sure of what she had to do in the world, and that knowledge suffused her with a good-humoured calm that bestowed a blessing upon all of us.

What Gran would make of a secret liaison between me and Nurse Melksham, I shuddered to think. Probably it would be so far beyond her wildest imaginings, she could only dismiss the suggestion as utter nonsense. That day in the rec, she had huffed in disapproval when I asked her for Nurse's name, as though the knowledge should be a prelude to some unpardonable intimacy. Had she but known that, by then, I had already touched the woman's naked breasts, she would quite likely have fainted away to a crumpled heap on the grass.

The last fishcake was one too many. I pushed my plate aside and studied a baked bean stain on the tablecloth.

"Something the matter, boy?"

"I said I wasn't hungry."

"I've never known you not to eat your fishcakes."

"There's more to life than fishcakes," I said, testily.

Gran lowered her head and peered at me accusingly. "Who told you to say that?"

"No-one."

"Hmmh. Sounds like you're quoting someone."

"I don't think so." I wiped a forefinger over the corners of my mouth. "Can I get down now?"

"What about your pudding?"

I stared glumly at my abandoned fishcake. There was nothing more to be said. Furtively, I glanced at my watch under the table.

"You'll be wanting to be off to the library," Gran observed, missing nothing.

"If that's all right."

She shook her head, sighing. "Go on then. You and your Martians!"

I wanted to be there in plenty of time. Sally was important to me, and I wanted her to know that. Hopefully she would be impressed by my punctuality. Some years before, I remembered, Dad had taken me to work with him; they were having some kind of 'open day' for families. As we prepared to leave the bus, a woman elbowed her way past us, jumped off at the traffic lights and ran breathlessly up the road. I pointed her out, as she scampered wildly between the strolling commuters.

"Aha. Does that every morning," Dad said. "Late for work five times a week."

"Doesn't she get into trouble?"

"Huh. She's making her own trouble. She doesn't need to get it from anyone else."

"How do you mean?"

He pursed his lips thoughtfully as he gazed after the running woman. "When you start work," he said, "always be on time. If you can, be early. Impress people with your enthusiasm. They will respond to it. Lateness is slovenly." He looked me quickly up and down. "Would you go to work in dirty clothes?"

"Course not."

"Well then." He nodded emphatically. "A clean and tidy mind."

"So that lady, she – "

"She starts every day by not getting out of the house at the right time. She starts every day by making a mistake." He raised a warning finger. "You cannot trust someone so manifestly unreliable. Never be late."

I wondered what Dad would think now about my clean and tidy mind, full of confusion, uncertainty and forbidden images. Still, at least I wasn't late. My watch showed ten to two as I cleared the railway bridge, dismounted and began pushing my bike up the slope towards the library. There was a church opposite, perched on a grassy bluff above the road. A wedding party was assembling, and I stood for a moment and watched. Large black limousines festooned with white ribbons glided up to the open doorway, disgorging outrageously overdressed people, who hugged one another and tottered about screaming. Buffoons in top hats appeared, slapping unsuspecting guests on the back, howling with laughter, preposterously desecrating the ceremony before it had begun. I waited, wanting to see the bride, to see if she was pretty, to reassure myself, perhaps, that chaos did not always produce ugliness. But the bride did not arrive, and I had to turn aside to keep an appointment of my own.

There was no sign of her in the courtyard. I found an empty bench in the shade of a tree and sat down with the box of chocolates in my lap. Even from here, I could hear the wedding guests screeching. Someone yelled, "Marcie!" and I supposed that was the bride, but it was too late to go back for another look.

I felt her touch before I saw her, a hand placed on my shoulder, light as a small bird, as she approached me from behind. Spontaneously, I turned my head to kiss her fingers, and she bent down, smelling musky-warm, compressing my lips with a liquid kiss that made my heart jump. Stepping around me, one hand trailing under my throat, she sat down at my side.

"You all right?" she asked.

I nodded.

"There's a wedding across the road," she said, matter-of-factly.

"I know. I saw it."

She tilted her head down. "What's in the parcel?"

I handed her the bag. "It's for you."

She slid the box out and smiled. "My favourites. How did you know?"

"I saw them on your sideboard. When I came round – remember?"

"How could I ever forget?" She squeezed my hand. "Thank you."

I looked around at the people going in and out of the library. "Are you getting a book?" I asked her.

"What? Oh – no."

"I borrowed Archie's ticket, just in case."

"Right. Are you going in then?"

"I don't know. I don't think so."

"What sort of books do you like, Neil?"

"Mainly astronomy. But I like stories, too. Mysteries and things."

"I see." She gazed around, looking worried. "Well, it's a lovely day."

"Yes. Sally, do you want – "

"Yes, I know. I'm sorry."

"It's all right. I like just being with you."

She sighed, and it sounded like a prelude. I saw her lick her lips. "Neil, I need to talk to you."

"There's something wrong, isn't there?"

Her eyes were on the ground, yards ahead of us. "Not necessarily. I'm not sure." She threw me a swift sideways glance, the flash of a chilled smile. "I'm sorry, I'm not making much sense."

"Is it about that man, that Mr Wicken? Are they saying we killed him?"

"What?" Now she turned to me and a little sunlight came back into her eyes. "No. No, of course not. The police are happy about it. We've nothing to worry about."

"What then?"

"Neil, I – well, I'm sorry. I think I'm, you know, quite late."

"Oh, that's all right. It doesn't matter. I'd just have waited anyway."

She shook her head, a kind of convulsive snap, as if she'd been shot. "No, Neil. You don't understand."

"Don't I?"

That sigh again. "Neil, what do you know about menstruation?"

"Menstruation?" The word came out in a spiralling yelp, and two women on an adjacent seat turned to stare at me.

Sally waited calmly for an answer, regarding me through lowered eyes.

"Some girls at school have got it," I replied.

A flickering spasm, almost a smirk, danced across her face. "Have they indeed? Let's hope they get better, eh?"

"I think you're laughing at me," I said, sullenly.

"Well, it's not a disease, Neil. It's not infectious."

"I know. It's – it's when they grow up."

"Hmm. Okay, I'll give you one point for that."

"I think it's like when we were in the bath together. It happened then."

"Yes, maybe you should keep your voice down, Neil."

"Sorry. Anyway – well, loads of blood comes out. It's called 'monthlies'."

"Right. What, is it a raging torrent, then?"

"Can be. Depends. Some of the girls, they have to bring spare knickers."

"Really? Must be inconvenient, in the middle of cookery."

I paused for a moment's thought. "I don't know. Boys don't do cookery. We do woodwork."

"Of course. So do you think I get regular 'monthlies', Neil?"

"I suppose. Does it hurt?"

"Never mind that. Tell me what you think it means if a girl – a woman – suddenly stops."

I shrugged. "Takes her knickers back home, probably."

"No, Neil," and she rolled her eyes skywards. "I mean, why would that happen?" She leaned closer, speaking quietly. "What's going on inside?"

"Can I get a drink, Sally? I'm really thirsty."

"Get you one in a minute. Come on, tell me."

"Sally, are you not well? 'Cause if you aren't – "

She covered my hand with hers. "Neil, what I'm trying to tell you is that I am very probably pregnant."

"Pregnant?"

"Sssh! We don't want half the town knowing!"

I gazed at her, open-mouthed. "Sally, that's amazing!" I glanced over at the women on the next seat. "I mean, that's really good."

Somehow, Sally didn't look happy. She was studying the ground again, and I could see the muscles in her jaw twitching nervously. I wondered if the bride had finished getting married yet. I bet myself she was really ugly. I wouldn't have wanted to see her, anyway. I was with Sally, and she was much prettier. Probably the bride's husband was quite ugly, too. The bridesmaids most likely had braces on their teeth and thin arms like white sticks. I was never going to get married.

"What does Archie think?" I asked her. "About being a dad, I mean."

So slowly, so very slowly, Sally lifted her head and stared at me. "He doesn't know," she said. "I haven't told him, not yet."

I frowned, flicking an insect from my neck. "You – ? Why haven't you?"

She waited for a few seconds before speaking again, and then her voice sounded soft and tired, almost apologetic. "Neil, you know perfectly well that Archie is impotent." She spread her hands in front of her. "Do you imagine all this is some kind of miracle?"

"I don't know. I mean, no. I – what are you saying?"

She puffed some air from the corner of her lips, blowing a strand of hair from her forehead. "I'll go to the snack bar. What drink do you want?"

"Um. Fizzy orange, please."

"Right you are. Don't go away."

I sat there in an emotionless daze. Sally was pregnant. Of course, it could be a mistake. Some sort of blockage, perhaps. Her tummy didn't look swollen. She wasn't wearing any funny clothes. I knew a bit about pregnant ladies. They wore smocks and walked about leaning backwards. I would watch when she came out with the drinks, to see if she was leaning backwards.

Why did she say that? 'We don't want half the town knowing.' '*We* don't want half the town knowing.' Who were *we*? Something didn't sound right. Something didn't feel right.

In Sally's progress back to our bench, I could detect nothing that varied significantly from the perpendicular. I took my orange and clasped the glass thoughtfully in both hands.

"Would you like one of my chocolates?"

"No thanks. Sally?"

"What?"

"I don't quite understand. If your baby isn't from Archie..."

"Which is why I haven't told him about it."

"Yes. Okay. Then who is its dad?"

She took a sip from her drink and put it down at her feet. "Neil," she said, flatly, turning to face me, "just how many men do you think I sleep with?"

"What?"

"You heard me. How many men do – "

"All right, I heard you." Despite the drink, I could feel my mouth going dry. "Sally?"

"It's all right, Neil. It's going to be all right."

"Sally?"

"Nothing bad's going to happen, Neil."

"Sally?"

She was nodding her head, reading my mind. "You always said you wanted to be grown-up. You didn't want to be a little boy any more."

"Sally!"

"Shush, Neil. There isn't anything you can do about it now."

"But Sally."

"There's my brave man. Yes, I'm carrying your child, Neil. Now I've told you. I couldn't tell Archie, you see, until I'd told you. It wouldn't be fair. You can see that, can't you, Neil?"

"Oh, Sally."

"Why the tears, Neil? No tears when you made love to me, were there? No tears when you were a big man inside me." She kissed me on the cheek. "We're going to have a baby, Neil. That's the biggest, most important grown-up thing you can do."

Some moments in our lives are destined to remain frozen in time. No matter how many years pass, distancing us chronologically from a traumatic event, that experience is always a malignant tumour in the memory, an incurable pain that can only ever briefly be anaesthetised by distraction. It is the pursuing demon that never goes away, the age-old horror that leaps out in the dark and happens again today and all our tomorrows. So Sally's revelation, quietly intoned in the leafy shade by the library, would be as a shrapnel fragment lodged inextricably in my brain, forever a living, livid part of me.

It was as though I viewed the people milling around us, the trees swaying in the breeze, the swing doors above the library steps, down a long glass corridor, a soundless, far-away vision as detached and unreal as a series of scenes cut from a film. It felt as if I were no longer there, no longer capable of knowing or feeling anything. I was that flying man again, hovering in space.

"...gone very pale." The words formed themselves out of a hissing nothingness, a volume control gradually adjusted into audibility.

"What?"

"Are you still here, Neil? I asked if you were all right. You've gone white as a sheet."

"I feel sort of sick."

"Well, don't be sick here. There's toilets inside."

"I said I feel sort of sick. I don't want to *be* sick."

"Good. You've got to ride back, remember."

"Sally."

"Yes, love?"

"I'm worried about Archie, about what he'll say. When will you tell him?"

"Soon."

"He'll be furious."

"I don't think so. Not if I handle him the right way. You leave that to me."

"Okay."

"You've got to trust me, Neil. Now more than ever."

"I know."

"I've made up my mind what I'm going to say. That this is his only chance. Between us, you and me, we're giving him a child, a son or a daughter, and he should look upon it as a gift."

"You make it sound very easy."

She put her arm round me and gave me a hug. Her hair brushed my face in a feathery kiss. "We can work this out, Neil. I know you're frightened, but if we just stay true to each other..."

"What happens next?"

"I'll talk to Archie, then we'll meet up – the three of us."

"He'll go mad," I said, darkly.

"Like I said, trust me. There'll be no-one going mad while I'm around. I won't stand for it."

"When can I see you again? I mean, in a private place."

"Come to my house next Saturday. I'll get Archie along. We'll talk about what we're going to do." She looked at her watch. "I have to go, Neil. Are you all right to go back on your own?"

"I love you, Sally."

"I know." She patted my hand. "It'll be all right. We'll make it all right."

The church stood quiet and deserted. I pushed my bike slowly up the steep path from the road. There was a weather-scarred bench against the wall by the doorway. I leaned the bike on the brickwork and sat down heavily. The ground in front of me was strewn with confetti, the frenzied dandruff of the celebrating hordes. On the grass lay a broken shoe, a pink slipper with the heel skewed sideways. I was surprised how muted the roar of the traffic was from this elevation, little more than a rush of air as each vehicle passed, faceless midgets at the windows, hurtling to nowhere under tin lids.

I pressed my back into the wooden frame and closed my eyes. A lingering wetness sealed the lashes together. I wanted my mother, the cosy feel of her arms around me, whispering that I needn't worry, she would take care of it, all the hurt and the fear and the badness.

More than anything else in the world, I longed to be a child again.

Chapter XI

Vexed at School

Peter Jessops pushed the bulging envelope into an empty pocket in his brown leather holdall. "Good, aren't they?"
"Yeah. Thanks."

"I can get more if you want."

"Not at the moment. I'll let you know."

He shrugged. "Up to you."

"I'll think about it."

"Not strong enough?"

"No, it's not that. Actually, my mum found them."

His eyes widened. "She never!"

"In one of my drawers."

"Cor! What she say?"

"Nothing. She told my dad."

"Hoo-hoo! D'e wallop you?"

"No. He shouted at me. Said it was filth."

"Huh. Didn't tell you you'd go blind, did he?"

"Not exactly."

Peter snapped the case shut and adjusted his cap to a rakish angle. "Come on. Bell's going in a minute."

Side by side, we hurried along the hydrangea walk towards the entrance doors. Ahead of us, Mr Glemser, the geography master, heaved open one of the heavy wooden doors and waited for us to pass through.

"Thank you, sir," Peter said.

"Put your cap on properly, Jessops."

"Yes, sir," said Peter, tugging at the cap.

Mr Adamson, our maths master, emerged from the next doorway.

"Good morning, sir," we offered in chorus.

"Take your cap off in school, Jessops," barked Mr Adamson.

Peter removed his cap and twisted it in his hands. "Sorry, sir."

We turned the corner, heading for the classroom. A group of boys came swaggering towards us, singing an advertising jingle. The deputy headmistress, Miss Quinn, walked behind them, taking quick, short steps. Peter Jessops smiled deferentially at Miss Quinn, who put up the flat of her hand to stop us and, with the forefinger of her other hand, jabbed menacingly at Peter's crushed cap.

"You, boy! That cap'll be ruined. It's not a dishcloth!"

"Yes, miss."

"Either put it on your head or carry it sensibly."

"Yes, miss."

Walking on, Peter cursed softly under his breath. "Bloody hat. Might as well stick it up me arse."

"Be a brown hat then," I pointed out. "Flagrant contravention of school uniform colour code."

The classroom was nearly empty. Kids were already on their way to assembly.

Peter threw his holdall down behind his desk. "Your mum."

"What about her?"

"Why'd she get upset?"

"Parents," I said. "They think they have to protect you."

"What, from people with no clothes on?"

"It's to do with pornography."

"That's stupid. Doesn't your mum ever take her clothes off?"

"Yes, when she goes to bed. Or if she has a bath."

"So then she's all naked, just like the women in the pictures. There's no difference."

I stood dumbstruck before Peter Jessops' desk and struggled valiantly to accommodate this parallel.

Mr Glemser put his head round the door. "Hurry up, you boys! You'll be late for assembly."

"Wouldn't want to miss that," Peter muttered, not loud enough for Mr Glemser to hear him.

All along the empty corridor, the sun was slanting through the tall windows, tilting incandescent panels of white light on to the polished floor. In the quadrangle, the school caretaker, George Mubble, was fishing paper darts out of the ornamental pond.

Peter stopped at an open window and cupped one hand against his mouth. "Morning, Mr Muddle!"

I tugged at the sleeve of his blazer. "Come on, they'll shut us out."

"Suits me. Why do we have to go to assembly, anyway?"

"To sing hymns and say prayers and atone for our sins. First day back, six weeks of sins to reflect on."

Peter appeared callously unconvinced. "Rubbish! We're just schoolboys. We haven't got any sins." He spread his hands loftily in front of him. "We are without sin."

I hung my head and nearly collided with a fire extinguisher. "Some of us might not be."

"Watch where you're going." He peered at me suspiciously. "What d'you mean, Robertson?"

"Nothing."

"No, go on."

I looked up and saw Mr Glemser come round the corner towards us, walking fast. "Speed it up, boys! No dawdling. Head's on his way in."

"Yes, sir," Peter said.

The teacher passed us at a brisk clip, his head rebounding in a double-take as he strode away. "Tie's all crooked, Jessops. Smarten yourself up."

The doors to the hall were ahead of us now, but Peter stopped and put his arm against the wall to hold me back. "Come on. You got a secret, an't you?" He leered up at me, and his breath smelled of bubble gum. "You look – kind of funny."

"So why aren't you laughing?"

"You know what I mean. Spit it out."

"What?"

"Been a naughty boy, I reckon."

"Might have." I looked hard into his eyes. "Please. Let me pass."

He bounced his hand against the wall and kept it there,

barring my way. "You have, haven't you?" His eyes gleamed. "Carnal knowledge, I bet."

I could feel my lower lip starting to tremble. "I didn't mean to."

He hopped excitedly from one foot to the other, a little jig of delight. "Hee, good old Robertson! Hoo-hoo! Girl from school, was it?" Suddenly he seized the lapel of my blazer, then loosened his grip and began stroking the crumpled grey fabric. "'Ere, it wasn't that Tabitha Gurney?"

"Who?"

"You know. Holes in her knickers and smells of cat's pee and tomato soup."

"No. No, it wasn't her," I said, wearily.

He was grinning at me broadly, and his approval seemed tantamount to envy. "Well, well, well! Robertson's finally done the business!" The grin faded like the sun going in. "Is it anyone I know?"

I shook my head, loosening the tears.

"Ooh, I get it! Outside girl-friend, eh? There's posh!"

"Can you just leave it, please?"

"Whatsa matter?"

The burning behind my eyes was finally too much to hold back, and a slow, inexorable, salt-sticky wetness lacquered my face.

A metal chair stood against the opposite wall, and Peter gestured vaguely towards it. "Reckon you'd better sit down, mate."

"We ought to go in," I said, choking.

He touched my arm protectively. "'S all right. I'll tell a teacher you're not well."

Before I could argue, he disappeared into the hall. There was no-one else in the corridor. Feeling vulnerable and slightly ridiculous, I sat down on the chair and wiped my face with my handkerchief. My lips began to quiver again, and however much I dabbed at my eyes, the more the tears flowed, until they trickled from my jaw, darkening my blazer. There was no point, now, in twisting my head about and gritting my teeth, and I slumped in the chair and let myself cry, moaning softly in the echoing silence.

I found myself envying Peter Jessops. His schoolwork was barely average, he had spots on his neck, and his father – as Mum had spitefully reminded me – was only a postman. Sometimes the collars of his white shirts were none too clean. Yet that, in a sense, was as far as it went. Peter went to school, fooled around with Tabitha Gurney behind the woodwork hut, went home and occasionally did his homework, and played football in the park with his mates, their coats and duffle bags left on the grass as goalposts. Life placed no other constraints upon him. His days were simple and undemanding. They asked him no questions, told him no lies. Once he had woken up in the morning, it was merely a matter of *being.* That youthful detachment conferred upon him an innocence, a freedom, I suspected had been stolen from me while my head was turned.

The door clicked open and a teacher's face appeared out of the gloom. It was Miss Quinn. She peered at me over her glasses. "It's Neil Robertson, isn't it?"

"Yes, miss."

"Not feeling well?"

"I'm all right, miss."

"Then why are you sitting out here?" She stepped forward, letting the door close behind her. "Have you been crying?"

"Sort of, miss."

"Well, come on. Either you have or you haven't. Your eyes are all red."

"Yes, miss."

"And is that all you've got to say on the subject?"

"No, miss."

"Is it a tummy ache?"

"No, miss."

"Hmm. Proper little chatterbox, aren't you?"

"Yes, miss. I mean, no, miss."

She bent down to inspect my face. "You haven't been fighting, have you, Robinson?"

"It's Robertson, miss. No, I haven't."

"And no-one attacked you?"

"No, miss."

"I see. Were you all right when you first arrived this morning?"

"Yes, miss."

Miss Quinn stood back and placed her hands on her hips. "You see, Robertson, I'm just trying to get to the bottom of this. I must say, you're not being overly co-operative."

"I'm sorry, miss."

"You sure you're not simply skiving off assembly?"

"No, miss," I said, my voice rising indignantly.

"Well, presumably you aren't crying for no reason. Have you a pain?"

"Sort of, miss."

"Sort of. Right. Where is the pain?"

I hesitated. "I can't say, miss."

"What do you mean, you can't say? Is it something private?"

I nodded, tears brimming in my eyes again.

"Is it something you would rather discuss with a man – with a male teacher?"

"I – I don't mean private like that."

"Well, what do you mean? At the present rate of progress, we shall both be here all day." She glanced up and down the corridor, her face contorted in exasperation. "Who is your form teacher, Robinson?"

"Mr Ransley, miss."

"Right. Would you like me to ask Mr Ransley to speak to you in confidence?"

I sighed. "I don't know, miss."

"Make up your mind, boy. Or shall I ask Mr Ransley to drive you home?"

"Oh no, miss."

Miss Quinn tugged thoughtfully at her earlobe. "I find this all quite surprising. Here you are, crying for no apparent reason, telling me you're not ill, suffering with a pain you can't describe, and yet reluctant to go home. What am I to make of it? Eh?"

"Please, I think I'd like to go to the toilet, miss."

"Yes, very well. Is that it? I mean, is the problem – you know – within the trousers?" She put one hand to the side of her face.

"No, miss. I just want to go to the toilet."

"Right you are. Run along. When you've finished, come to the first floor staff room. Tell them Miss Quinn sent you and you're to await instructions. Is that clear?"

"Yes, miss."

I got up and turned to go. I heard her call after me. "Robinson!"

"Miss?"

"Wash your face while you're in there. You look like a pink panda."

The boys' toilets stank ripely of stale urine and tired disinfectant. At the porcelain trough, I stood with my feet wide apart to avoid spraying my shoes. A previous user's thin golden channel inched fragrantly towards the drain. Above it, clinging to the base of the white splashback, a cluster of wiry, copper-coloured hairs lay coiled like watch-springs. Behind me, unseen, a boy came in and shut himself noisily in a cubicle. There was the clink of a belt-buckle, the rustle of discarded trousers, a grateful sigh, a series of preliminary farts.

I finished peeing and crossed to the wash basins. In the spattered mirror, my face appeared blotched and slightly swollen, my eyes bloodshot and vaguely smutty, as if I had been wearing make-up. I ran the cold tap and splashed my cheeks and eyes liberally with palmfuls of water, drying myself with a wad of paper towels from the battered dispenser hanging by one screw from the wall. Then I straightened my tie, combed my hair and hurried out, heading for the stairs to the first floor.

I remembered from a previous visit, delivering a sick note from my mother, that the staff room was a cold and gloomy place where shabbily-dressed teachers, drifting between lessons, encountered one another amid the acrid smoke from dirty ashtrays and the sickly-sweet pong of spilt coffee. They shambled about the untidy room, with its unmatching brown furniture, hanging their heads in an air of wordless regret, as though recalling someone close to them who had recently died.

I tapped two knuckles on the door and waited. A few seconds later, I dimly heard a voice call, "Yes?" and I eased open the door and crept inside.

The first person I recognized was my form teacher, Mr Ransley. I was relieved to see a familiar face. He was standing by the window, lifting a steaming kettle from a small gas burner. Between us, pushed at an angle across the floor, was a large brown leather settee, most of the cushions split and the stuffing poking out. Sitting at one end of the settee, her shapely legs extended and crossed at the ankles, was Miss Dutoit, our trainee French teacher, neat in her white blouse and tailored grey skirt. In the shadows beside a bookcase, one of the elderly English teachers, Mr Bradman, sat on a wooden chair, reading a newspaper by the curious method of holding his spectacles out in front of him.

Mr Ransley was stirring something in a cup. "Come on in, Robertson. Close the door."

Miss Dutoit looked up at me and smiled kindly. She had really nice legs.

Mr Ransley came towards me, carrying his drink. "What can we do for you, lad?"

"Please, sir, Miss Quinn said I was to come here and wait."

"Wait? What for?"

"Instructions, I think."

"Instructions? Hmm. All sounds very important. A coded message, perhaps?" He sipped from his cup, pulling a face. "You're not a special agent, are you, Robertson?"

"No, sir. Is it all right if I wait, sir?"

"I suppose so. Why aren't you in assembly?"

"I was excused, sir."

"Excused? On what grounds?" He bent forward and peered at me closely. "I say, you're not one of these blinkin' Buddhists, are you?"

"No, sir," I informed him, "we're Conservatives."

Miss Dutoit chuckled lightly and crossed her legs the other way. Mr Ransley moved back and took another drink. "Oh, I see. Well, good for you."

The door opened and Miss Quinn came bustling in. "Right," she declared, without looking at me, "I think we should start by giving this boy a drink."

Mr Ransley went back to the window. "We can make you a cup of tea. Or there's lemonade."

"Lemonade, please."

From the depths of a dark cupboard, he produced a bottle and set it on a trestle table next to a pile of magazines. I thought of the magazines distributed by Peter Jessops, and wondered if the teachers had anything like that. I sneaked another look at Miss Dutoit's legs. They were good enough to go in a magazine. I tried to see what the magazines were, and then I thought about Miss Dutoit's bosoms, only it would be too risky to stare at her again. On the bottle it said 'Robinson's Lemon Barley', which seemed oddly appropriate after Miss Quinn's mistake with my name. I wondered if Miss Dutoit had a boy-friend. I bet he knew all about her bosoms. Peter Jessops said French girls were easy.

"Wake up, boy!" Mr Ransley was holding out a tumbler of cloudy lemonade.

"Sorry, sir. Thanks."

I gulped a mouthful from the glass and wiped my lips. The juice made my teeth squeak.

Miss Quinn was standing beside me, staring at Mr Ransley. "I don't wish to seem overbearing, Edward – he is your pupil, after all – but I really feel this young man should go home."

"Yes, indeed." Mr Ransley gazed at me, sucking his teeth. "What exactly is the matter with him?"

Miss Quinn flapped her arms in frustration. "Why don't you ask him? Perhaps you'll get a more explicit answer than I did. Says it's private."

"Private, eh? Does that mean you can't tell us?"

"No, sir."

"No, what? No, you can't tell us or, no, you don't mean that, hmm? Make yourself understood, Robertson."

"I – I – " My voice faltered, my throat locked in a vice-like spasm.

"Well, there's a start, eh, Miss Quinn?" He reached for my empty glass. "Two words of explanation, neither of them very illuminating."

Miss Quinn turned to go. "Honestly, Edward, I can't waste

any more time on this. I suggest someone takes the boy home. Now, if you'll excuse me, I have a class to attend to."

She went out, slamming the door. Mr Ransley looked peeved. On the other side of the room, there was the swishing sound of the middle pages falling out of Mr Bradman's paper.

Mr Ransley indicated the space on the settee. "Sit down, Robertson. You look a little flushed. Are you running a temperature?"

I perched on the edge of the settee and tried not to look at the legs next to me. To my surprise and delight, Miss Dutoit put out a cool hand and felt my forehead. For the briefest moment, I inhaled the musky sweetness of her perfumed wrist.

"Well, Ginette?"

"I think he is a little hot. A little – moist."

"Right." He walked over and stared down at me. "There seems to be a lot of intrigue surrounding this incident, Robertson. I can't quite get to grips with it. If you weren't feeling well, why didn't you simply ask to go home?"

"I think maybe he has fever," Miss Dutoit said.

"Yes, quite. Haven't got this tummy bug that doing the rounds, have you?"

"I don't think so, sir. I don't feel sick."

"Good. But you feel – what?"

"Sort of funny, sir. I can't explain."

"Funny, you say? Well, you don't make me laugh." He raised his voice to Mr Bradman, still engrossed in his paper. "Make you laugh, Walter, does he? This boy?"

Mr Bradman dropped his glasses on the floor. "You talking to me?"

"It doesn't matter," Mr Ransley said, under his breath. "Now then, young man. Let's decide what we must do with you."

"I think we send him home," Miss Dutoit offered. "His mother look after him."

"Yes, I believe we have already arrived at that conclusion," Mr Ransley said. "For all we know, Robertson, you may be infectious."

"I don't think so, sir."

"Hmm. First a special agent, now a doctor. A man of many

parts, though most of them, sadly, invisible." He clasped his hands and rubbed them briskly together. "I have 3B shortly. I then have a free period, when I shall drive you home. How does that sound?"

"Yes, sir."

"That, Robertson, is an imprecise answer. Either you agree to the proposal, or you advance a better one of your own, so that we may consider our options. Now, which is it to be?"

Mr Bradman sneezed violently. "Speak up, boy!" he spluttered, and he began folding up his newspaper.

The truth of it was, I didn't know what I should do for the best. To concentrate on my classwork, with the emotional bombshell of Sally's revelation still reverberating in my brain, was almost unthinkable. On the other hand, to make a dramatic entrance at home, my education urgently abandoned, would inevitably invite all manner of wild speculation as to the state of my physical or psychological health. One interrogation would immediately be succeeded by another, of still greater intensity.

It was left to Miss Dutoit to save the day by easing me gently towards a decision. She ran a hand through my hair, brushing it from my brow, then playfully stroked my nose. "Poor boy! Not so well, I think." She crossed her legs the other way again, a pale flash in the corner of my eye. "You wait here for Monsieur Ransley. He will take you home. But first we will talk. I like to talk to English boys."

My teacher was pulling on his black gown. There were white patches of chalk-dust all over it. "Where do you live, Robertson?"

"Bottom of the hill, sir. First left after the bus station."

He stared at me in mock amazement. "Good Lord! That's the most you've said since you walked in here."

"Yes, sir."

"Very well." He picked up a pile of books and tucked them under his arm. "I shall leave you to Miss Dutoit's tender mercies. Pick you up at ten thirty."

I nodded as he opened the door and went out, a thin haze of chalk-dust hanging in the air behind him. That meant I had three-quarters of an hour to wait. Forty-five minutes in this cheerless room. I squinted over my shoulder at Mr Bradman. He was cleaning his glasses with his handkerchief, huffing on the lenses and polishing each one with the cloth between his thumb and forefinger. The newspaper was tented over his knee. We didn't have Mr Bradman very often. He taught Religious Instruction as well. He seemed to be in no hurry, and he had missed assembly, so I deduced that God was not very busy this morning. Still, in my mind I said a kind of feeble half-prayer, asking that Mr Bradman get up and go, so that I could sit a bit closer to Miss Dutoit and pretend we were friends. Of course, that might not work out, because some teachers returning from the hall would almost certainly come back to the staff room. Then I would be surrounded, and I would have to face more awkward questions. Why didn't people just leave you alone? Why did grown-ups insist on asking you questions all the time?

Miss Dutoit tapped my arm. "You want some more lemonade?"

"No thanks."

"Okay. How do you feel now? I can open the window."

"I'm fine. If I just sit quietly..."

"Of course."

I could ask her about her perfume, what sort it was, only that might seem rather – personal. Then she would go cold on me. I would have screwed everything up. You had to be so careful. I was learning about women, quite fast, but I didn't know that much really, not yet, not for a while yet. I liked it when they smelled nice. That made them seem kind of friendly. Warm. When they had perfume on and lipstick – Miss Dutoit wore pink, shiny lipstick – that meant they were looking for someone to be friendly with, someone who would like them and talk to them quietly and maybe touch them as the words came out, a sort of emphasis.

"I think I get some water." She stood up quickly and crossed to the window, where there was a small sink.

Now I could look at her legs while her back was turned. Her skirt hung just above her knees. I imagined some of the older women teachers probably disapproved of her. They thought, walking about like that, she might put ideas in the boys' heads.

Or somewhere else. Her legs were slimmer than Sally's, but shapely, with slender ankles. The sculpting of her ankles was complemented by the fashionable cut of her stiletto shoes, in burgundy patent leather. She was stretching over the sink. The back of her skirt rode up an inch, and I saw that pretty crease, shaped like a letter H, that ladies have behind their knees.

Into my cupped hand, I whispered, "Sorry, Sally."

"You are yawning?" Miss Dutoit was coming back, carrying a glass of water.

"No. Just thinking about something."

She smiled, took a sip of water, smiled again, showing white teeth. As she sat down, compressing the cushion, I lurched involuntarily towards her. Our arms brushed lightly together.

Mr Bradman was shuffling towards the door, buttoning his jacket. There was a God. "Going to the toilet. Take me paper."

Miss Dutoit acknowledged him by raising her glass. "All right, Walter. You take care."

He pulled the door open and half-turned to scowl at her. It looked to me as if he was eyeing her legs. I heard him mutter darkly, "Bloody French," and then the door shut with a thud and he was gone.

She shook her head and bent down to put her drink on the floor. "Funny old man." Squirming round in her seat, she laid one arm along the top of the settee and gazed at me inquisitively. "So? You have a name?"

"I'm Robertson, miss."

"Yes, I know this. But your first name?"

"Oh. It's Neil."

"Neil? Neil. I like that. Neil is a nice name."

"Thank you."

"Pleasure. And Neil is upset about something. Neil's eyes are a little – shotblood."

"Bloodshot, miss."

"Ah. I try to remember. See, you can teach me, too."

"If you like."

"Tell me – this upset…it is something we can talk about?"

"It's – uh –a bit complicated."

"Oh, but you are so young to have a complicated life."

I nodded at the floor between my feet. "I know. I have to think what to do."

"When you are so young, on your own, you can do nothing. There is not the experience. You share your problems with your friends, with your family, all the time they are getting smaller." She touched my hair. "But you must trust people."

I sat quietly for a while. My eyes slid across from my feet to hers. I swallowed, plucking up courage. "Miss Dutoit?"

"Yes, Neil?"

"I really like your shoes."

She swung her feet out, girlishly. "Yes? You are kind. You know how to make a good compliment."

"Did you buy them in Paris?"

"Ah, no. In London. They are quite new." She extended her legs, turning the ankles over, left, right, left. "With my mother, two weeks ago. We go shopping together."

"Have you been in England long?"

"Not long. About one month. But I like very much."

And so, with a gently disarming, lightly coquettish charm, Ginette Dutoit recounted to me how she had studied in Nantes and then received practical training at the lycee in her home town of Ploermel in Brittany. "I love these children," she said, and her dark eyes were warm and alive with memories. "But my fiancé, he is English, and so we decide I should take the job here if I can. Soon we are married, I hope."

"What is his name, your fiancé?" I asked her, feeling the tiniest pang of jealousy, the quick, soft puff of a bubble bursting absurdly in my brain.

"He is called Marc. Marc with a 'c'. He is lovely."

"That's good. He's lucky."

"Lucky?" She was gazing at me with her head on one side. "Why lucky, Neil?"

"Because..." I felt myself blushing. "Because he has you."

"Oh, Neil!" She reached out and squeezed my shoulder. "You say such nice things. I think you are a gentleman." Lowering her eyes, she added, "And there is no need to be embarrassed."

I nodded. "Okay."

"What about you? Do you have a girl-friend? I think you must. You are good-looking boy."

"Thank you."

"And so?"

I studied my hands, awkwardly. "I sort of do."

"Ohhhh," and she let out a slow, burbling laugh, as though to acknowledge that we had just shared a confidence. "She is at school?"

I shook my head, looking away.

"Ah, right." One finger moved to her lips and stayed there while she thought. "Maybe – I think maybe...no, no, I stop now, these things are private. Yes?"

Too late. I felt the tears coming again, ants nibbling at my eyes. Miss Dutoit's legs were a white blur, and bubbles frothed in my nose. In a hopeless attempt to conceal my distress, I got up and went to the window, keeping my back to the settee. I tried to look out on to the playing fields below, but the glass was nearly opaque with dirt. A sudden sweat was seeping into my armpits, making my shirt feel sticky. There was a grubby handkerchief in my pocket, and I yanked it out and wiped my eyes, and then I blew my nose.

As there was nothing to be seen through the window, I turned and looked at Miss Dutoit, grinding my teeth together to staunch the flow of tears. It made me feel better when I looked at her legs. There was a small brown mole above her left knee. She had uncrossed her legs, and where one leg had rested on the other, a red welt glowed on the pale flesh.

I read something meekly apologetic in the way she was sitting there, open-faced, spreading her hands towards me. "I say something wrong, Neil? I think I am bad person." She patted the cushion next to her. "Here."

I sat down, crouched over like a gnome. There were voices outside, and the door rattled, but no-one came in. I wondered what to say next. I had to say something; I didn't want her to think she had upset me. "Miss Dutoit?" I said, speaking to the floor.

"Oui, mon petit?"

I turned and offered her a strained smile. "I wish you took us for French."

She nodded slowly, sympathetically. "One day, perhaps. We see." The red mark on her leg was fading to a pink smudge. "Who is your French teacher now?"

"Mrs Tamblay."

"Ah, she is very nice." She flicked her wrist over, checking the time. "I think he comes back soon – Mr Ransley."

"Yes. Then I'll have to go home."

"You do not want this?"

"I think so. I don't know. My mother'll ask me lots of questions. She won't be pleased."

Her coral lips turned down doubtfully at the corners. "To see her son, I think a mother is always pleased. You will have a long talk."

"That's what I'm worried about."

It seemed to me she was going to laugh, and then thought better of it. Still, the bright spark of it lingered in her eyes, like when someone goes out of a pleasant room and leaves the light on so no badness can creep in.

The door banged open and Mr Ransley swept in, black cloak flying. "Where is he then?"

Languidly, I lifted my hand.

"Right, I haven't got long. Any stuff to bring?"

"In the cloakroom."

"Off you go then. Meet me in the car park. Green Zephyr, UUR 303."

I went to the door, stopped and looked back at Miss Dutoit. I wanted so much to say something, some special words that would mean a kind of 'thank you'; but when I opened my mouth, no sound came out, nothing at all, not even a whisper. I managed a smile, and hoped that said enough. Sometimes there are many words in a smile, because a smile can be a picture of what is in your heart, and then the words would not be good enough, anyway. So I felt all right about it, because I left Miss Dutoit my smile, and she might keep it close to her, and it would mean more than all the talking in the world.

Mr Ransley was sitting at the wheel with the engine running.

He reached across and pushed open the door. The radio was on, 'Workers' Playtime'. There was a fat blob of bird-shit on the windscreen, drying to a plastery crust. The car jerked uncomfortably as Mr Ransley selected first gear and let in the clutch.

"That door shut properly?"

I tugged at the chrome handle.

He darted a quick glance at me as we pulled out. "Don't need your cap on in the car, Robertson."

I removed my cap and held it in my lap. In the footwell, my bulging satchel leaned heavily against my left ankle.

I wondered what Miss Dutoit was doing right now.

"So what's this all about, lad?"

The Zephyr had a bench front seat in slippery tan leather, and I rode with my back against the door, right leg braced on the side of the transmission tunnel, to avoid sliding sideways and colliding with the driver. It made for an uncomfortable journey.

I couldn't explain my problems to Mr Ransley, so I said nothing, merely stared morosely out of the window.

My teacher cocked his head at me, mockingly. "Sorry, didn't quite catch that. Have to speak up a bit."

"I didn't say anything," I blurted.

"Sounds like the story of your life, Robertson. Straight on at the roundabout?"

"Yes. I know you're only trying to help me."

"Not my job, lad. I'm not a social worker." He pointed to the glovebox. "Peppermint in there if you want one."

"No thanks."

We cruised downhill to the shops. It seemed strange to be out in the main road at this time, and even stranger to be riding in Mr Ransley's car. I pulled down the sun visor. It had a mirror behind it, and I peered at my reflection to see if I looked ill enough to be taken home. My colour was quite good and the whites of my eyes were no longer pink. We were nearly there, so I leaned back and thought about looking sick. The trouble was, I could hardly remember why I wasn't at school.

"Directions, Robertson, directions."

"Sorry, sir. Next on the left, and it's number twelve, on the right."

As we turned, I put my cap back on, to save carrying it, and reached down for my satchel. The car squeaked to a halt opposite our house. Mr Ransley turned the radio off.

"Got a key, have you?"

"Yes. Anyway, I expect my mum'll be in." I fumbled for the door handle. "Thanks for the lift, sir."

He flapped a hand over me to gain my attention. "Hang on a second. You're not in a hurry."

I waited, staring ahead through the smeared windscreen.

"This – whatever it is. It's to do with a girl, isn't it?"

"Sort of."

"Everything's 'sort of' with you, eh?"

"Yes, sir."

"It's just – well, I'm not much good at these things, but the school does have someone who can help pupils with personal difficulties. She doesn't actually work for us, but she comes in when she's asked. You might have seen her about. She usually comes on Wednesdays."

"I think I know who you mean. She's got glasses and her hair piled up."

"That's her. Annie Fossett, her name is. Well, apparently her real name is Anemone, but everyone calls her Annie." He chuckled to himself. "Anemone. Parents must have been mad."

"Yes, sir."

"Anyhow, if you want to talk to her – if you think it'll help – just let me know. I'll get Mr Letts-Williams to book her in for you. You can have a quiet chat, just the two of you. Might ease your mind, eh?"

I didn't really want to get involved with Roger Letts-Williams. He was the deputy headmaster. He was always smoking a pipe. Mr Letts-Williams administered corporal punishment in his office with considerable zeal. I had never done anything to warrant such treatment, and I intended to keep it that way. Peter Jessops had been up more than once to receive a substantial caning from Mr Letts-Williams. The first time, it was for smoking behind the gymnasium. Peter Jessops was rather indignant about the punishment, because the man wielding the cane was smoking his pipe as he delivered the blows. The second time, Peter had been reported for masturbating in the lecture room. The violent reddening of his face, as he pumped his dangling dong beneath the panelwork, had given him away. His hopeful excuse, that the misdemeanour had occurred during a particularly interesting lesson in human biology, was not accepted in mitigation.

"Thank you, sir. Can I go now?"

"Very well, Robertson. Take care crossing the road. When you're ready to come back, get your mum to give you a note."

He watched me through the wound-down window. I looked both ways before hurrying across.

"Robertson!"

I wheeled round. "Sir?"

"You're practically in your front room, Robertson. You can take your cap off."

"Yes, sir."

I went in and leaned on the gate to watch him go. I thought about waving, but decided not to bother. I saw him stretch over and turn the radio on again, and a blast of music squealed from the window.

I turned to face the house. I hoped my mother was out. That would give me time to prepare my story. But I knew she would be in. Then the tears swarmed in my eyes again. I hoisted my satchel on to my shoulder. It felt like the weight of all the world.

Chapter XII

A Foiled Confession

I found her in the back garden, stretching up to the washing-line, grimly attentive. The old yellow plastic colander was between her feet, filled with wooden clothes-pegs. A pile of tangled sheets and clothing lay on a towel spread on the lawn. A single brown peg, bleached by the sun to the colour of driftwood, protruded ridiculously from her mouth, like a pale cheroot. Her hands were blotched red from the washing water.

I dropped my satchel on the path and waited for her to turn and notice me. When she did, the peg fell from her lips and she stood open-mouthed, staring at me incredulously.

"Hello, Mum."

"What on earth – ?"

"I've come home."

"I can see that. Whatever's the matter? Are you ill?"

"My form teacher brought me. He said I – he said..." I began to cry. The tears came streaming out of me, pouring down my cheeks.

"Oh, for goodness' sake!" Mum scooped up another armful of washing and, grabbing some more pegs, returned to her task. "You'd better go inside and sit down." A breeze sprang up, making the washing dance on the line. Mum's knickers with the long legs cavorted crazily in mid-air. "Just let me finish this."

I went up to my bedroom. I took off my tie and shoes and sat down on the bed. One of my socks had a hole in it, and my big toe was sticking through. After a minute or two I heard footsteps on the stairs and the thump of the door being shoved open.

"Now, what's happened?"

I turned towards her and then I looked away again. "Nothing's happened," I said.

"Oh, come on, Neil! You've been off for six weeks, and on your first day back they send you home again. Just tell me what's going on."

I had managed to staunch the flow of tears, but now I could feel the stiff crustiness of salt on my cheeks, and my eyes were pink again.

I couldn't say that I had never lied to my mother, but I had never told her a big, serious lie, and I wanted desperately to cling to that code of honour. That meant telling her the truth. That meant pain and shame and sadness. It meant growing smaller and less respectable – less lovable? – in her eyes, because I had failed to meet her expectations. I prepared to sacrifice myself on the altar of truth.

"I've got a problem, Mum," I told her, my voice breaking.

Mum rested her hands on her hips, invariably a sign that matters had taken a serious turn. "Right, well, I'm sure it can't be worth crying about. Just calm down and tell me."

"I can't go to school, Mum. I'm too worried."

"Worried? What, about your school-work?"

"No. I can't do it."

"You're not making sense, Neil. What is it you can't do?"

Like a dam breaking, the tears cascaded down my face. I felt her hand on my shoulder, just resting there. "Have – have a baby," I murmured, gulping for breath.

She leaned closer to me. "I can't hear what you're saying, boy. Something about a lady?"

"Baby!" I bawled.

She drew back from me, frowning. "Who's having a baby?"

The words trundled out in a low monotone. "Someone I know, a friend of mine."

"A girl at school?"

"No. Just a person."

"I see. And why does that upset you?"

I sucked in air until my chest fluttered. "Because it's all my fault," I replied, speaking to the floor.

"It's-all-my-fault." She repeated it like that, like someone slowly reading words they didn't understand. When I looked up at her, she fixed me with an unblinking stare, and there was a coldness in her eyes. "How?"

"What do you mean – how?"

"How can it be your fault that some woman's decided to have a baby? What's it to do with you?"

"Because I made her," I said, and it was hardly more than a whisper.

"I can't hear you, Neil," she said, irritably.

"I said I made her."

"You made her?" Mum sighed and scratched her head. "Neil, is this why they've sent you home from school – because you're bothered about some pregnant woman?"

"Sort of."

"You told this woman she should have a baby?"

"No. It's not like that."

"Well, what is it like?"

I started to cry again. While I struggled to find the right words, my weeping became a kind of convenient punctuation, even though I hated myself for doing it. Bubbles fizzed in my nose, and I could taste snot-slime in my mouth.

"Neil, talk to me, please."

"I am."

"Neil, who is this person you're worried about? Is she ill? Some women, when they fall pregnant, they do get bad spells."

"She's not ill," I croaked.

"Well then. I'm sure she'll be fine and have a lovely baby. Nothing to worry about."

"You don't understand."

"I'm trying to, Neil. You're not helping me. Just tell me who it is."

"How will that help?"

"If it's someone you know."

"Of course I know her."

"Then tell me who she is. It'd be a start."

I wetted my lips with my tongue, round and round. "It's Nurse."

Mum's eyes narrowed, the brows almost knitting together. "Nurse? You mean Gran's Nurse?"

I nodded.

There was a silence, and I wondered if she was expecting me to elaborate. "Nurse is having a baby?" she said, finally.

"Yes."

"Well, I must say I – who told you this?"

"Nurse did."

"When did you see Nurse?"

"I – I don't remember exactly."

"And she told you she was pregnant?"

"Yes."

"So – let me get this straight. Nurse is going to have a baby, and for some unfathomable reason that's got you all in a state, and now they've had to let you off school because of it." She hooked something out of her teeth with a forefinger, staring at me. "Neil, don't you see how ridiculous all this is?"

I went back to gazing at the floor. There was a dark, oval stain on the rug, and I wondered what it might be. Tea, perhaps? Or lemonade? Urine? Sick? I couldn't account for it.

Mum had moved to the window, standing with her back to me. "Grass needs cutting," she said. "Your dad's getting lazy."

"He's got to go to work," I muttered. "I'll do it if you like."

She turned round to face me, leaning back with her hands on the window sill, elbows out. "So Nurse is going to be a mother – well, well, well. I didn't even know she was married. Anyway, shouldn't be a problem."

"How do you mean?"

"If she's a nurse."

I felt as if I were standing, precariously balanced, with my toes projecting over the edge of a deep, dark precipice. Perhaps, now, it would be easier to close my eyes and topple effortlessly forward, than to struggle for a desperate equilibrium. There comes a time.

"It's not his," I said, quietly.

"What?"

"The baby. He's not the father – her husband."

She dredged up a thin smile, rolling her eyes contemptuously. "Oh, I see." She shook her head, loftily world-weary. "I might have known. Did she tell you who's responsible?"

"Yes."

"Oh, she did? She must think a lot of you – to confide in you."

"It's me," I said, through clenched teeth.

"What do you mean, it's you?"

"What I said." The tears welled up again. I had to stop the tears from coming. "I've – we did it."

Mum's face was contorted into a mask of piqued exasperation. "Neil, what are you talking about? Did what?"

"You know."

"Obviously I don't know, or I wouldn't be asking. Why do you keep crying?"

"I can't help it," I moaned.

"Just tell me what's happened – so I know what to do."

"Oh, Mum." I was sobbing now, fresh tears trickling down my face, dripping on to the floor. "I've done something really bad."

A short, impatient sigh. "Have you got a hanky?"

I nodded.

"Then use it. Blow your nose and wipe your face. I can't talk to you like this."

I did as I was told. I kept the dirty hanky out, twisting it nervously in my hands.

"Now then." Mum sat down beside me. "I want you to explain to me, very carefully, what bad thing you think you've done. Then we can start to put it right."

"You'll be really cross. You'll think I'm a bad person."

"I know you aren't a bad person."

"You won't say that when you hear what I've got to...say." The last word tailed off to a hoarse whisper. I felt alone and desolate. There was nowhere else to go, nothing left to do, but deliver the ice-cold, faith-destroying, stomach-wrenching truth.

She tapped me lightly on the wrist. "Come on then."

Just for a frozen moment, I thought I was going to wet myself. It would be like the incident in the wardrobe all over again.

"Neil?"

I could hear the blood kicking in my ears. My mouth burned

with a raw sourness, sucked dry. "Mum, you've got to help me. Please."

Again, she touched my wrist, as if feeling for a pulse. "It's all right, love. I'm here."

"Nurse – her name's Sally..."

"All right."

"Well, we went out. It was at night, you see. That's when it happened."

"What happened, Neil?"

"We spent the night. We were friends, so we did it. We still had our clothes on, mostly. But we did it – and now she – she's going to have a baby."

There was the slow, quiet, slightly laboured sound of Mum clearing her throat, as though this act might also clear her mind. I waited for her to say something, but no words came. The room hissed softly with our breathing.

"Are you going to tell me how bad I am?" I asked her.

She slowly eased herself up from the bed and stood there, staring down at me. If a human face can be totally expressionless, that was how hers appeared. It was as if I had suddenly ceased to be her son, and someone completely different, totally unknown to her, had materialised in the room as silently and mysteriously as a ghost. I gazed back at her, my eyes filled with fear and sadness, and I met no warmth or recognition.

"Mum?" The word floated formlessly on the air, light as a feather.

One hand moved up, a tent over her eyes, and she spoke from beneath it. "Neil, you haven't even got a girl-friend."

"No. What's that got to do with it?"

I wanted her at least to come out from behind her hand, but she stayed like that, not looking at me. I wanted to see her eyes, to read what was in them. I needed to know if she still knew me.

"Neil, why do you say these things?"

"What things?"

"You are a fifteen year-old schoolboy. You like playing in the park and – and riding your bike and looking through your telescope. You don't wash behind your ears and get holes in your socks. You draw silly pictures and stick them on the wall with drawing pins." Then she parted her fingers to look at me. "Isn't that right, Neil?"

"Well, I – "

"Isn't it?"

I shook my head. "Mum?"

"Answer me!"

"Yes, all right, I know."

"Of course." She leaned over and kissed me on the forehead. "You're a good boy, Neil. Aren't you?"

"Yes," I said, sullenly.

"That's what I thought." The merest flicker of a smile darted across her face. "And so. Now you're telling me how women fall for your worldly charms and throw themselves at you."

"I never said that!"

"They drag you to their beds, beguiled by your suave manner and manly prowess, and beg you to make love to them, so they can have your babies."

"No, that's not fair! It wasn't like that!"

"So what did you talk about when Nurse invited you to sleep with her, eh? Stamp-collecting? How to make a good catapult? What to do if the Martians landed?" The ripple of a smile upon her face had become a merciless wave, a scornful leer she could hardly contain. "You've been ogling too many of those magazines, boy!"

"You don't understand, do you? You'll never understand. She loves me. She said so."

"Don't be ridiculous!"

"She does! She's – we're really friends. She tells me things, and I make her smile."

"Hoo, I bet you do! Every time you walk past."

"You're being horrible!"

"Oh no I'm not! I'm being realistic, Neil – and it's high time you started doing the same." She stepped closer. She seemed to be shaking all over. "Sometimes you're just a stupid kid, Neil. What that Nurse thinks of you, I can't imagine, but I don't see her asking you to father her children. Not on any planet." The grin was creasing her face again, but the look in her eyes was wild and incredulous, and her nearness to me was intimidating, suffocating.

My mouth fell open in fear and rage. Nothing would come out of it now but tortured breathing.

Then my mother started to laugh. "If – oh, Neil – if you could see yourself! What a spectacle! Will you never grow up? You and your crazy inventions!" She was rocking back and forth with her arms folded under her chest.

I shrank back, clamping my hands over my ears.

The laughter seemed to echo in my brain, brittle, high-pitched yelps of cackling mockery that exploded around me and inside me.

I flinched, ducked aside, but not in time. Her hand lashed out, catching my cheek, smacking the flesh against my teeth. I tasted blood.

"There! That's for your lies!"

She was still shaking. A tremor ran through her whole body.

I licked my hand and saw the red saliva.

Again, she bent towards me. "Your dad'll be home soon. He'll want to know why you're not at school. You'd better think up a story he might just believe, or I won't be answerable for his actions."

I watched her as she went to the door. She turned to glower down at me. "Wash your mouth out! It's full of rubbish!"

I felt the room shake as the door slammed.

A few days later, I was called to attend a board meeting – or so it seemed to me at the time. Sally opened the front door, pecked me lightly on the cheek and quietly ushered me into the cool dining room, where the polished mahogany table extended before me. Archie sat on the left at the far end, gazing at the opposite wall. Rupert lay curled up on the chair at the head of the table, nearest me. I paused to stroke his glossy head, and he rolled on to his side to show me his snowy-white tummy.

Archie turned. "Neil, come and sit next to me." He patted the chair cushion.

I moved along behind the chairs, slid in and sat down.

Sally lifted her cat on to the floor and sat down at the head of the table.

Archie stared at her. "Surely you're not going to sit away up there? Are you expecting a committee?"

She got up and came to sit opposite me. Rupert sprang softly into an armchair.

There was a brief silence. I coughed into my hand. I wondered, idly, if either of them had prepared an agenda. Had a spiral notepad and pencil appeared, for minute-taking, I should not have been conspicuously surprised.

"Are you all right, Neil?" Archie asked me.

"Yes, thanks."

Sally smiled across at me, sympathetically. "Archie is fully in the picture, Neil."

"I know. You told me." I checked Archie with a nervous sidelong glance. "I'm sorry," I said.

"No need to be," said Archie. "What's done is done. Anyhow, it takes two to tango, as they say." He met Sally's gaze, then looked away. "I don't see it as a matter of culpability; if it were a time for apologies, then no apology would be adequate. Do you follow my meaning?"

"I think so."

"Right. So now we have to convert an unfortunate accident into something – beneficial. That's why we're here."

Sally clasped her hands together in front of her on the table, making misty smudges on the veneer. "Have you told anyone about what's happened, Neil?"

"I told my mum, that's all."

"Oh, I see. What did she say?"

"She told me off."

"Is that all?"

"She was really cross."

"With you or with me?" Sally ventured.

"With me. For telling lies."

"What do you mean, for telling lies?"

"She didn't believe me. She said I was making it up."

Archie scratched his head, thoughtfully. "So...so no-one except the three of us really knows the truth?"

"No. I mean, that's right."

"Well, hopefully we can turn that to our advantage," Sally said.

"How do you mean?" I asked.

"Damage limitation, Neil. Like Archie said, we need to rescue something from all of this, try to make a virtue of it."

"What, like – protect ourselves?"

"Not only that," Sally said. "We want to protect you, Neil, because you're under-age. We don't want you to get hurt, that wouldn't be fair."

It is, I think, a measure of my juvenile innocence, my naivete, that when they gave me this assurance, it did not occur to me that I was not the one most obviously in need of protection. The deduction would have required a degree of lateral thinking of which I was incapable.

"What about your father?" Archie enquired.

"Mum's not said anything. She thinks he wouldn't believe me either."

Sally and Archie exchanged wordless glances.

"Is there something you want me to do?" I asked, cautiously.

Archie widened his eyes. "Such as what?"

"I'm not sure. To do with money."

"And have you any money?" he asked.

"Only my pocket money."

"Well then." He touched my elbow, a brief moment of reassurance. "You're not to worry yourself about such matters. That'll all be taken care of."

Sally leaned forward over her folded arms. "There is something, Neil. We need your help – your agreement."

I wasn't sure what to say, so I said nothing. I heard Rupert roll over in the armchair and squeak as he yawned.

Archie looked at me quite suddenly, as if he had forgotten I was there. "What do you think, Neil? Are you with us?"

"I can't say 'no', can I?"

"You could do," Sally said, "but it would only complicate matters. Maybe they're complicated enough already."

I spread my upturned hands across the table. "So what do you want me to do? What am I agreeing to?"

Sally took hold of my right hand, clasping it between her palms. Her hands were very warm. "Archie and I have come up with – with a few…ground rules. They're a kind of code of behaviour. If we all three follow them, keep to them, I think – we think – we can get through this little crisis without anyone getting hurt."

"You mean about the baby?"

"That's right." She gave my hand a squeeze. "You don't mind, do you – that Archie and I have tried to formulate a plan?"

I shook my head.

"Very well." She glanced up at Archie. "Do you want to say anything to Neil?"

"What? No, no, you're doing fine."

Another squeeze from that warm, dry hand. I thought fleetingly of the other places it had been. "We have until May, Neil. That's when the baby will come. In the meantime, Archie and I will let a few people know that we are expecting – you understand this, that *we* are expecting – a baby, a very happy event after years of trying unsuccessfully. Now, what could be more natural? Our friends in Scotland, in particular, know very well that this is something we have always wanted. So, you see, no surprises."

Slowly, I withdrew my hand from her grasp. "But don't they know about the tests and things – that Archie and you couldn't get a baby?"

Archie shifted uncomfortably in his chair. "Possibly. But there was never anything conclusive, Neil. Nothing that would arouse suspicion."

I tented my hands over my nose. There was the sweet aroma of Sally's perfume, mingling with the thicker smell of my sweat. "So you want us all to say Sally's baby is just – normal? You'd be its mum and dad?"

Sally nodded brightly. "Exactly. And why should anyone suppose anything different? No-one need ever find out."

"It'd be our secret," I said.

"Are you good at keeping secrets, Neil?" Archie asked. "I think you are."

"What do you mean?"

"You never let on about any of this to me. You know, the sex and all that. Proper cunning, you were."

"Only because I was frightened to."

"All right, Archie," Sally admonished him. "I don't think we need to go down that road now."

Archie sat back, pinching the bridge of his nose. "Aye, well. Maybe you're right." He patted my knee. "I'm sorry, Neil."

Sally pulled a pink handkerchief from her cuff and wiped her eyes daintily. "Okay then. So no-one has to hide away or lose face. Life goes on as normal. And then, when the baby's born, Archie and I will choose a name and you, Neil, will choose a second name. Is that agreeable to you?"

"What, any name I like?"

"I suppose so. Just as long as it's a sensible one."

"All right."

"You can come and see your son or daughter whenever you like. We won't stand in your way. But we'll bring him, or her, up as our own, you understand. That means we'll make the rules about domestic arrangements, discipline, schools, clothing – all that kind of thing." She peered at me, a touch sternly, I thought. "You won't want to get involved in all that."

"Can I buy him – the baby – a present?"

"As often as you like," Archie said.

"Only no gifts of money," said Sally.

"I wonder if I'll love him," I said, absently. "I could try to love him."

Archie nodded thoughtfully. "I'm sure you will, lad."

"I've messed it up, haven't I?" I said.

There was a pause, a reflective silence. I studied my friends' faces, wondering if everything would be different from now on.

"We've all made mistakes," Archie said. "Water under the bridge now. Eh?"

"Do you think we can ever be normal again?" I asked.

A small, sad smile warmed Sally's face. "What's normal, Neil? What in the world is normal?"

"There's something else," said Archie. "I'm afraid you won't be seeing me quite so often, Neil. I'm leaving Mrs Blaney's. I'm moving in with Sally."

"Oh, I see." I was disappointed, but hardly surprised.

"But do you?" Sally asked me. "It doesn't sound that way."

"Nothing I can do about it, is there?"

"It makes a lot of sense, you see," Archie continued. "Sally and I – well, we'd like to make a go of it if we can. And she'll need some support over the coming months."

"What about Gran?"

Sally offered me a blank stare. "What about her?"

"She'll miss not having a lodger."

"Plenty folk looking for lodgings," Archie said. "One's as good as another."

I tried to fathom, without articulating the question, how much Gran knew of the relationship. She had never said anything to me about Sally being married. That day in the park, when I had asked her for Nurse's name, she had told me it was Melksham, which must have been her maiden name. Was this statement an economy of truth, or was Gran genuinely ignorant of her friend's background? Neither had I ever heard my grandmother say anything to suggest that she knew or suspected that Archie was married to anyone. It was all quite puzzling.

"Can I still come and see you?" I asked neither of them in particular, "when you're both at Sally's?"

"Of course, lad." Archie peered at me quizzically, as though taken aback that I had even asked such a question. "Come along whenever you can. The door'll be open for you."

"We can get him a key," Sally said, obliquely.

Archie nodded, closing his eyes. "Aye, so we can. He shall have a key of his own."

"Does that make you feel happier?" Sally asked me.

"Yes. Thanks."

"Perhaps you could stay over sometimes," she suggested.

"Stay over?"

"Yes. There's a spare room. Rupert usually sleeps in there." She smiled. "You could curl up together. He'd like that."

I remembered when I had curled up with Sally in the dark in the van that reeked of chickens. I remembered how she had touched me in the fusty warmth of the sleeping bag, making me grow like magic into her thrilling hand. I thought of the night sky's shimmering shawl draped over the jagged trees that guarded the clearing and the marbled moon's bright eye watching our soft tangle as we found each other at last.

Archie, I realised, was speaking again. "That sounds grand," he pronounced. "I like the idea of that. I know it'd work. We could all be there together, when it suited." He beamed down at me. "Would you enjoy that, Neil?"

"I think I would," I said, carefully.

"We'd be like a proper family," he went on. "I can just imagine it. You, and the two of us, and eventually a wee baby – we'd all get on like a house on fire."

The reddish-brown veneer of the table top swam before my eyes. I had the picture in my mind. I could see the house, and it was already ablaze. It was like when you rode in on the night train, out of the country into the town, and all the buildings with their lights on appeared as burning boxes stacked in a vast black hearth, glowing amber and yellow, their framework seeming to collapse into the darkness. I saw people at the windows, crawling like ants in glass cells. The people's faces were almost too small to be distinguishable, but some of them looked rather like us. I could even make out Rupert, a dark speck in the corner of the brightest window, a single flame at the tip of his tail, flaring like a lit fuse.

Inside my head, Archie said it again. *We'll all get on like a house on fire.*

Very well, I thought. I was there, in the house, and I was on fire. Recriminations, fears, anxieties, doubts, confusions…they were heating me to melting point. I was opening and closing my mouth, a goldfish drowning out of water, but no sound was coming out, no-one could hear my cries for help. My nostrils filled with the smell of my sweat, acrid as smoke. Searing pulses of venomous pain racked my body, as my clothes were infected by crawling brown stains, sputtering into flame.

Yes, I was in the house.

Burning.

Burning.

Chapter XIII

Gone Fishing

I think they call it 'shipping oars', don't they? Well, whatever, a sudden rumbling noise, loud enough to startle me, shook the boat, the percussion echoing across the water, as Archie dragged in both oars and let them fall on to the planking. Our rods and reels already lay in the bottom of the boat, criss-crossed like giant mating crane flies. A black, fine-mesh keep-net hung over the side, suspended from a brass hook, and the bottom of the net bulged with trout and brown eels.

"Ah, we've done grand," Archie pronounced, kicking the oars out of the way. "We'll have a rest. Drift a while."

We'd been out since first light. The sun was up now, climbing over the hills, and the loch's glassy surface was quilted with a rolling white mist. There was the occasional *plop* of a fish jumping for a fly, but otherwise the only sounds were those we made ourselves, as we coughed in the brittle air or slapped our hands together, urging the blood.

"You all right?" Archie asked. "You're not cold?"

My feet were almost numb and I was starting to shiver, but I wouldn't admit that frailty. I would be sixteen soon. I wasn't a child. "I'm fine," I said, but I blew into my cupped hands, relishing the warmth.

Archie slitted his eyes against the morning chill as he gazed out over the misted mirror of the loch. "Tell you the truth," he said, "I'm a wee bit surprised your father let you come up. He must be mellowing."

"Maybe," I allowed, though really this was just a way of

saying that I didn't think so. "My granddad died, and then I did quite well in these exams – mock GCEs, they call them – so I suppose he thought I should have a break, you know."

"Ah, I see. And he still doesn't know, your father?"

"What, about – about me and Sally?"

"Aha."

"No. I've kept it a secret."

"So – your daddy's going to be a grandfather in a few weeks' time, and he's completely unaware of it. That right?"

"I suppose so."

"Sounds to me like there's no 'suppose' about it. I can't help but feel – "

"It wouldn't work," I broke in. "You don't know him like I do. He couldn't cope with it."

"He's bound to find out eventually, Neil. You may think you're protecting him, but you're only delaying the inevitable."

"I'm not protecting him; I'm protecting *me*."

Archie rubbed one hand vigorously over his forehead. "All you're doing, Neil, is sparing him the present shock of confession by exposing him to the later trauma of accidental discovery. At best it's unfair, lad, and at worst it's – well, it's a kind of suicide."

I didn't want this, any of it, especially not now. Not here. Not in this place. We were having a good time together. We were feeling the same things, and words were superfluous. We didn't have to think about other people. This was like a secret world we could share, somewhere special that no-one else would know about. I didn't want anyone, anything to spoil it. Ever.

"If I tell him now," I said, sullenly, "he'll only say I should have done it earlier."

"You know that's a feeble excuse, Neil." He reached down for the oars again and began heaving them into the rowlocks. "Well, it's up to you, of course. I shan't interfere."

"You already have," I said, quietly, but my voice was lost in the clatter and rattle of Archie's exertions. His steamy breath plumed out in front of him.

"Right." He hunched his shoulders, ready to pull us forward. "What d'you say to a fine Scots breakfast?"

I nodded, unable to make the words. I tugged my woollen scarf up under my chin and sat, round-shouldered, huddled in my duffle coat, as the steely water began to slide past us, leaving a thin V-shaped crease beyond the squared stern.

"A braw morning," Archie exclaimed, panting as he hauled on the oars. "Rannoch's generally much rougher than this, even in calm weather. Have to drag through acres of choppy water, on the stillest day."

We glided past a stand of pines, and I looked up from my gently rocking wooden seat, cupped in the silver-furrowed water, and saw the sun hanging in the branches like a gold coin left dangling, a neglected decoration, the last foil-wrapped penny on the Christmas tree...when you carefully unhook it and use your thumbnail to peel aside the shiny case, seeing it silver inside, and there's the chocolate disc all soft and powdery-dry, lightly embossed with the shapes of animals.

"Can you grab that net?" Archie called to me. "Dump it inside. I want to pick up speed, and we'll lose it."

I lifted the hook and the net on to the floor. All the fish were dead now, crusty eyes staring icily into space. A pool of water spread towards my feet.

Archie was turning red in the face, pumping furiously at the oars, snatching deep breaths between strokes, spit flecking his lips and chin.

"It's like we're in a race!" I yelled, laughing.

"Good way to – keep warm." He grunted the words out as he found spare breath. "I'm starving – 'spect you are – want to get back – hot breakfast inside us."

I watched the water folding around the surging prow, streaming into flaring fans of hissing froth that raced wildly past us, before dissolving into dancing sunbeams. I trailed a hand in the water, and it came out pink and icy-cold, my fingers puffy as raw sausages. When next I glanced ahead, over Archie's shoulder, I saw the crooked legs of the wooden jetty, the edging boards painted yellow, nosing out into the shallows in the middle-distance.

For the last minute or so, Archie pulled the oars in so they fanned out under his forearms, and the boat just went gliding in towards the bank under its own momentum, spewing out little bursts of bubbles as the hull slapped on the rolling swell. The loch here was peaty, the colour of brown treacle, and I peered over the side, straining my eyes into the eddying gloom, searching for the bottom.

"How deep is it?" I asked.

"Under us here – maybe twenty feet. Out beyond, where we were fishing, could be as much as four hundred."

"Four hundred feet?"

"Aye. Maximum depth, four hundred and forty feet. The loch averages a hundred and sixty-seven feet."

Rannoch, the moor and the loch, was Archie's homeland – his playground, his back garden, his own quiet place. When he told me about the loch, its flora and fauna, its moods and characteristics, he did so with a calm, possessive pride which endeared him to me all the more, even as it surprised me that he could ever have deserted somewhere so special, so personal.

The boat's blunt nose bumped softly against the jetty, wood chafing warmly on wood, as we moved about, picking up our bags and fishing gear. The sun was stronger now, and I was warm at last. I felt a bead of perspiration trickle down my spine as Archie helped me up on to the dock.

A sandy path wound from the water's edge through a small copse, before broadening into a gravel track that climbed a bluff above the loch. There, on a hillside ridge, stood a pair of slate-roofed cottages, built perhaps a hundred yards apart. The cottages were virtually identical, each single-storey with a white-painted wooden gate opening on to a cinder path through a small garden. The path led to a tented porch, the roof in the same grey slate as the house, supported by red wooden pillars which, on closer inspection, were revealed as artlessly painted tree trunks, lacquered against the elements.

The gate to the first cottage stood open, and I saw the name plate: *The Eyrie*. When we arrived the previous evening, it had been dusk, too dark to read the name or to notice much about the little house at all. We had been on the train from London for most of the day, and I was tired, too travel-weary to do more than briefly acknowledge my surroundings before collapsing on to the settee, where Archie covered me with a quilt until morning.

I slept soundly, dreamlessly, and when he hissed at me in the unfamiliar darkness, I was already awake, trying to make my eyes decode the strange shapes and shadows filling the small room.

"You awake, Neil?"

"I think so," I whispered.

I heard him chuckle quietly in the dark as he bumped against the furniture, searching for the light switch. The room was suddenly bathed in yellow from an unshaded bulb above my head. I sat up, propped on both elbows, squinting up at him through foggy eyes.

"Time to go fishing, Neil. See, I keep my promises."

In the kitchen, Archie made tea and toast, while he told me about the two cottages. They had originally been workers' lodges, he said, one a gatekeeper's cottage, the other used by a ranger or gamekeeper, at a time when the entire hillside was part of a huge estate sprawling along the north shore of the loch. Most of the land-owning family had long since dispersed south, but the laird's granddaughter, Alice Minto, had been granted possession of the cottages and was living in one of them, having sold the other to Archie and Sally shortly after their marriage.

"You'll meet Alice today," Archie said. "She comes in to clean the place. She said she'd make us breakfast when we get back. She's – ah – well, you'll find her very plain."

The kitchen table was laid when we came in, and the cottage was warm with the thick fug of bacon frying. Alice Minto was standing at the stove with her back to us. She glanced briefly over her shoulder but did not turn round. Her broad back flexed as, head bowed, she shovelled food from pan to skillet to plate, pausing occasionally to brush damp strands of hair from her forehead.

"Morning, Alice," Archie said, pulling out a wooden chair and nodding to me to take the one opposite.

"Morning," came the reply, in a low, almost masculine voice, while no attempt was made to look at us.

I sat down and stared at Alice Minto's back. She was a big woman, surely six feet tall, with a square, hulking torso and muscular shoulders. Her grey hair, inexpertly hacked short at the nape of her neck, was held in place by a plastic band encircling her skull. She wore a grey cardigan and a grey pleated skirt, with a floral pinafore tied at her waist. Her grey-stockinged legs, unexpectedly slim, disappeared into large brown brogues.

I caught Archie's eye, and smiled when he winked at me. "What did you do with all the fish?" I asked him.

"In the fridge out back," and he pointed to the window with his thumb. "Alice'll get some ice to them later." He called over his shoulder. "Won't you, Alice?"

"What's that?" Alice replied, still bent to her task.

"I've put some fish out."

"Oh aye. More of your fish. I'll see to it."

Archie lowered his head and told me quietly, "Alice is a marvel. She turns her hand to anything."

A brimming plate in each hand, Alice Minto turned to face us. "I hope you're hungry," she said, in a tone almost threatening. "Plates are hot, mind." As she placed mine before me, she peered quizzically into my face, as though previously unaware of my presence. "And you must be young Master Robertson."

"I'm Neil," I told her. "I'm very pleased to meet you."

"Aye well. Enjoy your breakfast."

She moved across to the sink and began clattering the pots and pans. I gazed after her, fascinated by her sheer solidity. Something made me look down at her sturdy brown shoes. They were immense, bigger even than Archie's boots. To see Alice Minto standing with feet planted wide apart was to be put in mind of a woman momentarily interrupted in the act of transferring from one rowing boat to another.

Archie, watching me, tapped his fork against my plate. "Come on, lad, eat up. You'll need your strength."

I wondered why. "I'm tired, Archie," I said.

"That's why you need your breakfast. Busy day ahead."

"What are we doing?"

"Mmm. Going bicycling," he replied, over a mouthful of sausage.

"Bicycling?"

"Yes. You know what bicycling is?"

"Course. Where are we going?"

"You'll find out."

We came out into the crackling brightness of a Highland morning, the air sweetly redolent of pine and woodsmoke, squirrels racing in the trees, showering the dew. With Alice's gargantuan breakfast inside me, it was all I could do to walk, but Archie led me to the shed and pulled the tarpaulin off two bicycles.

"You take the smaller one," he said, "it's Sally's."

I wheeled it out, caressing the contours of the saddle thoughtfully with the palm of my hand.

"Ride beside me, Neil. There's no traffic to speak of."

"How far are we going?"

"You like trains, don't you?"

I gazed across the loch to the distant hills. "No trains out here," I said.

"Ah, that's where you're wrong. Be one along about lunch-time."

"Archie?"

He ruffled my hair in that affectionate way he had. Normally I didn't like it when people messed my hair, but I wasn't bothered when Archie did it. Funny, I didn't even care for it when my mum did it, but it was all right with Archie. It was being touched by a friend, something special, something that was almost like a secret.

"We'll ride along to Rannoch Station," Archie said. "Twelve miles. Think you can manage that?"

"Do we have to go over any mountains?"

"No," he said, laughing. "And the best part is, we might not even have to cycle back."

"What? Then how – ?"

"Ah-ah-ah!" He raised a finger to hush me. "Wait and find out. Archie always has a solution."

That ride along the loch shore keeps reeling through my head like a cine film in an endless loop. I believe it was one of the happiest days of my life. At first Archie rode quite slowly, and then, once he realised he was not about to lose me, he increased his speed, until it felt as if we were flying, our wheels whirring in the silence, the wind streaming through my hair. As for the traffic, Archie had been right about that, as he was about so many things. We had been out for twenty minutes before the first vehicle appeared, a red van approaching us. The driver slowed as he drew near and waved out of the window, waggling his fingers, touchingly, as he passed. It was the local postman, returning with the mail from the station. I waved back at him, and Archie rang his bell, the sound of it hanging crisply on the morning air, musical as birdsong. Round the next bend, Archie flung out a hand to stop me, lifting a finger to his pursed lips to keep me quiet.

He pointed into the trees at the foot of a rocky hillside. "See there?" he whispered. "Halfway up – red squirrel!"

I looked, and nodded, not wanting to break the silence. The squirrel sat facing us in the crook of a branch, tight against the lichen-crusted trunk, bright eyes feverishly alert, huge tail swishing, both front paws clasping some chance delicacy to his quivering jaws, while he darted lightning glances to left and right in that quaintly secretive manner which small animals display.

"I've never seen a red squirrel before," I said.

"Down south, you won't, except in a few protected areas. Greys have seen 'em off."

I remembered the squirrel that sat on Sam Wicken's head when we found him hanging in the woods. Then I reached out and, without knowing why, touched Archie's hand.

"You all right?" he asked.

I felt tears coming into my eyes, and I looked away. "It's a lovely morning," I said.

"It is, right enough." He steadied himself on the bike, bringing the pedals round with the toe of his boot. "Ready to move on?"

In a shallow pool below the road, a fish jumped with a fat *plop*, its tail a silvery arc, and I saw the spreading concentric rings creasing the water.

"Can I race you, Archie?"

"A race, you want? Where are we racing to?"

I pointed along the road. "That telegraph pole with the yellow box on it."

He shook his head, grinning broadly. "If that's what you want, lad." Leaning forward, he adjusted his grip on the handlebars. "You ready? Go!"

There was no way I was going to propose a race and not win it. I was a regular, enthusiastic cyclist, remember, and I was also a generation younger than my companion. Still, this was Archie's territory, and his gift to me, and so I let him sprint ahead for a few yards, before I caught him and streaked past, legs pumping furiously, a wide, frenzied grin splitting my face. I raised one arm to the sky as I pelted past the telegraph pole, braking to a shuddering halt immediately beyond.

Archie pulled up beside me, gasping for breath. "Whoo! Quite a turn of speed there, Neil!"

"I'd be even faster on my own bike."

"Aye, no doubt." He started coughing, and I slapped him hard on the back. He had to brace both legs to keep his balance then, and in the next instant we were both swaying and laughing, and I could feel the lightest brush of a breeze on the sweat on my brow and the sun seeping into my shoulders, thick as butter, like a warm stain.

"You're a good boy and no mistake," Archie said, and he leaned over and his bike tipped sideways, so we bumped heads, and then he bent down and kissed me on the side of the mouth. "Friends?" he asked.

"Friends," I said, and I wanted to wipe my mouth, only I didn't. The sun was striking bright sparks in the unshaven barbs on his jaw. "I'm glad you're my friend, Archie," I told him.

"Aye, I always knew we'd hit it off," he said.

"Archie?"

"Aha?"

"Sally will be all right, won't she?"

The brightness dissolved from his face, but that didn't scare me; I knew it was a sign that he valued my concern. "Of course," he said. "She insisted I bring you. It'd be difficult once the baby's born – to get away, I mean."

"She must be missing you."

"Ah, she'll be missing us both. There's two men in her life now, remember. Maybe there'll soon be a third – who knows?"

"She's not on her own, is she?"

"No, no. Her friend Millie's staying with her. Millie's a staff midwife at the hospital. They've been friends a long time."

I thought at first it was a bird's cry, a distant shriek, and then I searched towards the sound, and there, curling up from a cleft in the southern hills, was a grey tendril of smoke.

"Look, Archie!" I jabbed my finger at the horizon.

"Morning train to Inverness," he said, confidently. "Come on, Neil! Let's go and breathe some of that sweet, nutty smoke!"

He set off at a brisk pace, and I followed him. An AA patrolman swung round a bend towards us, wearing a brown helmet and thick gloves, the long toolbox beside his motorbike like a yellow coffin, and the rider saluted as he drew near, so we each waved back without reducing speed, as the wind carried the shrill chord of the engine's whistle warning the signalman. Then we were bouncing over the scree where the road ran out, and the crows pecking at a rabbit carcass scattered at our approach, squawking in flustered protest, as we came bumping and skidding into the station yard.

Archie propped his bike against a broken fence. "She'll be here in five minutes," he called, breathlessly. "Tea and a pie suit you?"

On that most magical of mornings, we sat on a scarred bench by the station garden while the station master's daughter served us tea in enamel mugs and piping hot mutton pies with a scoop of baked beans spilling from the hollow in the top, the oozing sweet sauce a perfect foil for the peppery nip of the minced meat under the pastry skin, and how I loved that special, pulpy, crammed-in-your-mouth feel of it, as the warm grease shone on my fingers in the sun, and soon there was just a fusty tang coating my tongue, while beyond the faded white line at the platform's edge I could hear the rusting rails starting to rattle at the train's approach.

Archie checked his watch. "She's right on time!" he shouted above the gathering din.

I scrunched back on the bench, my face suddenly smacked by fear and wonderment, as the huge black monster of the locomotive's boiler stormed into view, its vast, eyeless face wreathed in steam and flying cinders. I felt the platform shake beneath me as the great driving wheels ground, *chunk chunk chunk,* over the rail-joints, finally skidding to a graunching halt at the parapet downslope.

Archie reached for my hand. "Here, I'll take your mug."

I let it go and carried on gazing at the train. No-one seemed to be getting on or off, but a door opened in the guard's van and a short man in a grubby uniform began throwing out bundles of newspapers and an assortment of boxes and parcels. A breeze wafted down the platform, and I was enveloped in the sweetly smouldering incense of smoke and hot oil. The engine exhaled in an endless hissing breath, steam curling from the bogies, a sooty heat-haze dancing above the funnel.

I wandered down to the guard's van, where the railman was wedged in the doorway. "I could help you," I suggested, as he peered down at me.

"Ah, nearly done," he said, pleasantly. "There's a cat in a basket away up the end there, if you'd like to fetch it out."

I hopped on to the wooden step and went inside. It was quite dark in there, but I found the basket and brought it out on to the platform, next to the newspapers. The man smiled at me. Archie was putting the parcels on to a low trolley. The cat was mewing and scrabbling inside the wicker basket. Thin coils of smoke and steam drifted lazily past us.

"Thanks for your help now," the guard said, and he stuck a metal whistle between his teeth and searched along the length of the train. I walked quickly towards the engine. The driver wore a crumpled leather cap, and he was leaning out of the cab, straining to see back along the carriages. He looked at me sternly as I reached the tender, and then I waved to him, and he nodded and grinned and, reaching behind him, set off a fearsome blast on the steam whistle, making me jump with fright.

Coming up behind me, Archie laughed, clapping a hand on my shoulder. I sniggered to myself, as the guard blew his whistle and shouted something unintelligible, and the engine driver, adjusting his cap, vanished into his cab and shortly released a ferocious, deafening explosion of steam from the valve on the top of the boiler. When the valve shut off, the noise of the steam's escape seemed to carry on in muted register, for my ears sang from the shock of the pressure-wave. I pushed a finger into my right ear and wiggled it about, making a sound like the sea.

With ponderous slowness, as though a sleeping elephant awoke and rose laboriously to its feet, the big black locomotive inched forward, farting short, swift jets of boiling water ahead of its man-sized driving wheels. I watched the massive, oiled connecting rods, as thick as girders, surge forward, over and back, dragging the enormous wheezing, clanking weight of the engine, tender and coaches out of the station and into the green wilderness beyond. One more time, I waved at the driver, but he didn't wave back. I waited until the blunt back of the last coach had gone, then I stepped to the white line and lowered my eyes to the pit below, seeing the wet rails lathered with the greenish butter of warm grease from the leviathan's darkly suppurating belly.

Archie tightened his grip on my shoulder. "You ready?"

I turned to look at him. "Where are we going?"

"Not far. I've something to pick up."

We crossed the tracks where the platform sloped away and walked into what seemed to be someone's back yard, a rutted, earthy compound with a drooping wire mesh fence around three sides. Chickens strutted aimlessly about, pausing occasionally to peck unproductively at the ground, and next to a collapsing wooden garage an aged rear-engined Skoda stood forlornly in a large puddle of oil-streaked water. Out of sight, a door banged, and I heard the crunch of footsteps on gravel.

"Archie! You're back!"

"Aye, just for a few days." Archie raised a hand, more in acknowledgment than greeting. "Neil" – he touched my arm, a proprietorial gesture – "I'd like you to meet a good friend of mine, Michael Lomax."

"But you can call me Mikey," the man told me, "pretty well everyone does."

I reached out my hand, hoping it wasn't still sticky with mutton pie gravy. Mikey shook it, beaming, looking surprised. "Pleased to meet you, Neil." He glanced from me to Archie and back again. "Are you – uh – are you Archie's boy?"

I wasn't sure what to say. 'No' would have seemed a curt denial of friendship. I waited for Archie to rescue me.

"Oh, Neil's my boy all right," Archie said, placing one hand around the back of my neck. "He's real friend. We've laughed together, cried together, gone fishing together – haven't we, Neil? – but, no, he's not my son."

"Ach well, he looks a fine lad, right enough," Mikey said, rubbing his hands together. They were big, pale hands, mottled with freckles, and there were more freckles around his white neck, under the loose collar of his red shirt. The high sun shone through the thinning backsweep of his gingery hair, highlighting the curve of his skull.

"We've cycled over," Archie said. "I wondered if perhaps you – "

"Ah, you've come for your tools."

"That's if they're ready, Mikey."

"All done. A mower, a scythe and I've mended the handle on your saw. Grass cutters are as sharp as the devil."

"I'll settle up, then I was hoping you'd give us a lift home in the truck – you know, throw the bikes in the back as well."

"Aye, no problem. Come inside and I'll get my keys."

The pair of them threw me a backward glance as they walked to the side door, but I stayed where I was. The breeze was still carrying the rich, leaden smell of the train to me, and I wanted to stand and savour it. Past the side of the house, beyond the haphazard plot of Mikey's scruffy handkerchief of land, carelessly discarded amid all this uncompromising blue-and-green emptiness, a world moulded and compressed out of hills and sky and the broken mirrors of cloud-filled water, swelling over every fold and brook and gulley, as a silently engulfing invisible tide, the wild, peaty, feral smell of the moor rose up to meet me like the scent of some monstrous, formless animal. The unseen monster's breath enveloped me, and I was intoxicated by it, bright lakes forming in my eyes as though to reflect the shards of silvery water cupped in the wilderness that ranged to the far horizon.

When Archie and Mikey came out, I had not moved. They turned to gaze behind them, following my transfixed stare, as a sudden pulse of sunlight burned a gliding cloud-shadow across the flank of a treeless hill, like a spreading green stain.

Mikey swept a hand through his hair and down his neck. "You gonna help us, Neil?"

I nodded. "If you want."

"If we get this equipment loaded," Archie said, "Mikey'll give us a ride back to the cottage. Enough cycling for one day, eh?"

I asked to sit by the door on the way back, so I could look out at the scenery.

"You love the countryside, the wide-open spaces, don't you?" Archie said, with pleasure.

Mikey had an old Ford pick-up with dubious suspension, and he seemed to aim for every pothole. Our bikes, and Archie's lawnmower, rattled loudly behind us, and my teeth rattled in my head like castanets.

"Why do people leave places like this to go and live in towns?" I asked, between violent jolts.

Archie squeezed his nose, thoughtfully. "You meaning me?"

I was about to shrug my shoulders, but there was no room. "Not specially," I said.

"You know, I remember asking my mother that same question, God rest her soul. She said to me, 'Archie,' she said, 'you can gawp at mountains till they come out o' your ears, but you still cannae eat them.'"

I suppose Archie's response was a chilling reminder of the constant need to address the practicalities of life, no matter how unattractive they might appear. Already I was beginning to understand that this somewhat tedious discipline represented one of the fundamental differences between childhood and adult maturity, a time when dreams were tainted with dark bruises of suspicion and had frequently to be paid for with the leaden currency of disappointment.

These were thoughts which assailed me again in the torpid warmth of the bee-humming, bird-trilling afternoon, when we sat at the end of the wooden jetty alongside Archie's tethered boat, dangling our legs over the softly slopping water, the sun gently kneading our backs, and while Archie threaded a line listlessly in and out of the loch, I closed my eyes and watched the vivid pictures of the day go skittering through my mind. As I allowed the dark armies of the real world to converge upon my conscience, so contentment and euphoria became clouded by apprehension, and I remembered who I was and where I was heading. In the pit of my stomach, deep in the core of me, I felt the invigorating cocktail of wonder, surprise and excitement react to an infusion of fear, turning to a viscous bile that threatened to infect and inflame every fibre within me.

The few fish he caught, Archie threw back. "We've no need of any more," he said.

We waited there, not saying much, until the sun sank towards the horizon, its crimson rays spearing the clouds, painting the flag of Japan on the tinfoil water. The long day was dying, but it felt as if something inside me was dying as well. I was consumed with pain, and the pain was called knowledge.

"You've played hard today," Archie said, as we stepped into the cool gloom of the cottage. "You'll take the bed tonight. The settee's a bit lumpy."

"I don't mind," I told him, ambiguously.

On the back of the hob, Alice had left an earthenware crock of meat broth, a muslin cloth draped over it and the lid clamped down on the cloth. Archie removed the covering and peered inside. A dense aroma of stewed meat and vegetables permeated the kitchen. I realised how hungry I was.

"Smells good," Archie said. "I know what'll make it better."

I went to the toilet, and when I came back, he was mixing something in a bowl. There was flour down his front and on his face. He smiled at me and raised one forefinger.

He made six dumplings. Then he stirred the broth with a wooden spoon and, using a metal ladle taken from a hook on the wall, he decanted a generous portion of the thick, oily liquid into a pan, which he set to heat.

"Two of those large china bowls, please, Neil."

I lifted them carefully from the dresser and placed them on the table.

"Will you take a knob of butter on your dumplings?"

I smiled broadly and nodded.

"Sit down now. It's almost ready. Then I think we're for bed."

I could not recall ever having eaten anything so delicious. My eyes watered with the wonder of it. Brown juices oozed from the corners of my mouth and trickled down my chin. The plump dumplings soaked up the warm broth like fat, sticky sponges, each bite releasing a sweet flood of pulpy nectar, laced with a creamy froth of melted butter.

Sated, tired and drained, I fell face-down on to a soft, white pillow, taking no notice of my surroundings. There were framed photos arranged on a dressing table under the window, that much I remember, but otherwise the small room was just a dark box into which I gladly crawled to hide away until morning. Archie was there, behind me, pulling the blankets over my back, issuing quiet words of reassurance. My pyjamas smelled of mothballs. I could still taste the broth coating my tongue. It felt as if the whole world was slipping away in the dark.

I'm not sure how long I slept. I was woken by the bed shaking, something nudging my back. Someone breathing close to me. I opened my eyes, but I didn't turn over or look behind me. After a while I moved my head on the pillow to show that I was awake. A hand touched the top of my back, between the shoulder-blades. I could tell by the way the mattress had been flattened away from me that I was no longer alone in the bed.

Archie's voice was a hoarse whisper against my neck. "It's all right, Neil. Settee's damned uncomfortable. It's all right now. I won't touch you."

"Don't worry, Archie," I murmured. My heart was beating fast.

His hand touched my back again. "You're a good boy, Neil."

"Goodnight, Archie."

"Goodnight, Neil. I'm sorry I woke you."

I snuggled into my pillow, drawing my knees up towards my chest.

"Neil?"

"What is it?"

"Can I kiss you goodnight?"

I hesitated for a moment. "I suppose. If you want."

I waited tensely, holding my breath. I sensed him pulling closer to me, the warmth of his body against mine, how huge it felt, like something powerful that would envelope me, and finally the moist brush of his lips on the soft side of my neck and the quick scrape of bristles under my ear. He drew back, relaxed, and the dab of wetness below my ear felt cold, but I left it there.

The next I knew, I heard Archie's low voice, hushed but insistent, coming to me out of the shadows in my sleep, and I opened my eyes and saw him bending over me, silhouetted against a faint light from the window. I struggled to focus on the figure before me.

"Neil, are you awake?" he hissed.

"What? What's the matter?"

"I had a phone call."

"What? I didn't hear anything."

"You were dead to the world."

"Oh. Something wrong?"

"It's all right. Nothing's wrong."

I propped myself up on one elbow. "What then?"

"I had Millie on."

I stared at him out of sleep-fogged eyes. "A million?"

"No, Millie – Sally's friend."

"Oh, right."

"It seems Sally's started early."

"Started what?"

"I mean the baby – she's about to have the baby. Wise up, Neil." He reached over and flicked the light on. "I'll make you a drink."

I sat up, narrowing my eyes against the sudden glare. "So what's happening?"

"I'm sorry, lad," he said, sighing, "but we'll have to cut this short. We need to get back."

"Yes," I said, flatly, massaging the side of my head.

He went out to the kitchen, and I swung my legs on to the floor. There was only a thin rug over the boards, cold to the touch and slightly damp. I stood up and began to dress. Parting the curtains, I saw a pale, grey-blue haze dusting the black humps of the far hills. At the centre of the black ridge, a tiny yellow gem glimmered, perhaps the early light from a distant farmhouse. I imagined the burly farmer and his neat wife, already in her pinafore, moving to and fro in the warm, bright kitchen, resolute but calm, untroubled by the prospect of the day. Without seeing or knowing them, I envied them, because they were not about to tread an unknown path. They could reside in the comfort of goodness.

"Brought you some tea." Archie stood in the doorway, a steaming mug in his hand. "You all right?"

Slowly, I shook my head.

"What is it, Neil?"

"I – I think I'm frightened," I said.

"Oh, I see. But there's no need. We're all together. A family."

"Will we come back one day?"

"To Rannoch? Oh yes, Neil. You always have to come back."

I nodded and smiled, but I feared, in my heart of hearts, that I wouldn't be coming back. Not this way, at least, not like this had been.

"Archie, is it wrong to be frightened of things – things that happen?"

"Wrong? Of course not. Everybody gets frightened. We'd all be bad people."

"But what if, when everything changes, you don't know anything about it?"

"Neil, listen to me." He handed me the hot mug. "Do you remember when you heard the music in my room that time? You stayed to listen, remember?"

"Yes."

"Okay. I told you then about going on a long journey."

"I know."

"So you see, this isn't just about – about babies. It's more than that. It's to do with growing up and experience and life. It's about anything you can think of."

I was clasping the mug in both hands to warm myself up. "That's what frightens me," I said. "There's so much to learn."

"But that's what growing up is all about, Neil – learning. Even if there was no Sally, no baby, you'd have to do that anyway."

I hung my head and studied the cracks in the floorboards, as though I might find some kind of answer there. I saw a spider, but nothing else.

Archie checked his watch. "We haven't a lot of time. I need to ring for a taxi."

"Okay."

"Look at it this way, lad. You came to Scotland a child, and when you get home you'll be a man. That's one hell of a journey."

"And then, will I still be frightened?"

"I expect so. But you'll be a man, all the same. That's what you wanted, isn't it – not to be a child any more?"

I wondered if a frightened man was any better, any stronger than a child. Could he achieve any more? Would he walk any taller? Would people respect him and lean attentively upon his words?

Perhaps my friend had read my mind, unscrambled my confusion. "Let me tell you something important, Neil. Whatever you do, remember this: bravery is facing fear. That's what you have to do. Be glad of your fear, be proud of it. Without it, you'd have nothing to conquer."

I put my mug on the dressing table and reached out for Archie and let him hold me tightly with my face buried in his chest. Then I let him go, and I perched on the edge of the bed while he went to the telephone.

The light was coming up when we stepped outside, and already there were birds singing. In the air was that early morning earth-scent of grass and dew and electric mist. I heard the drone of the car's engine before I saw the headlamps cutting through the woods. They danced towards us, scratching fiery streaks on my vision, white-hot planets careering through the dark canyons of the trees.

There was the slithering scrunch of locked wheels on gravel. Then a man's voice without a face called out from a black window. A door slammed. Someone laughed. A bat flew past, startling me, a black rag thrown at the cloud-scudded wall of the departing night. I took a deep breath and walked towards the purring taxi.

I sat in the back seat and Archie sat next to me. "You sure you've got everything?" he asked me. "You sure you're ready?"

I swallowed hard. "Let's go," I said. "I want to see my child."

The driver spun two tyre-scrubbing arcs in the road and headed east along the north shore of the loch. I felt in the dark for Archie's hand and held it tightly. The sun was rising over the water, a pale peach glow, banded with dark bars of smouldering cloud the colour of smoke. It reminded me of the sun coming up over the trees in Croakers Wood after we found Sam Wicken's body. Then, I had wondered about the part I had played in his death; and now, as I faced another dawn, I realised that it heralded a day when a life was about to begin and, for that too, I was responsible. No, that did not make me feel powerful or even important, but it told me that I could make a difference. The morning sun was fire in my eyes, and in my heart was the best of me.

Chapter XIV

About Babies

To say that my knowledge of babies was limited would be a substantial understatement. I had seen them in photographs, of course, and occasionally yielded to vague curiosity by peering, with an air of nervous mystification, into the tall prams of friends or neighbours we casually encountered in the street. I recall how, in the course of such an inspection, it was generally difficult, if not impossible, to see a baby at all, for the infant was invariably shielded from public scrutiny by a large perambulator hood and an all-enveloping pile of blankets, for all the world as though the creature concealed within was of an aspect so horrendous that decent citizens should not be expected to confront the spectre without due preparation.

You can imagine, then, the depth of my apprehension at the prospect of becoming a father. It was more daunting by far than being sent on a cycling proficiency course without ever having seen a bicycle. The trouble was, this particular course was likely to go on for as many years as I had lived, requiring unremitting concentration and commitment.

We brushed lightly against these misgivings, Archie and I, as we sat on a wooden bench in the garishly-lit corridor outside the Maternity Ward in the East Wing of St Peter's Hospital. Sally had had the baby two hours earlier, and we had both been in to see her and the child, a little boy weighing six pounds and an ounce. A staff nurse told us that the new arrival was a little frail and would be put in an incubator for a while – "just as a precaution."

"The baby's going to be all right, isn't he?" I asked Archie. We were both perched on the edge of the hard bench, leaning forwards with our forearms balanced on our thighs, gazing at the polished floor. "He – my son's not ill, is he?"

Archie patted my thigh reassuringly. "Don't worry. He's just a wee bit premature, that's all. Nothing to get upset about. He was bawling lustily; that's a good sign."

Lustily. That adjective struck a responsive chord. Whilst I approved of the reconciliation forged between my two friends, a development without which I would surely have lost contact with one or the other, it inevitably meant that I no longer had the same ease of access to Sally, whose focus had now shifted to the reconstruction of her life with Archie. In the past few months, with one notable exception, I had been with Sally only as a platonic friend, and it irked me more than a little that the woman who was carrying my child should display such modest affection for me. We had seen each other, of course, and there had been trips to the zoo, to hear a brass band in the park, to the pictures – where we sat in a corner at the back, and she let me touch her breast in the dark – and we spent some lazy hours back at the Lido, when Archie came too, strolling by the water's edge, talking quietly of the future, and I had a radio-controlled boat which Archie had bought me, and we sailed it in the shallows. I loved that boat. I called it *Moonshadow.* Rather pretentious, I suppose, but I liked the name.

So you can see that, when I first went in to greet Sally after the baby had come, it was more than a surge of parental awareness that threatened to overwhelm me. After a few minutes, Archie had to go off to find a toilet, leaving me alone on a metal chair next to the bed. Sally was sitting propped up against three pillows. I kissed her, for the second time, and peered dutifully at the baby in its capsule alongside her. There were pink blotches on the baby's head and one tiny fist was curled by its nose. Some smears of blood showed on the blanket. It looked as if my son had been in a fight. I didn't think he looked like me at all. He could have belonged to anybody. I speculated privately that the hospital probably kept a supply of babies to be handed out to new mothers, who were simply told to push before being anaesthetised and subsequently presented with something suitable from the stock room.

Archie grinned, shaking his head, when I suggested this possibility. "Ah, and what would they do with the mother's own baby – the one she's delivered?"

"Go into stock, I suppose."

"Hmm. I think you'll find there are a number of practical flaws in your proposition."

This did not surprise me, for my life seemed full of practical flaws. I had made my friend's wife pregnant. I was a father with no means of supporting my child. Even to see him, I faced an endless round of excuses and subterfuge. And my parents remained blissfully ignorant of my precarious status. They did not know their own child. Moreover, *they did not know* that they did not know him.

When Sally leaned forward and asked me to plump up her pillows, two buttons on the front of her nightdress slipped open, revealing the full, pale melon of her right breast, with its taut red nipple distended. How I longed to slide my hand under the thin cotton and hold her there, if only for a fleeting moment. But Sally was in a public ward, and several of the nurses knew that she was married to Archie, who had introduced me as his nephew. There was no way I could submit to my desire and risk either discovery or Sally's indignant rejection of my advances. This, I reflected ruefully, was neither the time nor the place.

I mentioned an exceptional occasion, an all-too-brief oasis of bemused delight in the barren wilderness into which I had unknowingly, if inevitably, strayed once Sally and Archie had agreed to behave as a married couple once more. The word *delight* I use with caution. At the time, the incident pleased and even excited me, reminding me as it did of the days when Sally would tease me in what seemed mere harmless games, matters of no serious consequence. Later, I came to realise, or to suspect, that this was somehow a different kind of indulgence, something tainted with a pernicious aura of – impropriety? – that worried at my conscience.

How far Sally was into her pregnancy at the time, I cannot now remember, but I think it must have been about three months. There was, as I recall, an undecorated Christmas tree leaning against the fence by the back door, its needles rimed with frost. This was early on Sunday morning.

"Come round for coffee. We can play *Monopoly*, you like that. I'll get Sally to do early lunch."

Archie's invitation sounded innocuous enough, and vaguely attractive. Dad had said I could stay overnight at Gran's, so long as I was home in time to finish my school essay, which I had started on Friday night.

The back door was still locked, which surprised me, and there was no light in the kitchen. I tapped on the glass and waited for what seemed a long time. Then the light flicked on and Archie appeared, wearing a blue dressing gown over his vest, bare legs showing beneath. He unlocked the door, drew back the top bolt and let me in.

"Sorry, Neil. We slept in."

I hesitated in the doorway. "I can come back later."

"No, no, no, come in. It's fine. I'll make some tea."

"Where's Sally?"

He pointed at the ceiling, yawning. "You can go up. I'll not be long."

I trudged slowly up the stairs. I saw a half-open door and went in. Sally was lying on her back with the blankets up to her midriff and her arms stretched out on the counterpane. I could see the lightly-tanned tops of her breasts and the pale valley of her cleavage. Almost instantly, I began to get that funny feeling again.

She smiled at me, raising one hand. "Hello, Neil. You're nice and early."

"Sorry. I thought you'd be up."

"Don't go being sorry, Neil. I've told you before about that." She patted the bed beside her. "Come and sit down."

I perched awkwardly on the edge of the bed. Sally looked down at my legs and started laughing.

"What's the matter?" I asked, peevishly.

"You've still got your bicycle clips on," she pointed out.

I yanked the clips off and put them in my pocket.

"That's better." She touched my hand. "Aren't you going to kiss me?"

I could hear Archie clattering cups downstairs. Rupert came and stood by the open door, mouth opening and closing in a silent greeting. I leaned over to plant a kiss on Sally's cheek, but she intercepted my mouth and fastened her lips fiercely around mine, sucking the breath out of me. When I drew back to breathe, she grabbed my hair and pulled me back on to her, working her whole mouth over my chin and lips, thrusting her tongue behind my teeth. I hung against her, smelling her perfume, tasting the wet stuff sliding out of her. It felt like being swallowed by an animal, but a friendly animal that liked me and would never do anything bad, and I held my breath, liking it too much to want it to stop.

Archie's tread thudded softly on the stairs. Sally let me go, her eyes blinking rapidly, chest heaving. Her breasts looked wonderful. I wanted to kiss her everywhere, all the places she had, and not finish.

Archie, carrying a loaded tray, kicked the door open wide. "I expect you're gasping for a cup of tea after your bike ride."

My stiffening penis confirmed to me that tea was the last pleasure on my mind. I dared to hope that Archie might put down the tray and go, but I saw that he had brought three cups. He put two on the bedside table next to Sally and took the tray round to the other side of the bed. Uttering only small sighs and thin, wet intakes of breath, we sipped our drinks without speaking, while Rupert sat washing his face in the doorway.

I noticed, when I put my cup down, my hand was shaking. Sally looked into my eyes and smiled. She mouthed something silently with her lips, but I couldn't make out the words, so I just smiled back and touched her arm.

Archie was taking off his dressing gown. There were gingery hairs on the back of his shoulders where the vest straps exposed the flesh. He had on white, floppy underpants, the sort my father wore. "I'm for a wee while longer," he said, and he pulled back the covers and slid into bed.

Sally reached out and tickled my fingers. "It's a cold morning," she said. "You should keep warm. Come and join us."

"How do you mean?" I asked, nervously.

"You can climb over me. Take your clothes off first."

"Take my clothes off?"

"Neil, people don't get into bed with all their clothes on."

With trembling fingers, I undressed, put my socks in my shoes under the dressing table and laid the rest of my clothes on a chair by the window. I decided to keep my pants on, though in view of what appeared to be imminent, this seemed a faintly ridiculous modesty.

Sally flung aside the bedclothes so that I could roll over her to the middle of the bed. Archie was lying on his side, facing us, watching us. Sally's nightdress had ridden up, revealing her full, pale thighs and dimpled knees. A tuft of grey-blonde hair protruded from the folds of cream cotton covering her rounded belly.

"Soon have you nice and warm," Archie said, pulling the blankets back over us. "Three bugs in a rug."

I lay on my back, listening to the beating of my heart. The room seemed to swim around me, and a sour paste had risen into my mouth.

I could feel Archie's eyes on me. "Relax, Neil," he said, "we aren't going to hurt you."

"This is weird," I heard myself say.

"Look at me, Neil," Sally said, and I turned to face her. "That's better. There's nothing wrong, Neil, nothing at all. After all, if we're all friends together, what could be more natural?"

"I – I don't know."

She shook me gently, her hands on my shoulders. "What do you mean, you don't know? We are friends, aren't we?"

"Course we are. You know we are."

"Well then." With the edge of one finger, she stroked my cheek, the lightest caress. "At least we can have a cuddle, eh?"

I felt Archie moving up closer behind me, until he was resting against my back. At the same time, Sally edged towards me and hugged me more tightly to her, making room for Archie to press forward a little further, until I was sandwiched firmly between the pair of them. Sally raised her left leg and encircled me, and her warm hand reached for me in the dark burrows of the bedclothes, making me ache with my swift hardness. Then the room was spinning again, slowly rotating like a ferris wheel, and I was trapped on it, riding the big wheel, and Sally was urging me forward, reaching over me, reaching out for Archie, calling a name, but not my name, Archie's name, and she was drawing him in, hugging him, loving him, squeezing his fur-flecked shoulders, all the while crushing me harder, forcing me inside her until it felt like a solid bone there, and I caught the heat of Archie breathing on my neck as Sally lunged at him, trying to bite him, panting crazily, heaving, thrusting, calling out that she loved him, wanted him, and grabbing for his rough arms and holding on there, not looking at me at all any more, but working me up inside her, deeper and deeper, raking up sparks down in the dark, until I couldn't hold it any longer, didn't care any more, and I felt it all come drilling out of me, hot as blood-fire.

You see, all I ever wanted was to be able to love them unconditionally, and to have that affection returned. I could never understand why it should have to be complicated or compromised. The trouble was, of course, that it was a situation where I was never in control. I suppose I was a pawn in an emotional game, the complexity of which, through sheer lack of experience, I was quite unable to unravel. It was as though, from time to time, Sally and Archie went to the cupboard to take out toys, for themselves or for their baby – my son – and I was one of them. I was one of those toys.

"We can go in once more if you want," Archie said, "then I think we should let Sally rest. She's very tired."

"I know."

We went and sat with her for a few minutes more, Archie on one side of the bed and me on the other, each of us holding one of her hands. They had taken the baby away for routine examination. One of the nurses smiled at Archie kindly and assured him that, really, although his son was quite small, there was nothing wrong with him and no-one should worry.

My only concern was that they had put my child – I kept silently repeating those words to myself, over and over...*my child, my child, my child* – somewhere else in the hospital, out of sight, introducing the risk that a different one might later be returned to us, not maliciously, but by simple error. It seemed to me impossible that this mischance could be entirely eliminated, and the more I thought about it, the greater the likelihood became, until it assumed proportions tantamount to inevitability. Babies, I reasoned, by now in a state bordering on panic, were not readily recognisable. They were as indistinguishable as Chinamen. By one small, careless mistake, all hope of identification could be lost for ever.

A nurse approached and, glancing between Archie and myself, enquired if we would care for tea. I noticed that she didn't ask Sally. The nurse was brunette and pretty, her hair pinned back in a tight ponytail. I tried to read the name-badge clipped to her chest – it said Jane...and then a foreign-looking surname I couldn't decipher – but I didn't like to persevere in the attempt in case she thought I was staring at her breasts.

"We're going in a minute," Archie told her, and she nodded and left us.

A woman in an adjacent bed groaned loudly and wailed, "Nurse!" Curtains on rails around the bed were hurriedly drawn together, and a doctor wearing a crumpled white coat ducked in to investigate. I supposed the woman was having another baby.

Archie looked up at the clock on the wall. Standing, he leaned over and kissed Sally on the forehead. "You get some sleep now," he said, and she smiled and turned her head slightly, finding his lips, working them softly, insistently with her mouth partly open. I waited for them to finish, hoping she would kiss me the same way, with some warmth and wetness, but when my turn came, she just pecked me on the cheek and patted my hand. I tried not to feel jealous, told myself it really wasn't important, but all the way down the corridor afterwards I worried about it and even wondered if she would ever kiss me properly again or let me touch her like before and respond so that I got that funny feeling again, that magical feeling I couldn't describe or make happen in any other way, not even when I looked at one of Peter Jessops' magazines and rubbed myself.

"Very quiet," Archie said, as we walked towards the main doors.

"Perhaps it's the end of visiting."

"No, I mean you're very quiet."

"Can I come back with you – to the house?"

"I don't know. What about your gran?"

"What about her?"

"She'll be expecting you back."

"I told her where I was going."

"Aye. Sally said she telephoned Mrs Blaney from the hospital. Told her about the baby – that she'd had it, I mean."

"She didn't say anything about – you know?" I asked, in some alarm.

"No, of course not," he assured me, laughing. "Don't worry, you're still her wee boy."

"I don't want to be a wee boy," I said, tersely.

"Ah right. I remember now."

We caught the bus outside the hospital gates. I jumped up and sat on the long sideways-facing seat by the doorway, Archie next to me. I always liked this seat. If girls came and sat opposite, you could sometimes see up their knickers.

"I'm going to take you back to your gran's," Archie said, fumbling for his money.

"I don't mind," I said, carelessly.

"I won't come in. I'll leave you to tell her about Sally."

I took a deep breath. "Archie, I don't know if I can do this."

"Eh? Do what?"

"The baby thing. I won't be any good at it."

He sighed and sucked his teeth. "Oh, come on, Neil! Haven't we been through all this?"

"I know, but – "

"What's there for you to do? Help us think of a name. Keep your mouth shut. Smile at all the right times." He handed two fares to the conductor and took the tickets. "The rest of the problem's ours."

We carried on without speaking. I could hear the big double tyres whining on the tarmac, the pitch of the note rising and falling as the bus braked and accelerated. Soon the whine became an invasive drone, a relentless irritant that seemed to be boring into my skull.

Try as I might, I could not see how Archie's simplistic

assessment of the situation was anything less than alarmingly fanciful. A smile here, a whistle there, pat the baby on the head before waltzing off into the sunlight. How could this be? Did he really believe what he had told me, or was he simply trying to calm my nerves? However earnestly he might outwardly regard my future, there lingered the suspicion that, for his own peace of mind, he relied upon what he perceived as my naivete.

Without knowing exactly why, I felt ill-at-ease as I entered Gran's kitchen. I heard her moving around in the next room, where I found her laying the table, a task she did not interrupt when I walked in behind her.

"So how's the baby?" she enquired, speaking to the tablecloth.

"I think it's all right. Just a bit small."

"That's because it's early."

"I know."

"What do you want for your tea?"

I noticed she hadn't asked about Sally. This neglect hurt me a little, for it seemed like a kind of snub. I stood in the doorway, trying to decide whether I was simply misinterpreting an oversight, or if her reticence was deliberate.

"I don't mind. Some toast, perhaps."

She sighed, turning to face me. "Toast?" She shook her head. "He's been out for hours, and all he wants is toast. What's the matter with you?"

"Nothing."

"Have they thought of a name for it?"

"What?"

"The baby," she said, rolling her eyes. "Has it got a name?"

"Not yet. I'm go – " I bit my tongue, just in time, before I blurted out about my choosing a second name.

"You're what?"

"No, it doesn't matter. I'll go up and wash my hands."

"There's some nice ham. From the Co-Op. We'll have it with salad and bread and butter. I'll cut the fat off."

"I don't want beetroot, Gran; it makes it look like my gums are bleeding."

"Right. You can do your hands in the kitchen."

While I rinsed my hands at the big sink, Gran rummaged in the pantry. I felt a fart coming on, and I tried to slip it quietly, only I lost control of the muscles at the last second, and it came ripping out with a parping noise not unlike the horn on Noddy's car.

There was nothing amiss with Gran's hearing. "You can stop that nonsense right now. Go up to the bathroom if you want to do that sort of thing. There's food about."

"Sorry, Gran."

"You will be." A disembodied arm came out of the gloom. "Here, take this loaf and get a knife and put it on the table. Come back for the butter."

They said hospital food was horrible. I wondered if Sally would have something tasty for tea. She worked there, for goodness' sake. And what about the baby? I knew he couldn't have anything solid, because he had no teeth. Why did babies come with pretty well everything except teeth, and the teeth came later? It seemed a quite unnecessary complication, rather like if you bought a car and had to go back for the wheels. Probably Sally was going to feed the baby herself. I would like to see that, watch her unbuttoning her blouse and lifting out one heavy breast and sliding the engorged nipple lovingly into my son's mouth for him to suck. That would be wonderful. The more I thought about it, the stiffer I became.

Gran was calling me. "Neil, are you coming back?"

"All right."

She had laid out the rest of our tea on the kitchen table. There was a wooden tray for me to carry it on. The kettle was singing on the hob. Everything was comfortable.

"Archie gone home?" she asked, closing the pantry door.

"Yes. He said he had things to do."

"Got to make it all ready for the baby."

"Yes, and for Sally." Then I waited for a reaction.

"It's a boy, isn't it?"

"Yes."

"Ah well. You take what you're given." She pointed to the table. "Help me bring this through."

Gran and I seldom talked much during meals, but today I

would contrive an exception, for there were matters I wanted to clarify. Her stilted friendship with the woman whom she had always scrupulously referred to as 'Nurse' was a subject I had never heard discussed, something kept close to her chest. Inevitably, this reticence tended to invest the relationship with an air of mystery, and I knew that when adults nurtured these attitudes over many years, the truth would not be dislodged by a casual or oblique enquiry. This was a time for the fearless grasping of nettles.

I had missed my lunch to go to the hospital and had eaten hardly anything all day. Now I tucked into the sweet, crumbly ham, the tight, crackly florets of chilled lettuce, the neatly-cleaved tomatoes spilling their seeds in a golden bracelet on to fluffy hunks of fresh-baked bread, glossy with thick slicks of butter. Out of Gran's pantry came a lifetime of small miracles.

If I chose a deflection, Gran might not notice where the conversation was heading, and so I decided to ask her about Archie. With any luck, I would not have to mention Sally at all. She would sneak into the picture unobserved, through the back door of our awareness, to hover as a ghost in the shadows. Or so I hoped.

Gran told me off, of course, for speaking with my mouth full. I had to stop, chew my bread to a creamy paste, swallow hard, lick the crumbs from lips and begin again. At *Arcadia*, things always had to be done right.

"I – er – was wondering about Archie," I said, peering at my plate.

Gran stared at me, knife and fork upright in her hands. "What about him?"

"I mean, you know, now he's gone."

"Gone," she repeated, flatly, as if she had never heard the word before. "What, to the house?"

"Yes."

"So what are you wondering about?"

"I don't know. I was just thinking."

"Just thinking. You've interrupted my tea to tell me you're thinking?"

"No. Well, not only that. I sort of..."

"Spit it out, boy!"

"Do you – would you ever get another lodger, Gran?"

"Lord, I don't know. Can't say I've given it much thought."

This struck me as unlikely. If Gran had sought a lodger for economic reasons, surely she would need a replacement on his departure. The logic seemed unarguable. Here was a grown-up complicating matters again.

"Gran, do you remember, last year, when you said you wanted to put an advert in the paper – that day when you nearly lost your purse?"

"Oh, I don't know, boy. I can't remember that far back. What of it?"

"Well, was that when you advertised for a lodger?"

"I expect so." She tapped the table with the handle of her knife. "Why don't you try eating your meal? All these questions..."

I popped a tomato into my mouth and chewed it until it burst, a soft explosion over my tongue. "So if Archie replied, did he tell you he was – did you know – ?"

"Did I know what?"

"That he was married." I lowered my head. "To Sally," I added, quietly.

Gran stared at me for a moment. "Why do you want to know that?"

I shrugged. "I just do."

She tugged at one earlobe, gazing down at the floor. Something was going through her mind, requiring assessment. Watching her, I picked up a lettuce leaf in my fingers and vacuumed it into my mouth.

"Actually," she said, "Archie never replied to my advertisement. I took him in because I was asked to."

"Oh. Who asked you?"

"If you must know, she did."

"Who did?"

"Nurse did. Sally did."

Resting my elbows on the table, I propped my face on my fists. "So you knew then that – what, that they were married?"

"Of course. I was at the wedding."

I sighed and slumped back in my chair. I had rather lost track of where I was heading. But at least I had manoeuvred the conversation around to Sally.

"Something I don't understand," I said.

"Oh?"

"When we were in the rec that day, you told me her name was Sally Melksham."

"And did she tell you any different?"

"No. She never told me she was Sally McLeish."

All of a sudden, Gran looked tired. "She wouldn't," she said. "She got angry when it all went wrong, said she wanted nothing to do with him. That's when she started calling herself Melksham again."

"Sounds a bit hasty," I said.

"That's Sally for you. There's a spiteful streak in her."

We carried on eating for a while. I took another triangle of bread and butter, but I scooped some of the thick butter off and scraped it on to the side of my plate.

"I suppose it's all a kind of a miracle, when you think about it," Gran said.

"How d'you mean?"

"Well, all she ever wanted was a baby. He couldn't, you know, make it happen, and that's why they broke up. Then they ended up down here, obviously been seeing each other again, and – " – she flung out an exultant hand – "this is the result. Abracadabra! Unto us a child is born." Sniggering, she shook her head. "Doctors! What do they know, eh?"

"Right. Lovely ham, Gran."

"Only the best for my Neil. You're a good boy, going to see the baby like that. There's plenty your age wouldn't bother."

"I like Sally," I said, testing for a response.

"Ah, well just you be careful. She can eat little boys like you for breakfast. Wouldn't think twice about it."

"Gran, I'm not a little boy."

"No, all right. I'm getting old. I forget things."

"Will you be going to see the baby, Gran?"

"Me? Not likely. If I go into a hospital, I might not come out again."

"But when they're home?"

She pulled a hanky out of her sleeve and dabbed at the corners of her mouth. "If I'm asked." With thin, delicate fingers, she prodded the hanky back inside her wrist. "I wish the three of them every happiness," she added, icily.

As I had come down straight from Scotland, I had to use Mrs Cooper's phone to call Dad and ask for a lift home. I could have caught the bus, but I had a large bag full of dirty clothes, and I was tired. The half-term holiday was almost at an end, and on Monday I would be back in the classroom, a schoolboy father.

It was getting dark when the grey Hillman drew up outside. Dad hovered in the hall for a few minutes, making small talk with Gran, but he declined her invitation to wait for a drink. I was glad; I just wanted to go home and sleep.

We went grinding away in the wrong gear, the windscreen misting up. I had my bag on my lap.

"So how was it?" my father enquired.

"What, Scotland?"

"Where else?"

"It was super. We did loads of things. It was sunny and we went fishing and the day we arrived I think I saw an eagle."

"Ah. It was good of Archie to take you."

"Yes. Of course we weren't there very long."

"Why was that?" He started groping under the dashboard, a pained expression on his face.

"Watch where you're going, Dad. What are you looking for?"

"Cloth to wipe the screen." Then he reached up above the mirror and switched on the interior light. "Found it. Here, get rid of this mist for me."

I stretched across and rubbed at the fogged glass, creating an interlinked series of greasy swirls.

"That'll do, you're making it worse."

"Perhaps we should stop."

"What for? I want to get home."

"I can put the demister on."

"It doesn't work. Stop jiggling about. How's Gran?"

"I think she's all right. I haven't seen much of her today." I cleared my throat. "I went to the hospital with Archie."

He shot a quick glance at me. "The hospital? What's the matter with him?"

"Nothing. We went to see Nurse."

"At work?"

"No. She's had a baby."

Dad was peering up the road, tilting his head around the scuffs on the screen. "A baby, you say? I didn't know she was married."

"Yes." After some thought, I decided not to tell him she was Archie's wife. That could wait for another day. "She had a little boy."

"Oh, that's nice. Was the father there?"

"Yes. I mean, no. He's – I think he's coming tomorrow."

By now it was completely dark, and the multi-coloured glare from bright shop windows whooshed past me, an incendiary rocket trail instantly consumed by the night. Dad had left the roof light on, and as I gazed through the side window, I saw my own pale reflection etched on the glass, a spectral *alter ego* riding beside me. My companion's eyes were cold and nervous, disbelieving, accusing. I lifted a hand to shield my face. Then I reached up and flicked off the light.

"Thanks. No wonder I couldn't see properly."

"Dad?"

"Eh?"

"Does a baby always look like its father when it grows up?"

I heard that preliminary sniff again. "Well, they say babies have their fathers' noses or ears, or their mothers' hair or chins. You know how it is. Why do you ask?"

"No reason. I just wondered."

"You've heard these old biddies cooing into prams. 'Ooh, he's got his father's eyes!' All that kind of thing."

"Yes. But it doesn't necessarily happen?"

"It's to do with biological inheritance. The natural order."

"Did people used to say that about me?"

"What?"

"That I looked like you."

"Oh, I don't remember." He took one hand off the wheel and

slapped me playfully on the thigh. "If you ask me, it's all a load of codswallop."

He laughed, and I laughed along with him, until the tears brimmed in my eyes. I searched out his face in the dark, loving him.

Chapter XV

Noah

Gran eyed me reproachfully. "You want to what?"

"Go and see Sally and Archie. After lunch." I hesitated. "I didn't think you'd mind."

"Hmmh. I thought you came here to see me."

"I did. I do."

"Doesn't sound like it. I don't know," she sighed, "your granddad's gone, and I won't be long after."

Her response, although not entirely unpredictable, presented me with a dilemma, a crisis of conscience. It forced me to make a spontaneous decision: whether to yield to Gran's somewhat oblique emotional blackmail and postpone my visit; or to harden my heart and be resolute in the courage of my convictions, for my son had a right to see his father.

Whether it was mere curiosity that impelled me, was another matter. I think I wanted to find out what would happen to me when I had time to be with him, when I held him and gazed upon his tiny body. I had never held a baby before, anyone's baby, let alone one for whom I was – responsible. *Responsible.* The very word struck a dull, aching fear deep inside me. No, I was not deceived or encouraged by my friends' protestations, their cheerful insistence that the arrival of this child in all our lives would not cast more than a ripple upon the calm surface of my existence. That simply did not seem a reasonable submission. More than anything else, I anticipated my first days with my son as a way of finding out about myself, almost as if I could stand aside from those familiar parts of me that I knew intimately, and watch while another entity, dressed in my clothes and wearing a mask that resembled my face, went about the unfathomable business of fatherhood, unassailed by anxiety or doubt. I would watch him and learn my craft from him, and I would grow with my task until my emboldened stature filled every room of my life.

"I won't be gone long, Gran. An hour or two, that's all."

She sat down at the kitchen table, gently massaging the side of her head with her fingers. "Why this fascination with babies all of a sudden?"

"Not babies. Just this baby."

"So this is a special baby?"

I leaned against the door-frame and covered my eyes with my hands until red amoebae swam before my vision. "If you don't want me to go..."

"Did I say that? Have I told you not to go?"

It just happened without warning. There was no way I could prevent or control it. I suddenly burst into tears. Half-blind, I heard Gran's chair scrape the floor, felt her hand grip my arm, drawing me towards her. "Sit down, boy," she said.

I sat opposite her, cupping my face in my hands, my elbows propped on the table. My whole body was shuddering. After a while I managed to stop crying, but I still didn't want to uncover my eyes. I wanted to hide in the dark, where no-one could get me. The tears were running down on to my wrists, dampening my shirt-cuffs.

"Now then," Gran murmured, as I finally peeped at her between my fingers.

"Sorry, Gran," I whispered.

She was staring at me intently, not blinking. There was something about that penetrating scrutiny, a chilling reminder of the day when I had pretended to lose and find her purse. It was a look that made me fearful of breathing.

Gran was clasping her hands together on the table in front of her, thin white fingers interlocked, as if in prayer. "Before you even think of going anywhere, Neil," she said, "I want you to talk to me. I want you to tell me why you're upset. And I want you to tell me about the baby."

"The baby? I didn't think you were that interested."

"On the contrary, I am very interested."

I rolled my head slowly from side to side, making a sour face. "It's all right. It's a bit little. I don't think they've thought of a name for it yet. I expect they want to be home for a wh – "

"Neil, will you stop this, please?"

"What?"

"This prevaricating. You're insulting me – all this prattle."

"But you asked me."

"Yes, and I expect you to be truthful."

"So – what if I don't know anything?" I protested, frowning. "What is it you want me to say?"

"I'll tell you what I want, Neil." Gran folded her arms and leaned heavily on the table. "I want you to look me in the eye and explain to me how Archie McLeish, who is as impotent as a chocolate soldier, has suddenly managed to father a child." She shook her head as though the notion was as distasteful as it was implausible. "When you came back from the hospital, I talked about miracles – remember?"

"I think so, Gran."

"Right you are. Well, let there be no doubt about it, Neil; I don't believe in miracles, never have. You know something? When it all went wrong up in Scotland, and Sally walked back in my house with a long face and a tale of woe, we spent hours – d'you hear me? – *hours*, sitting in that room" – she jabbed her finger at the wall behind me – "while she told me every last detail of the tests and reports and examinations Archie had at the doctor's and the clinic, chapter and verse, and she made it perfectly plain to me that there was no way under the sun that man was ever going to give her the baby she wanted."

I felt my throat contracting, my mouth turning dry and acidic. "Doctors can be wrong, can't they? They don't know everything."

"No, and they're not magicians, either. They're just human beings like the rest of us."

"And human beings make mistakes. Don't they, Gran?"

With an almost unbearable tenderness, she reached out and gently stroked the back of my hand, her delicate fingertips tracing the bluish corrugations of my veins. "Oh yes, Neil," she said, "they certainly do; and very often they can be forgiven, especially when they're young and not used to the ways of the world."

I shifted uncomfortably in my chair. Gran seemed to notice this moment of unease, and waited for me to be still.

"You're very fond of Sally, aren't you?"

"I like her, yes."

"You seem to see a lot of her. Going round there, going out places."

"I can have friends, can't I?"

"Yes. Yes, you can have friends, but you have to be sure that they're trustworthy. Remember, there's always going to be people who hurt you, so what you have to do is keep on trusting and just be more careful about who you trust next time."

"Are you saying Sally's not to be trusted?"

"I don't know," she said, with a sigh. "There's something – complex going on there."

"That's because she's a grown-up," I said. "They always make everything complicated."

Gran smiled a knowing, slightly sad smile, slowly nodding her head. "Well, that's as may be. You'll be grown up yourself soon. Then you'll start to see things differently."

"I am grown up, Gran. I'm grown up now."

"Are you, Neil?" She touched my hand again. "Does that mean we can talk honestly about serious things?"

"I think so."

"That's good. I've always said you're a good boy, Neil."

"But I'm not a – "

"All right, I know, I know."

She paused and looked out of the window. It was as if she was trying to decide whether to mention something else, something that troubled or confused her. In the brief silence that ensued, I watched her face, the ruminative twitch of the muscles beneath her eyes, the way the spring sunshine highlighted the thinning tangle of her poorly-permed hair.

She drew her gaze back to me, her face sympathetic but

grave. "Neil, I'm going to ask you one more time – if there's anything more I should know about this baby."

"The baby's only just come, Gran. I've only seen it for a few minutes."

"Because if there is, if there's something in all this that you think is – private, then you should understand that you can tell me in confidence." For a moment she held both hands over her eyes, then lowered them back to the table. "I'm an old woman, Neil. I'm getting a bit tired. I think I'd rather like to go and join your granddad."

"But Gran, I can't – "

"Neil, listen! It's just that – whatever secrets you share with me now, or tomorrow, will remain exactly that – secrets. And then, when I'm gone, they will come with me, like little keepsakes."

"Yes, Gran."

"So long as you understand that."

I nodded.

"Perhaps you need a little more time," she said, after a silence.

"I don't know."

"So tell me. Have you talked like this with your mother?"

"A bit."

"I see. And what did she say?"

"She didn't believe me," I replied, and then, in an instant, my hand flew to my mouth.

"Hmm. Maybe I would believe you, Neil."

"No. There's nothing to believe. I mean, I got confused."

"Yes, that happens to us all from time to time. I shall say nothing to her, of course." She glanced up at the clock on the wall. "You might want to talk some more when you come back."

"When I come back?"

"Yes. You'd best be off now. Give Sally my love. And Neil –"

"Yes, Gran?"

"Don't be afraid. Be proud."

"Proud? Of what?" I asked her.

Gran offered no reply, but sat staring at me, her face oddly expressionless. Her eyes followed me as I stood up and went to the door, and not until I found myself in the side alley did I realise that I had been holding my breath.

How I loved my gran that day. I think, more than anything, I loved her measured, knowledgeable serenity, her seemingly infinite capacity to say something useful and reassuring simply by being there. Best of all, I knew that she could only do this because she loved me. Even as I eased my bike away from the wall and began wheeling it towards the gate, there festered in some small part of me the numbness of a nagging doubt, the germ of a suspicion that, loving me as she did, my grandmother deserved a little more than I felt able to give her, for I was driven by selfishness.

I had almost reached the pavement when I suddenly remembered the small teddy bear I had bought on the way over, to give to Sally for the baby. It was a little boy bear, soft and golden, with Black Watch tartan trews and bow tie. I had taken it indoors to remove the wrapping and price label, and then, in the heat of the moment, I had come out without it. Leaning my bike on the fence, I walked quickly back to the kitchen. Gran was still sitting at the table, her glasses upturned beside her, pinching the bridge of her nose between her thumb and forefinger.

"That was a quick visit," she said, peering over her shoulder.

"Forgot something," I muttered, and I went to pick up the toy from the hall table. When I turned back, she was gazing at me out of sad and empty eyes.

"Goodbye then," she said, tonelessly.

"Gran, I – "

"It's all right, Neil. I'm not wrong, am I? And please don't lie to me, I couldn't bear it."

"I haven't told you lies, Gran."

"That's as may be." She smiled briefly, something frail and uncertain. "But if you conceal the truth...well, it's a fine line, eh?"

"Yes."

"Yes, he says. That could mean anything."

"Gran, I have to go."

"To see your little boy? What's the matter, Neil? Don't you trust me?"

"Course I do."

She nodded, as though something important had finally been decided. "Then you've nothing to be afraid of."

"I'm not afraid," I said.

"No, all right. Scared stiff, perhaps. Terrified, bewildered, alone, helpless. It must be like your world's come to an end."

"Gran?" It was all I could do to make the word come out.

But that one small word was more than enough. My grandmother stood up, sending the chair toppling to the floor behind her, and in an instant I found myself folded effortlessly into her sheltering arms, where I hung, shuddering, limp as a rag doll, while my tears flowed. I cried and cried, until the salt-stickiness stung me, and I felt that scouring wetness sealing my face to the lavender-scented, crepe-thin tissue of Gran's cheek, like the sweet ache of a long kiss.

I don't know how long I clung to her. It seemed like a warm, fragrant, delicious eternity. My face buried in the shifting darkness of her neck, I felt that I floated weightless in time and space, mercifully disconnected from reality. It was almost as good as freedom.

"Come on now." She gave me final hug. "We've to get you sorted out, young man."

"Do you think I'm stupid, Gran?"

"What? No, I don't. I think you're vulnerable. I think you're trying to do too much on your own."

"I did try to tell Mum. It was months ago. She never – " I started to cry again.

"I know, I know. I believe you. She's my daughter, remember."

"Am I a really bad person, Gran?"

"Lord, no! You've always been a good boy, Neil. Nothing's changed."

"Oh, Gran! Of course it has!"

"The world changes, Neil. People don't change. People get hurt sometimes. They get left behind. They lose their way and don't know where they are any more. It's like a madness."

She took me upstairs to the bathroom and quietly sponged my

face with a soft flannel and warm water. I remember how comforting her ministrations felt, like a poultice to draw out all the pain and all the badness seething inside me. Anxious as I was to get away, to be with Sally and Archie and the small person I would have to learn to know as my son, I loved the slow, deliberate gentleness of Gran's touch upon my face, the steady, all-pervading sensation of *unburdening* that came from her caress, and so this moment, too, I hungered for.

Then she held me back from her at arms' length. "Tip your head up. That's it; you'll do."

"Now what?" I asked.

"What do you mean, now what?"

"Can – should I go out?"

"Oh yes," she said, with a sigh. "There's someone important you have to see – someone even more helpless than you."

I searched her face for a sign of bitterness or sarcasm, but there was nothing malignant to be seen. I smiled at her and nodded, and couldn't stop loving her.

"You give my love to that little boy," she said. "See he gets a nice name. Then when you come back, if there's time before you have to go, maybe we'll talk some more. What do you think?"

"Thanks, Gran."

Placing her hands on my shoulders, she turned me round to face the open door. "Okay. You take care on that bicycle." She leaned forward and kissed the back of my neck with her dry lips.

I went out through the front door, while Gran waited on the step, watching me. When I reached the gate, I turned and waved, and she smiled thinly, but didn't wave back. I set off along the road, the pedals feeling strangely leaden beneath my feet. The breeze quickly dried my damp face, chilling me until my eyes watered. The journey passed in a subconscious blur, as I reflected upon all that Gran had said to me and marvelled, with a kind of thrilling fear, at the quiet power of her intuition. My grandmother was, I suppose, inconspicuously remarkable. Then, as I turned into the avenue that led to the house, I thought about the nameless child I was shortly to see, and an idea came to me.

Archie answered the door. He was wearing that blue dressing gown again, the white sticks of his bare legs protruding beneath, which struck me as odd so late in the morning. I wondered if he and Sally had been attempting sex, but then I told myself that it would be too soon after the birth. A lady who had delivered a baby just days ago would still be red and sore; there would be bits hanging out, and stitches, and the discouraging possibility of plastic pants with elasticated legs.

He led me into the lounge. Sally, I was relieved to see, was fully dressed, relaxing on the settee in red trousers and a loose white roll-neck sweater that casually disguised the maternal swell of her breasts. On the coffee table in front of her, like some preposterous ornament, was a pale blue quilted carrycot, and nestling inside it lay my tiny son.

"Hello, Neil. Come to see your little boy?" She turned, glanced up at me, then reached protectively for the side of the cot.

I sat down beside her. "I brought this."

"What is it?"

I put the package in her lap, wishing I could leave my hand there. "You can open it. It's for – "

"I know," she said, smiling, "it's difficult when he hasn't a name." She tore off the paper and held the bear up for inspection. "He's cute. Thank you. His first teddy. Look, Archie!"

Archie nodded approvingly. "Aye, very good."

"Do you want to make us some tea?" Sally asked him.

He disappeared towards the kitchen.

I gazed at the baby, a mildly pungent disturbance under a candlewick blanket.

Sally leaned over and kissed me on the cheek. "You can hold him if you like."

"In a minute."

"We were talking, before you arrived, about – "

She stopped when she felt me touch her. My right arm seemed to have developed a mind of its own, and the next I knew, my hand was encircling her left breast, slowly caressing her through the soft fabric of her sweater.

The clatter of cups sounded from the kitchen, and Sally glanced across to the doorway. "I don't think this is the time, Neil. Not now."

I let go. "When is the time?"

"When I say," she said, quietly, not looking at me.

"So there will be a time?"

"We've got to work things out, Neil."

"What things?"

"Lots of things, Neil."

"What things?"

"Please don't be irritating, Neil," she rebuked me, with a sigh.

I waited silently until Archie returned with the tea. In a separate saucer there were arrowroot biscuits and some chocolate rolls in gold foil. I wasn't hungry.

Sally began again. "As I was saying..."

"I interrupted you," I said.

"Quite. Well, Archie and I were discussing names." She nodded at the carrycot. "For this little man."

"I thought of a name on the way over. You did say I could choose?"

"A second name, yes," she emphasized.

"I remember." I cleared my throat. "I'd like him to be called Pluto."

Archie coughed quietly.

"Pluto," she repeated, levelly. "Pluto. You mean" – she turned and stared at me – "like a crazy dog?"

"No," I countered, a defensive whine creeping into my voice, "I mean like the planet. Pluto."

Sally pulled the cot towards her and peeped in at the sleeping baby, almost as if she might consult him in the matter. Nobody spoke. Archie perched awkwardly on the arm of the settee, looking over her shoulder.

"You said it would be all right," I reminded them.

Sally was re-arranging the blankets around the baby's neck. Her eyes looked glassy, unfocused.

"If that's what the boy wants," Archie said. "Let him be."

Sally finished her fussing and sat back. "Well, anyway. He has to have a name, and Archie and I thought of Noah."

"Noah." I tried the name on my lips and in my mind. "Noah."

Archie stood up, one half-closed hand raised almost to his

chin. "Yes," he said, gravely. "I think that's it. I think that would suit him fine. Noah Pluto McLeish."

"Noah Pluto McLeish," I intoned.

Rolling back her head, Sally blinked thoughtfully at the ceiling. "Noah Pluto McLeish," she repeated.

"Why Noah?" I ventured.

"We like the name," Archie said. "And, for this wee man, it could be appropriate."

"How?"

"He means Noah was a saviour," Sally said. "Because of him, the lines continued. Through his foresight, the world and its creatures gained a chance for the future."

"I thought that was because of Jesus," I said.

Sally eyed me sternly. "You know what I mean, Neil."

So that was it. Instead of arriving as a blessing in his own right, this child would be retained as a travel ticket, assisting Sally and Archie to stations further down the line in their journey towards reconciliation. They hoped he would hold them together, give them a sense of purpose and direction. My son was a bonding agent. He was simply a function. What did that make me – an instrument?

"Why don't you pick him up?"

I stared at her. "He's asleep, isn't he?"

"No, no. He's just resting. Go on, you are his dad."

"Put him in my lap."

As she lifted him out, Noah squirmed in her arms, pumping the air with the tiny pink shells of his fists, while his cornflower-blue eyes blinked indignantly against the light. From his puckered lips issued a series of sibilant squeaks, like the protestations of some small, disturbed animal.

"Now, support his head," Sally told me.

"I know."

"Right. That's good."

He felt very warm, almost hot, like a comforter that had been heated up.

"You're doing fine," Archie said, quietly.

"What if he does a wee?"

"That's only to be expected," Sally confirmed, "but you won't notice; he's firmly packaged."

I cradled my son in my arms as best I could, feeling apprehensive and uncomfortably self-conscious. I even sensed a strong pink flush spreading upwards from my neck as I sat peering down at the trembling bundle nestling between my thighs.

Sally's sharply exhaled breath was almost a yelp of frustration. "For goodness' sake, Neil! Babies are made of flesh and bone; they won't break."

"If I drop him, he might."

"You won't drop him. Try to relax. Hold him a little closer to your body."

"Okay. Like this?"

"That's better. Just sit a bit more upright."

"I'm frightened he might wriggle. Something might happen."

"Neil, trust me, the baby will not explode."

"Better get used to this," Archie advised.

I wasn't sure if he meant holding the baby or Sally's instructions in the craft. A slow smile crept over my face, a mask for my confusion. I pretended not to notice the tears in my eyes, as I looked down and quietly made my peace with this child.

"I never knew babies came with hair," I said. A swirling tuft of pale blond hair sprouted from the middle of that tiny skull, fine as a curl of mist.

"Just like a wee onion," Archie said.

Without knowing quite why, or even knowing that I was going to do it, I lifted Noah carefully to the side of my face and bumped his soft, hot little cheek lightly against mine.

"That's right," Archie said.

"That's nice," Sally said.

Rising like an opening flower in my head was the smell of talcum powder mixed with buttermilk, something pure and untainted that the world had not touched.

Sally's hand was squeezing my shoulder. "You all right?" she asked.

One of my tears dropped on to Noah's cheek and I wiped it

away with my fingers, leaving a thin red mark like a brush-stroke.

"Don't you worry, Neil," Archie said, "you'll be just fine."

Rivulets of salt soured my lips. I saw my child's face as through frosted glass. In my arms I held something perfect, something amazing. It was too powerful to be imagined or believed.

I heard the clock ticking on the wall. There was nothing else. Just me and my child and a space filled with silence.

Then Noah slowly turned his head and opened his eyes wide. He looked up at me.

And I imagined he smiled.

Chapter XVI

Farewell

I don't remember much about the christening, because of what happened afterwards. It was a cold, damp day, and I remember how chilly and forbidding the church was. My feet went numb halfway through the service, and I wanted to stamp them on the stone floor, only I knew people would disapprove. Gran told me off for stuffing my hands in my pockets, but I simply wanted to keep them warm. There was a curious smell, a mixture of ink and potatoes, and I could hear birds fluttering high up in the rafters. The vicar's voice was a low drone, occasionally rising an octave before falling back again towards the floor, like someone flying a model aeroplane over our heads. The cold made my nose run, and I wiped it with my fingers. The vicar had bushy eyebrows and a red, mottled shaving rash that showed above his collar. I stared at him and wondered if he had ever had sex with somebody nice.

Noah started to cry when the man put water on his forehead. Archie laughed, but I was too cold to laugh, or even smile. I wasn't listening to the words, they could have been a foreign language; I was so uncomfortable. My willy had shrivelled up, and it felt like an icicle against my leg.

Somebody farted, but it wasn't me. Everyone must have heard it. I pursed my lips tightly together to stifle my amusement. That was the best bit of the service. I expect I'll always remember that moment. I looked at Gran, but her face was still and serious. Perhaps I would mention it to her later, and see if she smiled. I hoped whoever it was didn't do another one, because then I knew I would burst out laughing and be sent outside in disgrace.

It felt warmer in the churchyard than inside the church. Gran had hold of my hand, and I didn't want to pull away, though I would have liked to go up to Sally and Archie and touch little Noah. I searched them out and turned towards them, but then I felt Gran's grip tighten, and when I looked up at her, I saw how pale she was, almost swaying on her feet, with her eyes half closed. I asked her if she was all right, and she whispered something, just a few words I couldn't hear because of the breeze blowing in the trees.

A man I didn't know gave us a lift back to Gran's in his car. He had an Austin A30, a green one, like a jellybean. The interior smelled of tobacco. Sally was making tea and sandwiches at her house, but I thought I should stay with Gran. Suddenly she looked incredibly frail and she hardly spoke while we were in the car. She thanked the man as we got out, and called him Mr Corbishley.

We stood in the kitchen, warming up, and Gran asked me to put the kettle on for some tea. There was a noise outside, and I saw the shed door flapping to and fro in the wind. I said I would go out and lock it shut. At first I couldn't find the padlock, and I had to hunt for it among all the pots and bottles on the shelf, so I suppose it took me a few minutes to get the door secured.

When I came back in, the kettle was hissing on the hob but there was no other sound, and Gran had disappeared. I went straight into the living room, expecting to find her having a rest on the settee, but there was no-one there. Coming out, as I faced into the hall, I saw her.

The blood was all over the front of her face. She was lying at the foot of the stairs, her feet and ankles still on the two bottom steps, and her nose was pressed into a spreading pool of red oil on the wooden floor. I remember being surprised at how much blood had spilled out of her in so short a time, and how sticky it looked, dark and viscous. Of course, I knew I shouldn't move her, but she looked so uncomfortable, sprawled face-down like that, and I wanted to turn her nose away from the floor so she could breathe. Gran had always been slim and small-boned, and it took me hardly any time to ease her slightly to one side, so that most of her weight was on her hip. There was a hole in one of her stockings, her bare knee showing through, and something rough dug into my wrist – a glass bead from the necklace she so often wore. The other beads glinted on the stairs like hailstones.

I ran up to my room, pulled the blanket and a pillow off the bed and brought them down to the hall, where I covered my gran with the blanket and managed to squeeze the pillow under her head. Then I dashed back through the kitchen door and, shouting, waved my crimson hands at Mrs Cooper.

The ambulance came quite quickly. Behind it, a black Riley police car pulled up, its chirruping bell bringing the neighbours to their front gardens. I let the ambulance men in through the front door. One of them knelt beside Gran, opening his bag, while the other stood staring at me. "Best go wash your hands, son."

"Just a minute." His partner looked up at me. "What's your grandma's name?"

"Mrs Blaney. Jean."

"Thanks."

I stood at the kitchen sink, watching Gran's blood rush away in a pink whirlpool. Behind me, I heard the two men calling to her, but I knew she wasn't going to reply. My hands were shaking now, and my forehead felt icy-cold. I think I was too shocked to be frightened.

A policeman appeared in the doorway, turning his cap in his hands. "Are you Neil Robertson?"

I nodded.

"Are your mum and dad about, Neil?"

"They're at home. It's miles away."

"I see." He glanced into the hall. "Your grandma's going to hospital. We need to tell someone."

I gave him the telephone number, and he returned to his car, leaving his cap on the table. I stared at the upturned hat, grimacing at the line of smudged grease around the inner band.

None of this seemed real. A cold draught from the open front door wafted around me, its friendless chill intensified by the silence in the house. All I could hear was the quiet breathing and shuffling of the ambulance men as they crouched at Gran's side. They weren't trying to talk to her any more, and I knew that was a bad sign. The house was not friendly to me now; it had become a dark place.

It was the first time I had ever ridden in a police car. Some passers-by gawped at me as we drove up the road, perhaps thinking that I was under arrest for some act of juvenile hooliganism. After a few minutes I began to feel secure and cared for, and thus vaguely important, as though nothing bad could happen to me while I stayed in the car. As we neared the hospital, my mood changed, and the aching realisation dawned on me that, for all her reserves of inner strength and composure, my grandmother remained a small, lonely, vulnerable person who had already questioned her own capacity for endurance. My heart sank as I came to understand her gentle lamentations as a wistful prophecy.

She was still in Casualty when I arrived. The staff nurse said I could see her as soon as she was stabilised and transferred to a ward. The nurse looked stressed and pretty. Her brown hair hung through her cap in a ponytail. On her badge it said her name, Jennifer Peltzer. She smiled at me and – oh so briefly – touched my arm, and in that second I thought I loved her just a little and then tried to forget her.

They put Gran in a corner bed, tucked away at the end of the ward, with blue screens around her. Mum had arrived by taxi, and we waited in the doorway, looking down the expanse of polished floor, while she talked to the doctor. He looked too young to be a doctor, and he had dandruff in his eyebrows. I couldn't read his name, because his badge had slipped upside-down.

Mum kept glancing from the doctor to the distant bed and back again, saying "Mmm, mmm," over and over, interjecting an 'mmm' between each of the man's remarks, which made her sound both bored and impatient.

Once an orderly had provided us with two of the most uncomfortable chairs she could find, we sat inside the screens, facing Gran from opposite sides of the bed. I couldn't get over how small and fragile she appeared, as if a child had chanced upon an empty bed and thoughtfully slid her favourite china doll, a knotted hanky round its head, under the blankets to keep warm. My gran was miniaturised by trauma, white-faced and inexplicably tiny.

I watched my mother's eyes, seeing no fear there, no pain.

"Mum, will Gran die?" I whispered.

"How should I know? Don't ask questions like that."

"What did the doctor say?"

"Just medical things."

"I don't want Gran to die," I said, softly.

"She's an old lady, Neil."

I felt tears welling up behind my eyes, and I lowered my head.

Mum's short, sharp sigh was a contemptuous rebuke. "If you're going to start blubbing, you'd better wait in the corridor."

"No, I want to stay here. She might wake up."

"That could be any time. We can't sit here all night."

"People do."

"That's in plays on the television. This is real life now."

I bit my lip. That was the deal, my mother's version of events. My grandmother lay in hospital with a bandaged head and tubes coming out of her, hovering on the brink of death, and her own daughter told me this was real life.

"She wasn't well at the christening," I said, as much to myself as to my mother.

Mum sat there, gnawing the side of her thumb, staring morosely at Gran's chalk-white face.

"Can I have some change, Mum? I want to make a phone call."

"What? Who to?"

"Sally. You know, Nurse. She ought to know about Gran."

"Oh, she won't come over here. She's got the christening tea and all."

"But Gran's her friend."

She sighed, fumbling in her bag. "Here. Take my purse. Don't lose it."

The telephone was in an alcove by the fire exit. Opposite the exit was a little hospital shop. In the shop, peering at the magazines, stood a nurse. I saw black-stockinged legs with a smooth curve in the calves, and a dark ponytail dangling. There was no-one else, just her. Jennifer Peltzer. In the space of a microsecond, an icicle pricked my heart, suspending animation.

My dry cough was all I could manage, but it was enough. She turned her head, ponytail swishing, and darted a delicious double-take in my direction. "Hello. Didn't I see you in Casualty?"

"Yes. I'm Neil Robertson, Mrs Blaney's grandson."

"Oh yes, of course." She smiled. I struggled against cardiac arrest. "Have they made your grandma comfortable, Neil?"

I almost wished she hadn't done that, used my name. I mean, I could hardly return the compliment – I felt in my bones that she would not regard it as a compliment, more as a presumption or even an impertinence – by calling her Jennifer, and to address her as plain Nurse Peltzer would sound formal to the point of stuffiness. So I nodded gloomily at the floor, hoping to mask my disappointment.

"She's unconscious," I said.

"Hmm. That's not necessarily a bad sign, you know. She needs to rest. Her body's shut everything down – sort of to protect it."

"I see. Is she – do you think she'll die?"

She reached back to adjust the clip on her hair. "I really don't know, Neil. But perhaps you ought to be with her, eh?"

"Yes. I'm sorry I interrupted you."

I dialled the number, and Archie answered. I told him what had happened. In the background, I could hear people laughing. There was music playing, a repetitive, percussive beat. I could have been there with them, I thought. And then? Then Gran would have bled to death on the floor, and us all screeching and munching cake, tickling the baby and talking nonsense, making lunatics of ourselves, while Gran lay face-down in the wreckage of her spilled teeth, helplessly dying.

"It's a bit difficult, Neil," Archie said. "I'll tell Sally. We'll try to be there."

Gran was on her own when I returned, asleep with her mouth open, just a black hole where her teeth had been. I touched her cheek. Her skin felt crisply dry, like tissue paper.

"Do you know where my mother went?" I asked a black nurse, shuffling by. She was carrying a cardboard tray with a cloth over it. I supposed it was her tea.

"Toilet," the nurse said, without stopping.

The chair where my mother had sat was still warm, so she could not have been gone long. I sat down and put her purse on the bedside table. Then I gingerly picked up Gran's right hand and held it, firmly but gently, stroking one side with my forefinger. It felt loose and dry, like a small bag of thin twigs.

I leaned against her ear. "Can you hear me, Gran? It's me, Neil."

The faintest pulse flickered under my fingertip. Above the gabble of faceless voices and the clatter of trolleys, I could hear my own heart beating.

"Gran, please, open your eyes for me. Just for me."

The screen moved. Mum stood watching me. "What are you doing?" she asked.

"Nothing. Just talking to Gran."

"She can't hear you. She's out like a light."

"She might – it doesn't matter, I can try."

"Oh well. Do you want a drink?"

"What? No, I just want Gran to wake up."

"Hand me my purse. I need a cup of tea. There's a machine."

I gave her the purse. "Take your time," I said, under my breath.

"What?"

"Nothing."

This, I believed, was a special time, just me and Gran, the rest of the world a vague commotion in the distance. I pulled the chair closer to the bed and gripped her hand tighter. There was a hoarse rattle in her throat, but at least I knew that she was breathing.

I wondered if Sally or Archie would come. Perhaps they didn't even want to. They didn't need Gran any more. Still, if Sally were here, she could tell me what all the tubes and machines were for, what all the strange beeping noises meant. Above Gran's head was a white box with a screen showing coloured lights and bright, wiggly lines, and I was worried that no-one was reading the display. It didn't seem right.

My attention was diverted back to Gran's face when I heard her make a breathless snuffling noise. Her bandaged head jerked backwards in a brief spasm, and her mouth closed, then opened again. I could see her eyelids fluttering.

Bending over, I whispered in her ear, my lips trembling against that small, fleshy shell. "Gran, can you hear me? It's Neil."

A thin groan escaped from her parted lips.

"Gran, squeeze my hand if you can hear me."

I waited, holding my breath, but nothing happened.

"I'm holding your hand, Gran. You don't have to talk."

The black nurse peered round the screen, wrinkled her nose at me and vanished.

"I love you, Gran," I told her, raising my voice to a low murmur.

That was when Gran opened her eyes.

"Gran?"

"Where – where am I?" she asked me, the words scratched up from beyond the back of her throat.

"It's Neil, Gran."

"I know. Where is this?"

"You're in hospital. You had a fall."

"Ah. Silly."

I looked over my shoulder, unsure what to do next. "Look, I ought to get someone. They might – "

"No!"

She unfurled her hand from my grasp and clasped my wrist, squeezing it with amazing strength.

"What is it, Gran? Tell me."

Her head seemed to sink back, almost burying itself in the pillow. "Don't want anyone. Don't want anyone else."

"I could find a nurse."

"Don't want a nurse." Her tongue flicked out to wet her pale lips. "You listen."

"All right. I'm listening."

"Come closer. I'm tired."

I huddled tight against the edge of the bed and lowered my ear to Gran's lips.

"You mind what I said, now. You remember."

She crushed my wrist until I felt the bones would crack. I winced from the pain, but then, an instant later, she gasped, chest pumping, and let out a long, low moan.

"Gran, I'm a bit frightened. I think the doctor should come."

Fighting for breath, she tried to lift her head off the pillow. I saw a red coin of fresh blood imprinted on the side of the bandage. "I want – promise," she choked.

"Promise? You want me to promise?"

"Yes. That baby boy."

"His name is Noah, Gran. Noah Pluto."

"Noah. That's nice." She hesitated, coughing silently for a while, bringing a pink froth of blood to her tongue. "You hear me now."

"Gran?"

"You look after him. You love him. Do it for me."

I was weeping now, making no sound, collecting the tears in my mouth, tasting the warm salt inside my lips. "Gran, please."

"You have to promise."

"I promise, Gran. I'll try to love him."

"With all your heart?"

"With all my heart."

"You're a good boy, Neil. Now kiss me."

I bent down and kissed her softly, once on each cheek.

"I'll keep my word, boy. Your secret goes with me, see."

"Gran, no, you can't just – "

"Oh, come on now, no tears, no fighting. I'm tired. There's better places."

"Will you do one more thing for me, Gran?"

"Ah, if I can."

"Say 'Hello' to Granddad for me. Tell him I love him. Please."

Gran had almost vanished behind a veil of tears. I could feel their thin tracks crusting on my face, could hear the slick secretions bubbling in my nose. I wanted to go and get help, but I was desperate to stay with my gran for as long as she wanted me there, for in those few unforgettable minutes we were the only two people in the world. If I went away, Gran would be all alone, she would have no-one. And then...

"Don't cry, Neil. I'll tell him."

"Why did this have to happen, Gran? Why can't it all be like it was before?"

"But it will be, Neil, it will be. It all comes round again, you see. And I'll see you, and you'll see me, and then..."

"Then what, Gran? What happens then?"

She made no reply.

"Gran? Gran?"

Her hand slipped from my wrist and lay upturned on the blanket, like a small, white, hairless animal curled up in dreamless sleep.

Of course, I was submerged then, bewildered and drowning in an eddying tide, the relentless ebb and flow of wildly gesticulating robots, swerving this way and that, squawking instructions, frantic players in a cacophonous drama, suddenly self-important in their stark uniforms.

Without knowing who or where the exhortation came from, I heard someone shout, "Wait outside, son!" – and I found myself sitting, hunched and confused, on a wooden bench in the corridor, my bowed head clamped in shaking hands. Behind me, people barged in and out through a flapping door, and each time the door opened I heard the braying of urgent voices amid the stutter and whine of electronic instruments.

A hand touched my shoulder, but I didn't look up. The hand lifted, then settled once again, offering a squeeze of recognition. I turned to stare into my mother's eyes.

"Gran's gone, hasn't she?" My voice was hardly audible above the din. "She's died."

"I'm afraid so."

"You went away." I could feel my throat closing around the words, reducing them to a series of squeaks. "Gran died, and you weren't there."

"It can't be helped."

"What – that she died or you'd gone?"

She straightened up, letting her hand drop. "Neil, when bad things happen, you must try not to speak in that silly voice."

"I don't – you don't understand, do you?"

"What?"

"It doesn't matter. Nothing matters any more."

"Oh, now you're being ridiculous."

She turned away from me and went into the ward. The young doctor who had spoken to her when we arrived followed her in. I thought about joining them, but I suspected it would be too much for me. I had seen my grandmother seriously injured, I had seen her on the brink of death and I had seen her die. That was enough. I had no wish to see her dead body. What would be the point of it? We had been together at the end and talked and loved each other. That was all I could want now. It had to be enough. I would sit for a while longer, in case Sally or Archie came, but I would not go back to gaze upon Gran's lifeless body.

As I sat there, slumped back on the hard bench, my legs thrown out in front of me, I was brought to reflect morosely upon the nature of Gran's departure from the world, and I marvelled at her quiet courage. Once she had surfaced from unconsciousness, she knew that, without immediate medical help, she would fade and die; yet, when I tried to call a nurse or doctor, she fiercely insisted that we be left alone together, because she wanted to spend those last few minutes talking to me. She wanted to tell me that I must look after Noah, and to remind me of her promise to take our great secret with her and safeguard it always. Now, in a strange kind of way, the enormous intimacy of that understanding seemed to immortalize her, for although Gran's body had died, it felt as if her spirit would be sustained for ever by the knowledge we had shared, which could never be taken away from us. By confiding in each other in those private moments, we had achieved a humanity transcending death, and found something unique and special that was limitless enough to be called immortality. There was not the slightest doubt in my mind that Gran knew perfectly well that she was dying, but she was rational enough to foresee, also, that if she allowed me to bring strangers with machinery to her bedside, I would be banished from the room and the spell would be irreparably broken. So that was her great sacrifice. Rather than lose me with less than a *goodbye,* she had risked all she had to make a small, eternal peace out of our last few extraordinary moments together. In trying to save me from despair and even disaster, she had not thought to save herself.

I blinked back tears, but it was futile, and I felt my eyelids thickening and sticking. This was no place to cry, too public and too antiseptic, and so I got up and walked to the end of the corridor, where a patch of bright light, bisected by greenery and a low wall, suggested some kind of courtyard. The swing doors smacked my arms as I pushed clumsily into the daylight, lips quivering, eyes streaming. Against a curving, waist-high brick wall was a garden bench with a metal plaque set in the top of the backrest. The engraved words read: 'In Memory of Eliza Moulton. In Sickness and in Health, She Loved this Quiet Place'.

There were well-tended flower-beds inside the wall. I had no idea what the flowers were, but their vivid red petals, nodding in the breeze, and the thick, buttery sweetness of their fragrance, reminded me of the red flowers that grew outside the French windows in Gran's garden. Gran would have loved this place. A tree with shiny reddish leaves overhung the flower-bed opposite, and when the wind blew, the leaves hissed and rustled, sounding almost like music. Yes, I thought, Gran would have loved this place.

A small bird – a chaffinch, I think – settled on a spindly branch, the fluff-ball of its body see-sawing up and down on the springy perch. The little bird fixed me with a quizzical glint in its beady eyes and fluffed up its feathers, telling me it was not afraid.

"I'm sorry," I said, just loudly enough to be heard over the breeze, "I've got nothing to give you. I hadn't expected to be here."

The chaffinch chirped expectantly.

I looked around me. A few paces away, I saw a waste bin. I'm not sure what I must have looked like, rummaging in the rubbish, but as I had hoped, there was some discarded food in there, and I quickly plucked out the remains of a packet of cream crackers.

"Here! This is your lucky day!" I crumbled a piece of cracker and tossed it into the flower-bed beneath the tree. Quick as a flash, the bird hopped down and scooped the biscuit into its beak. Instead of returning to the tree, my tiny companion waited on the shadowy earth, bright eyes keenly anticipating more.

Engrossed in feeding the bird, I neither saw nor heard the movement behind me. I just felt the seat move as she sat down.

"You're a good boy, Neil."

I wheeled round, dropping the crackers.

"Did I startle you?"

"Oh – no. I was feeding that little bird."

"I know. I saw you through the window." She turned down her lips, apologetically. "I think I scared him off."

"Doesn't matter. He seemed quite tame. I expect lots of people feed him."

"I reckon." She had taken off her white cap and undone the top button of her uniform dress. Looking at her, I felt all melty. "How's your grandma, Neil?"

"She died," I said.

"I see. I'm very sorry."

"Right. It's okay. I'm sort of getting used to the idea."

"Yeah? That why your eyes are all red?"

I shrugged. "Well, you know."

"Of course I do. Hey, you don't mind me sitting here, do you?"

"No. It's nice."

"Only it's my break, you see."

"I said, it's all right."

"So where's your mum?" The breeze blew strands of her hair into her mouth, and she hooked them out again with her finger. "She still with your grandma?"

"I think so." I glanced at her, quickly, then examined my hands. Gran's death had changed my perspective. If it all went wrong now, I had nothing to lose. The courage was there. "Can I – would it be all right if I called you Jennifer?"

"Getting bold, aren't we?" she said, with a quick, artful smile. "Still, if I'm calling you Neil…"

"Only, Nurse Peltzer sounds a bit sort of stuffy."

"Thanks very much."

"No, I didn't mean you were stuffy."

"Hmm. Glad about that." Her hair was in her mouth again, a

thick U-shaped loop of it, climbing over her lip, only this time she left it there, wetting it with her lips and seeming not to notice, and I loved the small carelessness of it. "Okay, Neil, so while I'm off duty you can call me Jennifer."

"Thanks. That's good. Jennifer?"

"Yes, Neil?"

"Have you – has anyone close to you ever died?"

She opened her mouth, pausing to think. The curl of hair stuck to her lower lip, darkening as she dampened it. "Yes. I was engaged once. Sam, his name was. He came off his motorbike."

"Oh. And he was – ?"

"Instantly. Decapitated."

I fell silent, considering this jagged moment of terminal violence. Was it worse than what I had just experienced, more painful, more cruel, more icily unforgettable? Gran had at least lived a life, loved in the company of a husband, raised a child and seen her grow. Some things were simply, nakedly unfair.

"That's terrible. Was it long ago?"

"Long enough."

"Do you still think about him?"

"Most days. You never forget. I wouldn't want to forget."

I felt sorry for her now, and I couldn't help myself. I would use my courage again. Without even knowing exactly when I was going to do it, I reached out with one finger and flicked the loop of hair out of her mouth, shivering as my fingertip brushed her cheek.

"Thank you, Neil," she said, smiling. "I'm forever eating my hair."

"That's all right. I think you're really nice."

"You don't know me," she said, and I wondered if this was a warning.

"Do you – ever go to where he's buried?"

"Sometimes."

"I think I'll go to wherever my gran is. Then I can talk to her – tell her things."

"She'd like that, Neil."

"Maybe. Do you think, if you talk to someone when they're

under the ground, they can sort of hear you? It's possible, isn't it?"

"I don't know. But then, if we don't know if they can, we don't know if they can't. Yes?"

"Yes."

"You just have to believe, Neil. That makes anything possible. You know what my father said to me, when I told him I wanted to be a nurse – a good nurse? He told me, 'Belief is the engine of achievement.' So, remember that. You can walk on water."

I was still trembling from that touch. "Thanks, Jennifer. I'm glad I talked to you. I'm sure you're a brilliant nurse."

"I try to be."

"I don't know if I can walk on water," I said, checking my watch, "but I suppose I ought to walk back and find my mother. She'll be wondering where I am."

"Of course. You can look after each other."

"Something I need," I said, standing up.

"From me?"

I nodded. "I need a hug."

Whereupon Jennifer Peltzer stood to face me, wearing a smile and a beard of windblown hair, and I wrapped my arms around her, and she held me tightly for a few seconds that I would recall as hours, and I felt her breasts so firm against my chest, as I inhaled the warm, sweet, herby smell of her neck and hoped that time would stop and the world leave us alone.

I met Mum halfway up the corridor, looking confused and mildly irritated. "You just disappeared," she said, reproachfully.

"I needed some air."

"We should get back. I hate hospitals."

"What about Gran?"

"What about her? She's dead. We can't take her with us."

"I know. I mean, is there anything else to do? Forms or anything?"

She sighed. "Oh, I don't know, Neil. I don't think so. They'll let us know."

"Who's got her jewellery?"

"It's all in an envelope – in my bag. Neil, let's just go, please."

"I have to go back to the house."

"What? What house?"

"Gran's. My bike's there."

"Oh, I see. I never thought." She hesitated, fiddling with her handbag. "If I give you some money, can you get the bus round there? I really can't put up with any more of this; I just want to go home."

"I've got money," I said, beginning to walk away. I could feel the tears coming again. "I'll see you at home then."

I'm not sure why, instead of cycling straight home, I rode round to Sally's house. Perhaps I was looking for sympathy. Perhaps I was curious as to why neither of my friends – Gran's friends, for goodness' sake – had been to the hospital. Maybe I just needed time to think.

Archie let me in. "Sally's upstairs with Noah," he said.

"Has everyone gone?" I asked.

"Yes. All quiet on the western front. There's some food left if you want it."

"I'm not hungry." I sat down heavily in the armchair. "Gran died."

"Oh dear." He hung his head, gripping the temples in his fingers. "I'm so sorry, Neil."

"Sorry? Why? Sorry she died or sorry you weren't there? Sorry you might have to buy a bunch of flowers or sorry you never bothered to go and see her?"

He reached out for my shoulder, but I didn't want that, and I smacked his hand away. "Ah, don't be like that, Neil," he said, managing to sound hurt.

His reaction did not engage my sympathy. "I suppose one of you must have an excuse."

"As a matter of fact, there are two perfectly good reasons why we couldn't come to the hospital." He perched on the arm of the chair, looking down at his clasped hands. "One of us had to be here with our guests, obviously."

"Feed them their cakes," I said, but he appeared to ignore the sarcasm.

"Then poor Noah, well, he seems to have a wee bit of a temperature. Anyway, he was grizzling at first, then Sally couldn't stop him crying, and his little face, it looked kind of – blotchy, you know, like he just wasnae well."

"I see," I said, after a suitable pause. "Gran wasn't very well, either."

"I know, Neil, I know," Archie said, wearily.

"So how is he now?"

"He's away upstairs with Sally. She's put him in the big bed. You can go up."

I stood at the open bedroom door and looked in. Sally was lying on her back, Noah resting in the crook of her arm. He had a nappy on, nothing else. His face did look a bit puffy, and there were some red patches around his throat.

"Hello, Neil love." She sounded tired, but perhaps she had been dozing. A single sheet was pulled over her, though I could see her bare shoulders and the tops of her breasts. "How is Mrs Blaney?"

"She – she's died," I said, and I started to cry again, just quietly, just letting the tears run down my face and drip on to my collar.

"Oh Neil." One pale arm reached out from under the sheet, drawing her left breast out with it. The nipple was plump and distended, dark red. "Come here and let me cuddle you."

I sat on the edge of the bed. We held hands. Noah fidgeted in her other arm, whimpering softly, and she slowly freed her arm and rolled him on to his side. She sat up then, presenting her full breasts, and locked her arms around me, nuzzling my ear with her lips. "I've missed you," she whispered.

"A nurse was really nice to me," I said, wiping my eyes with a corner of the sheet.

"Was she? Was she, Neil? That's good." She stroked my forehead with a cool hand. "This nurse, she can be nice to you, too. Would you like me to be nice to you, Neil?"

I gulped and nodded.

It was the first time I had ever been completely naked in bed with Sally. I felt so many different emotions, all jumbled up inside me: sadness, confusion, fear, apprehension, excitement, despair, longing, regret, bewilderment. Most of all, I wanted to feel her arms about me, holding me, warming me, not letting me go.

The way the bed bounced, I realised Archie was climbing in next to me. I didn't turn to look at him. His forearm brushed my back, and a knee nudged my leg, so I knew he, too, was naked. Something hot snuffled in my ear, Noah half-asleep, Noah cradled now in Archie's arms, snugly embedded in the pillow.

"Noah feels hot," I murmured.

"Shush!" Sally said, and she kissed my lips. "Noah's safe. We're all safe, all four of us – snug as bugs."

I flinched when she cupped me in her hands but, funnily enough, I stayed soft for quite a long time, and I lay there, just thinking, just remembering the day. Sally was kind to me. She stroked me gently. I loved her very much.

Believe me, Archie never touched me. He lay there quietly, and after a while I heard his breathing change, not snoring exactly, more a rhythmic rumble that told me he was falling asleep with his son, *my son*, in his arms.

Even so, I tried not to move, in case I disturbed him. I let Sally be nice, oh so nice, to me. When I tried to speak, she put her hand over my mouth, and I could smell my penis on it, kind of a cream cheese smell. A private smell.

"Don't talk, Neil," she whispered. "You just lie back. Let it happen. Relax. I'll be nice, really nice."

I think most of it went in her hands. Anyway, she told me it would be all right. I felt easier then, all slack and unstressed and, somehow, weak as a kitten.

So I slept, held in her arms, and only Noah, of all of us lying together in that bed, was not naked. Only Noah knew nothing at all about any of it. I had dreams; good dreams, bad dreams, I don't know. I saw Gran's face – pale, accusing, hideously creased – staring at me out of the darkness, like a mask hanging from a tree in the night. When I spoke to her, she made no reply. I turned away, and in the light from lamplit windows, there she stood, offering me that sweet, delicate smile, Jennifer Peltzer, and I watched my own fumbling fingers peel open her small white buttons and her hand was on the back of my head, pressing my face into her perfumed valley – a lick, a kiss, the smooth, clean dryness of her – and I hung there, floating in time and space, and then the world seemed to roll over, I heard a baby crying, and my tongue came out, tasting something strange, a kind of sweet sick, and when I opened my filmy eyes I saw Sally smiling down at me, and she had my head between her hands, her fingers in my ears.

"Will you look at you?" she sang to me, shaking her head.

"What? What is it?"

"With your milky moustache."

I ran a finger over my top lip and tasted it again. Archie groaned and sat up. He rubbed the sleep from his eyes, and leaned towards his wife.

"Mind, don't squash the baby now!" She drew him close to her, guiding him down. Before he covered her, I could see the blue veins in her breasts.

There was plenty for Noah, of course. He should have been first, not last, but she had so much, it hardly mattered. We sat there, our sleep-warmed bodies chilling in the evening air, wearing our milky moustaches, smiling, not speaking. Noah, too, looked contented and at peace.

Finally, Sally hung her head, and I thought she was falling asleep again; but Archie put out a hand, supporting her right breast, and she let him hold her there, just working his fingers softly, and after a few seconds a light haze of milk touched her face. She smiled triumphantly. "Four milky moustaches," she said.

We began to laugh, the three of us. I only giggled to start with, but then my laughter swelled, shrieking, into the room, while Archie's deep bellow seemed almost to shake the furniture and, in high, pealing counterpoint, Sally squealed in falsetto, rocking, kicking her legs, until the house was full of the madness of our noise.

Then I saw Noah, lying there, gazing at the ceiling, licking his lips, balling his baby's fists. I thought, but for him – *but for you* – my gran would have passed serenely from this world in the company of friends. She had said nothing, made no reference, but she must have wondered why this should be. Why did this have to be? I took Noah's tiny hand in mine, and I squeezed it hard. Oh yes, I squeezed it very hard.

Noah began to cry. I cried, too. I cried out of love and fear and pain and terrible sadness. I cried until it seemed that nothing, and no-one, could ever stop me crying, ever again.

Among friends, I lay alone. In the evening's fading light, I had found a private darkness.

Chapter XVII

Talking to Gran

Strangely enough, I have always been rather fond of cemeteries. I have never found them in the least gloomy or sinister. In a cemetery there are stories on stones, sunshine and shade under dancing trees, bunches of fresh flowers, the calm traffic of caring visitors soothingly industrious with scissors and trowels and crumpled bags. Then there are the residents, quietly enjoying the unconditional luxury of togetherness. There is, in fact, a sense of life as we would want it.

This impression is reinforced, I think, by the vague suggestion that nobody there has actually died. Death and cemeteries do not appear to fit together. Dead people lie at the roadside, in burning buildings or on battlefields; once they reach the cemetery, they have mostly attained a modest resurrection. The headstones tell it all: *Now At Rest; Passed Away; Fell Asleep.* There are no dead people in a cemetery. Whilst I approve of these euphemisms, I also take due heed of them, lest when I fall asleep myself, perhaps in unexpected circumstances, I should shortly fall victim to a grotesque misunderstanding.

I rather believe Mum and Dad were surprised when I declined their invitation to attend Gran's funeral. Archie had already agreed to go. Perhaps he felt he owed his former landlady that much, at least, or maybe, like me, he enjoyed the ordered, secluded ambience of a good graveyard. Anyway, he described the event to me afterwards, in sufficient detail that I could almost believe I had been there. Archie, I discovered, as a seasoned traveller in his youth, had been present at burials all over the world, and I am sure that Gran's interment must have seemed quite tame by comparison with some of the ceremonies he recalled. For instance, there was a funeral in Kentucky – a close friend, killed in action in Korea, he said – where the mourners stood in a ring around the open grave and sang gospel songs in dialect to a concertina accompaniment; at a winter service in Poland, where the deceased was unknown to him and he had merely chanced upon the gathering, those assembled quickly despatched the coffin and proceeded to repel the bitter cold by imbibing copious draughts of vodka until they became insensible and forgot why they were there at all; and he had appeared at wakes in Ireland, not to mention, of course, the Scottish equivalent; also he told me of a visit to India, a village near Hyderabad, and a small gathering in the cool of the evening, the party standing respectfully with their heads down, backs to the wilderness beyond, while the children laughed and stamped their feet to shake the ground, because otherwise the preoccupied adults would not see a cobra gliding towards them – for families in India like to leave food at the graveside, whether to appease the gods or so that the departed shall not go hungry, and rats come to steal the uneaten food, and snakes follow, to take the rats.

"How come you didnae want to pay your last respects?" Archie asked me.

I told him, "I've paid them. For most of that last day, I was with Gran."

He nodded his head slowly. "Aye, right enough."

That I deliberately avoided seeing my grandmother stuck in a dark hole in a box – I did not consider that disrespectful. I wanted to remember her as she had always been for me. We had shared something special, and no-one could take that away. I saw her moving, smiling in my mind's eye, and I felt privileged and proud. If my gran was really dead, I had no wish to be forcibly reminded of it.

A week after the funeral, I decided it was time for me to go and talk to Gran. I was anxious to know if there was anything she wanted – some family photographs, perhaps, a trinket or keepsake from her dressing table or a book to read. If she liked,

I could sit for a while and read to her, as she had done for me when I was little. Gran was always a slow reader, sometimes not making out the words too well, but she would meander uncomplainingly through the pages, only the slightest expression in her soft voice, while I leaned contentedly against her arm until my eyelids grew heavy and my head dipped into a warm pool of sleep. Mum would read to me, if I asked her at the right moment, but there was usually a more brittle response, her stilted storytelling punctuated by a frequent riffling of pages as she raced ahead to check how much further she might have to go.

An idea came to me. On her bedside table, I recalled, Gran kept two small volumes of poetry – perhaps as much for decoration as for reading – next to a pink-shaded lamp. One book was *The Lake Poets – A Golden Treasury*, but I cannot remember the title of its companion. Anyway, I thought Gran might like a poem written specially for her. In English Literature at school we had explored poetry, superficially, and I had once been marked with an 'A' for my composition, a poem about our family holiday in the Channel Islands. Now it was time, I decided, to write something personal for Gran to keep.

I hate it when I am trying to write and someone peers intently over my shoulder. All brain activity, the whole creative process, seems to cease instantly, and I am left huddled over the paper, my pen dangling impotently in mid-air, in a state of suspended animation, like a dummy in a pointless photograph.

Mum, however, was insensitive to my discomfort. "What are you writing?" she asked, leaning into my light.

"Nothing," I replied, tersely.

"No-one can write nothing," she said. "That's stupid."

"If you must know," I told her, sighing, "it's for Gran."

She straightened up, blinking. "You're writing a letter to Gran?"

"It's not a letter. I didn't say it was a letter."

"Oh. So it's a sort of note?"

"Sort of. Actually it's a poem." I covered the paper with my hand. "It's going to be a poem."

"I see. Of course she may have trouble reading it."

"That's nasty, Mum, that's really nasty."

She raised her hands in a vague gesture of apology. "All right, I'm sorry. You go ahead. You always did write nicely."

"I'll put it in plastic when I've done, to keep it dry."

"Dad could get it typed out for you."

I thought about this. "Maybe it would be more personal if I just wrote it with a pen. He could have it photocopied, though. Then, if the first one got wet, I could replace it – so she'd always have one."

Mum smiled. "You're a good boy, Neil."

"Am I?"

"Course you are. You're too good for most of those you mix with."

"How d'you mean?" I asked, leading her on deliberately.

"Well, you know," she said, with a kind of forced weariness. "Your dad's got a good job in London. We've got the car and a television. I expect you'll pass your exams and go into the Civil Service. We're not jumped-up like some I could name."

"Oh, I see." I waited hopefully for her to name a few local wastrels.

"That Patrick you walk to school with. His dad's a plumber."

"Some boys in my form are quite clever. They could go on to university."

"Hmm. But what class are they, eh? Tell me that."

Inwardly, I was not so impressed with my own status. I was a lad of average academic ability who had had sex with a married woman in the woods and fathered a child without telling anyone. Correction: I had attempted to tell my mother, but I had made a hash of it, and I could not bring myself to confide in her again. Now I felt I was embarking upon a secret life, condemned either to live a lie or, in unburdening myself, suffer humiliation for my ineptitude.

It took me several evenings to get my poem right. Whenever Mum or Dad interrupted me, I covered the writing pad with my homework, so that they would not peer over my shoulder and distract me. I wanted it to be as good as I could make it; Gran deserved that much from me.

Dad took the poem to work with him and made some photocopies. I had sealed the sheet of paper inside a brown envelope, and Dad returned the original and the copies to me in the same envelope, the flap now stuck down with tape. Whether he had bothered to read what I had written, I don't know, for he never made any comment on it. In any case, my father was not a man to appreciate poetry.

When I told Mum that I intended to cycle over to the cemetery on Saturday, she stared at me blankly and shook her head, as though to dislodge a blemish in her vision. "It's a bit early," she said. "You'll have trouble finding her."

"How d'you mean?"

"There's no headstone yet. We haven't had time. Anyway, it's lots of money."

"But you must know where she is."

"I've got the plot number. I could write it down."

"There's usually a man there."

"What?"

"In the hut. He'll help me."

"He might not be there, Neil. He could be anywhere. It's a big place."

"Mum, I can do it. Please."

She went to her handbag, took out a slip of paper and wrote down the number on the back of an envelope. "Here. I still think you should wait. After all, she's not going anywhere."

"Don't want to wait," I said, sullenly.

"Oh, suit yourself. And don't make that face at me."

The sun was shining on the day I went, which was something of a relief, as I would not have wanted to stand about in the rain, and also there was no risk of my poem getting wet – well, not for a while, at least. I chained my bike to the wrought-iron gates and, opening the saddlebag, took out the foolscap sheet, which I had placed inside a clear plastic folder I had found at school.

My heart sank as I wandered along the cinder paths, for there seemed to be no pattern to the numbering of the graves and, stupidly, I had not thought to ask Mum to describe the exact location. I could have kicked myself. Walking up the steep slope towards the boundary railings, I found a long row of freshly-disturbed graves, the lumpy soil still brown and moist, with wooden markers stuck in the ground. Some of the markers bore no numbers at all, and those that were numbered were almost illegible. One plot had an abandoned spade thrust into the banked earth. I considered waiting for the tool's owner to return, but he might have gone to lunch.

Turning, I saw the dark block of the groundsman's hut against a distant hedge, the door standing partly open. Surely the occupant would not have gone out of sight and left the place open, so either he was inside or working nearby. The prospect of going home and admitting to Mum that I had not managed to find Gran appalled me; it was unthinkable. So I stepped out towards the shady bluff where the hut stood.

A thin whine of radio music drifted to my ears as I approached the dark cleft of the doorway. There had to be someone inside, someone who would offer me a reassuring smile and helpful directions. I pushed the door wide open.

Of course, my eyes were not adjusted to the dim light. At first I didn't see the man at all. I caught the smell of him, though, a high, almost palpable sourness that clung fiercely to the fabric of the room. He hadn't seen me, either, for he sat in a high-backed chair, facing away from the door, and his head hung low over something he was working in his hands.

"Excuse me!"

The man jerked upright, as if jolted by an electric shock. "Bloody 'ell!" He swung the chair round, tugging at his fly with one hand. "Don't you knock on doors?"

"Not in a shed, no. Sorry."

"This is private, mate. Supposed to knock." A white flash of his pants still showed. "What d'you want?"

I showed him the envelope Mum had given me. He snatched it from my hand and squinted at it. "I need to find this grave," I said.

"That a T or a J?"

"J, I think. It's my grandmother. Her name's Jean Blaney."

"Just a sec." He reached out and turned the radio down. "Um. J, J...right, all the Js are up the top, in the new bit."

"Have they got numbers?"

"Course they got numbers. 'Ere." He gave me back the envelope. I didn't like to hold it, now I knew what he'd been doing with his hands. "It's muddy up there," he added, looking me up and down.

"I don't mind. It's my gran."

"Yeah, yeah, you told me."

I looked back through the doorway. "Is it up that hill?"

"Yeah, you go – " He broke off when a box on the wall squawked at him. "'Ang about. I gotta get this." Scowling, he grabbed a walkie-talkie and fiddled with the buttons. "'Allo!"

I could make out the interior of the hut more clearly now. There was a window on one side and another, smaller one at the end. Next to the main window, a cork notice board was fixed to the wall. Forms, dockets and scraps of paper were pinned to the board in careless disarray. A workbench, doubling as a desk, ran from the board back towards the door, its surface cluttered with dog-eared files, pens, jamjars full of clips and nails, and a plastic lunchbox, the lid secured with a thick elastic band.

The groundsman was holding the walkie-talkie in front of his cheek, while whoever was on the other end gabbled at him. Every few seconds he blew out a deep breath and grunted into the speaker.

I carried on gazing around the wooden walls. Opposite the window was a poster, torn from a magazine, on which a girl leaned against a tree, grinning gleefully, displaying bare breasts. The picture made me smile, though I wondered whether it was entirely appropriate for the location. A tattered paper-covered book, an instruction manual of some kind, hung next to the poster, suspended from a drawing pin on a piece of twine. In a childish scrawl of uneven capitals, 'GILBERT' was written across the top of the book's cover.

"Yeah, yeah, yeah!" The man barked impatiently into the handset, clutched in chubby, grime-etched fingers.

A black-and-white photograph pinned to the cork board drew my attention. Quite why, I couldn't think, but I found myself staring in fascination at the two men in the picture. They were standing in the stern of a boat, beaming up at the camera, their broad, lardy faces split by leering, toothy grins. The men wore overstretched T-shirts, and each had an arm around the other's shoulders. A brief glance at the man panting in front of me confirmed that he was one of the pair in the photo – but there was something about the other that gnawed at my mind, a kind of ghostly familiarity about the face. This was someone I had seen somewhere before, a man I had met and touched and been troubled by.

"Okay, mate, let's go!" He tossed the handset on to the desk. "Just get me coat." Reaching behind the door, he took down a stained grey jacket and struggled into it.

"Where are we going?"

"Nowhere. I'm just gonna show you the way. Right?"

As he stepped into the doorway, the light glanced on the blue enamel badge in his lapel. The badge bore the council insignia, with the wearer's name in gold lettering below. His name, I saw, was Gilbert Wicken. A dry sourness tainted my mouth. I peered back over my shoulder at the photograph on the board.

"Sunnink wrong? What yer lookin' at?"

"That picture. That's you, isn't it?"

"'S right. Me an' my brother. We was on the Broads."

"I like the boat. When was that taken?"

Thoughtfully, he puckered up his fat lips. "Don't rightly remember. Three, four years back."

"Is it your boat?"

"Nah, mate of ours."

"Your brother looks just like you. Are you twins?"

"Just looked like me, that's all," he said, with a shrug. "Just 'ad that way about 'im."

"Had?"

"What?"

"You said 'had'. D'you mean…?"

"Yeah, sure, that's what I mean." He looked down at the floor, then back at me, biting his lip.

"What happened?"

"Ask a lot o' bloody questions, you, don't yer?"

"I'm sorry – Mr Wicken. I just wondered."

"Le's just say 'e came to a bad end, an' leave it at that."

"Okay. I expect you miss him."

"Course I do. We was close, me an' Sam, real close." He wiped his nose with his fingers. "Still, least 'e ain't far away."

"No?"

"Up the top there, under a nice shady tree. Got a view all around. I see 'im every day, pretty near. Funny, I still talk to 'im." I saw the muscles clench in his jaw, holding something back. "Yeah, well, 'e's still my bruv. Don't make no difference where he is."

With surprising gentleness, he put a hand on my shoulder and led me outside. I waited while he locked the door. There were some trees on a ridge about a hundred yards away, forming a leafy crescent with deep-shadowed graves tilting beneath, and I wondered if Sam Wicken lay in one of them.

"Don't tell no-one, will yer?"

"What about?"

"What I was doin' – when you come in."

I turned to face him. "Course not, Mr Wicken. You were right; I should have knocked."

"Ah well. Know 'ow it is. A man gets lonely."

"Specially now. When you lose someone close."

"Yeah. Sam, 'e was all I 'ad." He tossed the hut key in the air, caught it and put it in his pocket. "Come on, mate, I'll take you to see yer grandma. Then I'll 'ave a word wi' that brother o' mine."

Gilbert Wicken left me at the graveside and shuffled away. I thanked him, and he acknowledged me with a dismissive wave. The sun sneaked behind a cloud, and came out again. There was no sound, though high overhead the tiny silver blade of an aeroplane, trailing the long white scratch of its backdraught, sliced through the sky's blue parchment like a glinting knife-point.

Where Gran's headstone would have stood, if there had been one, a single wooden stake, resembling nothing more than a misshapen stick of firewood, protruded from a large brownish-yellow ball of clay soil. Some dried-up bunches of flowers, their colours faded almost into camouflage with the brown earth, lay criss-crossed over the rough plot. I pulled the crumpled envelope from my pocket and checked Mum's writing against the number scrawled on the stake. This was the place. This was my gran. I was back with her once more. This time, no-one would disturb us.

I knelt on the grass, though instantly I felt the wetness soaking into my knees. This was no act of homage. It was simply that, standing there, I seemed to tower over her – me standing up, Gran lying down – and so the sense of contact, or communion, was diminished. I just wanted to be close to her. She needed to feel me beside her, to know that I was there. I had to make her understand.

"Hello, Gran." I spoke the words in a firm, level voice, with no trembling. "It's Neil. I've come to see you."

Then I waited, saying nothing, allowing time for my greeting to sink down into the vault below. I knew I would have to be patient. Gran, after all, had plenty of time. I had plenty of time. Time was not important here. It seemed to me that, maybe, that was all there was to dying: the stopping of clocks. No more hurt, no more fear, no more anxiety, just a silence after the ticking.

"The sun's shining, Gran. It's a lovely day. It'll keep you warm, Gran."

If I closed my eyes and kept quite still, I imagined I could feel a kind of pulse in those deep recesses of my mind where anything is stubbornly possible, the low drone of a breath, the soft thud of a distant voice.

"Can you hear me, Gran? It's Neil."

Hello, Neil. I'm all right. I can feel you there. I hear you. Don't worry. There's nothing to worry about.

"I'll come lots of times, Gran, I promise. Next time I'll bring you some more flowers. I'll take away the dead ones now, they're ugly. There shouldn't be dead things here."

I'll always love you, Neil. There's nothing can take that away.

"I love you too, Gran."

The tears ran down my face like warm rain. Salt lakes shimmered in my eyes, making a sea of the sky, endless, unstoppable.

Don't ask me how long I stayed there. I found a metal waste bin nearby, and I upended it for a seat. I let the sun dry my face. Every so often I spoke to Gran and then I waited quietly and let her answer me. I was comfortable there, peaceful, relaxed in the rightness of it.

This had to be the moment to tell Gran everything about me and Sally and the baby. When, before, we had lightly touched upon the subject, it was as if I had given her the faintest sketch of what had happened, and now I would paint in the detail in the boldest colours I could imagine. It amazed me how easily I could talk to Gran in this clean, bright place, and I almost instantly forgot that she no longer sat beside me, listening and smiling, occasionally nodding her head as though to reassure me that, even as she remained silent, she was still attentive to my every word. So the fullness of my confession became a kind of purging, an act releasing inside me a thrilling physical pleasure, and soon I was emptied of my sadness, filled instead with a proud elation that came from knowing how completely I had shared myself, my real self, with someone I loved.

The trouble was, of course, I didn't want to leave her. How long did I sit there? I really can't say. When I stood up, the unforgiving steel rim on the base of that bin had numbed the backs of my thighs and my bottom, and I had to massage the creased flesh to restore my circulation before I could move. Through a gap in the hedge I saw Gilbert Wicken return to his hut, going in and out, stowing tools inside, and I realised that it was time for me to go. But not quite.

"I've brought you something, Gran," I told her, "for you to keep."

Something to remember you by? A photograph, perhaps?

"To remember me by, yes. Memories, sort of. Only the pictures are in the words."

That's nice, Neil.

"It's a poem. I wrote it specially for you. I'll read it to you. And I'll leave it here with you. Remember, the words are pictures and the pictures are in the words."

I knelt down again, and I read her my poem.

I'll miss your house
With its cool, dark places made of wood
And your big room with pictures round the bed

And the sunny kitchen where you stood
To watch as I explored the cluttered shed.

I'll miss your garden
With the summer roses and the wallflowers in spring
And Granddad's cabbages where caterpillars hid
Before his grimy fingers felt them cling
And pulped them swiftly like the starlings did.

I'll miss you in the rec
Where we would wave at trains beneath the trees
Or search for shiny conkers in the grass
Their husks green mines discarded by the breeze
Under hot silver skies like polished glass.

But most of all I'll miss your gentleness
That quiet way you had when things were wrong
The times your feathery touch would make me smile
And light a place where tears did not belong
With simple kindness innocent of guile.

I'll let you rest now
In time we pass to green and whispering places
Where after dark the moon paints cedar trees
The colour of electric dreams in furrowed faces
And hearts and minds hold memories as deep as seas.

Goodnight Gran.

There was one last thing I wanted to do before Gilbert Wicken locked the gate. Quickly, perhaps even a little carelessly – for I knew I could always replace it – I scrabbled away some loose earth and buried the plastic-sleeved paper for Gran to keep, and then I turned and made my way around the upper perimeter of the hill, staying close to the hedge, until I reached the patch the groundsman had indicated, where the trees stood folding their branches protectively over a row of sloping graves. There, in the dappled shade, a simple headstone marked the place where Sam Wicken lay. I would not stay long, in case Sam's brother saw me and became suspicious. Still, a minute or two wouldn't hurt.

"Hello, Mr Wicken. This is Neil Robertson. I expect you remember me."

I paused, almost as if I expected a reply.

"I came to visit my grandmother. Then I met Gilbert. He told me where you were."

Another pause, while I allowed my mind to slip back to the clearing in the woods and the icy flints of the stars and the black trees beyond.

"I just wanted to say, I'm sorry it – I'm sorry about what happened. You didn't have to do that, Mr Wicken. Really. We could have made it all right. Bad things – you can make them better. People'll help you." A sudden breeze raced through the branches above my head, tossing my voice away. "I hope you can hear me, Mr Wicken. I can't stay any longer, but I'll try to come back. You've got a nice place."

As I unchained my bike and levered the handlebars away from the gate, I realised that I had gone for a long time with nothing to eat or drink. Before cycling home, I ought to have something, a snack of some kind – and so I thought of Sally and Archie.

It took me only a few minutes to ride there. Archie let me in. I thought he would be surprised to see me, but he made no comment and there was no warmth in his gruff greeting.

Sally was sitting on the living room settee, feeding Noah, her hand cupping the back of his head as she applied him to her right breast.

"Sorry," I murmured, averting my gaze.

"In the circumstances, I think we can dispense with the modesty, Neil," she said.

Archie passed me on his way to the kitchen. "I'll make us some tea. Don't hover, Neil, sit down."

I sat in the armchair to one side of the settee. Noah, cradled at an angle between Sally's breast and her lap, was making little clucking noises as he sucked. Sally gazed fondly down at him, then her eyes assumed a glazed harshness as she peered across at me. "What are you doing over there? You look like you're waiting to be interviewed. This is your son, Neil. At least come and sit next to him."

"Sorry," I said, moving towards her.

She straightened up and made room for me against her thigh. "Yes, I've told you before about being sorry."

"I know. It's sort of – "

"Sort of what?"

"It's just something I say. It doesn't mean anything."

"A figure of speech?"

"That's right."

"Well, it makes you into a figure of ridicule, so stop it."

"I see." I sucked in a deep breath and let it out slowly. "So you think I'm ridiculous."

"That's not what I said."

"You came close. I can hardly tell the difference."

"Ah, don't you go all sulky on us," she said, frostily.

"I'm not sulking."

"No? You came close. I can hardly tell the difference."

"Now you're mocking me."

She sighed, manoeuvring the baby upright to face me while she rubbed his back. "Please don't let's be like this, Neil. You haven't even said 'Hello' to Noah."

"Hello, Noah," I said, deliberately not looking at him.

Archie called from the kitchen. "Do we have any biscuits?"

Sally's face seemed to suggest that she resented the interruption. "No. Just bring the tea." She shook her head as though to re-orientate herself. "I think you should hold him," she told me.

"In a minute."

"Why not now?"

"Because – I'm not ready yet. I went to see Gran. In the cemetery, I mean. I'm a bit mixed-up now."

"Oh, poor boy." She patted my hand.

Very carefully, I extended the little finger of my right hand and slid it like a pink peg into the moist, puffy curl of Noah's fist. With unexpected strength, he gripped this new plaything and held it tight.

"Did I hear you say you were at the cemetery?" Archie called.

"Yes. I went to my gran's grave."

"That's good," he said. "Everything all right?"

"Yes. There's no stone yet, but I found the place."

"Aha. And did you give her our regards?"

I stared at him blankly. "As a matter of fact, I didn't."

"Oh, right, I see," he said, with a wry smile.

I glanced at Sally, but there was no expression on her face. It was as though Gran was someone she had heard of but never known. Suddenly my grandmother's death seemed brutally, painfully complete.

"Here!" She held Noah out for me to take. "You can put him in his carrycot now he's been fed. He'll probably go to sleep."

I hoisted the little man on to my shoulder, as I had often seen Sally do before, and carried him to his cot. He struggled briefly as I lowered him under the hood, but I made him warm in his nest of blankets and his head lolled to one side as his eyelids fluttered into sleep. I stood and watched him for a while, feeling Sally's eyes on my back.

"He's not on his face, is he?" she asked.

"Course not. I know."

"Very well. Now come and sit next to me."

I sat stiffly beside her. She turned and kissed me wetly on the chin.

"Thanks," I said.

"You are a one, Neil," she observed, with a deprecating chuckle.

"What?"

"Time you loosened up. Let me make it better." Her hand crept out and settled warmly over my crotch. "There. That feel nice?"

"Don't." I brushed her away. My head was full of pictures of sun-lacquered trees, green baize buttons of moss on leaning headstones, sepia sprays of hopeful flowers, the musty claustrophobia of Gilbert Wicken's hut, the cool bower of his brother's final, merciful release and the sweetly aching silence where Gran lay smiling in eternal peace. All of that was inside me still, snapshots waiting to be shuffled and reviewed and rationalised into some kind of manageable, comfortable order. That much I needed, wanted, but not this, not this distracting, intrusive hand, not now. My thoughts and emotions were elsewhere, and the intimacy Sally proposed seemed almost obscene it its irrelevance.

She would not understand this mood, of course. I knew it instinctively, and I read it in her eyes and in the set of her jaw.

"Not like you to refuse an offer. You're normally keen enough."

"I don't feel like it, that's all."

"I see," she said, her voice clipped, tossing her head. "Pardon me for molesting you."

"I don't want to talk about it. Anyway, Archie's here."

"Huh. What's that matter? He knows the score."

"Maybe. But this isn't the time. I'm not..."

"Not what?"

"In the right mood."

"That's all right, love. I can help."

"It's not that simple. It's not like turning on a tap."

She inched closer to me. "Archie and me – we can show you all sorts of good times, if only you'll relax and forget your worries and – "

"And be your puppet! Is that it?"

I saw at once that this had not been a good idea. Sally leapt to her feet, her fists balled tightly at her sides. She met Archie carrying a loaded tray from the kitchen. "Oh, for Christ's sake! Will you just listen to this boy?"

"Where do you want this?" he asked her.

"Take it away!"

"What?"

"You heard me. Put it back in the kitchen. I'm going to sort this out first."

Now I heard the blood pounding in my ears. There was a crash from the kitchen as Archie abandoned the tray. I inspected my shoes through lowered, hooded eyes.

"What's going on?" Archie demanded from the doorway.

Without turning round, Sally jerked her thumb back at me.

"Our *friend* here reckons he's being put upon. He says we're treating him like a puppet. I can't believe it."

Her sarcastic emphasis of the word *friend* touched a nerve. My stomach lurched, but the sickness I felt was overlaid with a sense of anger and betrayal.

Though I hadn't looked up, I knew that Archie was standing in front of me. "What's this all about, Neil? What are you trying to do here?"

"I'm not trying to do anything. I just want to be left alone."

"You came to see us," Sally said. "You could have gone off on your own."

"Yes, I'm beginning to wish I had done."

"I'm trying to fathom you out, Neil." She and Archie stood side by side now, gaping at me indignantly. "We're doing all we can to shield you from harm, to divert attention away from you, and all you can do is accuse us of being manipulative."

"I didn't say that."

"Your meaning was perfectly clear," Sally said, and her tone had levelled off now, pitched an octave lower, yet somehow this equilibrium seemed to invest her words with a greater menace. "So what do you think, Archie?" she enquired.

"How d'you mean?"

"About this boy. He thinks he's a puppet."

"Aha."

"What do we do with puppets, Archie?"

Archie smiled, then the corners of his mouth turned down. When he looked at me, I saw sadness in his eyes. That frightened me. It scared me more than anything in Sally's voice.

She answered for him. "I think we make them dance, don't we, Archie? We pull their strings until they dance. Isn't that right?"

Despite his amenable grin, Archie retained the grace to appear a touch embarrassed. "Oh aye, I'd have to agree."

Sally nodded in satisfaction. "Well, in that case. Stand up, Neil."

"No, I don't want to."

"I said, stand up, Neil!"

I did as I was told, drawing myself upright on to quaking legs that felt, suddenly, as if they were not my own.

"What are you going to do?" I asked her, and my voice sounded small and far-away.

"What are we going to do? Oh no, Neil, it's not what we're going to do. It's what *you're* going to do."

"Please, Sally. You're scaring me."

Archie stepped forward, peering at me intently. "I'm afraid you've upset Sally, Neil. That's really rather bad of you. We've always thought of you as a good boy, you see. We're not angry with you, just disappointed."

"Archie? What's going to happen?" I asked him, my throat tightening.

"It's like you said, Neil." Sally's voice had fallen almost to a whisper. "You're a puppet. We'd like you to dance for us, please."

"But I can't. I'm no good at dancing."

"No good at dancing? Have you ever heard of such a thing, Archie – a puppet that can't dance?"

"We could teach him," Archie said.

"We could teach him a lesson," she emended.

"It'd be for his own good," Archie agreed.

"Let's do it." With one broad sweep of her arm, Sally sent a pile of magazines flying from the coffee table on to the floor. "Trousers off, Neil! Shoes as well!"

"No. I don't want to. This is silly."

"I'm not listening, Neil. Just do it. Then up on the table."

Archie slowly shook his head. "If you won't do it, lad, we shall have to debag you."

If the thought of removing my trousers in the middle of the living room, with Sally and Archie looking on, unnerved and embarrassed me, the alternative prospect, of being wrestled to the floor by grunting grown-ups and forcibly undressed, was infinitely more appalling. It was something I could not countenance. I stood up, kicked off my shoes and unzipped my trousers, feeling them fall loosely about my ankles. Sally told me to step out of them, and she picked them up, folded them neatly along the creases and draped them over the back of the armchair.

"Don't want to get them all crumpled, do we?"

I shook my head, gritting my teeth.

"You're a good boy, Neil," Archie said.

"What do you want me to do?" I asked, my voice full of tears.

Sally rubbed her hands together importantly. "We want to see this puppet you talked about."

"It was – only a joke."

"Oh, I see. A joke, was it? Trouble is, Neil, no-one's laughing."

I could not take my eyes off her, but I heard Archie speak softly at the corner of my vision. "Come on, Sally, I think maybe the boy's had enough now."

"Shut up!" she snapped back. "Put on some music!"

"What?"

"He can't dance without music. Even a puppet needs music."

They had a teak-veneered radiogram in the corner of the room. The name *Bush* was badged on the front. It was spotlessly clean, as though they hardly ever used it.

I think Sally expected me to try and run away, the way she came and stood in front of me. That would be futile, I knew, because they could easily overpower me.

"Here's a good one." Archie waved an LP sleeve at us – a photograph of a Scottish loch, framed in tartan, with a yellow slash across it. "Jimmy Shand and his band."

When the music started, I stood stock-still. I felt ridiculous. My legs suddenly felt very cold.

"Right, hop to it, Neil!" Sally clapped her hands in time to the music pounding across the room. "Get those knees snapping!"

I stared at her, but I didn't move. I couldn't move.

"I'll count to three," she shouted over the music, "and if you haven't started by then – "

I flung out one leg and nearly toppled over. My heart was a hot rubber ball, bouncing in my throat, choking me.

I never even heard her start to call the numbers, but suddenly she yelled "Three!" and then she screamed it again, and she was lunging at me, shaking my wrist, with this dreadful pent-up fury sparking in her eyes. I wanted to move now, to do something, anything, to get it over with, but fear rooted me to the spot, and my legs trembled and threatened to buckle under me, and then I was frightened of that, as well, and an ache swelled in my tummy, a sort of scalding wave that brought me out in a cold sweat.

I'd heard her shout something to Archie and, the next I knew, he was coming towards me, carrying in his hand the thick brass poker from the fireplace. I managed a few more desultory kicks, but you wouldn't have called them a dance, and then I felt the poker's cold tip against the back of my knee, sort of prodding me, the blunt stab of its vile metal snout – until Sally called out for him to stop.

"Eh? What's the matter?"

The first music track ended, marooning us in crackling silence. "I said" – she let her voice slide down in a gurgling *glissando* – "I said, not the poker. Too heavy, too hard. We don't want any nasty bruises, do we?"

Archie waved the implement ineffectually in the air. "What then?"

She indicated the kitchen. The music began belting out again. This time the tune was simpler, a chunky, rhythmic melody I had heard somewhere before, and I stood as tall as I could, pulling my shoulders back, and tried to forget I was in my pants, as I imagined my ankles were on springs, my feet darting artfully to left and right, a slicing kick here, a deftly pointed toe there, all the while my eyes fixed on the spinning black disc on the sunken turntable, as though the relentless rotation might gradually hypnotize me, so I would lose my fear, forget my shame.

Archie was back, looming in front of me. He held something in his hand, a stick, no, a wooden spoon. He showed it to Sally, and she nodded. Moving behind me, he tapped me on the knee-joints with the head of the spoon, not hard, more a series of coaxing slaps in time to the music – *pap pap pap.*

Sally was shouting again. "Faster, Neil! Come on! You can do better than that!"

That made Archie slap me harder, so it was starting to hurt. The pressure on the muscles was unnerving me now, and I could feel my legs trembling worse than before, I couldn't stop them, and I knew they were going to give up on me at any moment, unless I stood still and flexed them, but if I did that, Archie would hit me harder and Sally would yell at me. She would screech at me in that monstrous, animal voice.

He came round in front of me once more, and I could smell his sweat, the high, humid stink of it, and when he grinned at me I saw the yellow gasp of his teeth, and in that instant he whacked me on the knee-cap with that blasted spoon – yes, Archie did, my friend Archie, *my friend Archie,* while I stared into his eyes, deeper and deeper, the music nearly drowned out now by Sally's guttural screams, and it felt like I was falling, crashing down into Archie's eyes, tumbling, open-mouthed, wild-eyed, out of control.

And so it happened. You might have thought I did it on purpose, to get them to stop, to make them let me go; but I didn't. I never even thought of that. Even in the wildest, maddest part of me, I never thought of it. Still, the result was the same in the end. You see, I hadn't been all day, since leaving home in the morning, and my bladder was full. When he smacked me on the knee that last time, and it really hurt, well, then I just couldn't hold it any longer. I didn't even know what was happening at first, and I think I heard the noise before I actually felt anything. Of course, once it started, it wouldn't stop, it became a torrent. For a moment, I thought perhaps it was blood running down my legs – had he hit me that hard? – but then I sensed the scalding weight of it in my pants, and I knew that being watched attempting a crazy dance on a table top had become but a small disgrace.

They were worried about the table and the carpet, not about me. One on either side of me, they dragged me to the floor and pinioned me upright as I stumbled to the door, leaving a dark trail behind me. Idiotically, Archie had stuck the wooden spoon in the breast pocket of his shirt, as though it were a natural accessory. Neither of them had had a chance to turn the record off, and I remember a surreal terror surging inside me as I was bounced into the hall, my wee splashing my socks, to the cheery accompaniment of Jimmy Shand's wheezing accordion.

"Get him outside, for God's sake!" I heard Sally yell.

The acrid stench of urine rose to fill my nostrils.

"What about his trousers?" Archie said, breathlessly.

"What about my carpet?"

They shoved me through the front door, on to the doorstep. The door banged loudly behind me. I sat down on the tiled step, crouched over, gnome-like, so no-one passing in the road would see my sodden pants clinging to me. Through the window, I could hear Sally and Archie shouting at each other, and Jimmy Shand still defiantly pumping away at his accordion.

I wanted to ring the bell and ask for my trousers, but I didn't dare. It was easier just to sit there, huddled into myself, printing a spreading wet stencil on the cold tiles. The back of my right leg smarted where Archie had struck me, but that was a small, meaningless pain compared to the all-consuming ache I carried in my heart. I bowed my head and closed my eyes, encircled within a shrieking vortex of madness.

How I missed my gran. If only she had been at home now, whispering to herself as she busied her way through small tasks in the sunny kitchen, I believe I would gladly have rushed down the street in my half-nakedness to go to her and be held and comforted. She would have sat me down and cleaned me and, smiling with no need of words, made the bad places good again.

Death cannot destroy love, but it steals it away and hides it in the dark.

I wondered, too, about friendship, as Sally and Archie argued at my back. Yes, I thought, that also was a dead thing.

Through the open skylight, massed accordions marched gleefully into the street...*wee-waw-chunk-a-chunk-a-chunk.*

I opened my mouth to the sky, and a cry of rage came out of me.

Chapter XVIII

Forgiveness

I couldn't think what the building had been before. Some kind of lounge, perhaps, or even a stock room for the bowling club. Did you need stock for bowls matches? I really had no idea. I seldom came round to this side of the green, and I was only here now because I was hot and I had seen the metal ice-cream sign flapping in the breeze.

They'd put up a shiny new wooden sign over the doorway. It read *Ferdie's* in curly green lettering on a white background. I didn't know who Ferdie was, though presumably he owned the place. So I went in and sat at an empty table, which was easy, as there was hardly anyone in there. Each table was laid with a freshly-laundered cotton tablecloth in green-and-white gingham, while the crisply white-painted wooden chairs featured green leatherette seats. The sun slanted in through the white-framed windows, casting incandescent rhomboids randomly across the floor and furniture.

I thought perhaps they would have an attractive young waitress who would come across and simper at me, ready to take my order with head lowered attentively over budding breasts scarcely contained within her economical uniform; but very soon a raucous coughing echoed from the kitchen, and out waddled an elderly frump with wire wool for hair and an expression of resigned hopelessness. A notepad and pencil dangled on a frayed string from her apron pocket.

I ordered a strawberry milk shake and a sausage roll. The shake came with a maypole straw, but I couldn't quite suck up the dregs, and so I upended the glass and waited for the pink scum to slide slowly down to my lips, ending up with a milky moustache over my top lip, which reminded me of that time in bed with Sally and Archie and little Noah, and the strange, cloying sweetness that dribbled from Sally's swollen nipples.

As I was eating, I looked out on to the bowling green and the open grass beyond. It dawned on me then that I had never been in the rec alone before. I had always gone there with Gran or Sally. Now Gran was dead, and it was as though Sally had died also – for I had surely witnessed the demise of each of them. I had seen Gran fade away in her hospital bed and, hardly less poignantly, I had been with Sally and seen and felt the death of affection, that brightly bubbling stream of her smiling passion become a stagnant pool, a shadowed place, dark and dankly overhung with menace. In my own way, I questioned this eclipse and, perhaps self-pityingly, lamented it, but I could not understand what I needed to appreciate above all, that the dynamics and complexities of human emotions are not susceptible to rationalisation. They are limitlessly volatile forces answerable to no extraneous influence.

I had my head down, brushing away crumbs, so I didn't see them approach the door. Perhaps they had seen me through the window, or their arrival could have been mere coincidence. Anyway, I heard the clang of the pram wheels against the door-frame, and I glanced up and saw them standing by the till. Sally looked harassed, Archie gazed around vacantly and baby Noah was asleep, his head lolling to one side with his reddened cheeks puffed out like tiny apples.

I carried on eating, pausing occasionally to lick my fingers. Suddenly the food had no taste, and it seemed to lodge in my mouth like some kind of obscene discharge, constantly replenishing itself. Though I kept my head lowered, I knew they must have seen me. I just wanted to be out of there. Sweat thickened in my armpits and trickled down the hard flanks of my ribs.

A shadow loomed at the periphery of my vision. Archie was coming over to the table. "Hello, Neil. All right if we join you?"

No, go away. Leave me alone. I don't want you near me.

Well, that's what I wanted to say, but of course I didn't say it. I stared at him blankly, fighting to swallow the last of the sour paste that had been my sausage roll.

Sally came up behind him, Noah clutched to her chest, bare legs dangling. His eyes were partly open now, misty with interrupted sleep. Without speaking, I stretched my leg under the table and pushed out a chair with my foot.

The grey-haired waitress approached, scowling. "You can't leave that pram in here. No room."

Archie peered all around in mock confusion. "The place is practically empty. What's the problem?"

"Not my rules. If people come in for lunch..."

He sighed. "Okay, okay. I'll take it back outside."

Kicking off the brake, he slowly reversed the pram towards the door, while Sally carefully lowered herself and Noah into the chair I had eased out. I contrived to ignore her, feigning an improbably intense concentration by picking the last moist flakes of pastry from my plate.

"You're not going to talk, then."

I couldn't tell if this was an observation or a question, but I swiftly reminded myself that it didn't matter. Sally didn't matter. I didn't matter, either, if you looked at it in a certain way. I mean, I was an adolescent boy sitting in a café in the park. How important could that be? Where were the people to whom any of us could make a difference?

There was Noah. He lay opposite me, cradled neatly in the crook of Sally's arm. Noah, my own flesh and blood and sperm and breathless frenzy. I had to make more of him, somehow, than a nocturnal emission, a small accident at the front of my trousers, in a world too full of walking accidents. I studied his moon-like face, the pinkish opalescent paleness of it, light-washed in a colour that hardly existed, as surely unique as a fingerprint. In the blue-grey gemstones of his eyes, in the wheat-coloured wisps of his feathery hair, in the impudent upturn of his stubby nose, I thought I saw, almost as the merest mirage that was there in a certain light and quickly gone, a fragile reflection of myself, my face effortlessly submerged under water.

Archie was back, his vaguely grubby fingers fiddling with the typewritten menu card in its plastic holder. "I wonder what the fish is like," he said.

Sally seemed tired, preoccupied, her eyes unfocused. "Thin and dry, like the sole of your shoe. I just saw one go by." She reached for the menu, and Noah, jostled by the movement of her arm, began to snuffle and mew.

I remembered what Gran had said, when she had told me to look after the boy and love him. *You look after him. You love him. Do it for me.* I sat quietly, thinking about Gran, imagining her face. *Do it for me.* Noah's bottom lip was a curled pink worm, quivering, working up tears.

"Give him to me," I said.

Sally blinked elaborately. "Oh, it speaks," she said.

"Please."

"Come round to me."

"Good lad," Archie said, quietly.

They both ordered the same, chicken salad. I watched them eat, hugging Noah to my chest in folded arms, rocking him just slightly, enough to pacify him. I felt his body heat seep through to me like a warm stain. I inhaled the pure, buttery smell of him, the untainted odour of nothingness. How small and frail he felt in my arms, and yet how powerful, for throughout that tiny body hummed a vital charge of life and love and longing, suppressed by time, a long, wild scream unuttered, a whole world undiscovered. Noah. My son.

"You look easy with him, lad," Archie said.

I nodded, smiling down at the softly stirring bundle I cradled against me. "I haven't forgotten he's mine," I said. "I'll try to know him."

Archie's eyes roamed over us – my face, my faintly trembling arms, Noah's sausage-pink legs, quaintly akimbo. "I hope you'll do more than know him."

"It'd be a start, at least." Without even knowing that I would do this, I held my child under the arms and, lifting him level with my face, planted a hesitant kiss on the cool tip of his nose. "That's from your great gran," I told him.

Sally's eyes widened. "Not from you?"

Archie waved his fork lazily in the air. "Time enough for that," he said. "Give the lad a chance."

I had said so little, and yet it seemed enough. There was nothing more I wanted to say. This was like another funeral, the death of something thrilling and important that had become infected by deceit and mistrust. It briefly crossed my mind to ask the pair of them about the other day, the incident at the house, but surely there was no point. They would only laugh at me, or get angry. It would lead us nowhere, except perhaps into a dark morass of sullen contempt. I could do without that.

Sally dropped her knife and fork into the plate with a clatter and pushed the unfinished meal away from her. "I didn't enjoy that at all."

I studied her face. She didn't look well. Her skin, once suffused with a pale golden glow, now appeared grey and slightly greasy, reminding me of oiled putty. She seemed to have made no attempt to tidy or style her hair, and the darts that she used to wear cropped close to the nape of her neck were sticking out like fibrous wings. Even the whites of her eyes looked clouded, scratched at the corners by weary red threads. Inevitably, my attention fell to the vee of her white blouse, where the darkening slot of her cleavage opened and closed as she moved her arms or hunched her shoulders. To think that I had touched her there, stroked the cool, soft, dry flesh of those gourd-like fruits, taken the rubbery nipples in my mouth, raked them with my teeth. That seemed somehow unimaginable, incomprehensible. It meant nothing to me now, emotionally or physically. I gazed at the shapeless bulge of her breasts, remembering, visualizing, and it had no effect, I did not go hard under the table as I would have done a few months ago, I did not have to whisper an apology and lift Noah gently away from the bony thrust of my hungry penis. All of that was over, finished. Here was the death of it.

The trouble was, I would miss the excitement, the adrenalin-charged hypertension that flowed into me from Archie's knowledgeable manliness and from Sally's enigmatic sexuality. What had happened to me was that I had fallen in love with the experience of feeling in love. If I did not love – perhaps had never truly loved – the people themselves, their aura still surrounded me, and I was intoxicated and even sustained by it. Contemplating its loss, I felt as if the blood itself drained out of me.

I had already convinced myself I knew the reason for what I perceived as a fatal disenchantment. There was a flawless simplicity about it. I held the reason in my arms, and I raged inwardly at its innocence. Now, as I comforted my child, I had to find a new way of loving. I had to learn to be someone else.

Standing, I held Noah out to his mother like a cloth-wrapped parcel. "Here, take him back. He belongs to you."

I knocked my chair over in my haste to get outside, but I left it upturned on the floor. There was a low brick wall beyond the doorway with a small fountain playing behind it, and I sat on the wall in the sun, feeling the cold sparks on the back of my neck as the breeze carried water droplets towards me. Children on tricycles and scooters milled around on the sun-bleached flagstones.

If neither of them had come out, I suppose I would have felt indignant and disappointed. As it was, I didn't have long to wait. A shadow fell across me, and Archie sat down, loosening his collar against the sudden heat.

"You all right?" he enquired, not looking at me.

"Why shouldn't I be?"

"That's a question, not an answer."

I shrugged. "I was just thinking."

"Oh? What about?"

I looked him straight in the eye. "In my imagination, I was doing the Highland Fling. Only it wasn't just my imagination." Then I turned away, for hot tears were welling into my eyes.

At least he was gracious enough to appear uncomfortable. A tiny girl ran towards us, nearly overbalancing as she reached Archie's feet, and he put out a precautionary hand and gently supported her back, until she scampered away, laughing.

"We feel very badly, Neil," he said.

"*You* feel badly? How do you think I feel?"

His eyes were focused on something, or nothing, far away

again. "I know. Don't think we haven't talked about it, Sally and me."

"Oh, that's nice," I said, coldly.

He laid a hand on my thigh, but I swung my leg inwards, isolating him. It sometimes helped if I ground my teeth together, but not this time, and so the tears came again, turning the sunlight into blinding shards of broken glass. "It's all spoiled," I cried, "all of it, everything."

His hand reached for me once more, but then he seemed to think better of it, and drew back. "That's not true, Neil. It doesn't have to be like that."

"It's how it is, Archie. Don't you see?"

"Oh Neil. Don't cry here, in front of everyone."

"What's the matter? Am I embarrassing you?"

"No, no, it's not that," and he sounded almost philosophical. "I just wish you could try to be – more positive, more forward-looking."

"But I don't want something else, Archie. I want what we had."

"I understand. But that's just the problem; you're hankering after what we had before, whereas now we must work together with what we have from here on. There's no going back, Neil."

"You mean, just accept the change – make the best of it?"

"Well, I – " He looked downhearted and let out a short laugh. "It seems to me, when people say they'll make the best of a situation, it generally means they're only interested in the worst of it."

"Sometimes it means they're frightened, because they don't know how to change themselves into somebody else. They don't know how to start." I slipped him a quick glance, to see if he was listening and if he understood me. All the while, his blue eyes darted nervously from side to side.

I watched the door for a moment, in case Sally might come out, but there was no sign of her. "I really did love her, you know," I said, trying all I could to keep my voice from breaking. "I mean, it wasn't just a schoolboy thing."

I thought perhaps my use of the past tense might alert him to something, but if it did, he let it pass. "She's a complicated woman," he said, "but a strong one. Resolute."

"Do you think you'll stay together?" I asked him.

"No doubt about it." He laughed again. "United in a common cause, you might say."

Even as I uttered the words, I knew it was the wrong thing to say, but I said it anyway. "It's him that's broken everything up, isn't it? He's made it all different."

Archie fixed me with a caustic stare. "Ah, come on now, Neil. That's not fair. You don't go blaming a wee baby for your troubles." He shook his head in frustration. "I thought you were bigger than that."

I should have countered this reproach in some way, if only to uphold my self-respect, but when I opened my mouth, I could find nothing to say. I suppose I had no defence. Archie's statement was incontestable. In any case, the child was mine, so I was the architect of my own downfall. It was all I could do to force back fresh tears.

A whistle sounded in the distance, shrieking over the café roof, followed by the frantic metallic roar of an express hurtling past the chain-link fence. The building blocked my view, but I could see the thundering black engine in my mind's eye, a red-and-yellow ribbon of swaying carriages streaming behind the coal-crammed tender, the driver's grimy face dimly visible through the soot-smeared glass of the cab window. I would have waved at him, of course, or perhaps at the stooping fireman as he turned towards the tender, ready to replenish the livid, voracious firebox. At the flashing carriage windows I imagined all the stolidly impassive faces of the passengers, rushing past like truncated figures on a conveyor belt – some peering morosely at the jagged green blur of the trackside, some gazing as if transfixed at a book or newspaper quivering in their upraised hands, others in suspended animation, heads locked in a spasm of dreamless, ungainly sleep.

Picturing these spectral travellers, I found myself envying them. Unlike me, they were being swept not to some uncontrolled oblivion but to somewhere systematically defined in time and space, their journeys ordered and predictable, each encapsulated moment a component of a simple formulaic plan. *I begin, I go, I wait, I finish. I am in control.* I was the boy who waved at trains, the boy whose eyes were misted by the impossibility of being there, fearlessly cocooned in so much thunder. Under the whispering trees, with Gran or Sally beside me, I stood and watched the framed profiles cruising past in a torrent of noxious noise, bobbing like dim lanterns suspended in smoke-hazed windows. Their calm, wordless certainty was not for me; I was the boy who waved at trains, heart leaping in the infinitesimal flash of that light-splintered moment, and gazed with longing at the darkly expressionless hatcheted bulks of their receding tails, straining into an echoing vacuum where suddenly nothing remained but the sun's glint on steel and the smell of the wind.

"Probably the *Master Cutler,*" Archie declared, checking his watch as he tipped his head towards the subsiding noise.

"Usually twelve coaches," I informed him.

Apparently, he thought it safe to try a quick smile. "Class of locomotive, Neil? Wheel configuration? Type of valve gear? Smoke deflectors – yes or no?"

When he saw I wasn't responding, he fell silent and sat staring into his lap. I looked at the door again, but I didn't see Sally. Most of the children had disappeared, led away by mothers or aunts to play on the swings or in the sandpit.

I remembered that day in the rec with Sally, when she asked me to push her on the swing, and I felt the imprint of her bra as I pressed my hands on her back.

"I – I never paid for my food," I said, and I straightened as if to get up.

"It's okay," Archie said, "Sally'll see to it," and he laid his hand on my thigh to keep me there. This time I just let him do it, not bothering, and somehow I liked the warm feel of his palm on me, and I closed my eyes and half-turned towards him, wondering if he would do anything else, anything different from what he had done before. I could feel a funny fluttering in the tight part of my trousers, like a small bird waking up in the morning, and I wanted him to touch me, only we were outdoors and it would have been wrong and dangerous and quietly, gently crazy. But I did want him to love me, to make it almost like it used to be.

"We were going to ask you something, Sally and me, only then you ran out."

His hand was still on my leg, and I placed my hand on top of it. "Really? What's that?"

"Well, Sally could do with a break. She's tired. We thought we'd take Noah and go up to the cottage for a few days."

"You mean to Rannoch?"

"Aye." He freed his hand and used it to smooth back his hair where the breeze had ruffled it. "The thing is – well, would you like to come with us?"

I felt my heart skip, but I didn't want him to know that the idea excited me. "I don't know," I said. "My holidays end soon."

"That's all right. We'll go directly."

"Oh, right. Maybe I'd like that."

"What about your parents?"

I shrugged. "It was all right the last time."

"Aha. Sally, she'd probably rest up in the garden. You and me, we could go fishing like before – that's if you wanted."

"We could go out on the bikes again," I suggested, and I heard my voice leap at the memory of it.

He nodded emphatically. "We could, we could."

I glanced past him. "You'd better rescue your pram," I said.

"It's your pram as well, Neil. It belongs to all of us. Noah belongs to all of us."

"I know. Archie, will you do something for me?"

"What's that?"

"Will you go in there, please" – I nodded at the café door – "and tell Sally I forgive her and I still love her, and everything'll be all right. Tell her it's time for her to take Noah home."

"You think she's hiding?"

"I don't know. No, I don't think so."

He sat there a while longer, then he squeezed my leg and stood up. "I'll go inside," he said. I watched him, and he stood next to me, not moving, just standing by the wall, staring at the doorway. He turned and smiled at me. "Will I tell her you'll come with us?"

"If you want me." I reached out and he took my hand. I let him hold it for a while. Then he let it fall, and I lowered my eyes to the ground, just thinking, and when I looked up once more he had disappeared through the doorway.

I wasn't sure what to do then. I thought I should wait to see if they came out together, only they might sit inside, talking. I hadn't expected to meet them, in any case. So I moved away, back to the gate, where I had left my bike. Clutching both handlebars, I pushed it on to the open grass, where I could walk slowly along, skirting the trees, and watch the trains go clattering by. I stopped when I reached the place where I had found the slow worm that time, and I rummaged in the cool undergrowth, seeing nothing. I thought of Archie at the cemetery in India, keeping an eye open for cobras winding out of the long grass. I was glad there were no cobras in the rec.

Soon I was near the top gate. I carried on walking through the passage into Mandalay Avenue. I could have ridden downhill from there, but somehow that didn't appeal to me. I walked on down the pavement, slowing as I passed the spot where I had dropped Gran's purse behind the wall. The sun was hotter here, away from the cooling, heat-absorbing grass, and a fierce white light was reflected from the seared paving stones. Ragged moons of sweat bloomed in my armpits.

A breeze touched my face as I turned into the main road, chilling the moisture on my brow. I swung up on to my bike and rode slowly past the shops, curving through the traffic. I told myself that the tears in my eyes came from the wind.

That's how it was. That's how I came to be back at Rannoch. When I think about it, Dad could have said 'no'. That would have made a difference, all the difference in the world. Then it would never have happened, and probably I would not even be telling you this story. Of course, I wanted him to say it would be all right, and I was pleased and relieved when he did. Still, I don't want you to think I am trying to make out it was his fault for consenting. That would be unfair, worse than unfair. After all, I was old enough to take responsibility for my own actions, intelligent enough to make the decisions that naturally preceded those actions. It's just that you never know how things are going to turn out. I was the boy who waved at trains, only I never understood where my own train was going.

Chapter XIX

Dreams and Landscapes

What surprised me more than anything was the total silence. It was like watching a film with the sound switched off. And the people! They seemed to be everywhere, just shuffling aimlessly to and fro, mostly with their heads down, so that only through familiarity with their surroundings could they conceivably know where they were walking. I say, with their heads down; but – and I accept that you may have some difficulty in understanding me on this point – they appeared to me to have no proper heads, no heads constructed of flesh and blood and bone, at all. It took me only a short while to appreciate that, of course, they would need protection against the cold, which surely was why the domes above their collars were swathed in circular windings of cloth, woven from a material with a curious granular surface which looked almost as if it might be alive. When they turned towards me, I was afraid of their faces. I shuddered when I looked at the black ovals which should have been their eyes.

Although it was entirely logical, I was somehow taken aback to look down at my own body and see that I was dressed exactly as they were, in a long coat of a patchwork quilt effect, apparently made from any number of different coloured squares of a thick, coarse fabric, giving off the faint but unmistakeable odour of farmyard animals. The coat fell below my knees, where wrinkled black trousers or leggings rendered my legs all but invisible in the wretchedly poor light. My feet were encased in oversized, laceless black boots, possibly of thick leather or even rubber, while my hands were made shapeless and clumsy by leather mittens with pale fur at the cuffs.

There was a narrow pathway, twisting between outcrops of rock, and I was walking unsteadily over stony, pitted ground, my hips occasionally bumping against the dark boulders. To either side of me lay black, formless hollows, out of whose hideous depths fierce jets of a blinding blue light speared angrily upwards and then vanished – but no sound came from these eruptions, save in my tortured imagination. I watched my boots walking, and it was as though they advanced of their own accord, carrying me along with them, for I had no notion where I was going. The other people trudged inexorably towards me from the opposite direction, and I let my boots steer me around them. The people paid me no heed, as if they did not see me. A long, tapering geyser of glaring blue gas, incandescent as neon, shot from the ground beside my feet, and I jumped with fright.

Someone approached me and hesitated. I had no way of knowing if it was a man or a woman; it was just a person, just a shambling collection of rough clothes, decorated in coloured panels. The figure put out an arm, the hand palm vertical, gloved like mine. I took this gesture as a request, or even an instruction, to stop, and I waited where I stood, not knowing what else to do. The arm reached forward – it seemed to me to attain an almost telescopic length – and the leathery palm made contact with a blue square midway down one side of my coat, pressing the fabric against me, not hard, but firmly, very firmly. I braced myself, resisting the pressure – and something amazing happened. All the panels in my coat began to glow, emitting pulses of swelling, coruscating light, until I was engulfed from head to toe in a pillar of so dazzling a radiance, I felt I must lift a hand to my eyes to shield them from the glare. I was as a man on fire. Yet still I heard no sound, and I felt nothing, no pain, no vibration, no sensation at all.

But the colours! Never had I seen or imagined such colours. For a few seconds blue and gold were predominant, but then these were overwhelmed by a rising effulgence in which the colours were not fixed or primary, but streaked with dancing light and shadow in a form I cannot properly describe to you, a kind of granular, crystalline shroud that rose to envelope me in a mantle made of silently exploding suns, and the suns had a colour that was no colour I knew or could comprehend, my brain was not programmed to decipher it, and so it was delivered to me as a life-form, a creation, a texture constantly altering and revitalizing itself into different manifestations, each more incredible than the one before.

Then it came to me. No, not *to* me; *from* me. I am as sure as I can be that the extraordinary sensation accompanying the climax of the display of colours surged out from within my own body, like the birth of a creature freed, unfolding itself. Heat. This was not a fierce, alarming heat, but a steady current of glorious, all-pervading warmth that seemed to course, as blood itself, into every pore and fibre of my body. So, as the great light subsided, I felt myself empowered and rejuvenated by the life-sustaining miracle drawn from the bright patch on my coat which the traveller had touched.

All that time ago – I remembered. *Lirpa.* The colour that was not a colour. A colour unknown, unimagined. The colour I had tried to find for Archie. It had presented itself to me at last, and I would never forget it. The colour produced warmth out of nothing but itself, and now, of course, I knew at once where I was, who these people were. *Lirpa.* The colour that brought life to Pluto.

The man, if he was a man, had not moved away. He nodded his head and jabbed his gloved hand towards me, then drew back the dark glove to beat the front of his coat. Uncertain, I hovered there, motionless, and in the next instant his meaning dawned upon me. I raised my hand in recognition, and reached out for him. My aim was not directed at any particular panel, but I pressed a red square on his chest and stood back. The figure's arms rose stiffly, elbows out, the black eye-holes seeming to bore into me. In a frozen moment of horror, I realised my mistake. It was already too late for defence or avoidance. I watched, helplessly transfixed, as a quick spurt of flame darted from the dark wings of the coat, a red devil's tongue, and with terrifying speed more flailing tongues sprang towards me, lighting the darkness, until the silent form was cocooned in a blinding fireball. He tore frantically at the wrappings covering his head, dropping them into the fire, where they lay writhing like snakes, and I saw no face, only a ball of coiling smoke, angry orange lizards licking from the eye-holes, while the crinkling grey lip-worms oozed and shrivelled into the unmistakable shape of the words that could be neither spoken nor heard: *The Wrong Colour!* Then he was gone, subsiding into the ground with the awful finality of a building collapsed, and there was just the smouldering ruin of the tattered coat to mark the place where this had happened.

Reeling in revulsion, I turned away, but an unseen hand clamped my arm, gripping it hard, hurting me. Crying out, I tried to shake the hand away, but it held me fast, pressing my flesh against the bone. Twisting wildly, this way and that, I struggled to free myself from the vice-like grasp of my invisible captor, grunting, screeching – but now, somehow, I could hear noise, and the noises were of my own making, orchestrating my desperation, and there was a voice, too, a low, familiar monotone that gently, insistently called my name, over and over, urging me to listen and be still. Slowly, cautiously, I let the fight slip out of me.

He had hold of my arm. Archie was squeezing my arm.

"Neil, Neil, Neil. There, it's all right."

I jerked free, rubbing the place on my arm, blinking my eyes.

"Poor boy. You had a bad dream. It's nothing."

I lay on my back in half-light, trying to focus on the ceiling. My pyjama jacket was soaked in sweat.

"You're fine now. Only a dream. A nightmare, perhaps. You're safe now."

I glanced at him quickly, panting for breath. "I was somewhere else," I said. My eyes roamed the ceiling once more. "It was horrible. I burned a man."

"Neil, Neil."

"I don't want to be there, in that place."

He gave my arm a little friendly nudge. "Where were you? Do you know?"

"Pluto. I was on Pluto. It wasn't nice."

"Aye, that I can believe."

Carefully, he eased his arms about me and helped me lift myself up, turning me to face the window, where he drew the curtain aside so that I could look out and see the grey slab of the loch lightly stroked with the touch of morning. "See, it's real," he said. "That's no dream."

In one sense, it was, for I had come to love this place. I felt at one with the pewter water and the emerald stubble of forest on the far hills, the bulging laundry sacks of cloud drifting in from the west coast and Glencoe, carrying the soft rain that was gone almost before it had arrived. The animals, too, I loved – the tiny, flitting, multi-coloured finches, bright and nervous as butterflies; the impishly-dancing red squirrels racing through the trees at impossible speeds; a pine marten, sleek and dark as chocolate, arrowing across the road, into the waving bracken; a stag standing proud on a bluff beside a silver stream, his antlers black lightning against the sky. Yes, I thought, this was indeed the land of dreams.

Our movement had woken Sally, and she stirred, blinking open her eyes, and smiled thinly into the warm space between us.

Archie reached over me and touched her shoulder. "Boy had a bad dream."

I slid back down under the covers and lay still. Already I could hear birds singing in the trees bordering the road. A pale wash of actinic water-light filtered through the window, breathing a stain of morning on the walls.

"Poor boy." Sally rolled on to her side and kissed me on the cheek. "You're safe now. I've got all my boys with me."

I was still shaking from the dream, trying to re-orientate myself. Now I revelled in the warmth of two bodies close to me, enveloping me. They would protect me. Noah snuffled softly in his cot beside the bed, but he didn't wake.

"Sleep some more," Sally whispered in my ear, "it's early yet."

"Hold me," I said, drifting towards shadows again.

As a matter of fact, I hadn't meant that, hadn't deliberately sought that specific solace; but hardly more than a deep sigh later, I felt her hand steal down and enclose me, and somehow I was relaxed rather than aroused. All my limbs seemed to melt into the mattress. Her hand scarcely moved, just trembled lightly there, something tingling and feathery. I heard Archie clear his throat and take a breath. I suppose, after all that time, so much nearness, it wasn't surprising, and sure enough, as if I had always expected it, his hand crept under the blanket and the sheet, and I felt him touch me, his heavier fingers colliding softly with Sally's in the darkness. If the intrusion worried me, I chose not to show it, for the nightmare had disturbed me deeply, and I craved this quiet moment of comfort and reassurance, wanted them to do the most for me that they could. Yes, I questioned the rightness of it and, even as I allowed it, I was not proud of it. This was a time for needing to be loved, not a time for pride or self-esteem. It was the first time Archie had ever touched me in that way, in that place, and I could not find it in me to stop him. Lest he should think I resisted, I kept as still as I could, though my stomach fluttered and I felt myself growing larger with each caress, until my submission was total and complete, and I felt as if I floated upon a lilting, tranquil sea. At the end I had no notion whose delicately probing fingers brought about that sweet, aching fire, the liquid exhalation that briefly sent my body arching out of itself; but I could not make myself care any longer, as I subsided into the sweat-moistened softness beneath me, knowing that now I would sleep without torment.

Ever since that grey, brain-fogged morning, I have wondered, for no special reason, what my father would have thought or said if he had come to learn of my experience. Perhaps he would have disowned me. I cannot believe he would have understood. He could have sought Archie and attacked him, but Dad was never given to physical violence. In his world there was no swearing, no sexual reference, no overt aggression. Mainly, I think he would have been saddened and disappointed, and quite possibly he would have asked my mother where they had gone wrong. I drew comfort from the reflection that it was an incident of which he need have no knowledge.

The bright, tinkling bells of early birdsong rang at the sun-splashed window as I clawed my way upwards from the depths of slumber. I turned to look at Sally, and she smiled at me, whispered something inaudible and slipped out of bed, pausing just briefly to peer down at Noah, snug in his nest of blankets. She shortly returned with a tray of tea and toast, the warm butter seeping into golden pools on the plate.

"What shall we do today?" I asked her, between mouthfuls.

She sucked her teeth thoughtfully. "Don't know. What do you want to do?" Dark crumbs had settled like freckles on the tops of her breasts. Below the specks were spidery blue lines marbling the pale globes.

"We could go fishing," I said.

"*We* could go fishing?" she snorted. "Don't ask me to go fishing. I hate fishing."

"How can you say you hate something you've never tried?" Archie asked her. He had propped himself on one elbow, the pillow folded around his head. "There any toast for me?"

Sally took a butter-soaked triangle and fed it into his mouth. "Anyway, you went fishing yesterday. We hadn't been here five minutes."

"We didn't catch anything," I reminded her.

"Yes, I recall," she said, wearily. "It's a good job we're not relying on you to feed us."

"There's fish in the freezer box," Archie said.

She laughed, shaking her head. "I hardly think that's the point."

We carried on like that, bandying words and opinions, for half an hour or more, while the sun soared higher in the sky and the dewy dampness in the room succumbed to the warmth of the day. These were exchanges of view, not arguments, and I appreciated and enjoyed them, for amid this badinage I felt informally secure, part of a family. Five hundred miles from home, I felt at home.

Sally finished the toast, slotting a forefinger into her cleavage to wipe away the last dark crumbs. She used the same finger to clean the corners of her lips. I wondered if she had washed her hands earlier, or if, by forgetful transfer, we had all eaten my stuff with our treat.

Baby Noah began to cry. Sally ignored him at first, but then, when his wailing grew louder and more insistent, she lifted him from his cot and rocked him in her arms.

I sat up and perched on the edge of the bed.

"Here!" She held him out to me. "Take your turn. He's yours too."

I accepted the blanket-wrapped bundle. When I touched Noah's cheek, it felt hot and dry. "Perhaps he's feverish," I said.

She bent over us, rubbing the small, soft, roseate cheek with the backs of her curled fingers. My eyes moved away from the child's flushed, contorted face and roamed the ivory valley between his mother's dangling breasts. She wasn't beautiful any more, I thought, but she was proud and handsome, her sexuality diminished but still generous and open.

"What do you think?" I asked her.

"I'm not sure. He might just be wrapped up too warm." She peeled off the blankets and dropped them in the cot. "Hold him there. Let him get some air."

"He won't stop crying," I said, anxiously.

"He's a baby, Neil. They tend to do that. Birds sing, cats miaow, dogs bark, babies cry. It's the way of the world; don't worry about it."

I held my son close to me and rocked him gently from side to side as I had seen Sally do. His round, open mouth, with its thin pink ridge of toothless gum and curled wet lips, was like a fresh flower. I traced the outline of his lips with the tip of my finger, seeing my finger shake as I moved it.

Sally touched my arm. "That's good."

I felt Archie breathing on the back of my neck. "You're getting to look like a real daddy." His lips brushed my ear-lobe.

I lifted Noah a little higher, catching the buttermilk smell of him, and then something else besides. "I think he needs changing," I said.

"Very likely," Sally said, bending to sniff the nappy. "Will you help me?"

"Who, me?"

"Yes, you. Archie just said you were a real daddy."

"Yes. All right."

"There's nothing to be frightened of."

"I know."

"All fathers have to do it sometimes. It's only right."

"I suppose so."

"Bring him into the other room. The light's better."

"Do we – shall I put the kettle on?"

"Good gracious! What for? We're going to change his nappy, not sterilise him."

"Right."

Beyond the kitchen was the living room, which had an extra window in the side of the house. The sunlight was streaming in, casting bright frames of spotlit colour on the dusty rug. Sally spread a towel on the floor, and I carefully lowered Noah past my bended knee and placed him on his back. He screwed up his eyes as he met the light, but when we took off his cotton vest, the cool air seemed to soothe him, and his crying abated to a faltering whimper of complaint.

"Talk to him while I do this." She undid the safety pin and slowly peeled aside the folds of cloth.

"Ugh! Looks like Colman's mustard," I said, screwing up my nose.

"Come on, talk to him properly."

"He can't understand me."

"Doesn't matter. I want you to calm him down."

I knelt close to him, trying not to inhale too deeply. "Hello, Noah. That's a right mess you've made there. Pongs a bit." I flinched as a fountain of urine squirted into the air, narrowly missing my face. "Dirty little sod!"

"Neil, please."

"What's the matter?"

"Just – try and be nice to him."

"Okay," I said, inadequately. I stroked his anger-reddened cheek, cooing softly to him, tickling the pumping white sticks of his arms. "There's my Noah. It's all right, Noah. We'll soon make it better."

Sally had a jar and some cotton wool next to her. "Hold his wrists up," she told me, "above his head."

"How?"

She showed me. Noah started to cry again.

"He's still a bit fractious," I said.

"Well, he's a fraction."

"What d'you mean?"

"I mean, he's three months old today. So he's not one yet, but he's a quarter. He's a little fraction."

I smiled, clutching his tiny hands in my fist. "Hello, little fraction."

Sally was wiping Noah's bottom and minute, worm-like penis. She had made a neat parcel of the filled nappy and, with two fingers, rubbed cream into his crack and privates. His testicles hung like little acorns.

"There's really messy jobs with babies," I said.

"Next time you can do it on your own and I'll watch."

"I don't know. Maybe. I'd probably get it all over me."

"What, like this?" With one deft swipe, before I could even think of stopping her, she slapped the dirty nappy against my face, and instantly I felt the wet smear of Noah's yellowish turd upon my cheek.

I sprang to my feet, letting Noah fall back on to the towel. "What are you doing?"

Her brittle laughter seemed to drill into my skull. "Foretaste of things to come, Neil! Plenty more of that!"

"You're horrible! I hate you!" I prodded Noah with my foot. "And I hate you too!"

She leapt up, reaching out for me, but I had rushed to the door, impelled by rage and revulsion.

"Neil, wait! All right, I shouldn't have -"

Shut up!"

Dragging the front door shut behind me, I slid down on to the step. The sickening familiarity of the moment dulled my senses, and I was heedless of the early morning chill. It had happened all over again; I was sitting, soiled and humiliated, on the doorstep, without my clothes, Sally's screeching laughter jangling in my ears. I seemed to have shed so many tears for Sally and Archie, but now my eyes were stinging again, and there was no point in fighting my emotions. The teardrops were like dew on my cheeks, ice-cold in the crystal air. Don't ask me why, but I began unbuttoning my pyjamas, sliding free of them, finally tossing them aside. It was morning, brilliant daylight, and I found myself perched on the cottage step, as naked as the day

I was born. The cool air wafted over my body, drying my perspiration, prickling my skin, brushing away my tears. I felt something clean and pure wash over me in the morning's freshness, as though, just there and then, to be naked was the most natural thing in the world.

The red roof of the postman's van appeared at the side of the road below. The van door slammed and I heard footsteps on gravel. The postman came up the slope, walking briskly, and slowed as he caught sight of me. I waved.

"It's – it's Neil, isn't it?" he said, furrowing his brow.

"I'm Neil Robertson," I confirmed, "and as you can see, I've got no clothes on."

The postman pushed back the peak of his cap with the hand that held a thin bundle of mail. "Aye, right, I see. Will you not get cold?"

"Doesn't matter," I replied, with a shrug, letting my right hand drop to cover my dangling penis.

"Ah well, if you say so. Is – uh – is your uncle in?"

"He's in bed." I didn't bother to correct him, but held out my hand. "It's all right, you can give the post to me."

"Aye, I suppose." He handed me the bundle, secured with a rubber band. "Are you sure you're okay? Would you not be better off inside?"

I laid the post conveniently in my lap. "Inside I would be in greater danger," I told him.

"How so?"

"You don't want to know."

"Ah, have it your own way," the man said, adjusting his cap.

The door opened behind me. Archie stood at my back. "Neil, what on earth – ? It's okay, Sandy, I'll take care of this."

"Right you are, Archie. I'll be on my way then." He turned and headed back down towards the road.

Archie sat on the step beside me. "What's this all about, Neil?"

"Nothing."

"Come on, Neil. Sitting outside with no clothes on is never about nothing."

"I'm getting used to it by now, Archie."

"Eh?"

"At the house, remember? Dancing?"

"Hmm. Yes, okay. I remember." He shifted closer and wrapped an arm around me. "We can sort this out, Neil."

"Yeah, sure."

"Please. Just come inside. I'll make you a hot drink."

"I don't want a hot drink."

"What is it? Why are you out here?"

"Sally shit on me."

He screwed up his eyes, incredulously. "What?"

I cranked my head round to show him the scuff mark on my cheek. "See that?"

"Aye, what is it?"

"It's a bit of Noah's turd."

"Well – how did it get on your face?"

"Sally put it there."

"Sa – What on earth for? What's the point of it?"

"I don't know. She just likes doing things like that."

"Oh, this is all ridiculous," he said, and he hugged me more tightly. "Here's you sat out in the cold, stark naked, with baby shit on your face and your pyjamas chucked in the dirt. What's it all about, eh?" His arm fell to my hip and he tucked me up against him. "What's the world coming to?"

He reached down and plucked a large dock leaf from a rough patch under the window. I took it and folded it until some juice came out, then I used it as a cool pad to wipe the mess from my face.

"Now you'll have a green face," he said, "instead of a brown one."

We laughed. I leaned into him and closed my eyes. Archie's hand moved from my hip to my thigh, his fingers gently kneading the soft white flesh there. His touch felt strong, soothing, reassuring. I hung there, breathing deeply, lost in space. The warm pads of his fingertips sank against the muscle, inching gradually over the curve of my thigh and then upwards where the flesh broadened, a slow, rhythmic massage, its comforting glow amplified by a rocking, circular motion that enhanced its penetration.

"You all right?" he asked me, in a small, soft voice.

"Aha."

"Want me to stop?"

"No. I don't know."

I was glad I had put the letters in my lap. Whatever happened, Archie would not see. I didn't have to worry.

He kissed my shoulder, letting his lips linger just long enough to wet me. An electric pulse ran swiftly through the very core of me. I didn't look down, but I felt the letters shift as my excitement disturbed them.

Silently, I asked myself if I had stripped off my pyjamas by design, knowing that someone, and probably Archie, would be sure to come after me. My nakedness was hardly an accident. Only my true motivation was in question. Indoors, I might have allowed one of them to steal up on me in the act of dressing, and I could have claimed an element of innocence; but here, now, I had sacrificed that subtlety for an overt sexuality which troubled me even as I embraced it.

"Best give me the post," Archie said. "Not much use there."

"It's okay. It's no problem," I said, nervously.

"I'm expecting a cheque." He reached for the bundle, and I flinched as I felt his knuckles brush the stirring head nestling beneath.

I looked down, and suddenly I appeared more naked than ever. "I'm sorry," I said.

"What for?"

"You know."

"It's all right, Neil. It doesn't matter." He waved his hand towards the loch. "No-one can see."

I nodded. "Perhaps we should go in now."

"Aye, I dare say. No sense catching a chill." He stood up. "I'll make you some breakfast. And then – maybe we can go out on the bikes. What d'you think?"

Rising, I took his hand. "I'd like that."

"You're a good boy, Neil."

I remember he made me a huge helping of porridge. When I asked him for the sugar bowl, he scowled darkly. "Scots don't have sugar on their porridge," he told me, disdainfully. "You can sprinkle a little salt on."

"But I'm English."

"Are you? You've a Scots father. Don't you forget it."

Sally didn't come in. I could hear Noah grizzling in the next room, and her talking to him in a lilting, sing-song voice, trying to calm him.

I washed and dressed, then I went outside and started checking over the bikes. One of them, the one I had ridden last time, had a flat front tyre, but I pumped it up and it seemed airtight. Both chains looked oiled and secure, but I found a crooked brake-block, and straightened it with tools from the saddlebag. I tightened a loose bell and wiped each saddle with a muslin cloth. The sun was stronger now, and I looked forward to our excursion.

I heard the back door bang, and I looked up from my task to see Archie standing on the path, gazing at me with a sheepish frown on his face. With some small pride, I told him what I had been doing. His only response was a wordless nod.

"Archie, what's wrong?"

He let out an exasperated sigh. "Problem, lad."

"What problem?"

"Well, you see..." His voice tailed off, as he shuffled his feet awkwardly in the dust. "It's Noah."

"Yes? What about him?"

"The wee bairn's very hot and flushed just now." After a pause, he added, "You pointed it out yourself, right enough," as though by alluding to my paternal skills he might mitigate the disappointing decision he now had to announce.

I understood what was coming. "Why are you telling me this now? I mean, I already know." I heard the undertone in my voice betray my suspicion.

"In the circumstances...I think Sally's right. You can't be too careful."

"What are you trying to say, Archie? Whatever it is, just say it."

"Aye, okay. Look, sorry lad, but I'm afraid we'll need to get the doctor to have a wee look at him. Just to be sure, you understand. And so – "

"So we can't go out."

"Not just yet, no."

I smacked the saddle of the nearest bike, hurting my hand – a petulant, futile gesture, but it dispensed with the need for useless words.

"There it is," Archie said. He didn't meet my sullen glare. There were some pine cones on the path, and he began kicking at them with the toe of his boot. Behind him, in the cottage, I could hear Noah howling, his breath stopping and starting like bellows.

"Bloody baby," I muttered.

"What's that?" Archie challenged.

"Nothing."

I yanked the bike upright and wheeled it in a circle, nearly running over Archie's foot. I pushed it down the path, Archie staring after me. Pine cones popped under the wheels. I felt my friend's eyes boring into my back. When I reached the road, I swung my leg over, hoisted myself on to the saddle and sat there, gazing ahead into the distance. The sun was warm on my shoulders.

Archie was beside me, gripping my arm. "Where are you going?"

"For a ride."

"On your own?"

"Looks like it."

"I see. Where to?"

"Don't know."

"Will you go to the station?"

"Don't know."

"Well, are you just out for a ride, or heading somewhere particular?"

"Don't know."

"Will you be long?"

"Don't know."

"Shall we expect you for lunch?"

"I don't know," I said, irritably. "Please let go of my arm."

I stood heavily on the pedals, and when I looked back he was standing in the middle of the road, staring after me, one hand shielding his eyes. I made a point of not waving.

How long I was gone, I don't exactly recall. I suppose it was about six hours. After a while, I forgot about the disappointment of Archie not being with me, and I began to enjoy the freedom and solitude of the open road. I cycled along to the point where the loch narrows and there is a strange prison tower at Eilean nam Faoileag, a tiny islet in the middle, marooned in thirty feet of water. I dropped my bike down on the sandy shore and found a flat stone and skimmed it towards the tower, but it splashed and sank long before reaching the target. In the saddlebag I found a somewhat crumpled tube of fruit pastilles, so I sat on a fallen tree and ate half the tube, gazing out at the sunlight glittering on the steely water. Where it lapped at the sand, the water was shallow, rippled with tiny wavelets, and I took off my shoes and socks and paddled at the edge, feeling the tingly, ice-coldness nibbling at my ankles until they ached. When I padded back to my tree, my feet were smooth and white and clean, and I jumped, chuckling with fright, as a moss-green lizard scuttled over my toes and vanished under a boulder.

Behind me, a car engine revved in the clearing and doors slammed. I groaned inwardly. People were coming to pollute my tranquil oasis. I carried on gazing across the loch, but they appeared in the corner of my vision, a man and a woman, he in plus-fours, she in pink trousers, both with sun hats and binoculars. Silently, I cursed them, hoping my imprecations would send them in the opposite direction. They stood on the shoreline for a while, as if deciding which way to go, and then the woman turned and beamed at me, tilting her head so that the shadow of her hat angled away from her lower face, and the red of her lipstick, obscene as a bloodied gash in the dancing light, split in a lunatic smile that menaced my peace.

"Lovely day!" the woman called to me, extending her vowels with preposterous elaboration. *Laaaarvleey dayyyy.*

Grinning back perfunctorily, I worked my lips around a soundless response. "It was until you got here."

"Sorry?"

"Good morning!" I called back.

"Yes, isn't it?"

Not wishing to appear rude – though there was no doubt that my disgruntled contempt at the intrusion was tantamount to rudeness – I walked quite slowly back to my bicycle. Hauling it from the sand, I fairly leapt to the saddle, and at once pedalled off westwards, the breeze tearing at my hair.

Laaaarvleey dayyyy.

Almost as an antidote, I had to find a place where I would be on my own again. This was not a day or a time for other people. This was my place, my time – my space in the universe. So I rode on another four miles, past the shallows at the end of the loch, only slackening my pace when I reached the open moorland where the River Gaur winds along beside the road. A man in a telephone engineer's van came towards me, honking his horn, and I rang my bell, and then I braked hard and bumped down off the road, and the sloping grass bank was as soft as velvet under my tyres.

The hills had receded to the horizon now, and the river cut through a stark wilderness of tawny grass bluffs, stunted trees bleached white by sun and wind, and jagged outcrops of slate-coloured rock. I laid my bike on the ground and sat on a sun-warmed boulder, and all I could hear was the busy chattering of the river as it tumbled over the polished stones. I watched the water cascading silver over jutting ledges of gleaming rock, sluicing into sudden pools of still, tobacco-brown darkness, then spilling out again in a silken curtain, seeking the next twisting channel, the next frothing, gasping cataract on its way to the hills and the dark chasm of Rannoch.

There was a big flat rock at the water's edge, and I moved down the slope and sat on it, pulling off my shoes and socks once more so I could dangle my feet in the swirling water. I loved the fierce, chilling bite of that water. Its razor-sharp teeth raked through to the bone, yet miraculously drew no blood. The pain quickly subsided as my senses were numbed with cold, but I stayed immersed, grinding my teeth against the icy fire of it, and as the veins glowed blue in my ankles, my feet shone pure and bright as marble, like the sunken feet of a statue. When finally, with one last aching surge, I pulled my legs up and clear, the air was as a warm poultice wrapped around my feet and ankles, and I took the handkerchief from my pocket and bent to dab dry my frozen, chicken-white flesh.

As I dried myself, I glimpsed a movement in the corner of my eye. On the opposite bank, a grey rabbit hopped over the stones, hesitating here and there to nibble at the interstices of sprouting grass. Watching the creature's easy, careless lollop, I never noticed the kestrel until it was too late – too late for me to scream a warning or for the rabbit to run to earth – and the bird's dark shadow was plunging like a thunderbolt, kicking up dust as it snatched its helpless prey. In seconds the kestrel had soared high over the water, and I saw the white glint of the rabbit's incisors as it squealed in death against the sky, and then my hand jerked in shocked spasm as a hot gout of blood splattered it, a thick slap of scarlet rain. I dunked my hand in the running water and watched the blood spiral away like red smoke.

On the slope where my bike lay, the grass was soft and warm, and I stretched out on the green carpet, the sky quivering red behind my closed eyelids. Soon, I slept in that wild place, one arm thrown behind me, cushioning my head. In my fractured dreams, a train ran through the station in my brain, and I waved at the driver, and he stopped the train to let me climb aboard, where it was dim and cool, and in the quiet compartment there she sat, her face lit by the perfumed candle of a smile, Jennifer Peltzer, and I lay against her, hearing the whistle blow, and our bodies bumped softly together as the carriage jolted.

The cold woke me. I lay there, grit embedded in my arm, blinking at the sky. Huge grey clouds were massing, sailing in from the northern horizon. A gusting breeze, smelling of rain, ruffled my hair. I sat up, stretching my cramped limbs, wiping the sleep-seeds from my eyes. My watch showed half past three. I was getting chilled, and I was hungry. If it rained, I would be drenched, as I had no coat. I ate the remaining fruit pastilles. Then I stood with my back to the road and peed against a rock. Even my penis felt cold. The sun slid behind a cloud, emerged briefly, and was snuffed out again. It was time to go.

I didn't hurry back, for the sky ahead of me was clear. With the wind at my back, and the effort of the ride, I kept warm. Nothing approached me or overtook me the whole way. It took me two hours to reach *The Eyrie.* I put the bike away in the shed and went in through the back door.

Big Alice Minto was working in the kitchen. "Afternoon, young Neil," she said, not looking up.

"Oh. Hello, Alice."

"Go on, say it."

"What?"

"You didn't expect to see me here."

"I didn't expect to see you here."

"Right enough." She banged a mixing bowl down on the table so hard, I thought it might shatter. "People coming. Archie asked me to stop by and cook."

"I see. What people?"

"Well, me for a start."

Alice emptied a bag of flour into the bowl and a white cloud rose in the air. Something was bubbling in a pot on the stove, the metal lid lifting and clinking as the steam escaped.

"Shall I turn that down?" I asked.

"Don't you touch ma cooking."

"Sorry."

"They're gone out."

"Who?"

"What d'ye mean – who? Who's here, for goodness' sake?"

"Sorry."

"Nothin' to be sorry about." She wheeled round and lowered the heat under the pot. "They've taken the bairn for a walk."

"Good. I mean, is he all right?"

"Oh aye. It's nothin'. Doctor came and left some jollop."

"Right. So he's not ill, then?"

"Seems not. Panic attack, I reckon."

"Hmm. What are we having?"

"To eat?"

I nodded.

"Nothing at all if you don't get outa ma road."

"Sorry."

I went to the bedroom and lay down on the unmade bed.

Sally's pink bra was draped across her pillow, so I picked it up and sniffed it, inhaling the faintest hint of her fragrance. Without moving off the bed, I removed my shoes and trousers and tossed them to the floor. The cool air in the shaded room soothed me. For a moment I considered clenching Sally's bra between my legs; but I reasoned that Alice Minto might come in to ask me about the meal and, as Alice seemed to like me, the discovery could tragically compromise my credibility.

Quite why or how I fell asleep I cannot say, for I had rested by the river for hours. Of course, I had spent the day in the fresh air, cycled twenty miles and eaten no real food, so as soon as I relaxed on a comfortable bed, I suppose exhaustion overcame me. The shapes and shadows grew indistinct and the room swam into blackness.

The voices woke me, booming softly through the closed door. Once or twice a peal of laughter sounded in counterpoint, a timbre I couldn't identify. Outside, darkness had fallen, and I watched the skeletal reflection of a tree branch scratching the ceiling.

Sally came in, flooding the room with yellow light. "You're awake then."

"I am now."

She stared at my legs. "Why have you no trousers on?"

"I'm in bed."

"Well, make yourself decent. We've got guests."

"Why would they come in here?"

"They might. Then there's you, lying in the middle of the room, a kid displaying his pants."

I sat up, sighing, and swung my legs to the floor. "Is Noah all right?"

"Yes, yes. The doctor came. He left some medicine. It's nothing serious."

"Where is he? Where's Noah?"

"He's in the other room, meeting the people – like you should be. If you come out, I'll put him in here so he can sleep." She slid down the side-rail of the cot. "Come on, get dressed!"

No doubt I looked a sight, with my crumpled clothes, puffy eyes and dishevelled hair, but they all nodded and smiled pleasantly at me – Alice, still wearing her floral-print housedress, Michael Lomax, whom I remembered had driven us back from the station that day, and a tall, slim girl in leather trousers, with sallow skin and a straight-cut helmet of black hair, who must have been the source of the unfamiliar laughter I had heard from the bedroom. Sally introduced me to Mikey, presumably not realising that we had met before, and then to the tall girl, who turned out to be his fiancée, Louisa. I nodded to each in turn, offering a tight-lipped smile and a perfunctory, half-hearted flick of the hand.

"You'll have to excuse Neil," Sally told them, "he's in a bit of a sulk."

Instantly, I felt insulted and humiliated. "Excuse me!" I retorted, "I am not in a sulk!"

"Don't patronise the boy," Archie said, in a low voice.

Sally raised her hands defensively to her face. "Okay, okay. What he means is" – she threw me a deprecating glance before facing her friends once more – "he was sulking earlier but he's getting over it now, so he's gradually learning to be sociable."

Louisa shook her mane of lank hair and I heard that high-pitched laugh again. Her fiancé grinned, struggling to mask his embarrassment.

I sucked in a deep breath, avoiding their eyes. "Don't listen to her," I said. "She doesn't know me. I don't know her. She's a different person."

"Sounds complicated to me," Mikey said.

"Now Neil's here, maybe we should eat," Archie proposed.

"I'm not hungry," I said.

Alice regarded me sternly. "You've been out all day, boy."

"I said, I'm not hu – "

"Very well, suit yourself, go without," Sally countered.

"Right, I will."

"Are you going to stay and spectate while we eat? You know, like at the zoo?"

"Now you're just being silly," I rebuked her.

She taunted me then, with a shallow, girlish giggle and a facile shake of the head. "I don't think it's me who's the silly one, Neil."

"I'm not going to argue. Where's Noah?"

"Like I said, I put him in the bedroom."

"Then I'll go and see him. I haven't seen him all day."

"But you've just come out of there."

"It doesn't matter. I want to see him." I drew myself up, clenching my fists. "I want to be with my son."

I have no doubt that I said it for a reaction, but I didn't hang around for one. I strode to the bedroom and shut myself in.

As I had expected, Sally burst in after me, her face pink with fury. She slammed the door and leaned against it, her eyes blazing at me. "What the fuck d'you think you're doing? Are you completely mad, for Christ's sake?"

I was sitting on the edge of the bed, staring up at her; I could feel my hands shaking against the mattress. "What did I say? What's wrong?"

Her voice was quavering, quaking out in short, convulsive gasps. "You-know-perfectly-well-what-I-am-talking-about." She jabbed a finger at my face. "You-will-blow-this-whole-sorry-affair-wide-open! And-make-no-mistake. You-will-be-the-loser! And-I-mean-*loser*!"

I shrugged, stalling for time, wanting her to calm down. I hated it when she was angry. It frightened me. "I know all about losing," I said, trying to keep my voice level. "After all, I've lost you."

She breathed deeply in and out again, leaning against her hands. There was a slick of sweat beneath her hairline. "Lost? Look what you've gained, Neil!" She reached out and rattled the cot. "Just remember – if it wasn't for us, you wouldn't have him!"

"No Sally! If it wasn't for *me, you* wouldn't have him!"

"Oh please! Don't kid yourself you're indispensable!"

"How can I be anything else? When your old man fucks you, all he can get up is a fart!"

She lunged forward and smacked me across the face with the flat of her hand. It was the speed, more than the force of it, that took me by surprise. I didn't move, just sat there, feeling my bottom lip going numb. I knew I wasn't going to cry, wouldn't give her the satisfaction. So I sat staring at her, saying nothing, not even breathing much.

A strange, ringing silence pervaded the room. I heard the others talking quietly as they prepared for dinner.

Noah stirred under his blanket, grumbling to himself. The small sound made me look at him. That was when it happened. That was when I made up my mind. Because it was all gone now, everything. The holiday, Sally, Archie, Noah, everything. In a way I didn't even care. It didn't matter to me. Or if it mattered, I could make it not matter. I had the power to change it. I felt strong. I could seize the day. So I sat there and I smiled at her, because she didn't know. At last, I had the game won.

"What on earth are you grinning at, you idiot?"

"You'll see."

"Oh, I'm scared. Oh dear, I'm really frightened. Grow up, Neil, it's about time."

"Leave me."

"What?"

"Go. Leave me with my son. Just for a few minutes. Please."

She screwed up her eyes, peering at me intently. "What's that in your hair?"

"What?"

"There's red in your hair. I didn't do that. It's on the pillow, look."

I ran my fingers through my scalp, feeling a resinous crust, seeing red dirt on my fingertips. "Yes. A rabbit."

"A rabbit?"

"A hawk got it. By the river. It flew over my head."

She straightened up and pulled the door ajar. "Better wash it out. Five minutes. Noah needs to rest. He's not been well, remember." The door swung open and a cool draught blew in. "I'll go in and make my peace. Tell them you're poorly."

"Tell them whatever you like, I said. "It won't matter."

After a while I heard the door close in the other room. I looked at Noah, and he seemed to be asleep. He looked so peaceful, with one puffy pink fist curled under his nose, it would be a shame to disturb him. Still. It was for the best. I leaned into the cot and, oh so carefully, looped my arms around that warmly pulsing bundle and slowly, slowly lifted him out. I held him against me. The tears coursed down my cheeks like hot rain. I kissed the flat button of his nose and the lightly-furred curve of his skull, smelling the creamy sweetness of him. My son. My Noah.

Then I was in the hallway. Cradling my child briefly with one arm, I bent to pick up something I needed from the kitchen floor. That was all I had to do. I hoped it wasn't raining. I didn't want him to get cold. The back door was bolted against the encroaching night, and my heart beat faster as I was obliged to put Noah down on the floor while I cautiously slid back the bolt. It was all right; Noah was in another land.

Five minutes, she had said. I would have time enough.

The night's cold breath momentarily startled me. I hugged Noah closer, making him as one with my body. I pulled the door until I heard it latch. The air felt damp, and I knew the pathway under the trees would be slippery. My arms were beginning to ache. With short, flat-footed steps, I trod the sloping path, wary of rolling pine cones and dew-mulched leaves.

There wasn't far to go. The dangerous part was almost done.

Noah shifted slightly in my trembling arms.

I bent to his ear. "It's all right my darling. Your dad's here. Hush little baby, don't you cry..."

I crossed the road. The night was black as pitch. An owl hooted, scaring me, reminding me of Croakers Wood, death in the night.

We were nearly there.

Hush little baby
don't you cry
I will sing you
a lulla-by.

Chapter XX

Loch Rannoch

The breeze had dropped. With the deepening of the night, a flat calm had settled over the silent water. The surface of the loch, once mobile with roiling channels of energy, seemed now to have collapsed in on itself, a dense black pool, inert and formless.

I knelt on the slats of the jetty and lowered my precious bundle into the bottom of the boat. Then I stepped down, carefully judging my tread in the darkness, grateful for the smoothness of the water. Behind the rough plank of the rearward seat, a wooden locker ran across the stern. I pulled down the flap and my urgent fingers found a coil of thin rope and Archie's battery lantern. Flicking the light on, I set the lantern down next to Noah. I dragged the oars up, slotted the left-hand one into the rowlock and pulled it in towards me so that it wouldn't fall over the side. Standing up, I reached for the mooring rope and untied it, tossing it down into the hull behind me. I sat down then and, with the blade end of the second oar, punted the boat away from the jetty. It slid soundlessly towards the open water. As quietly as I could, I secured the oar and eased its companion back over the side.

We were ready to go.

The tops of the cottage windows were dimly visible above the shoreline, two amber eyes peering into the gloom. Five minutes, Sally had said. It had taken me all that and more. They would be out soon, once she had found the room empty and raised the alarm. Still, no matter; we would be in the middle of the loch, and I had the boat, so there was no way they could reach us.

Noah squeaked and wriggled, flapping one arm out of his blanket.

I gripped the oars and pulled us away from the outline of the shore. After four strokes, I lifted the blades and waited, listening to the hiss of the bow cutting through the water. The boat glided on under its own momentum, untroubled by wind or current. I looked over my shoulder, and a stand of trees had obscured the light from the cottage windows. There was nothing to be seen anywhere, except the thin white glow from the lantern at my feet. I reached down and pulled it back towards me in case Noah knocked it over. His little arm waved in the light, and I reached out for it, feeling the dry coldness of his skin.

"It's all right," I said, "we're almost there, Noah. It won't be long now."

Something feather-light, a fly or a moth, flickered over my face, and I brushed it away, and in that instant I heard the dry slap of a door slamming, a soft percussion carried effortlessly over the water. A hoarse cry rang out like a fractured bell.

If I put out the light, we would be invisible. They might not think to look for us on the water; but if they saw the boat was gone... I switched off the lantern, plunging us into impenetrable darkness. Anxious that he might be afraid, I clasped Noah's hand, squeezing it gently, making it warm.

"You need to be a brave boy, Noah."

The boat turned lazily about itself, pointing at the opposite shore.

We were safe. I wasn't frightened, not any more.

"Far enough, Noah, far enough."

Away in the woods I heard Sally screeching in that hideous voice of hers and, twisting round, I saw their torch-beams painting green stripes in the trees. One of them screamed my name.

I lifted my son on to my lap. I could just make out his face in the dark. His eyes were open. He gazed at me, working his lips. I put my little finger in his mouth and felt his hot, slippery gums chew at the fleshy pad.

"I can't feed you, Noah. I'm sorry."

Somebody shrieked. There were dancing lights in the woods. A fish jumped close by, scaring me.

It felt colder now, with a cutting edge of dampness in the air, and I drew Noah's small, firm body into my belly and wrapped the blanket more tightly about him. Time and again, his right arm popped out from its coverings, and I folded it back into the warmth, only for him to thrust it out defiantly, and I sat there, hugging him, smiling to myself in the dark.

"Listen to me, Noah." I raised my knees to bring his face a little closer to mine. "This is important. You have to understand."

Sally and Archie had disappeared. I imagined them crashing about in the undergrowth, scaring small animals with their torches. I knew they would be back. They would not give up.

It was no good; I needed the light. I couldn't talk to Noah without seeing his face. Anyway, I deserved to see him, if only for a short while. The face of a baby is the purest, most perfect creation in the whole world. And this was something I had made – not on my own, but still with love and some strange, elusive conviction.

So I fumbled for the lantern, and the pale light brought us back together again. When they emerged from the woods, they would see us for sure, a bobbing glow in all that blackness, but they would not be able to interfere with us any more.

Noah looked so snug in my arms, his chill-pinked face peeping out at me from the encircling folds of his blanket, like a fleshy kernel protruding from the furred leaves of a ripening fruit. The tight comb of that miniature hand pawed the air close to my nose, and I gave him my forefinger to clench.

"I want to tell you about a lovely lady called Jean, Jean Blaney. She was my gran – your great grandmother. Oh, you would have loved her, and she would have adored you. She was kind and quiet and gentle and caring, which is why she's gone to Heaven. That's a place where good people go to be happy for ever. Your great grandmother never did get to see you, Noah, but she knew about you. She cared about you."

A cry in the distance diverted my attention. I heard Sally call my name three times. After a moment's silence, she shouted for

Noah. I shook my head. How would a baby answer her? I struggled to imagine Noah yelling 'Here I am, mother!' as he dashed from the bushes and leapt headlong into her arms. It sounded as if she was getting hysterical.

I bent down and planted a kiss on the ice-cold button of Noah's nose. "I was with your great grandmother the day she died," I told him. "I was the last person to see her alive. I remember something she said to me. She talked about you, Noah, and she said, 'You look after him. You love him. Do it for me.' And I promised her, Noah, I promised her. I loved my gran, so that's a promise I can't break. You have to keep your promises, you remember that. She was a good person, but not everyone's like that. I have to protect you, because that's what Gran would have wanted. There's people out there you have to be protected from, people who'll hurt you and try to take you away from those who really love you." I lifted him up in front of my face. "You listen to that noise, Noah. That's the noise of bad people howling in the dark. I can't leave you to them. I won't do it."

The tears felt like fiery sparks on my cheeks. Noah's face dissolved into a blur, and I rubbed my knuckles in my eyes. With trembling fingers, I began to unwind the coiled rope, balancing my child in my lap.

"You see, I'd take you away with me, only there's nowhere we could go. They'd be sure to find us. I've got to make you safe. The bad people would steal you, and then I'd never see you again. I'd never know where you were, in all the world. That lady, I know she's your mother, but that doesn't mean – well, she told me I was a loser and I would lose everything, that's what she said, and I know what she meant, she'd be all wrong for you, Noah, she'd hurt you like she hurt me, I just know she would. 'You look after him,' Gran said, so I have to do this, Noah, I don't have any choice."

I choked on the scalding in my throat, and the words wouldn't come out any more. With the palm of my hand, I scooped some water out of the loch and drank it gratefully. Then I drew a deep breath and let it out slowly, in a long, despairing sigh of resignation.

A light flashed in the corner of my eye. They were on the

shore, playing their torches on the water. Sally was screaming into the darkness. "You're a bad boy, Neil! You're a bad boy!" Her voice was horrible, unearthly, strangled by madness.

I knew I had to stay calm. They couldn't get to us. Even if they did, it would be too late. I didn't care what they did to me now, it wasn't important.

"Noah, listen. After this, I shall be going away for a while. I know you can't see it in the dark, but this is such a beautiful place. You just wait for me here. There'll be the sun in the morning, dancing on the water like golden fire, and the birds swooping over your head, and all the painted dreams of mirrored mountains. If I can't give you anything else, little Noah, I'll give you that. At least, here, I'll know where to find you, and I'll come back, I promise, and we'll talk some more, and I'll tell you what I'm doing and you can tell me about what it's like to grow up without fear or danger or sadness. And remember, Noah, I always keep my promises. Always. Always, my Noah."

"You're a very bad boy, Neil!"

I clapped my hands over my ears to blot her out of my life.

Then it was time. No more delay, no more words.

Do it, Neil. Oh, sweet Jesus, just do it.

It was the moulded weight they had used to prop open the kitchen door, and I looped one end of the rope through it and knotted it tight. It wasn't perfect, but it would do. I yanked it as hard as I could. After that, I had about twelve feet of it left. I lifted Noah out of his blanket, laid him on the floor and passed the rope underneath him so I could knot the other end at the front. It looked quite secure, right under his tummy button. He never cried, never even whimpered.

"You are such a bad boy, Neil! Do you hear me? Neeeeeil!"

I smiled. "It's all right, Noah. They're too late. We've done it. You're safe now."

So I picked him up and watched as his eyes flicked from side to side, almost as if he was judging me. Quickly, so I didn't have to think about it, I kissed him lightly on the forehead, but I didn't hug him any more. That would have hurt too much, and I had had enough of pain. There were no more words to say, and nothing left to do. This was it, all over. Everything. In the black of the night, the world stopped. I moved to the edge of the seat and faced the water.

He seemed to float for a moment. He was my brave boy. His arms and legs thrashed for a second or two as the cold hit him, and then, curiously, he stopped fighting and just lay there, wallowing on his back in the boat's shadow, and I lifted the lamp to show him where he was, where he was going, and his tiny hand came out of the water, opening and closing like a pale, pumping heart, and I reached down and touched it, as I lowered the weight over with my other hand and carefully let it go. I shall never forget the gentle, feathery touch of that waving hand, light and sweet as a blown kiss. He began to go down, and I tried to follow him with the light, his eyes wide open, gazing up at me so trusting and unafraid, his face tinted gold in the peaty swell, and then of course the weight grabbed him and it was as if he kicked under the water, trying to get up again, but the lead lump took him, and I saw him turn over and go down fast, head first, with his white feet flailing soundlessly into the dark. A stream of bubbles rose softly to the surface, marking the place where he had gone, and then there was nothing, only the hollow slapping of the water on the boat's hull and the strange unbelieving wonder of it, a wild ringing in my ears, in the heart of the night.

I thought I might keep the blanket, but there didn't seem much point. It was just an old blanket; it didn't mean anything. In any case, it would be difficult to smuggle it ashore. I knew they would be waiting for me. I turned the light out and took hold of the oars, and when the boat was under way I struck out with my feet and kicked it overboard. It floated away and was soon lost in the darkness.

As I neared the jetty, I looked behind me and saw the beams of their torches slanting down on to the planking, and then, when they picked out the shape of the boat, they shone both lights on me, two cold white eyes glaring out of a black void. I dipped the oars in the water to decelerate. I felt perfectly calm.

"Throw me the rope, Neil." Archie's voice was a flat monotone, almost a growl.

"Where have you been?" Sally demanded, the words screeching out, taut as a wire about to snap.

"I've been rowing," I said.

"Don't get cl- Where's Noah?" She scanned the light across the boat. "Where's my baby?"

I took Archie's outstretched hand and he hauled me up. "It's all right," I told her. "He's safe."

"Safe? What d'you mean, safe? Where is he?" She grabbed my shoulders and started shaking me, and Archie gripped her arm, trying to separate us.

"Don't start on me," I said, averting my eyes. "I've had enough. It's finished."

She let go of me and stood there, panting for breath, making a strange wailing noise in her throat, like a trapped animal.

"I'm cold," I said. "I want to go in."

I began to turn away, but Archie clamped my arm, squeezing the flesh hard on to the bone. "Where's the wee boy? Where is he, Neil?" He pressed harder, making it hurt. "What have you done?"

I reached across and started to unpeel his fingers. "Let me in the warm and I'll tell you."

He raised his hand to my face, and I flinched, thinking he was about to hit me, but instead he wagged a rigid finger menacingly close to my nose. "If you've hurt that wee boy or hidden him away, I warn you I'll – "

"You'll what? You'll fuck up my life or shit all over me or make me do somersaults just to keep the pair of you happy? Tell me something I don't know, Archie."

His hands dropped to his sides and he flapped them angrily against his legs. "All right." He was almost whispering now, shaking his head. "Just tell me. No more games. Where – where is that child? In God's name, what have you done with our child?"

Over his shoulder, I could see Sally staring at me, waving the torch to and fro in frustration. She was crying with her mouth open, a child-like bleat of fear and despair. I gazed at her huddled outline in the dark. In the past, I thought, I had hated myself for loving her; and now I loved myself for hating her.

I started to walk up the jetty towards the road. Archie came after me, feet stamping loudly on the boards, cursing softly under his breath. When I reached the top of the bank, I stopped and turned, staring back down the grey spear of the loch. In my mind's eye, I travelled back over the glassy water, searching for the place.

I'll come back, I promise, and we'll talk some more.

Archie was standing so close to me, I could smell his breath. I slitted my eyes against the cold, biting my lip. "Help me, Archie," I said.

"What is it, lad?" he murmured.

"Call the police. I want it to be over."

He went up to the cottage, leaving me alone on the bank. When I looked back at Sally, she was standing motionless on the jetty, her arms hanging limply, staring out over the silent water. That was the last time I ever saw her.

Chapter XXI

Sternley Hall

I rather liked my room. I had the upper bunk bed, so when I lay in it, I could see out of the window. I liked that. I could see the sky and watch the clouds go by. Sometimes I liked to try and make faces out of them, or the shapes of countries. There were two lockers as well, and one of them was mine to keep my personal things in. Between the lockers was a small table, positioned directly under the window. I was in room number 28. There was always an odd smell in there, a mixture of urine and disinfectant and shoe polish, but I soon learned to live with it. After all, it was only a smell.

It's funny about the bed. My room-mate was there when I arrived – I think he came in two days before me – and he had taken the top bunk. So I put my bag on the lower one, and he looked down from above my head, where he was reading a magazine, and asked me, quite politely, if I would prefer the top. I said it didn't matter, as he was there first; but he scrambled down, pulled the covers straight and indicated his bed, rather grandly, with an elaborate flourish of his hand. He told me it was now mine, and he was happy to sleep below. Sometimes, he said, the height made him feel dizzy, so he would rather be nearer the floor – if I didn't mind. I said thanks, I didn't mind. So that's how we arranged it, sort of like gentlemen.

He was fifteen. His name was Graham McLarty. I didn't know much about him at first, except he seemed friendly enough, in a cool sort of way, and he had quite a lot of spots on his face and neck. He had a tube of green stuff, which he squeezed on to his fingers every night to rub into the angry pimples. I didn't like to ask him about the spots, in case he was self-conscious about them. I wanted to stay on the right side of him, at least until I knew him better. One thing I knew about Sternley Hall: it was not a place to make enemies.

"What shall I call you?" I asked him on the day we met.

"How about 'sir'?" he said, and I studied his face nervously to see if he was joking. "Best if you call me Malarkey," he emended, with a flicker of a grin, "all me mates did. 'Cut the malarkey, McLarty.' Even me dad used to say it."

"Okay. Is that why you're in here – too much malarkey?"

"They don't lock you up just for messin' about."

"No."

This seemed an appropriate moment to ask him exactly why he was here; but somehow I felt that, at this formative stage in our relationship, I ought not to broach such a potentially emotive subject. He would tell me in his own good time. It was important not to rush matters.

"You don't snore, I hope," he said.

"I don't know. I can't hear if I'm asleep."

To my considerable relief, he laughed. "S'pose not." He stared at me, as if measuring me against his own temperament. "Reckon you'll be all right, you."

That evening, he asked me about the wall. It was pale green, finger-marked, pitted with old pin-holes. "D'you want that wall?" he asked.

"What?"

"You got stuff in your bag. I seen it. Pictures and stuff. Put 'em up there if you like."

"You were here first. Don't you want it – some of it?"

He pulled a face. "No. I ain't got no pictures. What do I want with pictures?"

"I see," I said, nodding sympathetically. "Actually, I thought I'd put them up by the bed."

"Up to you, mate. Not much room."

"I just – I think I'd like to have them near to me. I've got pictures of my mum and dad, you see. It'd sort of be nicer." I felt myself colouring up. "You know, like I wasn't really that far away from them."

The hell with it, I thought, but it was too late, and I started to cry. "What am I gonna do without my mum and dad? Eh Malarkey? What am I gonna do?"

With his hands on my shoulders, he pushed me gently down on to the lower bunk, then he sat beside me, one arm draped lightly but protectively around me. "Come on, mate. Long way to go yet."

"My name's Neil," I said, in a quavering voice.

"Yeah, okay. Neil. But you've not been 'ere five minutes. You 'ave to work out a way of 'andlin' it. Cryin' only makes it worse. Cryin's like rubbin' a sore."

He gave me a quick hug, before crossing to his locker and opening the door. When he came back to me, he held a shoe box half full of oddments. "Got most things in 'ere," he said, with a smile.

I pulled a handkerchief from my pocket, blew my nose and dried my eyes. "What things?"

"Sticky tape, for a start. I'll 'elp you. We'll soon 'ave those pictures up. We'll do 'em real nice, you'll see."

Mum had sent the photographs in. There were five of them, all black and white, a couple of them a little crumpled. They straightened out quite well once we had taped them to the wall. It was a thoughtful, well-chosen little gallery. There was one of Dad sitting on the garden bench behind the garage in his cardigan and slippers; one of Mum stretched out on the beach somewhere in her swimsuit, her eyes made into black holes by unflattering sunglasses; another showed the three of us grouped round the huge iron wheel of a traction engine outside a farm we had stayed at in Cornwall; in another, my guinea pig Hector was crouched on the roof of his cage, nibbling a large carrot; and then there was Gran, sitting by the hearth on a winter's day, one hand resting lightly on the top of the fireguard, over whose wire mesh a pair of bloomers had been hung to dry.

I could lie in bed and see my pictures quite clearly. On a cloudless night, when the moon rose, a shaft of bluish light fanned through the window, illuminating those scenes from the past, and I reached up until my hand grew white in the moon's glow, and traced my family's faces, round and round, with just the merest tickle of my finger, making the tears brim in my eyes as I recalled the days of innocence gone by.

Malarkey laughed at me about that window. The bars frightened me. The bars said to me: *Trapped for ever. No escape.* So, in my mind, I simply took the bars away, and changed them into stripes. Stripes on my pyjamas, stripes on the pen and pencil case I kept in my locker, stripes in my toothpaste, stripes on the window. Some nights, the big moon painted stripes on my wall, putting a cage around my pictures, keeping them safe. I didn't mind the stripes. I could live with the stripes. When I see stripes, I think of tents at a fair, or zebras in the zoo, or seaside rock. I like stripes. Stripes are fun.

"What d'you mean, stripes? Think you need to ask the medic about a pair of glasses." He shook his head affectionately. "You're mad, you!"

"Probably am," I said. "Maybe that's how I got here."

He gazed at me levelly. "Why are you here?" he asked, quietly.

"Same as you, I expect." I wasn't sure I was ready to go through it all, to relive the experience.

"Don't muck about." He tapped my forearm with his fingers, a small gesture of conciliation. "We're mates, aren't we? We don't 'ave no secrets."

So I told him. I told him about Archie and Sally and Noah. Then I told him about Sam Wicken dying in the woods. And Gran. I told him about Gran and what a special person she was, even now, even afterwards. I even told him about the cottage by the loch, and going out in the boat. I described how it had been that night. I didn't leave anything out. I told him everything.

He was silent for a long time, just sort of pursing his lips, gazing ahead of him. "That's amazin'" he said, finally.

I shrugged. "It seemed amazing then," I said. "But now it just feels – pointless."

He nodded thoughtfully. "So you – you actually done it with her? With a nurse?"

"Yes."

"Cor!"

"What about you?" I enquired, cautiously.

"Me? I never done it with a girl, least not properly."

I found his honesty rather touching; but he had missed my objective. "No, I mean, what did you do that they put you in here?"

"Oh, right. That"

"It's all right. You don't have to tell me if you don't want."

"Yeah. Well, if we're gonna be – "

"Mates."

"Right." He scratched the side of his head and looked puzzled, as if trying to remember what it was that he had done. "Well, trouble was, I – I didn't get on with me brother. Trouble was, I liked not likin' him."

"I see."

He paused, gazing anxiously at the floor. Someone shouted in the corridor, leaving a thin metallic echo. I waited patiently for elaboration, until the delay assumed a semblance of absurdity.

"Look, if you don't want – "

"No," he blurted, "it's okay. You ought to know. I mean, if we're sharin' like."

"Right. And I did tell you about me."

"Yeah. That's amazin'."

"Tell me later, if you like."

"No. It's not that I don't want you to know. It's just – I don't like talkin' about it. Gives me the shivers." He shook his head in distaste. "Daft."

"You're not daft, Malarkey."

"Huh. You don't know me. You just met me. I'm just a spotty stranger."

"You can tell me when it's dark, if you want. If that makes it easier."

"Yeah, okay. When it's dark."

"Sometimes it's better to talk in the dark," I said. "Stops you thinking. You can get lonely in the dark."

"There's nothin' worse than bein' on your own in the dark. It's like you've died. It's like it'll never get light."

"You won't be on your own, Malarkey. I'm here."

"Tell me again," he said. "About them people. Sandy an' that."

"Sally."

"Yeah, her. I can't believe it."

"Neither can I, Malarkey, neither can I."

So I told him again. I went through the pain of it all over again. This time I mentioned my granddad, and I talked about Jennifer Peltzer and about Sam Wicken's brother in the cemetery. I recited my poem from memory, the one I had left for Gran to read when I wasn't there. I told him how good it was to go fishing on Rannoch with the warm shawl of the sun on your back and the water glittering like quartz and all the trees standing there on the far shore in the deep shadows, silent as soldiers in green uniforms. I told him about the sun coming up over the mountains in the morning, throwing golden spears into the valley. For a moment, I lived it all again.

"That's beautiful, he said. "Do you think – ?"

"What?"

"Do you think you'll ever go back?"

"Oh yes," I told him. "I've got to go back. My little boy's there."

Later, in the fading light, we lay on our backs in our bunks, muttering softly in the gloom. Through the window, I could see stars slowly imprinting themselves on the darkening sky, but there was no moon.

"Are you all right down there?" I called out.

"I'm tired," he replied. "I think I'll go to sleep."

"Goodnight then. Mate."

Very soon I heard a change in the depth and rhythm of his breathing, yet from its regularity I gathered that he was not dreaming. The sound was of a stalled engine, chuffing restfully in the sidings of his sleep. I found it comforting, somehow.

Even so, I couldn't sleep. Malarkey's questioning had forced me to revisit my past, and I could not at once claw my way back to the present. I was a lonesome time traveller, stumbling along the road between what had once been and the unimaginable here and now. I lay there for perhaps half an hour, staring at the grey ceiling not far above my head, and then I swung my legs out of bed and dropped lightly to the floor.

In the darkness and the deeper shadow of the upper bunk, I could barely make out Malarkey's face, but I saw a stab of white as his eyes opened. "Hullo mate," he grunted.

"Hello there."

"What d'you want?"

"Are you asleep?"

"Well, I bloody was." He rolled over on to his side. "What is it? I'm tired."

"Yeah. I'm sorry. Stupid. I just..."

"Just what?"

"No, it doesn't matter. I couldn't sleep, that's all."

He sighed, eyes flickering. "Try countin' stripes."

I reached out and patted his shoulder. "Goodnight, Malarkey." I waited for a moment, trying to see his face in the dark.

He moved again, groaning quietly. "Okay. D'you want me to do you, is that it?"

"What? No, no, it's all right."

"You sure?"

"Course."

"'Cause I will if you want. I ain't shy. It's easier in the dark."

I swallowed hard. "Goodnight, Malarkey. I'm sorry I woke you."

"Yeah, yeah. G'night mate."

I lay back in my bed, listening to my heartbeat. I wondered what it would feel like if Malarkey held my penis. But there would be time enough for that. I counted the stripes on the window, then I multiplied them by three and subtracted my age and added the number of the room. My eyes fluttered and I slipped towards fitful sleep.

Dad came to see me when I'd been there a week. The whole time he was with me, he looked nervous and uncomfortable. I'm sure he hadn't wanted to come at all. I expect Mum had nagged him to make the effort.

"What's the food like?" he asked me. His eyes were hooded and lifeless.

"All right," I said. "Better than school."

"Aha." He cast his gaze slowly round the blank white walls of the visiting room, past the guards standing stock-still, as if mummified, at their pre-selected posts, hands clasped non-committally behind their backs. "Ah. Right."

I pointed out Graham McLarty sitting a few tables away, talking to a blonde woman. "I'm sharing with that chap. His name's McLarty."

Dad looked where I had indicated. "Aha. What's he like?"

"Seems quite nice. We get on all right."

"Well," he said, with a sniff, "if he was that nice, he wouldn't be in here."

"So what does that make me?" I asked him.

He pursed his lips reflectively. "No comment," he said.

Malarkey glanced across and waved, nodding his head towards his visitor. His lips mouthed, "Me mum."

I nodded back and smiled at Malarkey's mum.

"Will mum be coming?" I asked my father.

"She's got a headache. She's lying down with a flannel on her head."

"I didn't mean today. Some other day."

"We'll see. It's difficult."

"It's difficult for me," I said.

"Aha." He glanced surreptitiously at his watch. "Do you want anything brought in?"

"Cake with a file in it."

Dad stared at me lugubriously. "Hardly a joking matter," he said.

Malarkey's mother stood up and kissed him quickly on the forehead. She turned and waggled her fingers at me.

"Who's that?" Dad asked.

"That's his mother."

"Looks like a tart to me," he said.

"She's still his mother," I offered.

"Ah well. So you don't want anything?"

"Ask mum if she'll come. Or you could both come. I'd like to see her."

"Aha. It's a bit difficult."

"Why? Why is it difficult?"

"You know – this place. People."

I nodded solemnly at the table top. "Right. I suppose I've made her really ashamed. Like she'll never be able to hold her head up again."

He sat there, drumming his fingers on the table. "Like I said."

"Difficult."

"Yes."

Malarkey got up and left, slapping me on the back as he passed.

Dad peered up at him. "Why's he got all those spots?"

"I don't know. Just spots. Does it matter?"

"Huh. Better not let your mother see those spots."

"Well, she won't if she doesn't visit me," I said, sullenly.

He sighed and his eyes took on a hollow glaze. "I don't understand – any of this." His hands spread towards the four walls. "How did this happen, for goodness' sake?"

I shrugged. "You were in court."

"Yes. A most distressing experience. Most distressing."

"I didn't like it much, either."

"This baby..."

I covered his hand with mine. "Please, Dad. Don't. I don't want to talk about it. We can't change anything."

He opened his mouth to say something more, then fell silent. There was moisture in his eyes.

"How's Hector?" I asked.

"Hector?"

"Yes. The guinea pig you bought me."

"Oh yes. He's fine, as far as I know."

"Someone'll have to clean him out. Now I'm not there."

"Aha. I know."

"And don't give him too much lettuce. He gets the runs."

"Neil, why did you do this?"

"Not now, Dad, please." I touched him again. "Just

understand. It wasn't your fault, Dad. You couldn't have prevented it. It wasn't your doing."

He stood up suddenly, nearly capsizing the chair. "I'll get your mother to come. Maybe she'll get some sense out of you." He thrust out a hand, and I shook it firmly. "Watch out for those bloomin' spots."

"I love you, Dad," I told him, and a single tear rolled down my cheek. "Tell Mum I miss her."

He was buttoning his coat. "Don't go all to pieces," he said, gruffly. He walked up to the nearest guard. "You can tell me how to get out of this damned place."

When I received Mum's letter, I felt strangely glad. Not about the content, of course, but because I had said those last words to him, and meant them. That was important, somehow.

Apparently Dad had gone out to buy a set of windscreen wipers, even though he said he wasn't feeling well. When he drove back into the open garage, he stopped neatly alongside my bike, switched off the engine and remained in the car. Mum became suspicious after ten minutes had passed, and went out to find him. He was sitting slumped over the wheel with his eyes open. She felt his neck, and knew that he was gone.

They let me out for the funeral. It rained the whole time. There weren't many of us there. He had never had a lot of friends. Other people were to be discouraged, in case they made a nuisance of themselves. I tried very hard to cry, but the tears wouldn't come, and all I could summon was a dry burning in my throat, a taste of slow, inexorable sadness, the stuttering machine of my life running down into inexplicable seizure. As the small party moved away, and the guard with the navy blue ribbed sweater and the body odour sidled up to escort me back to the van, I asked my mother for a hug; but she only pecked me on the cheek and drew back to recompose herself.

"No, no. You're all grown up now."

"You mean, I'm old enough to be imprisoned."

Malarkey, in his own way, did his unwitting best to salve my disappointment. A touch on the arm, a wink, an artless smile;

that was Malarkey's way. "You look done in, mate," he said. "Musta been grim."

"I'm all right. Could have been worse."

"How'd yer mum take it?"

"She looked pale. She'll manage."

"No man in 'er life now, eh?"

He stood watching me as I changed into some dry clothes. He waited until I was dressed, then he came towards me and put one arm around my shoulders, holding me against him as my body shook with weeping. The minutes passed, and as my tears subsided, he turned my face between his hands and kissed me moistly on the lips. As his skin brushed mine, I smelled the residue of the cream he used on his spots, but I felt no dismay or revulsion, only a deep and warming sense of peace and gratitude, a reminder of the sweet, aching surge of love.

I knew, when the dusk came, that we would not fall into our separate beds. That discipline would have seemed as ridiculous as it would be improbable. I would not, could not, go into this night lonely in the stifling dark. It was not something we had planned or discussed, and it had no connotation of a sexual act. There was, instead, a kind of quiet purity about it, a stillness.

"We'll be warm," he said, pointing at my pyjamas. "You won't need your stripes."

We lay on our sides, facing each other, and he pulled the thin blanket over us. "Comfy?" he asked me.

I nodded, momentarily unable to speak.

"You smell nice," he said.

"It's only soap."

"Your legs are all smooth."

"Malarkey."

"Yeah?"

"Hold me. Please."

"Yeah, right." He put his arm between my legs and I felt his hand hot in the small of my back, tugging me towards him. I stirred against the inside of his elbow. "It's all right, mate. Malarkey's here. Malarkey's got you."

We leaned together and kissed softly, until the wetness lay on our chins. When we moved apart, I asked him if he thought we might still be friends when we gained our freedom.

"Don't see why not. We could be as much friends as we liked. There'd be no-one could stop us."

"I'd like that. And we'd have no secrets, right?"

"Not if we was best friends."

I thought for a while. All I could hear was our breathing, small, wordless whispers in the dark. Every now and then, a tiny sound of pleasure would escape from our lips as our warm bodies, lightly oiled by perspiration, bumped together, parted, bumped together once more. This I would remember. This was our beautiful time.

I propped myself on one elbow and searched for his face in the darkness. "You still haven't told me your secret," I said, stroking his neck with my knuckles.

"You what?"

"Why you're in here. What you did."

"Oh, that."

"Yes. No secrets. You agreed."

"Yeah, right."

"I told you what happened to me."

"That was amazin'. Go on, tell me again. Tell me about that woman, that Sally. About when she p – "

"Don't, Malarkey! I don't want to keep going over it. It's done now."

"All right. Keep yer 'air on." He gasped. "Move yer leg, me 'and's goin' to sleep."

"Better? Now you can tell me why you didn't like your brother."

I felt him stroke the inside of my thigh. "It was more than that," he said.

"I know."

"What d'you mean, you know?"

"You went to bed with him, didn't you? Malarkey?"

There was no reply, and I couldn't see properly in the dark, but I felt the bed shake as he nodded his head. "His name was Brian," he said. "I loved 'im."

"You loved him? You just said you didn't like him."

"You can not like someone and still love them deep down."

"Mmm. So you wanted to hurt him?"

"Not at first. Not when it started."

"What did he do, then? To make you hate him so much."

"I never said that. I never said I 'ated 'im."

I sat up, nearly banging my head on the base of the bunk above. "You killed him, Malarkey! Didn't you? You killed him!"

"All right!" he shouted. Then he went on, in a smaller voice, "But I didn't 'ate 'im. Honest. I never 'ated 'im."

Someone banged on the door. "Keep it down in there!"

We lay quietly, holding our breath. Keys jangled in the distance, and a door slammed.

"They find out, they'll split us up," Malarkey whispered.

I rolled on to my back, thumping my head against the pillow. "What made you do it? You have a fight?"

He exhaled slowly, blowing my hair. "Not exactly. More of an argument."

"About what?"

"I dunno. I can't remember. Nothin', prob'ly."

"You're in here because you disagreed with your brother over nothing?"

"No! Don't – you're twistin' everythin'!"

I sighed, tugging at the blanket to cover my bare shoulders. "I just want to find out if it's safe for me to be in this bed with you."

"You jokin'? Course it is. We're mates, aren't we? I'd never 'urt you."

"You hurt Brian. You more than hurt him."

"He threatened me."

"What with?"

"He said – he was gonna tell me dad, tell 'im I'd raped 'im. Then I'd get thumped and we'd 'ave to stop, we wouldn't be able to do it no more." He choked on his words, starting to cry. "But I loved 'im, see. I couldn't bear it."

"There's different kinds of love, Malarkey." I turned over and pulled him towards me and held him while he sobbed, wetting my chest as he shuddered against me. "The wrong kind of love, Malarkey."

"What about this, then?" he moaned. "Is this wrong too?"

"No, because we're trying to help each other. That's not wrong."

"So I got a blade, see."

"A blade? What sort of blade?"

"From me dad's razor."

I heard him panting in the silence. "Go on."

"I 'ad it in me fist, y'see. Just stickin' out. I didn't mean to push so 'ard." He was crying again, shaking uncontrollably. "It was 'is – what is it, cartoid? – no, c-carotid artery, I got 'im there, I bloody ripped it, 'eard 'im scream out like – "

"Oh no, Malarkey! You're making this up! Tell me you're making it up!"

"I put me 'and over 'is gob to shut 'im up. We was starkers, see. I didn't want me dad to come and find us. 'E was always wallopin' me. Only it started shootin' out, it was like everywhere, like a red fountain, so I put my 'and on 'is neck, but it weren't no good, Neil, it was in me 'air, in me eyes, I couldn't make it stop, an' 'e was makin' this 'orrible noise, sorta like a sheep bleatin', only real loud, an' me dad come in an' pulled me off 'im and started shakin' im, an' then this huge spout come out and it done a sploshy red sunflower down the wall, an' Brian, 'e was jerkin' up an' down like 'e could be electrocuted, an' it was just 'orrible, Neil, it was just – just..."

"Shush, shush, shush! It's all right, mate, it's all right." And so I held him tight in my arms, my chest and my shoulders soaked from his tears, and I said nothing more, just waited for what seemed like an age, until he was quiet and not shaking any more. I held him there, not moving, not speaking, until a patch of grey light stained the morning sky.

When I was certain he had fallen asleep, I climbed back into my own bunk and lay there, wide awake. Every so often, I leaned over to look at him, to make sure he was all right. As the dawn came up, I looked at the pictures on my wall, and I ran my finger round my father's face and thought about him, trying to think of something to say to him. I wanted to tell him we were still friends.

Malarkey was quiet that day. He wasn't rude or sullen, just calm and uncommunicative. Now and then he would stop what he was doing, as if he had suddenly thought of something, and smile at me, only he wouldn't say anything. Perhaps he just thought he had said it all. Each time he did this, I smiled back, and once or twice I touched his arm or his shoulder, giving it a little squeeze, as if to let him know I was still there for him. I wanted him to know that it hadn't all been just a dream.

After supper, when they locked us in, he perched on the edge of the bed, gazing at the floor. I asked him if he was all right.

He shrugged, glancing at me briefly. "I dunno," he said. "I just feel – sort of empty."

"Does it feel any better, now you've told me about Brian?"

"Maybe. It was right to tell you."

"Yes. Was he – was Brian the first?"

"The first person I've done in?"

I allowed myself a short laugh. "No, daft. The first boy you'd been with. You know."

"Yeah. An' you're the last."

"How d'you mean?"

"'Cos we're best friends, right? So there's not gonna be no others. Never."

"Never's an awful long time, Malarkey."

"Don't look like I'm goin' nowhere."

"You will be, when you get out of here."

He looked at me properly then, a strangely earnest expression on his face. His eyes roamed over me, from head to toe and back again, and he seemed to be searching for something, some kind of reassurance. He narrowed his eyes, tipped back his head and assessed me, almost as if seeing me for the first time.

"What's the matter, Graham?" I asked.

"Don't call me that."

"Sorry. You look – lost."

"No. I was just thinkin'. About when I've done me term. What it'll be like."

"Planning for the future, eh?"

"Do I 'ave one?" He peered at me fiercely. "Well, do I?"

"We all have a future. It's a blank canvas. It's up to us what we paint on it. Some of us create a beautiful picture. Some of us, we just spill the paint pot. Then you spend half your life trying to find a clean sheet of paper, so you can start again."

"I reckon I crapped on mine."

I sat at the table under the window and watched the sky turn from cerulean to grey to indigo. A painting, perhaps. If only I could colour my future on the sky. A misshapen moon appeared, tilting at the glass like an old man with a black hat on, peering in. I thought of the same moon hanging over Rannoch, a luminous disc floating on the water, and Noah reaching up for this shimmering plaything.

"I'm talking to you."

I turned to look at him. "Sorry, Malarkey, I was miles away."

"Looked like you was in outer space."

"What were you saying?"

"Just – well, you been around, done loads more than me. You know about things."

"Do I? What things?"

"No, straight up. Don't muck me about."

"I'm not. What's bothering you?"

He chuckled. "You don't 'alf talk funny sometimes."

"Do I? Okay, Malarkey. What's fucking you up? Is that better?"

"Yeah, that's better," he said, slapping his hands on his thighs.

Don't ask me how long we talked that night. Time was meaningless in there, something that went on for ever. Malarkey seemed to hang on my every word. I suppose I was flattered by his attention. It was odd, really; I was only a year older than him, yet he would turn to me for advice in all manner of things, as though, in me, he recognized someone invested by experience with a worldly wisdom scarcely invalidated by its abrasive prematurity. I think he respected me, perhaps he loved me, but I could never quite fathom exactly what I felt for him. It could have been gratitude, amusement, friendship, or possibly some kind of subliminal yearning, a fragile tethering to the forbidden excitements of the past. All I know is, we never argued or fought or ridiculed each other, and I never feared him. For weeks at a stretch, our small worlds might simply brush without colliding, and there would be only a fleeting physical contact between us, hardly more remarkable than the soulless space we occupied;

and then, for night after languorous night, we would sleep together, wrapped in each other's arms, peaceful as babies.

So I touched him with my heart and cared for him and told him no lies. No, I told him no lies. I told him all that I had learned of the ways of the world which, however incredibly, he evidently believed I had unaccountably mastered. Time and again, but now without bitterness or rancour, I retold the story of Gran and Sally and Archie and Noah; the rattling trains by the park in the dappled sunlight; the silver pistons of leaping fish trailing their jewels of spray over the wind-ploughed acres of Rannoch. We talked of my son, the boy who lived on in dreams under the water, and we wept together as we saw him reaching for the moon. Safe at last.

Something else I told him; perhaps the most important part of all that I had to say. I wanted to warn him about the perversity of dreams.

"When you go free into the world, Malarkey, go down the road where you see a light to stand in."

He stared at me. "A light to stand in," he repeated slowly.

"What I mean is, don't hurry by, searching for a distant crock of gold. Don't be blinded by the brighter light of your dreams. Maybe they're already behind you."

He frowned. I persevered. I had to make him understand. If I was to be his mentor, his *guru,* I mean. I owed it to him to get it right. One day, after all, he would be on his own. So I reminded him that dreams are inventions of the night. They come and go in darkness.

One thing I knew for sure. The light on the far horizon is not there. We can be so brave and hopeful on that road, following that mirage.

And then the darkness comes for us.

Chapter XXII

1970

Epilogue

I rather like my room. I use it as a study, my private place, the only room in the house that is entirely, exclusively mine. If it gets dusty or untidy or the window needs cleaning, I have to leave my other work and attend to these more menial tasks. It is a very small room; but then, this is a very small cottage. Come to that, we are only small ourselves, tiny people living in a big country. We are content, though, with our smallness. By mutual consent, we have adjusted to our surroundings, retreated into ourselves.

She will be back soon. She went into town in the Land Rover an hour ago. I kissed her lightly as she left, marvelling quietly at her childish excitement.

"Sure you don't want me to come with you?" I asked her.

"No, no. You've got your writing to do. There's a deadline."

"You're all right to drive?"

She laughed, that wonderful high, squealy, girly laugh. God, how I love that laugh, those happy bells! "Course I am, dopey! I'm only five months gone."

She's going to pay the man for the photographs, do a little shopping, perhaps stop for a coffee, then come home. At least, that's what she told me. Knowing her as I do, I suspect it won't quite work out that way, and she'll take one look, flicking through the photos, and have to come rushing straight back, bursting to show me – to share them with me. It'll be like she'd gone out and got married all over again.

"Have you enough money?" I asked, as she was putting her coat on.

"Nope," she chirped. "You and me, we'll never have enough money."

"You know what I meant."

She tossed her pretty head in mock frustration. "Here, give me your hand!" She hitched up her T-shirt and placed my hand on the cool hummock of her rounded belly. "You've given me this," she said. "It's all I want."

I love that smooth white inflation, dimpled with her belly-button that seems to change shape almost daily. Making love to her was never so good, feeling that glossy hillock gliding under me as we move. In the early morning light, the covers thrown back, the exposed skin has a brilliant translucence, irresistible. I woke her, once, licking her tummy. Yummy.

We don't mind if it's a boy or a girl. How can that possibly matter? If you've created a human being, for God's sake. If you've made a whole world. If it's a boy, we think we'll call him Daniel Mark. If it's – she's – a girl, perhaps Ruth Anne. Whichever. Whenever.

She yelled at me yesterday, something she's never done before. We were out in the range warden's boat – he lets us borrow it sometimes, until we can get one of our own – and the loch was flat as glass. I had a rod, but the fish could easily see my reflection, so it was futile. In two hours, I caught nothing, never even came close.

"Perhaps you'll take your little boy fishing," she said. "He might actually catch something."

"What if he's a little girl?" I countered. "Maybe you'd prefer a girl."

She swung her chocolate-coloured hair in the sunlight. "No. I think you'd like a boy. You'd be good with him, a good father."

"Are you sure?" I gave up and dropped the rod in the boat. "Look what I did to the last one."

That's when she exploded. I even saw her spit fly out against the light. "Don't you say that! Don't you ever say that! You hear me? Don't you *ever* say that!"

My hands flew to my face, palms out, to placate her. "All right, all right! I'm sorry. I shouldn't have said it. It was a stupid thing to say."

She waited, taking a deep, shuddering breath. "Too right it was. Don't you dare say such a thing. That's awful."

"Why? I couldn't blame you if you said it to me."

"No, I would never say that to you." Suddenly, almost ferociously, she grabbed my hand, twisting my wrist, and her eyes blazed into mine. "Neil Robertson, I fucking love you to fucking bits! Do you hear me? I fu-"

"Yes, okay, I hear you. I told you, I'm sorry."

"Well, all right then." She let go of my hand, an impish smile on her face. "Did I scare you?"

"Only a bit. Only half to death."

"It's just – when I think of all you've been put through. All the things those – those bastards did to you, and you ending up in that place all those years, because you saved a child the only way you could see...when I think about that, Neil, it makes my blood boil." She shook her head, tight-jawed. "Don't belittle yourself, you're too good a man for that."

I had nothing to say then, no adequate response. I felt warm and humble, quietly elated in the piercing magic of that moment. How much can you love someone and not burn up inside, spontaneous combustion? Where do you put all that glorious pain?

I dangled my hand in the water, gazing down into the gold-webbed depths. My imagination was my eyes.

"This is the place, isn't it?" she said. "That's why you always come here, to this spot."

I nodded, clenching my teeth, watching her face. "Who cares about the fish?" I said. My eyes were filling up, breaking the sky into fragments.

Again, she reached for me. "Don't," she said. "No more tears, brave boy. You've shed enough of those for a lifetime. You've got me now. Don't cry for him. He's safe. No-one can hurt him, ever."

She squeezed my arm, little pumping pulses to tease the blood. I moved to draw it back from her, but she grinned, tugging at her sweater and the shirt underneath, and her swollen belly, flashing stark white in the sun, filled my vision, as she dragged my hand on to her chilled fullness, urging me to feel where our baby lay. I let her clasp me against her, warm hand on cold tummy, while the boat rocked on the current. "Touch me," she said, "put me in the sun," and I slid my hand down under her waistband until my fingers found a warm crevice, probing that puffy pinkness out into the light.

Anyway, as I said, she'll be back soon, and we can look at our wedding album together, just taking our time. Our time. It sounds strange, but wonderful, when I say that. Our time. Our time. I just want to go on saying it.

She had only been gone five minutes when my mother rang. We'd told her she could come up whenever she wanted, as we couldn't afford a honeymoon. I hadn't expected to hear from her so soon.

"I was thinking of next Friday," she said. "I'll stay till Monday."

"That's fine," I said. "We can pick you up from the station."

"I should hope so," she huffed, "after I've come all that way."

"We'll be there. Jennifer's out, by the way."

"I see. Working?"

"No, gone into town."

"She's on the district now?"

"Yes. She's liking it. She gets around, sees the people."

"What is it with you and nurses?"

"Mum, please."

"Well, I only asked."

"I'll tell her you rang."

"I don't know how the pair of you are going to make out, really I don't. Her with just a nurse's wage and you scratching along on articles for a paper no-one's heard of." I caught a quick sigh of disappointed exasperation. "You'll never be rich, that's for sure."

"Probably not, Mum. But we'll be happy. That's what counts. That's what's important."

"And when the baby comes, that's another mouth to feed."

"Well, I know that, don't I!"

"Yes. Well, I daren't think what you're your dad would have said."

"Mum, we'll pick you up at the station. Okay?"

"Well, it's not much to ask."

I put the phone down. She had me all wound up, tight as a drum. My hands were shaking. It was ridiculous.

I thought what she had said about being rich. I wondered what it was she imagined you must have to be rich. What wild dreams did she expect me to chase, leaping at shadows?

In the next room, up a small wooden step much weathered by the years, our bedroom door stood open, shielding from view Jen's kidney-shaped dressing table, brought from her flat down south. It has a glass top, and the inlay underneath is a ruby colour, reminding me of flock wallpaper from an Indian restaurant. Whenever my wife – and I am barely accustomed to the idea of calling her that – is out of the house, I find a quiet consolation in going to her dressing-table and picking up the small personal accessories of her existence, one by one, for they carry her fragrance, her indelible imprint: a pot of cold cream of inexhaustible size; a vanity set comprising hand mirror, comb and two hair brushes, each piece backed in hallmarked silver decoratively inlaid with curlicues – these a wedding gift from her best friend; a tiny amber bottle of Patou's *Joy*, with which I remember she freshened the channel between her breasts the night we made our baby; and her duty fob watch, resting on a scrap of grey velvet. Also, this morning I noticed, at the edge of the table, her dog-eared diary from the hospital, used now to record her district appointments. Vaguely curious, but intending no invasion of privacy, I picked it up, weighed it in my hands and opened the cover. Her photograph, full face and shoulders, was stuck to the cardboard inside – and beneath it I saw, with a quickly fluttering heartbeat, that she had fixed a recent picture of me, so that she could carry me with her each day. I traced my finger over her gentle, querulously posed face and then over the already-smudged name badge below: Jennifer Amelia Rebecca

Peltzer. Then I closed the book and replaced it exactly where I had found it.

By the time I had returned here to my study to watch through the window for the Land Rover, I knew what I will say to my mother when she pays her first visit to Acorn Cottage. It is all so simple. I can play the scene through in my mind right now.

"Very nice, dear," my mother says, "but I really don't see how you're going to manage."

"Oh, we haven't come here to manage," I reply, "we've come here to live."

Her face clouds with that ungenerous cynicism engendered by old age. "Huh. A bit put by, a bashed-up old Land Rover, two jobs struggling to make one. Poor kid, when it comes."

"We'll do well, Mum. We'll have enough, more than enough."

"Well, I hope it makes you happy," she says, doubtfully.

So then I smile at Jennifer and pat the fleshy fruit of her tummy. "Our future's in here, Mum."

Then I turn her around and point to the garden with the apple trees and the vegetable patch and the compost heap and the rusty wheelbarrow. "See, our own little acre, Mum. The soil is beautiful."

She remains stolidly unconvinced. No matter. I am saving the best till last. We each take one of her hands and lead her to the window. She blinks at the view but says not a word.

"Look Mum! Out there, in all that wild space – riches beyond compare! There's your riches!"

And Jennifer's eyes go misty in the steely light, and all down the valley the mountains are white-crowned teeth reflected in the loch, a timeless canyon full of pictures of another country, and perched on the hillsides the squat sheep are scattered sugar cubes, and our eyes, unbelieving, trail down to the place where Noah sleeps, and the wind cleaves the grass like green fire.

END

Printed in the United Kingdom
by Lightning Source UK Ltd.
103021UKS00001B/445-453